Hearts of Gold

ReGENERATIONS

AFRICAN AMERICAN LITERATURE AND CULTURE

Regenerations is a new series devoted to reprinting editions of important African American texts that have fallen out of print or have failed to receive the attention they merit. *Regenerations* encourages research that develops and extends the understanding of African American literary and cultural history, by promoting regional and local research that represents the complex dynamics of African American experience.

"[Regenerations: African American Literature and Culture] has the potential to be a vital, exciting series that will make available neglected texts that can help us to rethink African American literary and cultural traditions."—*Robert S. Levine, Distinguished Scholar-Teacher, University of Maryland*

"[This] series will expand the scholarly discussion about the ways in which such texts help us to rethink the field and insure that the books will be taught in the classroom and thereby be sustained for the next generation."—*Sharon Harris, Director, Humanities Institute and Professor of English, University of Connecticut*

"As the editor of *African American Review*, Joycelyn K. Moody has had her finger on the pulse of new scholarship. . . . . [while] John Ernest [is] a scholarly editor whose work is careful, insightful, and accessible."—*Frances Smith Foster, Charles Howard Candler Professor of English and Women's Studies, Emory University*

A Novel by J. McHenry Jones

Edited By
John Ernest and Eric Gardner

West Virginia University Press
Morgantown

West Virginia University Press, Morgantown 26506

Originally published 1896 by Daily Intelligencer Steam Job Press.

Printed in the United States of America
18 17 16 15 14 13 12 11 10   9 8 7 6 5 4 3 2 1
ISBN-10: 1-933202-52-1   (pb) 1-933202-53-X
ISBN-13: 978-1-933202-52-5   (pb) 978-1-933202-53-2
(alk. paper)

Library of Congress Cataloguing-In-Publication Data
Jones, J. McHenry.
Hearts of gold : a novel / by J. McHenry Jones ; edited by John Ernest and Eric Gardner. -- 2nd ed.
p. cm. -- (Regenerations ; v. 1)
1. African Americans--Appalachian Region--Fiction. 2. Appalachian Region--Race relations--Fiction. 3. Southern States--Race relations--Fiction. 4. African Americans--Social conditions--19th century--Fiction. I. Gardner, Eric. II. Ernest, John. III. Title.

PS2151.J28H43 2010
813'.54--dc22

Library of Congress Control Number:
2009032571

CONTENTS

Acknowledgments ix

Introduction 1
by John Ernest and Eric Gardner

Hearts of Gold 55

Appendices 273

Appendix A 275
The Speech of James McHenry Jones, Wheeling's Magnet Colored Orator, Seconding the Nomination of George W. Atkinson for Governor, at Parkersburg (1896)

Appendix B 278
Jones's speech to the British Grand United Order of Odd Fellows 1897 Annual Conference

Appendix C 288
Advertisement from the Charleston Advocate (1907)

Appendix D 291
Jones, "*The West Virginia Colored Institute*" (1907)

Appendix E 297
Jones, "*Biographical Sketch of S. W. Starks*" (1908)

Appendix F 302
Jones, "*The Epworth League and the Enthronement of Christ*" *(1909)*

According to historian John Jones, his brother J. McHenry Jones was feted at twenty-one banquets (including three given by members of Parliament) and "treated more as a prince than a common citizen" when he visited England in 1897 and sat for this portrait, which the British Oddfellows featured in their 1897 annual conference proceedings. *Photograph reproduced courtesy of the Library of Congress, Rare Book and Special Collections Division, Daniel A.P. Murray Pamphlets Collection.*

ACKNOWLEDGMENTS

JOHN ERNEST

West Virginia University Press's *Regenerations* series is devoted to collaborations among scholars working to recover and broaden our understanding of African American literary and cultural history, and I have benefited greatly from those collaborations in playing my part to prepare this edition of *Hearts of Gold.* When I first encountered this novel, I knew that few were likely to have read it and that fewer still would be at all familiar with J. McHenry Jones's extraordinary career. Still, I was sure that Eric Gardner would know of him, and I imagined that Eric probably had already done some archival research on Jones. I was right. I was grateful, then, when Eric agreed to co-edit this volume. All of the biographical background in the introduction is the result of Eric's exemplary research, and it has been a real pleasure to work with him on this project. I'm grateful as well to Pat Conner for his initial enthusiasm and support for this project, and to Carrie Mullen for continuing and extending that support so substantially when she took over as director of the WVU Press. It is my honor to co-edit the WVU Press *Regenerations* series with Joycelyn Moody, and her commitment to this project and her editorial and general guidance have been essential to this book's development. I'm deeply indebted as well to Luminita M. Dragulescu for her scrupulous assistance in researching this project, as well as her expert reading of this manuscript against the original. For access to that original copy, I owe a debt of gratitude to the staff at the Rare Book Room at the Wise Library of West Virginia University, and for a good copy to work from in preparing this manuscript, I am indebted to the Ohio County Public Library of Wheeling, West Virginia. While I cannot acknowledge everyone who has played a role in this project, let me say that various friends and colleagues have expressed interest in this project as it has developed, and one in particular has helped me though numerous conversations about *Hearts of Gold.* They know who they are, and I hope they know how much those conversations mean to me.

Eric Gardner

I'm thankful for the chance to acknowledge, first, the great benefits John Ernest's spirit of collaboration, deep determination to expand our sense of African American letters, and imagination have given to this project, to our field, and to me personally. John's rich sense of the contexts surrounding *Hearts of Gold*—and nineteenth-century African American literature more generally—continues to impress and inspire me. Like John, I deeply appreciate also WVU Press's commitment to this project. In addition to those noted above, librarians at the Appalachian State University Library, Houghton Library at Harvard University, the Ohio County (WV) Public Library, the Ohio State University Library, the Saginaw Public Library, Saginaw Valley State University's Zahnow Library, the Southern West Virginia Community and Technical College Library, the University of Michigan Library, and the Virginia Historical Society Library answered queries quickly and helpfully. The Ruth and Ted Braun Fellowship program at Saginaw Valley State University helped free up both time and resources for my work on this project. My colleagues and students at SVSU have been uniformly supportive; special thanks are due to Pat Latty and Sharon Opheim for assistance in preparing some of the appendices to this volume. And, as always, I am grateful beyond measure to my family—especially Jodie, Abby, and Libby.

INTRODUCTION

In 1989, the historian Dickson D. Bruce Jr. observed that although scholars have learned a great deal about "the dynamics of post-Reconstruction white racism," there was still a great deal to learn about "black responses to the racism of the period," and he noted especially "a need to go below the surface of black thought and action in the post-Reconstruction period and to explore the underlying structures of ideas and feelings behind the more visible responses to white racial oppression."[1] Bruce turned to literature for that underlying story, exploring the "unprecedented burst of literary activity among black Americans" from 1877 to 1915. But relatively few scholars have followed Bruce to this body of literature that offers such a significant perspective on what was, on the one hand, one of the most murderously racist periods of American history and, on the other, one of the most remarkable periods of determination and achievement in all of African American history. This period was long known to students of American history and literature primarily by way of two dominant figures: W. E. B. Du Bois and Booker T. Washington, with Du Bois representing the forward and militant advance and Washington representing an accommodationist strategy that increasingly has seemed rather too accommodating to a dominant culture characterized by overt white supremacist ideology. But the dominant themes of two leaders do

---

A Note on the Text

This edition of *Hearts of Gold* is based on a first edition housed in the West Virginia and Regional History Collection of the West Virginia University Library. We have quietly corrected obvious spelling, punctuation, and typographical errors, but otherwise we have maintained the spelling, punctuation, and phrasing of the original edition.

not begin to account for the diversity of African American experience, organization, and thought during this period.

Especially over the last thirty years, scholars have started to take a closer look at the unique insights into history and cultural life afforded by literature. Many African American texts from this period were republished in the 1960s and 1970s, and many more texts are available online today. At least a few writers from this time are now recognized as major writers in the African American literary tradition, though only a few—most prominently, novelist and short-story writer Charles W. Chesnutt—have received broader attention. Pauline Hopkins—novelist, playwright, short-story writer, editor, singer, and performer—has started to earn a reputation as an especially important writer of this time. Novelist, poet, and orator Frances E. W. Harper has been recognized as a significant writer as well, and her novel *Iola Leroy; or, Shadows Uplifted* (1892) was for a time considered the first novel by an African American woman. But Harper is instructive in many ways, for subsequent research revealed that Harper had published three earlier novels in serial form in the A. M. E. *Christian Recorder*, and that there were other and stronger claims to the first novel published by an African American woman in perhaps Harriet Wilson's 1859 publication *Our Nig; or, Sketches from the Life of a Free Black* or Julia Collins's novel (also published in serial form) *The Curse of Caste* (1865). In short, the more we look, the more we find, and the more we understand about African American literary and cultural history—making it difficult to even map out the literary surfaces, let alone explore the depths that await.

The book that you are about to read is, like many books published during this period, a novel that has been hidden in plain sight. Literary historians have long known about J. McHenry Jones's 1896 novel *Hearts of Gold*, but very few scholars have lingered over the novel for a closer look, and what is believed to be Jones's only published novel has long been virtually unavailable to readers. Those readers who have lingered over the novel have generally either anticipated or echoed Dickson Bruce's claim that *Hearts of Gold* is "one of the more romantic novels of the period," and that "there is little original in the novel."[2] Interestingly, similar judgments have been rendered on virtually every other African American novel published in the nineteenth century—William Wells Brown's *Clotel; or, The*

President's Daughter (1853), Harriet E. Wilson's *Our Nig*, Frances Harper's *Iola Leroy*, and Pauline Hopkins's *Contending Forces* (1900), among many others—some of which are now recognized not only as major achievements but also as challenges to our assumptions about how to approach literature and how to evaluate aesthetic quality. And just like the important work of Harper, Hopkins, and Chesnutt, *Hearts of Gold* offers an intriguing examination of the relationships among love, life, politics, racism, economics, cultural life, and violence in American life after the Civil War. This is, after all, a story that involves black education, the black press, lynching, the convict labor system, and black fraternal organizations. This is a story that features a black doctor reduced to unjust imprisonment and unimaginable suffering, and it is a story that features a black journalist who uses the newspaper to exert political leverage. This is a story of a woman who could pass for white but chooses not to and of an African American whose skin was "as free from pigment as an Albino's." This is a story of a white man pressing for interracial marriage in an effort to acquire a woman's wealth, and it is a story of an elite class of African Americans who sacrifice their advantages to teach and serve poor African Americans in the rural South. More than many novels published during this period, *Hearts of Gold* brings together the products of African American achievement—its doctors, newspaper editors, and educators—and places them within a threatening cultural setting that is governed by the priorities of violent racism and institutionalized white supremacist ideology.

This novel that deals with one of the most horrible forms of exploitation—convict labor in the coal mines of the South—is itself devoted, in short, to mining "below the surface of black thought and action" in the last decades of the nineteenth century. And yet both *Hearts of Gold* and its then-prominent author, educator J. McHenry Jones, remain virtually unknown—markers on a few historical charts, a presence among the occasional homages to the literary sons and daughters of West Virginia, an interesting footnote in African American literary history. The book you are about to read is the first edition of *Hearts of Gold* designed to reach a broad reading public, and in the pages that follow you will encounter our attempt to gather what is known about J. McHenry Jones, a man whose remarkable life has itself been largely relegated to footnotes. Much work remains, and the editors of this volume hope that this edition of *Hearts of Gold* and this account of Jones's life will provide inspiration and a reliable map for that remaining work.

History of the Jones Family

When Jones dedicated *Hearts of Gold* "To my parents, bending under the cares of three score years and ten whose lives have been a constant sacrifice for their children," he was invoking more than the domestic ideals (and idylls) stamped on most of the novel's pages. He was paying homage to a family story emphasizing education and community work that shaped much of his life, a story that his brother John Lysandrous Jones found important enough to record in a c. 1930 pamphlet titled simply *History of the Jones Family*, and that has drawn the attention of local historians in Ohio and West Virginia even though J. McHenry Jones and his novel remain absent from most major reference sources on African American literature and culture.

John Jones placed the Jones family's beginnings in a ten-year-old "son of an African prince," who reportedly, though taken to Jamestown, Virginia, aboard a slave ship in 1754, nonetheless avoided slavery because the Virginia whites supposedly had "respect" for his "royal blood."[3] Jones asserted that this "prince" married a free black woman and that they had several children including Reuben Jones in Henrico County, Virginia. In their immensely valuable annotated reissue of the *History* (which also contains a collection of memorial pieces on J. McHenry Jones, "In Memoriam," Ohio historians Nancy Aiken and Michel Perdreau argue that this story is largely apocryphal, and they are most likely correct in this, as well as in their suggestion that Reuben Jones was likely born a decade earlier and may have been "one of the 31 slaves liberated in Henrico County in 1800."[4]

Reuben Jones's life remains sketchy, although Jones, Aiken, and Perdreu agree with extant records that Jones married Elizabeth Ailstock and that the couple had four children.[5] Their second son Joseph, born c. 1825 in Virginia, had moved to Ohio by at least the 1840s, when his marriage to Temperance Reed was recorded in Lawrence County—on the far southeastern edge of the state—on November 16, 1847.[6] Temperance Reed, according to John Jones, was born 15 May 1824 in Burlington, Ohio, to farmers William and Nancy Reed.[7] The 1850 Federal Census of Lawrence

County places the Reed family in Fayette township, notes $200 in real estate holdings (likely a small farm and home), and lists five children living with them—all younger than Temperance.[8] Aiken and Perdreau rightly note that the census lists William and Nancy Reed's family next to Joseph and Temperance Jones, who did not yet own real estate and who had just recently had their first child.[9]

That both the Jones and the Reed families chose to migrate to Ohio from the upper South is not surprising. While Ohio's state constitution and early Black Laws drove some black immigrants further West or further North, as a state close to eastern "civilization" but still part of the Old Northwest Territory, Ohio continued to offer great promise.[10] Pioneering higher education efforts at Oberlin and Wilberforce, a series of state conventions about African American issues, black leaders ranging from journalist William Howard Day to colonizationist H. Ford Douglass to later politician John Mercer Langston, and active abolitionist efforts on the part of both some African Americans and some whites would have also made staying in Ohio attractive.[11] Ohio was certainly no paradise, though—especially in the southern counties where the Jones and Reed families settled. While the scale of violence in a series of race riots in Cincinnati's "Little Africa" in 1829 (and then again in 1836 and 1841) was not duplicated in the counties that these families chose, southern Ohio's racial attitudes and practices sometimes made it look much more like the upper South than the "Old Northwest." Especially after the passage of the Compromise of 1850—including the accompanying tougher Fugitive Slave Law—tensions remained high. Still, by 1860, the state's 36,000 black residents (about 2 percent of the state population) had succeeded in convincing state legislators to repeal some of the Black Laws and to begin to fund (separate) schools for African American children.

Joseph and Temperance Jones stayed in Lawrence County for only a few years after their marriage and then moved between Lawrence County, Gallia County (one county to the north), and Meigs County (just north of Gallia County). They would go on to have ten children, though only seven lived to adulthood. Though Joseph had learned coopering, he also seems to have worked extensively as a whitewasher and a boatman—living under the maxim, in the words of the *History*, that one should "never wait for a job. When one gives out, go after another one."[12] John L. Jones remembered his father as "a man of large ideas" and describes him as "a constant reader" who followed antebellum politics closely—even naming his first son after William Henry Harrison.[13] Joseph and Temperance were, the *History* continues, also "ardent Christians" who "established the family altar in their home, and prayed earnestly"; while there were several nascent black churches in the area, they most often chose Baptist groups.[14] Jones's *History* adds that the family—and especially his father—saw music as "a gift from Heaven" and thus became deeply involved with church music and church-related singing clubs.[15]

The young family saw great trials: in addition to increasing racial tension in the area, their son William died c. 1857, and their fifth child was either stillborn or died in infancy. They also saw a handful of celebrations, as when Joseph's parents Reuben and Elizabeth moved to Ohio, where, though "old and broken in health," they shared a reunion for which Joseph had "prayed earnestly."[16] By 1858, according to the *History*, Joseph and Temperance Jones had saved enough money to buy a "double lot" in Gallipolis and to build "a five-room brick house" with "a large porch extending across the front."[17] Soon after completing the home, Joseph began work on a cooper shop and storage facility next door. While the 1860 Federal Census of Gallia County lists him with only $50 of personal property and leaves the space for real estate valuation blank—and while the 1870 Census of Meigs County offers no notation on the family's economic status—several factors suggest that, even if the *History* exaggerates, the Jones family was moving toward the middling classes. Both of these censuses shift the job listing for Joseph to "cooper" from "laborer" (his marking in the 1850 census and the moniker most often assigned to black men by racist census-takers). The 1860 listing notes two children as attending school, and the 1870 census notes three children in school.[18] In short, as a propertied tradesman, Joseph Jones was building the home J. McHenry Jones would later praise. John L. Jones asserted that his parents used their growing resources to actively aid fugitive slaves crossing into Ohio on their way to Canada. "The store room on the corner," he says, "was built with . . . an especially prepared room to feed and house the fugitives" because "Joseph Jones was the conductor for the Gallipolis station" and "never left home without his two ominous-looking guns" so that "there was no chance to take possession" of the fugitives in his care "without first killing him."[19] Area historians Aiken and Perdreau are relatively silent on these claims, and Joseph Jones appears in none of the histories of the Ohio Underground Railroad. He is also absent from various county histories' sometimes-hagiographic accounts of the anti-slavery contributions of their residents—some of which do mention black abolitionists and Underground Railroad operatives.[20] It is certainly plausible that John L. Jones embellished the family's engagement—especially given the fact that he was writing as part of the last gasp of firsthand Civil War memorialization. It is just as likely that some or all of Jones's claims are true: as several historians have demonstrated, black aid to fugitive slaves often went purposely undocumented because of both the risk to such heroes and the lack of coordination within the movement. What is clear is that the Jones family's racial consciousness was deep, centered on a sense of racial elevation, and communitarian.

Joseph and Temperance Jones's sixth child, James Henry—he would not add the "Mc" for several years—was born in Gallipolis on August 28, 1859.[21] "In Memoriam" claims that he "spent his early boyhood with his grandmother"—likely, Nancy Reed[22]—"on her farm in Lawrence County," that he moved "with his family to New Richmond," and that "during his ninth year, the family took up its residence at Pomeroy, Ohio."[23] His brother's *History* says little more beyond noting that Gallipolis, which was close enough to the upper South to see the edges of the Civil War, "was not a very desirable place in which to live" because "the soldiers from the convalescent hospital" nearby "frequented" a saloon "near our home."[24] The family's October 1869 move to Pomeroy seems to have been Joseph and Temperance Jones's attempt to settle the family for the long term.

John Jones described Pomeroy as "a string town with one long street"; he said that "the hills come out almost to the river, leaving just a narrow place" for that street.[25] The "one long street," however, did not stop the town from having some notable segregation: more than half of the city's residents marked "black" or "mulatto" in the 1870 census—including the Jones family—lived in Pomeroy's First Ward, where they made up almost three-eighths of the population; conversely, only sixteen residents of color lived in the second of the city's four wards. Still, African Americans made up almost a tenth of the city's 1870 population of 5,824, and the broader Meigs County area was home to 2,000 black Americans. Very much an Ohio River town, Pomeroy gained some black residents because of various occupations related to the river trade; there were also plenty of hard labor jobs in the coal and salt mines in the area. Coopers were thus, of course, consistently in need.

The cluster of African Americans in Pomeroy also allowed some educational and religious opportunities. Pomeroy had, in John Jones's words, "a one-room frame structure" that functioned as a school for area black children "with one very good he-man teacher."[26] The younger Jones children—including J. McHenry, who his brother reports was called "Jimmy"—attended this school. Decades later, John Jones was rightly proud of that small school, asserting that he had never seen "children more eager for education" and noting classmates including his brothers J. McHenry, Fleming, and Charles E., local orators Joseph Spears and Ollie Wilson, several teachers (both men and women), and poet and teacher James E. Campbell.[27] The Jones family initially struggled to fit in with the Wesleyan Methodist Church in Pomeroy, but doctrinal and practical differences drove them to leave that church and organize a Free Will Baptist Church. For much of his youth, J. McHenry Jones thus attended Sunday services led by Thomas Jefferson Ferguson.[28] Ferguson would become a key figure in J. McHenry Jones's early development—and he was an area powerhouse. Praised by no less than Carter G. Woodson as one of the Ohio men who devoted their lives to "contending for the enlargement of freedom and opportunity for their race," Ferguson had already helped found both the Albany Enterprise Academy (a black-owned and operated school in nearby Albany, Ohio) and the Ohio Colored Teachers' Association and had authored an 1866 pamphlet *Negro Education: The Hope of the Race* by the time the Jones family had settled in Pomeroy.[29] Historian Adah Ward Randolph notes that well into the 1880s, Ferguson served as the Albany Academy's "agent, teacher, principal, and board president" and so "raised funds for the institution, taught courses," and led most school efforts.[30] Like many black educators of the period, Ferguson maintained close church ties and preached regularly. The Jones family would have been not only attracted to his theology and his emphasis on literacy but also his deep investment in "voice culture and music."[31] J. McHenry

Jones moved across denominational borders a bit more easily than his parents, though, and, in addition to learning from Ferguson, both he and brother John participated in "a revival started under the leadership of Rev. Donaldson, pastor of the Wesleyan Methodist Church" in the mid-1870s, and there knelt "at the mourner's bench" and "professed religion."[32]

By all accounts, J. McHenry Jones was a precocious child, and his brother's *History* reported that "Jimmy" was "the foremost scholar of the little frame building," was "a bright and shining Christian boy and [a] very forceful speaker," and "had gone over the lower grade books until he knew them by heart."[33] Pomeroy schools offered him nothing in terms of continuing education, so by age sixteen, he was already teaching in Meigs County schools for young black children and investigating a potential career as a minister: "In Memoriam" says that he was also licensed to preach c. 1877, after completing "a preparatory course in theology . . . given him by Prof. T. J. Ferguson."[34]

While various accounts disagree on the details, all are clear that Jones chose to leave teaching—and, apparently, preaching—to enroll in Pomeroy's previously all-white high school. One of the earliest published biographies of Jones, a laudatory piece in the 26 January 1889 *Cleveland Gazette,* simply observes his status as the first black graduate. "In Memoriam" suggests that Jones—almost on a whim—"while passing the high school building," entered, went to the principal's office, and asked to be enrolled. When "the principal hesitated" and asked the city superintendent, Jones reportedly told him that "the State of Ohio owes me an education; you must either allow me to enter this school or hire a special teacher to instruct me."[35] John L. Jones's *History*—the account that early Jones biographer Ancella Radford Bickley accepts—offers this more elaborate story:

Father concluded that it was about time for the whites to open up central high school for our people. Superintendent Flannigan was in school one Friday evening, Jimmy had read a paper just before he came in sight, giving the school authorities a good raking for not allowing him to go to high school. When the superintendent came in, Mr. Thomas Carr called Jimmy up and had him read the paper over again for Flannigan's benefit. When he had finished the paper, the superintendent came to him and congratulated him on his paper and told him to meet the school board Tuesday night and take the matter up with them, as he had his consent to enter high school. On Tuesday night Father and Jimmy met the board, Father brought up the matter and asked them to allow his son to make a statement. They gave him permission, and when he had finished his plea, the entire board gave their consent and sent him to [the principal] Mr. Pace, who readily gave his consent by telling him . . . that he was glad to have him enter.[36]

The truth of what happened is likely somewhere in the middle of these accounts: Aiken and Perdreau do not favor one over the other, and there are enough commonalities to suggest a hybrid. Whatever that truth, these events would also have to be figured in dialogue with Ohio blacks' increasing efforts during and after Reconstruction to gain civil rights. While we have not yet definitively identified the Thomas Carr—who appears to have been an area teacher for black students—or "Mr. Pace" noted above, Thomas C. Flannigan (sometimes spelled alternately) was indeed Pomeroy's superintendent.[37]

The Jones family was well positioned to make a case to Flannigan and other school personnel: Joseph's coopering business was well-established; his religious ties were deep and well-known; the family's two youngest children, Charles E. and Thomas Jefferson, were currently successful students in the school system; the elder sons had completed common school with distinction; and J. McHenry (listed as James Henry) and younger brother Fleming were already, in the 1880 Federal Census, listed as schoolteachers.[38] Still, their case would have played differently in other locations in Ohio: the state was less than willing to accept the Radical Republican sense of Reconstruction many of its politicians advocated for the South. The state rejected a constitutional amendment allowing black male suffrage in 1867 and even initially refused to ratify the Fifteenth Amendment, which nationalized such suffrage in 1870. While some of the Black Law provisions were revised as early as 1849,[39] measures governing social interaction—including the integration of schools—proved much thornier. It was not until 1884 that Ohio began passing legislation guaranteeing equal access to "places of public accommodation and amusement" and public transportation, and it was not until 1887 that the state passed a bill—co-sponsored by black legislator and A. M. E.

minister Benjamin W. Arnett—that phased out school segregation and repealed the last of the state's Black Laws.[40] It was likely a combination of J. McHenry Jones's own abilities and experience as a teacher in the Meigs County schools paired with his family's reputation in the city and the willingness of some whites to move toward more egalitarian education that allowed him to enter Pomeroy High School—and to then graduate, first in his class of seven students, in June of 1882. His brother's *History* reported that Jones took as the subject of his valedictorian address "Iconoclast." The text does not seem to survive, but the *History* asserted that it was "a big hit," "capturing the entire town both white and black."[41] He thus paved the way for future Pomeroy High School black graduates like the poet James Edwin Campbell.

Jones had already passed the state's examination for his teaching credentials in April of 1882, and, according to the 26 January 1886 *Gazette*, was chosen from among six candidates to become the principal of Lincoln Grammar School across the river in Wheeling, West Virginia.[42] Jones flourished at Lincoln School, as Wheeling's black community had already built a base he could improve on by securing the Second Ward school building, which had initially been a white school in the Madison District of Wheeling. Recognizing West Virginia's separate but (un)equal approach to education but in possession of a serviceable building and budget, Jones worked to strengthen the curriculum and the school's public presence, and the 26 January 1889 *Cleveland Gazette* praised especially the fact that, because of Jones's "untiring efforts and energy," Lincoln "graduated colored scholars in the same class at the same time and from the same stage with the whites"—perhaps "for the first time" in "schools south of Mason and Dixon's line." Enrollment increases seem to have given Jones a further impetus for arguing for broader support and for secondary opportunities for his students. The 1882–1883 Wheeling city directory notes Jones as having only one "assistant"[43]—that is, teacher—under his supervision and an enrollment of only 114 students; the 1888 city directory places the school's enrollment at 230 and Jones's number of "assistants" at four.[44] Enrollment would hover around 200 for the rest of Jones's tenure at Lincoln, and he would generally have between five and seven teachers under him depending on enrollment—a ratio roughly equivalent to that at the district's nine white school buildings.

In addition to increasing his staff, in the late 1890s Jones succeeded in establishing a program that paralleled Wheeling's white secondary education by offering, in Carter G. Woodson's words, "practically the same course of study taught in the white school, though at times some classes were too small to justify instruction in certain phases of specialized work."[45] By the publication of the 1907 *History of Education in West Virginia*, two dozen African Americans had received their high school diplomas through this program. In short, Jones was growing into a clear leader in black education at the local and state level.[46]

It was also through Lincoln that Jones met his first wife, Carrie M. Harrison, who accepted an appointment as a teacher in 1885. Harrison has received only brief mention in works on J. McHenry Jones, but extant records suggest that she was from a family much like his. Born in or near Marietta, Ohio, c. 1861, her father George W. Harrison was a mill worker who had amassed both significant real and personal estate in the Harmar district of Marietta, and her mother Maria Blackstone Harrison seems to have been of mixed racial heritage—as the 1880 census lists her father as having been born in Ireland.[47] The 1870 census lists all five of the Harrison's school-age Harrison children—including Carrie—as attending school, and the family's 1880 listing marks one of her older brothers as a druggist, two other brothers as teachers, and four younger children as attending school.[48] Congregationalists who had been in Marietta since at least 1855, the Harrison family seem to have been as deeply tied to the ideals of elevation through education and faith as the Jones family.

According to his brother's *History*, Carrie Harrison may well have brought about Jones's shift from "James Henry Jones" to "J. McHenry Jones," as supposedly "there was another James H. Jones living in the city who had the pleasure of reading his mail and returning it to the office 'opened by mistake.' At the time he was corresponding with" Carrie Harrison and "to have this man reading those adoring passages was, to say the least, annoying."[49] Jones thus supposedly added the "Mc" prefix to his middle name, and, though a handful of records as late as 1888 refer to him as James or James H., he went by J. McHenry for the rest of his life.[50] Jones and Harrison married on 27 December 1887, probably in Ohio, and John L. Jones's *History* says that they lived an "ideal" life together for five years."[51] They took a home at 22 Vermont Street in Wheeling—

likely larger quarters than either had been used to, as prior to their marriage both had boarded in various black rooming houses: Jones, at 1208 Byron and 1119 Eoff, and Harrison at a rooming house on Delaware.[52] Their time seems to have encouraged Jones to explore new possibilities, and he even reportedly wrote a novel during the period titled *A Strange Transformation*—although according to his brother's *History*, the novel "was in the hands of the publisher when he failed, and the manuscript was misplaced."[53] Jones also seems to have sought additional education opportunities during the period—and reportedly did work with, among other institutions, the University of Michigan.[54] However, as John Jones writes, "at the table one morning" Carrie Harrison Jones "took suddenly ill and died before the doctor could reach her."[55] The couple had no children, and by all accounts Jones was devastated.

While, given his family's emphasis on religion, one might have expected Jones to turn to the church after his wife's death, biographers say relatively little about his faith—beyond its presence. In his eulogy to Jones reprinted in "In Memoriam," Atkinson says that "his religion was a real and practical thing. He found his creed in the Sermon on the Mount rather than in the dusty tomes of theologians."[56] As a black leader—and especially an educator—Jones would have had to maintain ties with an organized church, and he did, according to "In Memoriam," join Wheeling's Simpson Methodist Episcopal Church soon after moving to the community.[57] However, the evangelism that marked his late teen years seems to have become much more focused on the secular—or, at least, been relegated to a supporting role within his larger educational and socio-political activism.

"Our Party": Jones and Post-Reconstruction Politics

That activism increased over the years. Having entered the state as an educator, Jones discovered in West Virginia an increasingly promising field for African American men of his caliber. While the tragic death of his wife undoubtedly marked Jones's time at Lincoln School, it was also during these years that he grew to regional prominence—in part because of his achievements as an educator, but also because of his oratorical abilities and his savvy negotiation of the social and political opportunities available in the Ohio/West Virginia border region at the end of the nineteenth century. Jones was not alone in recognizing such opportunities. As Douglass C. Smith has noted, "from the post-Civil War period until the 1940s, the black minority in West Virginia increased at a rapid pace . . . . In 1870 the black population was 18,000. By 1920 it had increased to 87,000 or some 480 per cent."[58] Smith presents these figures as "the best indication of black opportunity and acceptance," which might best be viewed as an optimistic spin on a difficult national and regional situation for African Americans. Still, while one can only note that African Americans still faced racism and all of the challenges that followed from a white supremacist cultural order in West Virginia, the origins of the state (a break with the slaveholding capital of the Confederacy during the Civil War) and its consequential unique position in the newly ordered Union sometimes made for a quirky twist on at least some of the usual patterns of racial politics that plagued African American life after the Civil War. Jones's education and talents made him a notable force in the state's small but growing black minority—both in interracial politics and in efforts to organize the African American community and connect it with national self-organization efforts. Such efforts were necessarily at the heart of Jones's rising status as an educational leader, but they became important as well in his increasingly prominent role as an African American representative in the state's political scene.

Described by the *Gazette* as "a strong advocate of Republican principles," Jones began to address political questions of the day directly, and, at the request of the West Virginia Republican Party, he stumped for Benjamin Harrison and Republican candidates for state office across West Virginia in the election of 1888. The invitation likely came as the result of Jones's interactions with George Wesley Atkinson, a white attorney and politician who had moved to Wheeling in 1877, spent two years editing the *Wheeling Standard* (and would later spend five more editing the *West Virginia Journal*), served as both an internal revenue agent and U.S. marshal in West Virginia, and grown into a leader among West Virginia Republicans, who would send him briefly to Congress in 1890 and elect him Governor in 1897. Jones was, according to the 15 September 1888 and 22 September 1888 *Wheeling Daily Intelligencer*, a driving force behind the organization of "the Atkinson Republican Club," a group of over 100 young black voters. At times both more Southern and more segregationist than some of the Ohio Republicans Jones grew up watching, Atkinson's faction still offered Jones and select African Americans some opportunities, especially those beginning to be advocated by figures like Booker T. Washington, whose work was beginning to be known across the South.

Jones's efforts for the Republican party in West Virginia were part of a difficult struggle—at the state, regional, and national levels—to establish African Americans as a political force, a struggle complicated by the inevitable compromises and power struggles of one of the most racially charged periods of American history. "Reconstruction in West Virginia was, like in most border states," notes Stephen Engle, "a struggle between conservative whites and liberal whites with blacks becoming the object of abuse and political leverage."[59] During and beyond the Reconstruction years, African Americans needed to negotiate with often complex and deceptive political dynamics—and many African Americans were uncertain about the advantages of playing along with a Republican party that had once stood as an advocate for African American rights and opportunities but increasingly seemed more concerned with the shifting currents of political advantage. As Gordon McKinney has observed, "West Virginia Republicans encountered much dissatisfaction among black voters. Many black supporters seemed willing to leave the party in 1888 because they did not feel that they were receiving fair treatment."[60] Some African American voters broke off into the Colored Independent party in 1888, and others made their dissatisfaction with the Republican party evident in other ways. Through such efforts, as McKinney notes, African Americans in the Mountain State showed their willingness to "break from a mountain Republican organization, and they thereby forced the mountaineers to make adjustments." While the Democratic party still dominated much of the state's politics, West Virginia Republicans voted in four congressmen and the governor in 1888, enough for the state's Republicans to believe "that they were on the verge of a great breakthrough,"[61] a breakthrough that depended in some measure on the cooperation of the state's African American population and of leaders like Jones.

Jones's political activities were part of his increasing prominence as a black leader, through and beyond the organizations he helped develop in the state. His brother's *History* says that J. McHenry "became very restless" after his wife's death, and that "he was constantly on the go during the period of vacation"—and cites obligations with the Odd Fellows, a fraternal organization, and religious meetings, but emphasizes a broader and growing career as a public speaker, both lecturing and offering stump speeches in Ohio, Pennsylvania, and especially West Virginia. Perhaps spurred in part by the press coverage of Booker T. Washington's Atlanta Exposition address in September of 1895, Jones, according to a brief biography in the *Negro History Bulletin*, "became a speaker on the Chautauqua circuit."[62] While few of his speeches from the period seem to survive—or to even have been transcribed—the titles listed in "In Memoriam" and the *History* offer some sense of the topics of his lectures: John L. Jones lists "Is the Good Time Coming?"; "Frederick Douglass"; "Don't—Danger Signals"; "The Triple Tie"; "The Negro Problem Solved"; "The Silent Voter of the Silent South"; and "Abraham Lincoln." While some of these titles are relatively ambiguous, it is clear that others focus on constructing a specific sense of national and racial memory that could create opportunities for racial elevation and broader civil rights. This is also likely the approach Jones took in organizational speeches—like the address on "the fifty-three years' history of Odd Fellowship in America among his race" that he offered a Wheeling Odd Fellows audience in late February 1896.[63]

While some of these speeches clearly advocated acceptance of a partially Washingtonian framework, Jones never became and does not seem to have been inclined to be one of Washington's anointed disciples like, for example, Robert Russa Moton. While Washington and Jones clearly knew of each other and likely knew each other at least in passing, Jones is not included in the extant Washington correspondence and appears only once in Washington's major published works—as one of a number of signatories (including Atkinson) on a invitation asking Washington to speak in Charleston reproduced in *The Story of My Life and Work*.[64] The absence is especially curious given the fact that several men—Byrd Prillerman, who would later work with Jones at the West Virginia Colored Institute, and James Monroe Hazelwood, a childhood friend who would also work with Jones at WVCI, key among them—did engage Washington.[65] We could theorize that Jones was close enough to several of Washington's key stances (and simultaneously far enough away geographically) that he did not constitute a threat, that Jones was already well-established by the time the Washington machine was in full power, or that for other reasons the two decided consciously or unconsciously simply to co-exist, but the simple fact is that we do not yet know enough about Jones's biography to move beyond such speculation. Perhaps some indication of what we will discover through further research is Louis R. Harlan's comment about Washington's views on Jones in his important 1983 biography, *Booker T. Washington: The Wizard of Tuskegee, 1901–1915*. Harlan notes that the Tuskegee Machine looked for "a suitable black man to make the traditional seconding speech for Taft's nomination" at the Republican national presidential convention of 1908, and that Jones, then president of the West Virginia Colored Institute, was mentioned as a possibility. According to Harlan, Washington rejected the suggestion because he "thought Jones too dull a speaker."[66] Given Jones's reputation as a speaker, one can only wonder whether there is a larger story behind Washington's decision. In any event, Jones's presence as a political figure never extended far beyond the state level, though it was quite strong there.

Indeed, and in sharp contrast to Washington's views, Jones's subject matter, oratorical power, professional success, and place in the state were undoubtedly factors that led the West Virginia Republican Party to invite him to give a speech seconding the nomination of Atkinson as the Republican candidate for governor in July 1896. In that speech—published in the 31 July 1896 *Wheeling Daily Intelligencer*, reproduced in the appendix to this volume, and headed in part "The Speech of James McHenry Jones, Wheeling's Magnet Colored Orator"—readers will see traces of Jones's sense of both the past and the future of the nation. After invoking Gettysburg and so the American Civil War, Jones told his fellow Republicans that

> The history of our party is simply a record of triumphs of right. We were right in 1856, at the birth of the Republicanism. Right in 1860, under the leadership of the immortal Lincoln, right in '61, when it was determined that one flag should wave over an undivided county and liberty should not perish from the face of the earth. Doubly right in 1863, when it was finally concluded that the life of the nation demanded the freedom of the slave. Right under the peerless leadership of that matchless soldier, Grant. . . . .

Constructing a sense of the Republican party as the party of Lincoln, anti-slavery, and brave patriotism, Jones proved himself an able advocate for the role of black voices within the American political system. It was *those* Republicans who, Jones asserted, could stand "against the tumult and above the roar of populism"; Atkinson, who he described as both an "idol" and a "friend," thus could "pilot" that state "with a cool head, discerning eye, pure life, strong arm, open hand, and patriotic heart."

Jones likely walked a similar line in his role as planner and master of ceremonies for the September 1896 Emancipation Day celebration in Wheeling—a large gathering labeled a "tri-state affair" and including community members from Ohio, Pennsylvania, and West Virginia. Jones opened the day by reminding the primarily black attendees of the millions "of their number" who "had been set free by that illustrious statesman and martyr, President Abraham Lincoln." In both planning and probably in his transitional remarks between speeches, Jones then balanced a welcome by Wheeling's mayor—B. F. Caldwell, who, though a Republican, awkwardly mixed racism, paternalism, and the day's demands by referring to "colored troops" who "fought nobly" for the Union, but also asserting that "the war was not waged in the interest of the colored man, but for the maintenance of the union"—with a speech by black former congressman John Roy Lynch of Mississippi, who not only placed the nation's sacrifices as directly related to the need for emancipation but also blasted colonizationist efforts.[67]

It was at this time of political influence and his increasingly prominence in the state that Jones published *Hearts of Gold*. No doubt, he hoped that the novel could extend his efforts to gather an African American readership into an increasingly focused social and political force. He might have hoped as well that the novel would provide his white associates with a deeper understanding of the possibilities of black self-reliance and organization, given the novel's emphasis on black fraternal organizations, educational outreach, and the power of the black press. He might also have hoped that the novel's attention to mixed race characters—demonstrating "a century of miscegenation of the best blood of the Caucasian, Negro and Indian races"—would highlight a racial past that made the easy divisions of black and white less of a potent force in state and national politics. Whatever his hopes, the novel fell short of Jones's ambitions. Still, even though *Hearts* failed to gain much of an audience—in a white-dominated publishing and reading complex that, if it talked about African Americans at all, favored easy stereotypes—it did become another accomplishment on Jones's already impressive resume, and it undoubtedly joined with his political clout in West Virginia, his continuing power in the Odd Fellows, and his growing reputation as an orator to lead to two key opportunities in the late 1890s: the chance to address a British Odd Fellows gathering as black America's national representative and the appointment as president of the West Virginia Colored Institute.

Odd Fellow

It is significant that *Hearts of Gold* begins with characters "dressed in the fatigue uniform of the Knights of the Red Cross" to attend a "reunion of the Knights Templars," for African American fraternal organizations played an important role in early black efforts to organize communities and to shift the terms by which those communities were identified and understood. The most prominent of these fraternal organizations were the Grand United Order of Odd Fellows and the Prince Hall Freemasons, though there were many such organizations before the Civil War and a grand flourishing of them after the war. The draw of fraternal organizations was that they provided members with a fundamentally different orientation to the social order than was generally available to African Americans of this time.

At the most basic level, fraternal organizations were community networks offering access to opportunity and power, places where men could collaborate in business and politics, extending their economic and political reach by connecting with economic and social partners. Fraternal organizations also allowed members and communities to present a unified face to the broader public. The regalia that they featured identified a common bond among members, an internal discipline that countered the stereotypes and caricatures that dominated the mainstream press and minstrel stage, and those bonds were strengthened by the private rituals so central to fraternal organizations—the means by which men measured their achievements and progress in relation to one another and in relation to an established tradition of advancement. Indeed, the fraternal organizations' unique marriage of secrecy and public display provided African Americans with important ways to negotiate their way through a world in which privacy was often violated and public space often restricted.

These organizations were important, too, in countering the force of racism, for by becoming Freemasons or Odd Fellows, African Americans claimed membership, a fraternity, with men around the world. Of course, despite the ideals of brotherhood so central to fraternal organizations, there is little question that U.S. fraternal groups have been marked by racism, and that African American fraternal organizations developed in large part due to racist exclusions by white organizations. In the early twentieth century, the tensions between black and white fraternal orders erupted into a series of lawsuits over the right to claim certain affiliations. In the early years of black fraternal orders, the tensions were more fundamental—and African Americans gained membership through these organizations only by affiliating themselves with fraternal lodges beyond U.S. borders. Still, through fraternal rituals and celebrations, African American men (and women, in sister organizations) relocated themselves both culturally and historically, identifying themselves with a transnational tradition of brotherhood and with observances and a historical tradition of at least theoretically universal meaning and significance. Against the pressure of the world seemingly determined to reduce the meaning of their lives to the absurdities of racial ideology and law, they created, participated in, and inhabited (both in the lodges and in their public displays and acknowledgments of brotherhood) a world of meaning that was both wholly in their control and connected to a broader, transatlantic community.

Jones's sense of the possibilities of fraternal associations is clear in the opening pages of *Hearts of Gold*, where the global brotherhood of the Knights of the Red Cross seems to represented by the very bloodlines of its African American members. "Every kind and condition of the better class of Afro-Americans were here represented," Jones writes, and adds, "What a strange variety of human beings, what a panorama of the races of the world! In color, every nationality from Northern Europe, shading down through France, Italy, Portugal, across the Mediterranean into Egypt, Morroco, and then to Equatorial Africa. Perhaps not a man, woman or child of all these strangely dissimilar types would have hesitated a moment to answer to the name of 'Negro.'" Just as the long history of racial mixing had exposed the absurdities of neat racial distinctions, so their participation in a proud tradition of global brotherhood allowed African Americans to change their racial designation from a badge of degradation to an emblem of pride.

Jones was affiliated with various fraternal organizations, but the one in which he became most prominent was the Grand United Order of Odd Fellows, an organization that began in determined resistance to American racism. At the center of the story of this organization's development is Peter Ogden, a black man who served as a steward on the ship *Patrick Henry*, and a literary club, the Philomathean Institute, which included the influential African American printmaker Patrick H. Reason and James Fields. The members of the Philomathean Institute petitioned to become a lodge of the Odd Fellows, but they were refused—so they turned to Ogden, whose travels had taken him to Liverpool, England, where he had joined the Grand United Order of the Odd Fellows. Odgen took the group's request to England and obtained a charter on March 1, 1843. Fields became the first grand master of the lodge, and Ogden was honored as past grand master. Reason, who was also an influential Mason, served as grand master and permanent secretary of the black Odd Fellows in the 1850s. By the late 1850s, the fraternal order had made much more conscious moves toward communal activities—insurance, self-help, etc.—and had increased to over two dozen chapters. In the later nineteenth century, the Order spread not only west but especially south, and it boasted several thousand male members as well as a women's auxiliary, the Households of Ruth. Although the black Odd Fellows did not have the same struggle as the Prince Hall Freemasons in establishing their origins or legitimacy (a story in itself), they too faced significant challenges over the years. An early scholar of the Grand United Order of Odd Fellows in America, writing in 1902, looked back to Peter Ogden's initiative revealingly, suggesting that Ogden "thought it folly, a waste of time, if not self-respect, to stand, hat in hand, at the foot-stool of a class of men who, professing benevolence and fraternity, were most narrow and contracted, a class of men who judged another, not by principle and character, but by the shape of the nose, the curl of the hair, and the hue of the skin."[68] This statement speaks volumes about the racial tensions behind the organizations claiming fraternity and mutual support as their guiding ideals.

Jones began his long affiliation with the African American Grand United Order of Odd Fellows organization in 1877, when, at age eighteen, he was allowed to join with his father's permission. As African Americans in the middling classes, both Jones and his father were similar to many members—and especially many leaders—within the organization, and they would have been attracted to the Order's non-denominational Christian ethos, its sense of community elevation and race support, and its emphasis on history, oratory, and service.[69] Unsurprisingly, then, Jones became very important in the organization. The 26 January 1889 *Cleveland Gazette* asserts that J. McHenry Jones was already involved at the district level by 1880 and helped form the Ohio District Lodge in Columbus that year. Elected the District's Deputy Master in 1882 and then District Grand Master in 1883 and 1884, he was awarded a gold medal in 1885 for his "excellent management and . . . faithful performance of his duties." He was again elected District Grand Master in 1888 and served in this role until 1891. Both "In Memoriam" and the *Cleveland Gazette* credit him with making major changes in the organization's governance, and he continued to be active with the Order after stepping down as District Grand Master.

Through the Odd Fellows, Jones was able to reach a broad and international audience in furthering the ideals that began with Ogden, Fields, and Reason. The 290 men who attended the black Odd Fellows national convention in October 1896 in Indianapolis elected Jones their "fraternal delegate" to the upcoming British annual meeting; he thus became, according to Odd Fellows historian Charles Brooks, "the first delegate ever sent over to England by the Order."[70] In May of 1897, Jones duly applied for his passport, noting that he intended to return to the U.S. "within six months" and listing his job simply as "teacher."[71] Soon after, he traveled to Britain, where he arrived in Bolton in either late May or, more likely, early June.

He was welcomed by Britain's current Grand Master William Elliff and past Grand Master Richard Hill-Male. Hill-Male seems to have become his escort, and the two may well have been renewing an acquaintance made when Hill-Male toured the U.S. in 1894, visiting black Odd Fellows chapters across the East and receiving accolades for the British Odd Fellows' support of their African American compatriots. John Jones's *History* claims that J. McHenry Jones "was treated more as a prince than a common citizen. He was given 21 banquets, three by members of Parliament, he spoke at them all, not because he wanted to but because they insisted."[72] The *History* even claims that Jones rode in the Queen's Jubilee and that "the people along the line of march mistook him for an Indian prince and ran after his carriage cheering the prince."[73] In this, Jones likely sensed the differences in the ways Europeans could treat African Americans, and at an "informal dinner" with his British hosts offered a tellingly open joke that "he thought his presence amongst" the British Odd Fellows "would add colour to their meeting."

His introduction to the annual meeting's delegates, though, was much more formal—if just as positive. His speech (reproduced in Appendix B of this volume) was published in pamphlet form with a picture of an almost-dashing Jones in full evening dress. The speech's opening lines of his speech loftily describe "the deep and rolling ocean" he had crossed in order to demonstrate that both the black American Odd Fellows and his British audience were "plighting their vows at the same sacred altar, drinking from the same perennial stream at the fountain of Friendship . . . and worshipping at the Shrine of Truth." In a variation of the narrative common to his speeches discussed above, Jones briefly (although in more heavily metaphorical language) traced the history of the connection between the Odd Fellows on the two sides of the Atlantic.

But the speech quickly became a chance to showcase the achievements of black America—and especially the several thousand black Odd Fellows Jones had been chosen to represent. In this way, as in other aspects of his public career, Jones was a proponent of what is known as uplift ideology prominent among African Americans at the end of the nineteenth century and well into the twentieth. The politics of uplift ideology are highly contested, since it involves a reliance on the influence of race and class in a culture that often seems to be in denial about the centrality of the interlocking structures of race and class as driving social forces. But the most basic hope behind black uplift rhetoric was that through the associations of class, and especially middle-class values and morals, African Americans could decrease the force of racism and acquire acceptance in the social order. Kevin Gaines's explanation of uplift ideology is particularly pertinent to Jones's career:

Racial uplift ideals were offered as a form of cultural politics, in the hope that unsympathetic whites would relent and recognize the humanity of middle-class African Americans, and their potential for the citizenship rights black men possessed during Reconstruction. Elite blacks believed they were replacing the racist notion of fixed biological racial differences with an evolutionary view of cultural assimilation, measured primarily by the status of the family and civilization. Cultural differences, then, rather than biological notions of racial inferiority, were said to be more salient in explaining the lower social status of African Americans. And a middle-class consciousness stressing racial solidarity and self-help, uniting blacks across class lines, promised a more legitimate basis for social differentiation than color.[74]

The Odd Fellows offered an ideal forum to promote such views, and particularly an international audience, and Jones took advantage of the opportunity, placing African Americans not simply as supplicants for acceptance but as leaders in the work of uplifting the masses. He offered summaries of property ownership, activism, educational advancements, and professional achievements. But to these summaries, he added analysis that may well have been more radical than that his mixed American audiences heard: he told the British Odd Fellows that "the world has but one new woman—the Afro-American woman," that "the progress of the American Negro during the last generation finds no parallel in the history of the world," that "the work of educating and uplifting the masses has been largely done by our own people," and that "we have made bricks, gathering our own straw." While he certainly—as would black thinkers from Washington to Du Bois—addressed the self-sufficiency common in uplift rhetoric, his emphasis on the "self" of that concept (as a communal "we") is striking.

The British Odd Fellows received both Jones and his words warmly and quickly moved to publish his address. His contributions were also celebrated in the U.S. when he returned in late July after visiting Scotland, Wales, and Europe. "In Memoriam" and the *History* both note that Jones published letters "describing his travels" in the Odd Fellows *Journal*, although no extant copies containing such have been located.[75] The 30 July 1897 *Wheeling Register* reported that Jones was given "a royal welcome by his colored and white fellow citizens" on his return to the city—one that included a parade of both black Odd Fellows "in all the splendor of regalia and full dress suits" and "a platoon of police." Jones shared a carriage in the parade with Wheeling's mayor, and the festivities continued into the night with a banquet—at which Jones spoke.

Educator

That Jones was approaching national—indeed, international notice—was also confirmed by his appointment to lead the West Virginia Colored Institute. For all of its importance in his life, though, the events surrounding that appointment remain cloudy. John Jones's *History* claims that he was "elected to the presidency of the school at Institute, West Virginia" well "before leaving for England."[76] The Wheeling press did not report on the matter until a brief item in the 16 September 1898 *Wheeling Intelligencer* that claimed that the school's regents had just, by "special dispatch," named Jones to the position—replacing John H. Hill, who was supposedly leaving for "a first lieutenancy in the Eighth United States Infantry."

Subsequent newspaper coverage suggested a more complex story. Hill did leave—along with select students—and did enlist, serving as a First Lieutenant in the Virginia Sixth Infantry in the Spanish-American War.[77] But the 17 September 1898 *Wheeling Register* asked "Has Jones Been Elected?" and went on to describe "a queer proceeding on the part of a committee of the Board of Regents of the Colored State Normal School." Specifically, it asserted that "Republican members of the Executive Committee of the Board of Regents" hatched a "scheme" to "oust Hill and put Jones in as his successor"; apparently, the two Republican members of the three-man committee failed to notify the third member of a meeting date and, at that meeting, issued "the statement . . . that Prof. Jones had been chosen." The *Register* quoted the *Charleston Gazette*, which argued that this was "a slap in the face, direct and hard, of the colored people of this part of West Virginia" because the position "belongs and has practically been promised to a man in this section"; Jones was a "Panhandle" man and was apparently receiving the appointment because "Ohio county is going to cut quite a figure in the contest for the United States Senatorship. Too many plums cannot be distributed in that section." "The fine Italian hand of [Republican] Chairman Dawson and the John Hancock of the Governor [Atkinson] is in the transaction," the paper concluded. For his part, Jones told the local papers, including the *Register*, that he was "well pleased with Wheeling" and "had received no communication of any kind bearing on the subject."

Years later, Governor Atkinson was fittingly vague on the subject, saying that a "vacancy occurred" at the Institute, that the "regents sought about for an established educator," and that Jones was "unanimously chosen"; Atkinson's "recollection" was that "this took place during my term, but whether it was or not, I know I endorsed him as a suitable and worthy man."[78] Whether through the governor's hand or simply through a majority of the regents making the selection, the tempest was quickly placed in a teapot. The 22 September 1898 *Wheeling Intelligencer*—probably gloating a bit after the competing *Register*'s claims—told readers that Jones was introduced to the staff and students of the Institute "as their president. Formerly the head of the institution was the principal, the higher office of president has been created for Prof. Jones" who "has been a power for good in his social, scholastic, and religious connections" in Wheeling.

As Jones readied himself to leave Lincoln, he likely saw the move as a new beginning in more ways than one: some time in either late 1895 or early 1896, he had hired Elizabeth S. Moore as a teacher at Lincoln; at some point in late 1897, they married.[79] Little is known about Moore, who was fifteen years Jones's junior. Born in Ohio, with parents from Kentucky, she is occasionally listed with the middle initial "M." John Jones's *History* and "In Memoriam" both say she was from Cincinnati, but the commonness of her last name makes finding record of her there difficult. The 1910 Census—taken less than a year after J. McHenry's death—lists her specifically as a "music instructor" at the Institute and as living next door to her brother-in-law Charles Jones, who began teaching at the school late in his brother's tenure as president. J. McHenry and Elizabeth Jones had no children, and both seem to have devoted their lives to the Institute.

If Jones's ascension to the presidency of the Institute was a patronage appointment, he was nonetheless one of the most qualified men in the state for the position and was well-suited to take on its challenges. If there was actually "a man in this section" that residents thought should have the job—perhaps Byrd Prillerman, a Knoxville College graduate who had helped establish the Institute and served as head of the English department under both Campbell and Hill—Jones seems to have quickly smoothed over any concerns. Prillerman, a friend of both Booker T. Washington and Carter G. Woodson, remained at the Institute throughout Jones's years as president and worked closely with him.[80] Hill himself even, according to Bickley, "returned from military service and became the Commandant of the Cadets" and instructor in military science, "a position which he held until 1903."[81]

Jones quickly moved to use his connections for the Institute's benefit. West Virginia's state appropriations for the school, for example, went from $29,000 in 1897 to $39,000 in 1899; by 1905, they were at almost $68,000.[82] Enrollment went from around 100 students in 1897 to 225 in 1906.[83] Jones pushed for state legislation to fund military training at the Institute, and in 1899 the "Cadet Bill" began supporting up to sixty male students in a program "both theoretical and practical" that existed well into the twentieth century.[84] Jones also garnered support to add to the Institute's physical plant. Easily the gem among these improvements was the 1903 A. B. White Trade School building, which Jones described as "the most commodious and by far the largest building connected with the school . . . with ornaments" that "would be a credit to any institution."[85]

"This building," Jones continued, "erected at a cost of thirty-five thousand dollars" was "finished by the students of the school" and, "if we except the Armstrong-Slater Trades School at Tuskegee," was "the largest building of its kind in the United States"; it was also "without exception" the "best lighted and most convenient" industrial training building in the nation.[86]

Clearly, Jones saw these measures as the maturing of a much-needed institution that had only begun offering classes in 1892—after being created by the West Virginia legislature in 1891. The logical end—one which Jones did not live to see—was growing the Institute into a fully fledged college.[87] Still, he made significant strides toward that goal and held fast to the sense that WVCI should never be simply a school of industrial and domestic arts. Bickley notes revisions during Jones's tenure to the Institute's catalogs, entrance exams, and especially its curriculum—which "under the [faculty] leadership of Charles E. Mitchell, a graduate of the Boston Commercial College" included new "courses in bookkeeping, shorthand, banking, transportation, commercial law, dictation, orthography, and economic history."[88] These revisions and Jones's emphasis on a normal school structure suggest that Jones took the model of Tuskegee and equally emphasized teacher training; he asserted in 1907 that "the course of study in the West Virginia Colored Institute is the same as that which is pursued in the other normal schools of the State. In addition to the book-work, every student is required to learn some useful trade before graduation."[89] So successful was Jones in teacher training that, in 1908, the state legislature "exempted Institute graduates from the state teachers' examinations," giving them, in Arline Thorn's words, "the same privileges as those with diplomas from white normal schools."[90]

Jones had reason to be proud of the Institute's results, as he emphasized in this summary of the Institute's alumni in a 1907 essay:

> In all one hundred and sixty-one students have graduated from the school since 1896; of these eighty-five are engaged in teaching, three are successful pastors, two are machinists, one an attorney at law, sixteen are carpenters, six blacksmiths, and twelve are dressmakers. The remainder are leading useful lives. A casual glance at the above figures reveals the fact that by far the larger half of the graduates from our school have devoted their energies to teaching. This is true of the first graduates from nearly all institutions for normal and industrial training for negroes. It grows out of the great demand among us for trained teachers. Many of these teachers, however, follow their trades during vacation from school duties.[91]

The 1900 Federal Census listing of the Institute expands on this snapshot. The 125 students listed—probably a bit lower than the full enrollment, given that the census-taker visited in mid-June—were all African American.[92] The vast majority were between the ages of fifteen and twenty-one, although there were seventeen students over twenty-one, three thirteen-year-olds, and even ten-year-old Ida Harvey of Powelton, West Virginia. Fifty-five of the students were male, and seventy were female. They came from larger cities like Wheeling and Charleston, but also from towns like Mount Carbon, Red Sulphur, and Winifred. While almost all were from West Virginia, there were a handful from Ohio and even one from Chicago. The census says nothing about their fields of study and next to nothing about their backgrounds, but their geographical range strongly suggests Jones's commitment to expanding educational opportunities for

African Americans throughout the region. He was always reminded that his teachers were working "with the children of race scarcely a generation removed from slavery" and that he was trying to help in "fitting" those young people "for the complicated economic and moral duties of life" and to "inspire" them "with the spirit of real liberty and true citizenship."[93]

Jones was also fully cognizant of the importance of promoting his school—a role through which Booker T. Washington, of course, seized national prominence. Jones continued speaking widely, wrote occasionally (including a piece for the 1904 *History of Education in West Virginia*, which he revised and updated for the 1907 edition), and, according to Bickley, "sent exhibit items to the Jamestown Exposition, the first such activity in which the Institute's students are known to have participated."[94] However, unlike Washington, Jones seems to have set aside desires for national fame—though he did serve time as a national officer of the Odd Fellows (rising, in 1902, to the position of National Grand Master). Again unlike Washington, with the exception of his Odd Fellows work, he seems to have focused his energies within his adopted state.

Jones joined Charleston businessmen Samuel W. Starks and James W. Hazelwood in what Bickley calls a "triumvirate" of black leaders in West Virginia who worked closely together on a range of issues. Starks operated a number of businesses and, after founding the West Virginia Grand Lodge of the neo-Masonic secret society the Knights of Pythias in 1892, eventually rose to the rank of national chancellor of the Knights in 1901—with a membership (including Jones) that grew to rival the numbers of black Odd Fellows. Hazelwood, an immensely successful barber and entrepreneur who grew up in Ohio and knew Jones from his youth, became the first black regent of the West Virginia Colored Institute—even serving for a time as the Board's treasurer.[95]

All firm Republicans, the trio played party politics well: Starks, for example, was appointed as the State Librarian in 1901 and held that position until he died in 1908, and Jones was, according to Bickley, named an Alternate at Large to the 1908 Republican National Convention in Chicago.[96] The trio, along with John C. Gilmer (who seems to have done the lion's share of work with Starks), was also involved in the founding of the *Charleston Advocate*. Jones also rose to a leadership role in the West Virginia State Teachers Association. In short, these figures, along with

Christopher Payne (prior to his 1903 appointment as Consul General to the Virgin Islands), were recognized as "race leaders"—with all of the complexity and richness of that term in the early twentieth century. Jones also seems to have explored various business ventures. Aiken and Perdreau note that Jones "was a member of the board of directors of the first oil company in the United States to be owned and operated by African Americans."[97]

During these years, Jones never forgot his family ties. Brothers Fleming and Charles followed him to West Virginia: Fleming replaced his brother as principal at Lincoln Elementary, and Charles would teach at the Institute for more than three decades. Alexander similarly followed and worked in Charleston as a barber. As their parents aged and then both suffered bouts with pneumonia, the family decided that J. McHenry's situation at the Institute would afford the best care for them. John Jones's *History* says that there "they had a nice home with everything a heart could wish, the faculty and student body made much over them, everybody was kind and affectionate. . . ."[98] Joseph Jones died that on 13 December 1904, and Temperance followed on 13 July 1905.

Approaching sixty, Jones seems to have begun to consider retirement and seems to have renewed his interest in literature. Bickley reports that Institute students and staff staged *Hearts of Gold* as a five-act play in May of 1907, and both his brother's *History* and "In Memoriam" claim that he authored another novel titled *The Bluevaynes* that was "ready for publication at the time of his death"—though no other record of this novel has been found.[99] The *History* asserts that Jones planned "to give up school work, build a home in Wheeling, West Virginia, and write for the rest of his time."[100]

Still, he continued to lecture and was especially invested in an invitation to speak at the annual meeting of the International Epworth League, a primarily white Methodist Episcopal youth ministry organization that was founded in Cleveland in 1889 and grew into a large movement that flourished until the 1920s. African Americans were generally skeptical about the League's early work, in part because, like the broader white Methodist Episcopal Church, it was uneven on race and civil rights and in part because most black churches were actively advancing their own youth organizations (like the A. M. E. Church's Christian Endeavor Society).[101]

Still, Jones was both tied to the Methodist Episcopal Church and consistently interested in building cross-racial relationships; he also knew that the 1909 conference held in Seattle would be a massive event. Extracts of his 8 July 1909 speech there—included in "In Memoriam"—suggest that it was fairly tame and focused on the League's potential to inculcate youth with the morality Jones found so essential. That said, Jones did remind his listeners that "neither Saxon Christianity nor Saxon civilization can make of my race a simple reflex in ebony of itself. Race ideals and race distinction must not be ignored."[102] According to former West Virginia Supreme Court Judge H. C. McWhorter—in a letter first published in the 24 September 1909 *Charleston Gazette*—Jones "was the last speaker, but one," and, though "the hour was getting late and the people wearied," he held "that vast audience" of "6,000 or 8,000 in undivided attention to the close of his magnificent address."

He used his return trip to move across the nation at a more relaxed pace, stopping along the way to visit friends as well as an Ohio District meeting of the Odd Fellows. His health worsened quickly, though, and he died on 22 September 1909 of Bright's Disease; his brother's *History* notes that he was scheduled "to make an Emancipation Day speech in Pittsburgh on that day."[103]

Jones's funeral was a massive affair—featuring addresses by the sitting West Virginia governor William Glasscock as well as former governor Atkinson and a host of black and white dignitaries. Glasscock called him, as reported on the front page of the 26 September 1909 *Charleston Gazette*, "a big, broad-minded, well-liked, and patriotic citizen of West Virginia." Family friend (and probable cousin) I. V. Bryant of Huntington, West Virginia's First Baptist delivered the central eulogy, but the personal remembrance by National Odd Fellow Grand Master W. L. Houston—which asserted that "the greatest men are the tenderest" and that Jones was both—was perhaps more memorable.[104] In part because of the cluster of voices at his funeral, Jones was remembered as an educator at the national level for several years; Roscoe Conkling Simmons, for example, named him (along with Daniel Payne and Booker T. Washington) as one of history's "great educators, race or no race" in a 8 June 1940 *Chicago Defender* piece. Still, J. McHenry Jones and his single published novel sank into obscurity.

Hearts of Gold and the Challenge of Racial Justice

As noted above, Jones reportedly wrote a novel, *A Strange Transformation*, during his first marriage, and for reasons as yet unknown—but likely related to both the political and social arguments noted above and his longstanding commitment to education generally and literacy specifically—Jones returned to the idea of a novel during the height of his influence in West Virginia. The result was *Hearts of Gold*, which Jones arranged to have published through the Wheeling *Daily Intelligencer*'s offices in 1896. The book's print run seems to have been small (as very few copies are extant), and its reception limited, even though John Jones's *History* claimed that it "was widely distributed and eagerly read by all classes."[105] The Indianapolis *Freeman* included a front page picture of Jones in its 24 October 1896 issue with this caption:

> J. M'Henry Jones, Ex. D[istrict] G[rand] M[aster], Author of "Hearts of Gold." The book treats the Negro as an American. Hitherto the writers who have told the story of the Negro, have confined their efforts to the Uncle Toms. These stories served their purpose, but there is a new Negro, not peculiar or particularly different from other Americans who loves, hates, suffers and succeeds, in common with their fellows. Mr. Jones assumes in his well told story that the characters in "Hearts of Gold" are simply Americans. The style is commendable, the plot interesting and the book as a whole is a valuable contribution to the realm of fiction.

Still, the *Freeman* said nothing else about the novel except for a brief mention of it in a short summary of Jones's accomplishments in a 27 May 1899 report on one of his lectures. Given the *Freeman*'s place in black letters, it seems likely that Jones himself sent the paper a copy in hopes that they would promote it. The Black Periodical Literature Project also identifies a brief notice of the book in the 23 April 1898 Kansas *American*, but scholars have found no other contemporary reviews.[106]

Of the eight extant copies examined in preparing this introduction, four were presentation copies, likely sent in similar fashion to the copy that the *Freeman* used in its short review. The most notable of those presentation copies is now in Ohio State's Charvat collection; it went to I. Garland Penn, one of the most important figures in the world of the black press, whose 1891 *Afro-American Press and Its Editors* is still recognized as a crucial early effort in the history of black journalism.[107] We have yet to locate a written response by Penn, although his copy does contain some marginalia (mainly underlining) that suggests that he read at least part of the book. While *Hearts* is mentioned in a handful of recent critical works, it was, soon after its publication, essentially ignored and then quickly forgotten.[108]

Such neglect of African American literature was hardly rare during the closing decades of the nineteenth century, even though African Americans were a frequent presence in literature by white writers. The Civil War was among other things a conflict of various narratives—national, regional, religious, and racial. Its influence on American literature was profound, as various studies have demonstrated.[109] It was also a time when the significance and centrality of race in the United States was variously exposed and veiled, and in the wake of the Civil War the course of racial history was altered in significant ways. Following the Civil War, the racial presence in literature by white Americans became increasingly pronounced. During this period, Joel Chandler Harris produced his famous series of stories about Uncle Remus, drawn from black folk culture but geared towards the tastes of white readers—a series of stories and poems that included *Uncle Remus: His Songs and His Sayings* (1881), *Nights with Uncle Remus* (1883), *Uncle Remus and His Friends* (1892), *The Tar-Baby and Other Rhymes of Uncle Remus* (1904), and *Uncle Remus and Br'er Rabbit* (1906), leading to the founding of Harris's *Uncle Remus's Magazine* in 1907. These stories of the wise and earthy wisdom of Uncle Remus, presented in dialect and set in an idealized world of plantation slavery, romanticized the system of slavery and produced a stereotypical vision of black life and thought that has remained potent in American culture ever since. That idealized vision of the Old South—later made one of white American culture's most powerful obsessions through Margaret Mitchell's novel *Gone with the Wind* and the film that followed—was powerful in part because it appealed to both white fantasies about the past and white fears about the black presence in American politics and society. The romantic vision was provided by such writers as Thomas Nelson Page in such books as *In Ole Virginia* (1887), *The Old Gentleman of the Black Stock* (1897), and *Red Rock* (1898), all of which promoted the vision of the grand lost cause of the honorable Old

South—which of course meant the *white* Old South, with a supporting cast of dialect-speaking and happy slaves—and the perceived loss after the Civil War of what Page and others promoted as a Golden Age in the South. The major contributor to the other side of the this idealized story, playing to white fears, was Thomas Dixon, who in a series of novels—*The Leopard's Spots* (1902), *The Clansman* (1905), and *The Traitor* (1907)—told a threatening tale of the Civil War and Reconstruction so as to tell the tale of those he presented as the guardians and saviors of Christian order and western civilization, the Ku Klux Klan.

In the context of such portrayals of American history, African American writers faced one of the most significant battles that followed the Civil War—the battle over the public imagination through literature. For African Americans, the Civil War was both the fulfillment of a long-developing story of liberation and justice and, following the abandonment of Reconstruction efforts to provide African Americans with rights and opportunities, a forceful reminder of the limitations of a linear, progressive narrative of history, albeit a reminder not evident to many at the time. Progress was both everywhere and nowhere, a new set of paths to follow and a series of familiar dead ends in a virulently racist culture. Similarly, African Americans were everywhere in American literature, but they were usually enslaved blacks speaking dialects and happily gesturing to a romanticized past that had been lost with the southern cause. In such a culture, how could African American writers, with limited access to the usual and white-controlled publishing venues, get a fair hearing? A great deal of African American literature published during this period, accordingly, was necessarily devoted not only to envisioning a self-reliant and thriving black community but also to deconstructing white images (literary and otherwise) of black identity and potential. For example, one character in Frances Harper's intricate novel *Trial and Triumph*, published serially from 1888–1889, complains to a white merchant with whom he shares "kindred intellectual and literary tastes" that books by black authors go unread by white readers; and of the "unaspiring" inhabitants of one depressed neighborhood, the narrator explains, "The literature they read was mostly from the hands of white men who would paint them in any colors which suited their prejudices or predilections."[110] Similarly, in "The Negro as Presented in American Literature," an essay included in her 1892 book

A Voice from the South (with the author on the title page listed only as "A Black Woman of the South"), educator Anna Julia Cooper discusses the role literature plays in the promotion of distorted and essentialized images of races and cultures. Noting the tendency of white writers to base their black characters on the writers' perceptions of whatever black people they happened to encounter, Cooper complains that "a few with really kind intentions and a sincere desire for information have approached the subject as a clumsy microscopist, not quite at home with his instrument, might study a new order of beetle or bug. Not having focused closely enough to obtain a clear-cut view, they begin by telling you that all colored people look exactly alike and end by noting down every chance contortion or idiosyncrasy as a race characteristic."[111]

This consistent concern with misrepresentations that defined the purpose of the overwhelming majority of nineteenth-century publications produced by African American writers operated within a national context defined by the instabilities of what is too often taken to be a stable and even self-evident category of identification: race. Of the many changes wrought by the Civil War—and by the economic, industrial, and political developments that followed in the war's wake—one of the most significant was that of race itself. As Matthew Frye Jacobson has demonstrated, from the 1840s to the 1920s U.S. culture was characterized by a "spectacular rate of industrialization," a corresponding "appetite for cheap labor" that encouraged migration, and a "growing nativist perception of these laborers as a political threat to the smooth functioning of the republic."[112] Responding to such changes and the shifting politics of American demographics, the nation moved "from the unquestioned hegemony of a unified race of 'white persons'" to "a contest over political 'fitness' among a now fragmented, hierarchically arranged series of distinct 'white races.'"[113] These changes in conceptions of whiteness naturally presented challenges to black Americans in their efforts to define the terms of their collective identity. While many of the most prominent African American writers and political leaders had long argued against the relevance and even the existence of race, they had recognized as well that those of African heritage were subject to prejudices, laws, social practices, and scientific theories that insisted on its existence and relevance. African Americans were defined by simplified conceptions of their complex relations with

Africans, other African Americans, white Americans, and various immigrant groups, conceptions that often were played out in political articles and books, scientific treatises, literature, drama, popular song, and the minstrel stage. It was virtually impossible for African Americans to escape the pressures of racial thought, and it was therefore imperative for African American writers to deal with that thought in literature—often matching romanticized and idealized white portrayals with corresponding romances that accounted for racial violence and offered possibilities for envisioning a more just future.

But as Jones's approach in *Hearts of Gold* indicates, African American writers felt a need to challenge the stereotypical portrayals of happy slaves with complex portrayals of the absurdities of race and of the diversity of the African American populace. Certainly, this was a time when the absurdities of race were quite obvious, since the legal system struggled, through the one-drop rule and other measures, to even define who did and did not count as white. Indeed, Mark Smith has argued that, while many discussions of race work from the default mode of visual markers, increasingly race was identified and experienced by a broader realm of sensory characteristics. These other racial markers, Smith notes, became increasingly prominent toward the end of the century, a time when "many whites worried that blackness was in danger of becoming whiteness."[114] "The number of visually ambiguous 'black' people," Smith observes, "increased (the great age of 'passing' was 1880–1925), and sight became ever less reliable as an authenticator of racial identity."[115] While sensory perceptions in interracial interactions had played a role in antebellum racial politics as well, their importance increased during these years, to the point of constituting a significant reconfiguration of the dynamics of racial thought and experience:

> Ascertaining racial identity was even more important under segregation than under slavery because race had to be authenticated on a daily basis between strangers in a modernizing, geographically fluid South. The basis of segregation, a system that argued for the utter, intrinsic, static, and meaningful difference between black and white, was a product of a late nineteenth-century, largely Western questioning of vision, in which Western elites generally, southern segregationists included, found they could no longer rely solely on

their modern eyes to verify all sorts of truths, racial ones included. Segregationists faced this visual tremor with aplomb. The problems with seeing gave further authority to nonvisual sensory stereotypes, such that smelling, tasting, feeling, and hearing race were now more important—and, whites liked to believe, more reliable—than ever.[116]

The effect was to centralize racial affiliation in the imagined racial consciousness or even subconsciousness, that complex of factors that theoretically made one comfortable or uncomfortable, attracted or repulsed, empathetic or distanced in social encounters—both those encounters that took place in a racial theater of sorts (that is, those segregated areas where one could be theoretically confident about those whom one might encounter) and those that took place in less certain interpretive contexts.

What Smith calls the "emotional, visceral, and febrile understanding of racial identity" was often a prominent presence in late-century writing by white writers, constituting one of the many concerns African American writers needed to address in turn.[117] When Thomas Dixon Jr., for example, did all that he could to demonize African Americans in his pointedly white supremacist fiction at the turn of the century, prominent among his literary devices were appeals to the senses of smell and touch, appeals brought to a visceral point in the threat of interracial rape. In his own commentary on social divisions within the black community, African American writer Charles Chesnutt similarly appealed to the senses in his complaint against the Jim Crow cars on the train, and in his story of light-skinned African Americans, "The Wife of His Youth," Chesnutt contrasts social divisions based in part on visual distinctions with the tug of a felt allegiance to a historically constituted network of affiliations. One thinks as well of the exchange in Frances Harper's *Iola Leroy* between the white Dr. Latrobe and the African American Dr. Latimer, whom Latrobe believes to be white. Latrobe boasts, "The Negro . . . is perfectly comprehensible to me," and he claims that he can always identify a "nigger," no matter how white he or she may appear, for "there are tricks of blood which always betray them."[118] When Latimer points out Dr. Latrobe's error, Latrobe disappears from both the scene and the novel itself. The increasing prominence of dialect, too, in its appeal to the ear, helped to serve as a racial marker and a racial boundary, indicating a more primitive, essential consciousness that spoke of a fundamentally different world and mode of understanding. From Uncle Remus to the ongoing insistence that Sojourner Truth is somehow more authentic when speaking in a stereotypically black southern dialect (she was raised in a Dutch-speaking community in upstate New York), white representations of black identity in literature specialized in the transformation of visual difference into that world of intellectual and sensory cues by which such differences are represented on the page.[119] The experience of reading, one might say, involves always the illusions of visual experience presented by way of verbal appeals to a broader realm of sensory and psychological experience, and the representation of race in literature by white writers of this time is a particularly insistent example of this, whether the purpose of that literature is to celebrate black folk wisdom or caution readers about threats to white civilization.

As Smith argues, and as the ongoing appeal to white readers and audiences of late-century representations of race suggest, the very instabilities of racial thought led to a new and increasingly insistent stability, for these instabilities led to an understanding of racial identity that was "immune to logic, impervious to thought, and, as such, a perfect foundation for segregation."[120] The white rage to explain the perceived necessity of black subordination was the subject of numerous books, both fiction and nonfiction, a tradition that has had considerable influence and ongoing appeal. From such overtly racist nineteenth-century books as J. H. Van Evrie's *White Supremacy and Negro Subordination; or, Negroes a subordinate race, and (so-called) slavery its normal condition* (1868) to *The Bell Curve* in the twentieth century, from Uncle Remus to Disney's *Song of the South*, from Thomas Dixon's fiction to the film *Birth of a Nation*, and then to *Gone with the Wind*, popular also as both novel and film, white culture has long provided space for essentialized representations of black identity that fall into familiar patterns. "Segregationists," Smith observes,

> lived an illogical, emotionally powerful lie that relied on gut rather than brain to fix racial identity and order society. Their ability to make solid what was always slippery is annoyingly impressive. When it came to race, ordinarily thoughtful people contorted reason to fit a system of racial segregation riddled with so many exceptions and nuances that it should have

imploded under its own nonsense. But that is not what happened. Sensory stereotypes—and the unthinking, visceral behavior they encouraged, even required—helped make the system seem entirely stable, reasonable, and appropriate to the people who sponsored it. This tension, along with the ability to reconcile the ostensibly contradictory, was present from the very beginning of formal segregation."[121]

In such a chaotic social system, defining the course for African American uplift, individual and collective, involved much more than direct political action or intraracial organization. Before the Civil War, African American abolitionists understood well the ways in which slavery, racism, economics, and politics were intricately related, and the history of the black convention movements, fraternal societies, press, and educational initiatives demonstrates both their awareness of the comprehensive efforts required as well as the overwhelming complexity of the task. It is no wonder that so many black abolitionists viewed the Civil War as the second American Revolution. But the nation awaiting at the other side of that revolution was more complex still than the one that preceded it, and it was a nation in which race played a new, if familiar, and even more threatening role than it had before the war.

The effects of the racial landscape that supported these multiple wars, this national community organized by way of its own instabilities, were inscribed in turn in black expressive culture. Observing that "terror, organized and random, was a persistent part of politics in the postwar South," the historian David Blight rightly notes that these conditions defined the needs of African American expressive culture, and that, accordingly, "black folklore, fiction, and reminiscence have reflected the legacy of violence that began during Reconstruction."[122] Bernard Bell similarly notes the challenges faced by black American writers of the time, observing that "as twenty-first-century readers, we are inclined to forget the tenacity of the tradition of white supremacy with which postbellum and post-Reconstruction black novelists had to contend and the gravity of their dilemma."[123] As Trudier Harris has noted, "between 1882 and 1927, an estimated 4,951 persons were lynched in the United States. Of that number, 3,513 were black and 76 of those were black women."[124] Harris argues persuasively that these lynchings were significantly symbolic of white fears. "Historically, in their ritualistic lynchings of black people," she asserts, "white Americans were carrying out rites of exorcism in which they seemed determined to eradicate the black 'beast' from their midsts, except when he existed in the most servile, accommodationist, and helpful of positions."[125] As we have suggested above, this led to a white obsession with black characters in literature ranging from servile and happy black slaves to threatening black soldiers and rapists after the Civil War, literature that often either led to or promoted the cause of white violence against blacks. And such representations required a response. As Jerry Bryant has argued, by the end of the nineteenth century,

> lynching had acquired a symbolic power far greater than the numbers involved. It demonstrated the total political, social, and economic powerlessness of the African American, representing the most vindictive of all the forms of violence whites invented for terrorizing blacks, restoring white supremacy, and identifying blacks as sinister, subhuman threats to the racial purity of the southern Anglo-Saxon. By the end of the nineteenth century, when the post-Reconstruction white supremacist campaign had become most intense and most successful, lynching, though hardly the only form of violence in black life, had become the most conspicuous and dramatic. Thus, though they also deal with rape, beatings, and riots, lynching is the principle symbol of white violence the African American novelists treat in the first decades of the novel's development.[126]

Through their writings, African Americans tried to both expose the injustice of lynchings and force white American culture to come to terms with a new world populated by black Americans unlike anything found in the popular literature written by white authors.

The threats to black liberty and life extended far beyond overt acts of murder, however. As Leon Litwack has observed, "In what has been called the 'nadir' of African American history, a new generation of black Southerners shared with the survivors of enslavement a sharply proscribed and deteriorating position in a South bent on commanding black lives and black labor by any means necessary."[127] Among those means was a reconstruction of the legal system to create a new form of slavery in the form of forced labor, particularly though not exclusively in the South. As Martha

Myers has documented, "The link between the penitentiary and the development of a capitalist political economy was particularly close in the South, which long relied heavily on a different organization of convict labor known as the lease system. In 1885, only a minority of all productively employed convicts worked under this system. In the South, however, 65 percent of all productively employed convicts were so engaged. Alternatively put, of all convicts leased to private entrepreneurs, a full 96 percent were in the South."[128] As Ron Lewis puts it, "Under the convict-leasing system, a white power structure benefited financially from forcing black prisoners against their will to labor under physical and psychological conditions that were all too reminiscent of slavery."[129] The crimes by which African Americans might land in such circumstances were many, but it is not a stretch to say that many were simply convicted of being black and powerless. "Instead of thousands of true thieves and thugs drawn into the system over decades," Douglass Blackmon observes,

> the records demonstrate the capture and imprisonment of thousands of random indigent citizens, almost always under the thinnest chimera of probably cause or judicial process. . . . Instead of evidence showing black crime waves, the original records of county jails indicated thousands of arrests for inconsequential charges or for violations of laws specifically written to intimidate blacks—changing employers without permission, vagrancy, riding freight cars without a ticket, engaging in sexual activity—or loud talk—with white women. Repeatedly, the timing and scale of surges in arrests appeared more attuned to rises and dips in the need for cheap labor than any demonstrable acts of crime. Hundreds of forced labor camps came to exist, scattered throughout the South—operated by state and county governments, large corporations, small-time entrepreneurs, and provincial farmers. These bulging slave centers became a primary weapon of suppression of black aspirations.[130]

Many argue, and with good cause, that these practices have been immensely influential in the subsequent development of the American legal system, accounting for the current prevalence of non-white prisoners in a penitentiary system increasingly under the control of private corporations.

While a great deal of African American literature addresses the abuses of the American legal system, though, Jones is singular in devoting a significant plot line to the convict mining system. Lewis observes, "Leasing, which evolved out of the heritage of slavery as an adaptation to the needs of a nascent industrial capitalism in its aggressively exploitative stage, may have sprung from habits of thought and attitudes rooted in agricultural slavery, but it took nourishment and flourished in the New South's most dangerous labor-intensive industries, especially mining. Slaves had, after all, worked in the region's coal mines, so it was an easy progression to send convicts into them after the war. Just as slave owners desired a cheap and tractable labor force, so did industrialists."[131] In having a black physician unjustly accused, convicted, and sent to almost certain death in the mines under this system, Jones follows the development from slave labor to the convict leasing system that Lewis examines—placing a symbol of African American achievement, strength, and hope in a system designed to obstruct achievement, exhaust strength, and discourage all hope for a more just future. As Lewis notes, among its other purposes "leasing was also an important pillar of the South's racial hierarchy. Whites who were afraid that the hierarchy of the Old South was beginning to crumble took aggressive action to reinforce the edifice of white supremacy through the now familiar mechanisms of segregation."[132] By manipulating the legal system, whites created a new form of racial control deeply linked with the old, as if to both assert and assure that the Civil War had changed nothing. "Consequently," Lewis observes, "the prison population became overwhelmingly black, and disproportionately, blacks were leased to do the hard, dirty, and dangerous work of mining coal."[133] The result of this "unholy alliance between government and capital was a labor system with a mortality rate three times higher than the rate in northern prisons, and at certain mines ten times higher,"[134] a result that Jones depicts with vivid clarity.

Hearts of Gold, then, is much more than "one of the more romantic novels of the period." It is a novel in which Jones draws from his extensive experience in public and private spheres to expose the injustices of a murderously threatening culture while also responding to white misrepresentations of black life. Against the Uncle Remus school of idealized earthy slaves with amusing folk wisdom, Jones offers readers physicians, newspaper editors, Odd Fellows, and strong women who represent in their bloodlines, their families, their educations, and their social affiliations a proud African American community that cannot be reduced either to stereotypes or to the neat boundaries of the color line. This is an African American community defined not solely by the racial absurdities of American culture but also by the tradition of African American self-determination and community service. Against the idealized Old South of Thomas Nelson Page, Jones explores the challenges and opportunities of a new South guided by a quest for educational, economic, and social justice. And against the terrorizing depictions of a threatening black mass that would soon dominate the fiction of Thomas Dixon, Jones draws his readers to other terrors and locates the security of civilization in the cause of African Americans struggling against white manipulations of the economic and legal systems. Offering one of the most horrific scenes of lynching in American fiction and an extended portrayal of the murderous machinations of the convict mining system, Jones balances romance with harsh realities—a classic story of separated and reunited lovers tainted by a white supremacist culture that makes theirs a story of the chaotic entanglements of a culture that has gone violently astray from its proclaimed ideals.

The story of mining hearts of gold in Jones's novel takes us to other mines and other hearts, and to a depiction of late-nineteenth-century life that draws readers "below the surface of black thought and action in the post-Reconstruction period" and into "the underlying structures of ideas and feelings behind the more visible responses to white racial oppression." Over a century later, we still have much to learn from the singular excursion into fiction of this remarkable African American educator and leader.

Notes

1 Dickson D. Bruce Jr., *Black American Writing from the Nadir: The Evolution of a Literary Tradition, 1877–1915* (Baton Rouge: Louisiana State University Press, 1989), xi.

2 Ibid., 138–139.

3 John Jones, *History of the Jones Family*, in *Annotated Edition of the* History of the Jones Family, *by John L. Jones & In Memoriam: J. McHenry Jones*, by Nancy E. Aiken and Michel S. Perdreau (Bowie, Maryland: Heritage Books, 2001), 1. All references to *History of the*

Jones Family and *In Memoriam* are to this edition. For the sake of clarity, all references to Aiken and Perdreau and to *In Memoriam* will be listed under *History of the Jones Family.*

4 *History of the Jones Family* (53–54n1). Perdreau's contributions to local history re: southeast Ohio are significant, especially in terms of rescuing the history of the region's African Americans from relative oblivion. For an introduction to this work, see "African Americans in Southeast Ohio" online at <http://www.seorf.ohiou.edu/~xx057/>.

5 There is more disagreement, however, on Elizabeth Ailstock's ethnic background. John L. Jones says that Elizabeth was the daughter of the Englishman Joseph Ailstock and a woman he refers to as a "squaw" (2). Aiken and Perdreau, citing the "Memorial to J. McHenry Jones" included in their reissue of the *History*, similarly place Joseph Ailstock as white and his wife as "half Indian" (54n2). Various family trees posted on ancestry.com assign Elizabeth Ailstock Jones—sometimes called "Sally"—to various racial backgrounds, including Scot, English, Native American (Shawnee), and African. Contrary to all of these claims, however, it is fairly clear that Joseph was one of the children named in the will of Michael Ailstock, who was most often listed as "mulatto." The extended Ailstock family had deep ties to other tri-racial (African/Native/white) families in Virginia, and thus Elizabeth Ailstock's marriage to Reuben Jones is not surprising. Terry E. Davis's Ailstock research is among the best-documented of the online sources; see < http://www.tedmrd.com/AILSTOCK/Ailstock.htm >.

6 Aiken and Perdreau, viii, cite the 1860 Census of Gallia Co., Ohio, 196, as well as Lawrence County, Ohio, marriage records, 4:90. See also 1850 Census of Lawrence County, Ohio, 441.

7 Jones, *History*, 6–7. The date of Temperance Reed Jones's parents' move to Ohio remains in question, though William likely came from Virginia, and Nancy, from Kentucky. The *History*'s references to Temperance's "Uncle George Bryant" and "aunt" Sarah Bryant (6, 8) as well as its claim that "most of the people . . . through the county were related to Mrs. Jones" (7) augers strongly for the possibility that Nancy's maiden name was Bryant, and that she was connected to the large family of free African Americans in southeastern Ohio bearing that surname.

8 1850 Federal Census of Lawrence County, 441.

9 *History of the Jones Family*, 55n4.

10 James Oliver Horton and Lois E. Horton offer this succinct summary of Ohio's racist laws in their *In Hope of Liberty: Culture, Community and Protest Among Northern Free Blacks, 1700–1860* (New York: Oxford University Press, 1997): "The Ohio state constitution of 1802 denied black residents the right to vote, hold public office, or testify against a white person in court, and in 1803 blacks were barred from service in the state militia. In 1831 jury eligibility was changed so that only qualified electors could be considered, effectively excluding blacks from such service" (102). See also David A. Gerber, *Black Ohio and the Color Line* (Urbana: University of Illinois Press, 1976), as well

as J. Reuben Sheeler, "The Struggle of the Negro in Ohio for Freedom" in *The Journal of Negro History*, 31.2 (April 1946), 208–226, and Stephen Middleton, *Black Laws: Race and the Legal Process in Early Ohio* (Columbus: Ohio State University Press, 2006). Stephen A. Vincent provides a wider context for black migration to, from, and through Ohio in *Southern Seed, Northern Soil: African-American Farm Communities in the Midwest, 1765–1900* (Bloomington and Indianapolis: Indiana University Press, 1999).

11 In addition to the sources cited above, see Levi Coffin, *Reminiscences of Levi Coffin, The Reputed President of the Underground Railroad* (1898); Larry Gara, *The Liberty Line: The Legend of Underground Railroad* (Lexington: University of Kentucky Press, 1961); George W. Knepper, *Ohio and Its People* (Kent: Kent State University Press, 2003); Keith P. Griffier, *Front Line of Freedom: African Americans and the Forging of the Underground Railroad in the Ohio Valley* (Lexington: University Press of Kentucky, 2004). The online "Ohio History Central" at <www.ohiohistorycentral.org> provides a useful introduction.

12 Jones, *History*, 8.

13 Ibid.

14 The A. M. E. Church, for example, had active congregations throughout the area, some of which are briefly mentioned in the church's weekly newspaper, the *Christian Recorder*.

15 Jones, *History*, 8, 5.

16 Ibid., 11, 8.

17 Ibid., 10.

18 1860 Census of Gallia Co., Ohio, 196; 1870 Census of Meigs Co., Ohio, 137.

19 Jones, *History*, 12–13.

20 The Jones family is not mentioned in Gara, Knepper, or any of Wibur Siebert's extensive work on the Underground Railroad in Ohio. Black conductors related to the area include Gallia County's Elijah Anderson, Hiram Davis, and John Gee; Meigs County's Adam Smith was also active.

21 John L. Jones's *History* places J. McHenry Jones's birth two days later on 30 August 1859 (12), and Aiken and Perdreau accept this date (viii). The "Biographical Sketch of J. McHenry Jones" in the "Memorial" gives the birthdate of 28 August 1859 (68). We favor the 28 August date because the only record of Jones giving his birthdate in his own hand is a 22 May 1897 passport application (US #3607), which lists his birthdate as 28 August.

22 See Aiken and Perdreau's edition of the *History*, 55n4.

23 *History of the Jones Family*, 68.

24 Jones, *History*, 16.

25 Ibid., 20.

26 Ibid., 21.

27 Ibid. On Campbell (1867–1895), see Joan R. Sherman, *Invisible Poets: Afro-Americans of the Nineteenth Century*, 2nd ed. (Urbana: University of Illinois Press, 1989),

186–192, and Joan R. Sherman, ed., *African-American Poetry of the Nineteenth Century: An Anthology* (Urbana: University of Illinois Press, 1992), 306–324.

28 Jones, *History*, 22–23. Joseph started each evening "by reading a chapter in the Bible and winding up with prayer," and John L. Jones later wrote that "even when we were thoughtless boys we loved to hear our father pray" (22).

29 Jones, *History*, 29. On the Albany Academy, see especially Adah Ward Randolph, "Ferguson, Thomas Jefferson," in *African American National Biography, Volume 3*, ed. Henry Louis Gates Jr. and Evelyn Brooks Higginbotham (Oxford: Oxford University Press, 2008), 251–253; Adah Ward Randolph, "Building upon Cultural Capital: Thomas Jefferson Ferguson and the Albany Enterprise Academy in Southest Ohio, 1863–1886," *The Journal of African American History* (87 (Spring 2002), 182–195; Ivan M. Tribe, "Rise and Decline of Private Academics in Albany, OH," *Ohio History* 78.3, 188–228.

30 Adah Ward Randolph, "Ferguson, Thomas Jefferson," in *African American National Biography*, ed. Henry Louis Gates Jr. and Evelyn Brooks Higginbotham (Oxford: Oxford University Press, 2008), 252–253.

31 Tribe, 200.

32 *History of the Jones Family*, 25. James Donaldson, an English immigrant and long-time clergyman was still living in Pomeroy in 1880, when the Federal Census of Meigs Co., Ohio, recorded him as a "minister gospel" living with his wife and daughter (2B).

33 Ibid., 23.

34 *History of the Jones Family*, 68. Whether Jones actually attended the Albany Academy or studied privately (for whatever duration) with Ferguson remains unclear. The "Memorial" actually claims that Jones taught at the academy for a year, and Tribe lists a "Mr. Jones" as an instructor in 1880 (68, 200 page #?).

35 *History of the Jones Family*, 69.

36 Ibid., 23.

37 According to the 1880 Federal Census, which lists him as "superintendent of schools," he was born in Ohio in January of 1829, and he and his Massachusetts-born wife Margaret had four children, the eldest two of whom attended Pomeroy schools (138A). Flannigan had a long association with Meigs County schools; he is listed as a teacher in the 1900 Census of Meigs Co., Ohio, 7B. He also had at least some (however limited) interactions with the black community, as the 1880 Census also lists a live-in African American servant, the West Virginia-born Charlotte Strauder (138A).

38 1880 Census of Meigs Co., Ohio, 12D.

39 Led in part by future Ohio governor and then-antislavery Whig state legislator William Dennison, Jr., this legislation was a product of a series of trade-offs with state Democrats. See Knepper.

40 Arnett, who was elected by the primarily white Greene County by eight votes, in part because of his ties to the state Republican Party, walked a tightrope when he helped

introduce this legislation soon after his election. Arnett initially pulled back some of his calls for equal education that some whites objected to, only to have those actions cause an outcry in some sectors of the black community. Still, he helped push the bill through the State House in early 1886 and then the State Senate in early 1887. Although the "Arnett Bill" resulted in wide celebration among Ohio's black residents, its enforcement remained uneven—as when the city of Xenia, per a report in the 15 September 1888 *Cleveland Gazette*, "redistricted so as to evade the provisions of the Arnett School law" with "a zig-zag line so skillfully run that all of the colored children are thrown into one district and all of the white children into another"—with "the few white children who live in the colored district . . . given permits to go to the white schools." On Arnett and this legislation, see Stephen D. Glazier, "Benjamin William Arnett," in *African American National Biography, Volume 1*, ed. Henry Louis Gates Jr. and Evelyn Brooks Higginbotham (Oxford: Oxford University Press, 2008), 170–171; Middleton, *Black Laws;* the 23 August 1884, 12 December 1885, 30 January 1886, 21 August 1886, and 19 February 1887 issues of the *Cleveland Gazette*.

41 *History of the Jones Family*, 27.

42 John L. Jones says that there was only one other candidate, J. J. Lee, who withdrew because of another contract and who "threw his influence to Jimmy" (27).

43 Mrs. Leona Gaskins, the widow of the previous principal that Jones had replaced, was listed in the directory as Jones's assistant; subsequent directories unfortunately do not name staff in school listings.

44 W. L. Collins, *Wheeling City Directory for 1882–1883*, 49; W. L. Collins, *Wheeling City Directory for 1888*, 29.

45 Carter G. Woodson, "Early Negro Education in West Virginia," *The Journal of Negro History* 7.1 (January 1922), 39.

46 He also worked with the early iterations of the West Virginia Teachers' Association, an organization of black teachers that presaged later teachers' unions. Woodson, for example, notes that he attended the organization's third annual meeting, held in Parkersburg, in 1893, where his colleague from Pomeroy, James Edwin Campbell was elected to the group's presidency.

47 1880 Census of Washington Co., Ohio, 253D.

48 1870 Census of Washington Co., Ohio, 288; 1880 Census of Washington Co., Ohio, 253D.

49 *History of the Jones Family*, 27. Throughout the period, there was, indeed, at least one other James Jones listed in the city directories. A black barber named James Jones actually lived in Wheeling longer than J. McHenry Jones, and, in 1886, he lived less than a block away—at 1034 Eoff, while J. McHenry was boarding at 1119 Eoff; see W. L. Collins, *Wheeling City Directory for 1886*, 239.

50 Jones is not listed individually in the 1888 city directory, though the school listing

refers to him as "James H." Directories after 1890 consistently name him "J. McHenry."

51 *History of the Jones Family*, 31.

52 See W. L. Collins's Wheeling city directory listings for Jones in 1882–1883 (240), 1884 (250), 1886 (239), 1890–1891 (240), and 1892–1893 (244). Harrison is listed in only the 1886 Wheeling directory (204), and is not to be confused with the other (white) Carrie Harrison in other directories.

53 *History of the Jones Family*, 36. "In Memoriam" dates this novel to 1890 (71). No other record of *A Strange Transformation* exists, and, given the successes of Lincoln School and his broadening personal and professional life, Jones may have chosen not to pursue the literary life at this point.

54 "In Memoriam" notes the work at the University of Michigan (71). Aiken and Perdreau, citing Bickley, also note work at Mt. Hope Episcopal College in Alliance Ohio (91n1). "In Memoriam" lists honorary master's degrees from Shaw and Wilberforce Universities as well as an honorary doctorate from Rust University (72). Aiken and Perdreau, again citing Bickely, add West Virginia Baptist Seminary and College to the list of honorary degree grantors (91n1).

55 *History of the Jones Family*, 31.

56 Ibid., 82.

57 Simpson is listed as an A. M. E. Church in several Wheeling directories, but this is an error likely perpetuated by white directory compiler's ignorance of black denominations.

58 Douglass Smith, "In Quest of Equality: The West Virginia Experience," *West Virginia History* 37.3 (April 1976), 212.

59 Stephen D. Engle, "Mountaineer Reconstruction: Blacks in the Political Reconstruction of West Virginia," *The Journal of Negro History*, 78.3 (Summer, 1993), 141.

60 Gordon B. McKinney, "Southern Mountain Republicans and the Negro, 1865–1900," in John C. Inscoe, ed., *Applachians and Race: The Mountain South from Slavery to Segregation* (Lexington: The University Press of Kentucky, 2001), 204.

61 Gordon B. McKinney, "Southern Mountain Republicans and the Negro, 1865–1900," in John C. Inscoe, ed., *Applachians and Race: The Mountain South from Slavery to Segregation* (Lexington: The University Press of Kentucky, 2001), 207.

62 Anonymous, "J. McHenry Jones," *The Negro History Bulletin* 5.4 (January 1942), 94.

63 See 2 March 1896 Wheeling *Daily Intelligencer*.

64 Booker T. Washington, *An Autobiography: The Story of My Life and Work* (Naperville, IL: J. L. Nichols, 1901), 156.

65 On Prillerman's comments on Washington, see his December 1902 article for the *National Magazine*, "Booker T. Washington among his West Virginia Neighbors," in the *Booker T. Washington Papers*, 6: 617–621. For Washington's Comments on Hazelwood, see Washington, *The Negro in Business* (Boston: Hertel, Jenkins, and Co., 1907), 251–255. On Moton, see Maceo Crenshaw Dailey Jr., "Moton, Robert Russa," *African American*

National Biography, Volume 6, ed. Henry Louis Gates Jr. and Evelyn Brooks Higginbotham (Oxford: Oxford University Press, 2008), 71–73.

66 Harlan, Louis R. *Booker T. Washington: The Wizard of Tuskegee, 1901–1915* (Oxford: Oxford University Press, 1983), 329.

67 These events are discussed in the 11 September 1896 and 23 September 1896 issues of the Wheeling *Intelligencer*. On Lynch, see Rodney P. Carlisle, "Lynch, John Roy," *African American National Biography, Volume* 5, ed. Henry Louis Gates Jr. and Evelyn Brooks Higginbotham (Oxford: Oxford University Press, 2008), 338–340.

68 Charles H. Brooks, *The Official History and Manual of the Grand United Order of Odd Fellows in America* (1902, rpt. Freeport, New York: Books for Libraries Press, 1971), 13.

69 On the black Odd Fellows, see especially Brooks; David M. Fahey, "Grand United Order of Odd Fellows," in *Organizing Black America*, ed. Nina Mjagkij (New York: Taylor and Francis, 2001), 252–253; and the special issue of *Social Science History* (28.3, Fall 2004) focusing on "African American Fraternal Associations and the History of Civil Society in the United States" and edited by Joe W. Trotter. While differing from the Masons in that they were more a fraternal organization than a secret society—even though those distinctions break down quickly in terms of studying white and especially black organizations of the period—it should be noted that many Odd Fellows also belonged, as Jones did, to both masonic and neo-masonic organizations (like the Knights of Pythias).

70 Brooks, 271.

71 The section of the application calling for a physical description gave his height as 5' 8½", described his forehead as "high," his eyes as "dark brown," his face and chin as "round," his hair as "black (curling)," and his complexion as "brown" and duly noted his moustache.

72 *History of the Jones Family*, 31.

73 Ibid. Jones was in the country during Queen Victoria's Diamond Jubilee.

74 Kevin K. Gaines, *Uplifting the Race: Black Leadership, Politics, and Culture in the Twentieth Century* (Chapel Hill: University of North Carolina Press, 1996), 4.

75 *History of the Jones Family*, 72. Only a handful of issues of the *Journal* are listed in WorldCat.

76 Ibid., 31.

77 Hill had taught at Storer and at the WVCI prior to being named the Institute's second principal, after the 1894 resignation of founding principal James Edwin Campbell. See Willard B. Gatewood, Jr., "Virginia's Negro Regiment in the Spanish-American War: The Sixth Virginia Volunteers," *Virginia Magazine of History and Biography* 80 (April 1972), 193–209; Edward A Johnson, *A History of Negro Soldiers in the Spanish-*

American War (Raleigh, NC: the author, 1899), 118, 123–124.

78 *History of the Jones Family*, 80.

79 The 1896 Wheeling city directory is the only such volume that lists Moore (368).

80 Prillerman was named President of WVCI after Jones's death. See "Byrd Prillerman," West Virginia Division of Culture and History website at <http://www.wvculture.org/History/histamne/prillerm.html>.

81 Ancella Radford Bickley, "James McHenry Jones: Pioneer Black Educator, 1859–1909," in *Honoring Our Past: Proceedings of the First Two Conferences on West Virginia Black History* (Charleston, WV: Alliance for the Collection, Preservation & Distribution of West Virginia Black History, 1989), 80.

82 Jones, "The West Virginia Colored Institute," in *The History of Education in West Virginia*, revised edition (Charleston, WV: Tribune Printing, 1907), 103.

83 Arline R. Thorn, *West Virginia State University: A Brief History* (Institute, WV: West Virginia State University, nd), citing Hill, places the 1897 enrollment at 100; a 23 September 1909 *Charleston Gazette* obituary places it at 90. The latter number is from Jones, 103.

84 In addition to Jones, 103, see Lewis Keefer, "On the Homefront in World War II," *West Virginia History* 53 (1994), 119–132, and John C. Harlan, *History of West Virginia State College* (Dubuque: William C. Brown, 1968).

85 Jones, "West Virginia Colored Institute," 101.

86 Ibid.

87 The West Virginia Colored Institute became the West Virginia Collegiate Institute in 1915. It granted its first degrees in 1919. Carter G. Woodson would later teach briefly at the College. See Thorn 7 and Jacqueline Goggin, "Woodson, Carter Godwin," *African American National Biography, Volume 8*, ed. Henry Louis Gates Jr. and Evelyn Brooks Higginbotham (Oxford: Oxford University Press, 2008), 437–439.

88 Bickley, 78.

89 Jones, "West Virginia Colored Institute," 102.

90 Thorn, 6.

91 Jones, "West Virginia Colored Institute," 102.

92 See 1900 Federal Census of Tyler, Kanawha County, West Virginia, 9A, 9B, 10A, and 10B.

93 Jones, "West Virginia Colored Institute," 100.

94 Bickley, 80.

95 On Starks, see "Samuel W. Starks," West Virginia Division of Culture and History website at <http://www.wvculture.org/HISTORY/starks.html> and Connie Park Rice, "Starks, Samuel W.," *African American National Biography, Volume 7*, ed. Henry Louis Gates Jr. and Evelyn Brooks Higginbotham (Oxford: Oxford University Press, 2008), 381–382. On Hazelwood, see "Samuel W. Starks"; Jones, "West Virginia Colored

Institute"; Washington, *Negro in Business*, 251–255.

96 Bickley, 86.

97 *History of the Jones Family*, 92n4.

98 *History of the Jones Family*, 34.

99 Bickley, 82; *History of the Jones Family*, 36, 72.

100 *History of the Jones Family*, 36.

101 On the Epworth League, see various Methodist Episcopal publications including *The Doctrines and Discipline of the Methodist Episcopal Church 1896* (New York: Eaton and Mains, 1896), 176–179, as well as the A. M. E. *Christian Recorder* for 7 September 1893, 21 March 1895, and 24 July 1902.

102 *History of the Jones Family*, 90.

103 *History of the Jones Family*, 38.

104 Ibid., 79. Bickley provides a detailed discussion of the services (68–69).

105 *History of the Jones Family*, 36.

106 A multi-year project directed by Henry Louis Gates Jr., and the W. E. B. Du Bois Institute at Harvard, the Black Periodical Literature Project combed extant African American periodicals for poetry, fiction, and book reviews, microformed what they found, and, in so doing created one of the most valuable and comprehensive tools in the field. While new texts and additional extant copies of periodicals will surely be discovered, the BPLP search gives the fullest sense of what scholars are currrently aware of.

107 On Penn, see Jennifer R. Thomas, "Penn, Irvine Garland," *African American National Biography, Volume 6*, ed. Henry Louis Gates Jr. and Evelyn Brooks Higginbotham (Oxford: Oxford University Press, 2008), 302–303.

108 John Jones does say that he "heard Judge Morris Donahue of the Federal Court make during a speech, three quotations from *Hearts of Gold* . . . during a period of controversy over sending a Negro back to Africa," though he provides no additional information (36).

109 The scholarship on literature related to the Civil War is extensive. For studies that represent a broad period of scholarship, see Daniel Aaron, *Unwritten War: American Writers and the Civil War* (Madison: University of Wisconsin Press, 1987); Kathleen Diffley, *Where My Heart is Turning Ever: Civil War Stories and Constitutional Reform, 1861–1876* (Athens: University of Georgia Press, 1992); Alice Fahs, *The Imagined Civil War: Popular Literature of the North & South, 1861–1865* (Chapel Hill: University of North Carolina Press, 2001); Drew Gilpin Faust, *Southern Stories: Slaveholders in Peace and War* (Columbia: University of Missouri Press, 1992); Sarah E. Gardner, *Blood & Irony: Southern White Women's Narratives of the Civil War, 1861–1937* (Chapel Hill & London: University of North Carolina Press, 2004); Jennifer C. James, *A Freedom Bought With Blood: African American War Literature from the Civil War to World War II* (Chapel Hill: University of North Carolina, 2007); Shirley Samuels, *Facing America: Iconography and the*

Civil War (Oxford: Oxford University Press, 2004); Lyde Cullen Sizer, *The Political Work of Northern Women Writers and the Civil War, 1850–1872* (Chapel Hill: University of North Carolina Press, 2000); Timothy Sweet, *Traces of War: Poetry, Photography, and the Crisis of Union* (Baltimore: The Johns Hopkins University Press, 1990); and Elizabeth Young, *Disarming the Nation: Women's Writing and the American Civil War* (Chicago: University of Chicago Press, 1999). For a useful sampling of southern fiction related to the Civil War, see Gene Baro, *After Appomattox: The Image of the South in its Fiction, 1865–1900* (New York: Corinth Books, 1963); for a still-more useful sampling of historical interpretations of the Civil War, see Thomas J. Pressly, *Americans Interpret Their Civil War* (Princeton: Princeton University Press, 1954).

110 Frances E. W. Harper, *Trial and Triumph*, in *"Minnie's Sacrifice," "Sowing and Reaping," "Trial and Triumph": Three Rediscovered Novels by Frances E. W. Harper*, ed. Frances Smith Foster (Boston: Beacon, 1994), 222, 240.

111 Anna Julia Cooper, *A Voice from the South by a Black Woman of the South*, The Schomburg Library of Nineteenth-Century Black Women Writers (New York: Oxford University Press, 1988), 186–187.

112 Matthew Frye Jacobson, *Whiteness of a Different Color: European Immigrants and the Alchemy of Race* (Cambridge: Harvard University Press, 1998), 41.

113 Ibid., 42–43.

114 Mark M. Smith, *How Race is Made: Slavery, Segregation, and the Senses* (Chapel Hill: The University of North Carolina Press, 2006), 7.

115 Ibid.

116 Ibid.

117 Ibid., 47.

118 Frances E. W. Harper, *Iola Leroy, or Shadows Uplifted*, The Schomburg Library of Nineteenth-Century Black Women Writers (New York: Oxford University Press, 1988), 227–29.

119 On the cultural politics of the use of dialect in literature at the end of the nineteenth century, see Gavin Jones, *Strange Talk: The Politics of Dialect Literature in Gilded Age America* (Berkeley: University of California Press, 1999).

120 Smith, 47.

121 Ibid., 66.

122 David W. Blight, *Race and Reunion: The Civil War in American Memory* (Cambridge, MA: Belknap, 2001), 108. For background on the culture of racial violence, including its representation in literature, see Jeffory A. Clymer, *America's Culture of Terrorism: Violence, Capitalism, and the Written Word* (Chapel Hill and London: University of North Carolina Press, 2003); Mark Nathan Cohen, *Culture of Intolerance: Chauvinism, Class, and Racism in United States* (New Haven: Yale University Press, 1998); Susan Gillman, *Blood Talk: American Race Melodrama and the Culture of the Occult* (Chicago: University

of Chicago Press, 2003); Sandra Gunning, *Race, Rape, and Lynching: The Red Record of American Literature, 1890–1912* (New York and Oxford: Oxford University Press, 1996); Trudier Harris, *Exorcising Blackness: Historical and Literary Lynching and Burning Rituals* (Bloomington: Indiana University Press, 1984); Andrew Silver, *Minstrelsy and Murder: The Crisis of Southern Humor, 1835–1925* (Baton Rouge: Louisiana State University Press, 2006); and Bertram Wyatt-Brown, *Hearts of Darkness: Wellsprings of a Southern Literary Tradition* (Baton Rouge: Louisiana State University Press, 2003).

123 Bernard W. Bell, *The Contemporary African American Novel: Its Folk Roots and Modern Literary Branches* (Amherst: University of Massachusetts Press, 2004), 98.

124 Trudier Harris, *Exorcising Blackness: Historical and Literary Lynching and Burning Rituals* (Bloomington: Indiana University Press, 1984), 7.

125 Ibid., xiii.

126 Jerry H. Bryant, *Victims and Heroes: Racial Violence in the African American Novel* (Amherst: University of Massachusetts Press, 1997), 74.

127 Leon F. Litwack, *Been in the Storm So Long: The Aftermath of Slavery* (New York: Knopf, 1979), xiv.

128 Martha A. Myers, *Race, Labor, and Punishment in the New South* (Columbus: Ohio State University Press, 1998), 7.

129 Ronald L. Lewis, "African American Convicts in the Coal Mines of Southern Appalachia," in John C. Inscoe, ed., *Applachians and Race: The Mountain South from Slavery to Segregation* (Lexington: The University Press of Kentucky, 2001), 259.

130 Douglass A. Blackmon, Slavery by Another Name: The Re-Enslavement of Black People in America from the Civil War to World War II (New York: Doubleday, 2008), 7.

131 Lewis, 261.

132 Ibid., 262.

133 Ibid.

134 Ibid., 263.

HEARTS OF GOLD.

A NOVEL,

BY

J. McHENRY JONES.

"Yet, by your gracious patience
I will a round unvarnished tale deliver;
Nothing extenuate or set down aught in malice."

—SHAKESPEARE.

WHEELING
DAILY INTELLIGENCER STEAM JOB PRESS,

1896

TO MY PARENTS,

Bending under the cares of three score years
And ten whose lives have been a con-
stant sacrifice for their children,
this volume is lovingly
dedicated.

CONTENTS.

Chap. .... Page

A Temporary Exodus 61
Knights in Line 66
The Prize Contest 72
Mrs. Underwood's Charge 83
The Flambeau Drill 98
From Lake to Lake 98
The Fete Terpsichorean 107
Seven Corners 114
Homeward Bound 120
The Shadow of a Dream 126
Lucile and Regenia 132
The "Events" 138
Wedding Bells 142
A Compulsory Desertion 148
Disinherited 154
Alone and Penniless 161
At Work 168
Teaching the Young Idea 174
An Old New Friend 181
The Close of School 187
Mrs. Levitt 194
A New Experience 200
Behind Prison Bars 206

The Lynching Bee 215
At the Tribune of Justice 221
The Convict Mines 226
"Forty-seven" 233
Clement St. John 238
Executive Clemency 246
Clouds Lifting 252
Hearts of Gold 259
By the Restless Sea 265
The Convocation 271

HEARTS OF GOLD.

A TEMPORARY EXODUS.

Chapter I.

"We cannot stem the tide. The cumulative force of discouraging circumstances stands as a bar sinister to every new fledged hope. I wish I had your sanguine disposition, Lotus, but five years of buffeting with the white caps of real life, destroy many of the sea-sand castles of our old high school days," said Clement St. John.

"I am five years older as well as yourself, you must remember, but my faith in the fickle future of which you speak so disparagingly, is as bright as it was when with our diplomas we marched home from commencement," replied the young man addressed as Lotus.

"Your life has been so different from mine," Clement continued; "you have not been ground between the upper and nether stone of men's constant faults and occasional virtues. You have lived so long in Washington, oscillating between the Pension Office and the Medical School, that you imagine the whole world to be peacefully swinging within your arc."

"I hope I am not quite so circumscribed," said Lotus, laughing. "You news-gatherers are too apt to conclude from a pessimistic contact with the dark side of life that those who do not readily accept your views are rainbow chasers."

"No, no; you judge me too harshly. The shell has not quite grown over me. I am still able to award credit where it is due. Contemplating myself from your standpoint, I feel like an antiquated mote between two hills, with only a patch of blue sky to canopy my narrow world. While I am free to admit, I can not see a heaven as resplendent as your telescope compasses, still a few brilliant twinklers linger to give the hoped for better day at least a melancholy welcome," replied Clement, earnestly.

"Give me your hand, comrade of my youth, you begin to talk like my St. Clement of old. We were to be knights in the real work of life, do you remember?" asked Lotus feelingly.

Clement St. John and Lotus Stone, for this was the name of the other disputant, had not met for nearly two years. As intimate as brothers for the most of their lives, they had lived next door neighbors from boyhood in the city of Minton. Graduating in the same class, Clement St. John had drifted into the newspaper office, his friend into a departmental clerkship in Washington. The two young men were remarkably unlike, in appearance, disposition and character. Afro-Americans both, they were as dissimilar as the Polish Jew and his brother of the same lineage in the streets of Cairo.

In complexion, Clement St. John was fair, in truth, too fair for an Afro-American, or any other American to the manor born. His skin, save here and there marked by an ugly freckle, was as free from pigment as an Albino's. His white face, with undoubted African features, was crowned with a shock of reddish-brown hair, stiff and bristly. A sickly mustache, of faded red, which the wearer, fearing it would lose its curl twisted nervously, gave to his angular features a decidedly unique expression. From beneath a scanty row of disarranged eyebrows, peeped a steel gray eye, which, under certain surroundings, shaded into a faded blue. His eyes possessed a daring twinkle at utter variance with the insipid color of his face. Large hands, which in reality were not mates; tall, narrow-shouldered and awkward, Clement St. John was a young man with a clear head, stout heart and upright disposition.

Lotus Stone had that peculiar complexion seen in no land but our own, and among no other people but Afro-Americans. His complexion was a transparent brown, without the swarthiness which is noticeable in the other dark races of the world.

His color was the product of a century of miscegenation of the best blood of the Caucasian, Negro and Indian races. His features were regular. Black eyes, black mustache, heavy eyebrows within a line of meeting, made a face that one might dwell upon restfully, after contemplating for a time upon the singular looks of his companion.

His hair, which was closely cut, had a wiry tendency which proved that through a century of infiltration the Negro was still on top. He wore a pair of gold-rimmed glasses, made secure by a black silk cord. The latter appendage was indeed necessary, as the glasses, for want of sufficient bridge, sat awkwardly upon the saddle which nature had designed for spectacles of a different make. He was dressed in the fatigue uniform of the Knights of the Red Cross.

The two friends, after the greetings common to men who are renewing old and agreeable acquaintance, dropped into the subject always nearest the intelligent Afro-American heart, "the race outlook."

After the conversation, the conclusion of which is given, the two friends sat for some time looking into the restless water, frisking in joyous buoyancy in that August sunshine. Each occupied with his own thoughts, gazed out upon the lake, where outlined in the dim distance against the clear blue sky, two tireless lake steamers oscillated with arithmetic precision.

"What a perfect day!" said Lotus breaking the silence, "just breeze enough to ruffle the lake and break the monotony that contemplation of endless wave and sky produces."

"I have been watching those whale-backed lake boats with the black smoke streaming far out behind; they move, like Indians, single file. How patiently they seem to bear their burden from far off Superior," Clement replied.

"They move as stately as if conscious of good work almost completed. See," continued Lotus, "the flock of long-winged lake birds circling around the main mast, darting now and then toward the water, laving their breasts anew in nature's baptismal fount."

"A picture from which we must take fresh courage, my friend," said Clement, placing his big, awkward hand upon the shoulder of his companion.

"Our hilarious friends are not worrying over the outlook for the race," said Lotus, looking toward the quay, where a noisy multitude of laughing Afro-Americans awaited the arrival of the "Carrier Pigeon." On this boat they were to complete their journey.

Lotus Stone and Clement St. John were part of that grand number of Afro-Americans who engaged in a temporary exodus, by way of the lakes, to attend the reunion of the Knights Templars, at Mt. Clare during the summer of 188–. What a crowd of them hurrying to Mt. Clare. Many of them hope to set foot for the first time upon the region of the Queen. Where else on earth could be found so large a number of people so unlike in appearance, yet each claiming blood relation with the other. Every kind and condition of the better class of Afro-Americans were here represented. What a strange variety of human beings, what a panorama of the races of the world! In color, every nationality from Northern Europe, shading down through France, Italy, Portugal, across the Mediterranean into Egypt, Morroco, and then to Equatorial Africa. Perhaps not a man, woman or child of all these strangely dissimilar types would have hesitated a moment to answer to the name of "Negro." Old men and women who had come north in the days immediately preceding and after the war, with their grown sons and daughters, stop the pendulum of their busy lives and take advantage of the opportunity to sail across the lakes.

The picturesque knights, in their jaunty fatigue uniforms, lend martial splendor to the occasion. Here the beau and belle with many an honest glance, pass and re-pass each other as they gaily promenade up and down the quay. A notable feature of the assembly is the universal cheerfulness that characterizes it. A like number of no other race in our country, their equals financially, could approach these Afro-Americans in gallantry and orderly demeanor.

Many of them are from the far South, and for the first time taste the only hospitality that the North gives or the Afro-American wants: "Pay for what you get, and get what you pay for." Many of them for the first time sit unmolested in a restaurant or hotel.

Fine fellows these, who would pass for men in any country in the world, with possibly one exception. Here are men from almost every state in the Union; men who have held high places among their fellows, and filled those places with marked distinction.

The shrill scream of the "Carrier Pigeon" warns the happy excursionists that they must prepare to resume their journey. After much ado, the last of the crowd get aboard and the boat turns her bow away from land and the familiar hills of the best loved state fade from sight. Clement and Lotus, seated well toward the front, observed the crowd with growing interest. The merry laugh of happy contentment rang out over the lake.

The brass bands, good, bad and indifferent, mostly indifferent, succeeded each other with tireless regularity for the first few hours; but as the boat got further away from the shore and the waves increased in size, it was noticeable that the music grew more subdued, or rather more religious in character. As darkness came on, the wind raised and shifted. The lake became boisterous; the good ship lurched and trembled at every revolution of her wheels.

The moon, as it now and then swept into view, revealed an angry, threatening storm. Supper was eaten in silence. Each mouthful of sweetmeats was taken with a furtive glance at the clouds. Now and then beneath the hush which followed the roll of the steamer, a popping cork recorded the fact that some one of the fearful many, was determined, in one way or another, to keep up his spirits.

The storm spent its force in threatening; the moon again silvered the tossing waters and the cheerfulness increased as the roll of the waves subsided.

So the night passed until just as day crept slowly up from the surrounding hills the lights and steeples of Mt. Clare, the beautiful, came into view.

KNIGHTS IN LINE.

Chapter II.

Mt. Clare was literally alive with visiting Knights and their friends. Each new arrival was met at the depot with a band of music, the Committee of Reception, and an escort of their fraters. Music filled the air. The streets were lined with people decked in holiday attire. The citizens, white and black, vied with each other in open-handed hospitality.

The little city had donned its national dress for the occasion. Streamers of red, white and blue accompanied by flags of welcome, duly bespeaking the insignia of knighthood, everywhere flaunted to the breezes the good will which the people bore toward their sable guests. Every precaution necessary to the comfort and pleasure of the visitor was duly provided by the Committee of Arrangements. The hotel proprietors met the incoming guests with a reassuring smile. The "White Elephant" was the headquarters of the Grand Commandery. The Knights and their friends, like a victorious army of invasion, took complete possession of the place.

Conversing in groups in the office, filling every corridor and promenading along every balcony, quiet, genteel and unobtrusive, the visitors, in sober earnest hold sway.

Fraternity hall, the most commodious audience room in the city, was gratuitously tendered as a rendezvous for the commanderies. Here on the first day of the conclave, the mayor of the city spoke his words of welcome and the Eminent Grand Commander delivered his opening address. To these ceremonies the great majority paid but little attention; sight-seeing, boat-riding and crossing the narrow way that connected the two inland seas and separated our country from the dominion of the English, possessed for them, a greater fascination. Canada, to the average Afro-American, is a land of never-ending interest. The English ensign, to these Knights, is only one degree less sacred than the flag of the "stars and bars."

The supreme interest of the conclave week revolved about the second day's proceedings—the street parade and the prize drill. Long ere the morning cock called the earliest risers from their night's repose, the hotels were alive with bustle and excitement. Each company that had entered the list of prize contestants spent two hours before breakfast, on the morning of the parade, busily executing the prospective programme.

Each commander's face wore an air of triumph, as his men filed in to partake of their well-earned repast.

During breakfast, the sound of martial music seemed to echo from every point of the compass. Long before the last Knight had folded his napkin and drawn his knees from beneath the table, the clattering hoofs of the all important marshal of the day's horse, were heard frantically galloping through the streets. Of all the officials that form a part of these gatherings, the marshal of the day is generally the most excited and useless ornament. Armed with a little brief authority, this self inflated personage, with the airs of a major domo, and the gilded trappings of a field marshal on muster day, delights to see his manly shadow in the sun. Ordinarily he is a useless appendage, but in this occasion he exceeds in supercilious stupidity the arrogance of his kind. Galloping his foam-flecked jade, from right to left of the rapidly forming line, he gave his orders in a stentorian voice, always careful to halt where he could be most advantageously observed by the admiring multitude.

Glancing from side to side as he passed, he searched furtively the faces of the bystanders for a smile of approval, which might be appropriated as complimentary to the wisdom of the committee, in appointing a man so eminently fitted by nature, to fill with grace a position demanding such rare and versatile accomplishments.

After three or four excursions from the head to the foot of the line, it dawned upon the marshal of the day that the procession waited only his orders to move. Putting spurs to his horse, he once more made his way to the public square, where, after gallantly saluting the ladies standing upon the steps of the city building, he waved his hand to the cannoneer to fire the signal to start. The sight was imposing. A cordon of mounted police led the parade. The Grand Officers, contrary to their general custom, followed on horseback the city's protectors. Not less than three thousand Knights, each commandery headed by a band, marched to the inspiring music with military precision. Chapeaus enriched with ostrich feathers, black coats, silver trimmings, gay uniforms and swords glistening in the sunlight, made a spectacle that must be seen to be appreciated. Along the entire march the citizens lined the streets and openly demonstrated their delight as the intricate movements of the drill were executed. Proud of the approval of the beholders, these black Knights lost no opportunity to show themselves worthy of the kindly consideration being accorded them.

Lotus Stone, although Grand Generallissimo of the Grand Commandery, marched as Eminent Commander of the Knights of the Red Cross. Whether riding or walking he was the most knightly of all that knightly throng. Five feet and ten, his military bearing and symmetrical form, made him easily six feet to the admiring crowd that jostled each other on the curb stones along the line of march.

Clement St. John, who would have made any sacrifice for his friend, blushed at the momentary thrill of jealousy which he experienced as Lotus Stone, in the front of the Red Cross Commandery, passed his point of observation. At the outskirts of the city, the line halted to take the street cars for Recreation Park, where the outing and prize drill were to be held. Here the street became a road, shaded on one side for some distance by giant elms. On the left hand side of the road, surrounded by trees, stood the home of the late Judge Underwood.

Mrs. Underwood, anticipating that the marchers would be thirsty from their long dusty tramp, had placed a barrel of cool water in the front yard, and standing at the gate as the Knights halted under the inviting shade, asked them to walk in and slake their thirst. The men did not wait to be asked a second time. Filing through the open gate, each gracefully lifting his chapeau to the kind old lady as he passed, they soon filled the inclosure. Clement and Lotus were the last to enter.

"See what the tardy bird always finds," said Lotus, with unmistakable disappointment, as he tilted the barrel, only to learn that the last clear cupful had been dipped by the man who preceded him.

"Your bread shall be given," remarked Clement slowly. "Has the water failed?"

"There comes our car, we might as well catch it," replied Lotus, as he turned to retrace his steps.

"Wait, I'll bring you a drink," said a girlish voice from the porch.

Lotus turned just in time to see a sylph-like form disappear through the open door.

"Shall we wait?" asked Lotus, "our car is moving?"

"There are other cars, my unsophisticated friend, and if that were the last, we had better walk out to the park miss the sight of such disinterested loveliness," said Clement, with a knowing wink.

"I am not so sure about the loveliness, but there is little doubt about the disinterestedness," said Lotus with a smile.

He had hardly finished the sentence before there appeared at the door, pitcher in one hand and glass in the other, a vision of beauty that caused both of the young men to forget the moving car, and the hilarious knights waving their gauntleted hands from the steps and windows at their friends left behind.

Clement and Lotus rushed simultaneously up the steps to relieve the blushing girl of her burden. Clement reached the place where she stood first.

"Allow me to relieve you," he said, bowing and ordering out his holiday smile. "I am sorry," he continued, putting forth his hand to take the pitcher, "that our negligence has caused you so much trouble."

She drew back, and smilingly poured out a glass of water, and as she presented it to the over-gallant young man, said: "Let me serve you, Sir Knights. To-day your bread shall be given and your water shall be sure," she continued archly, finishing the quotation which Clement had doubtingly made a short time before.

Clement received the glass and with a deferential bow, passed it to his friend. "Your kindness will not be forgotten," said Lotus, returning the glass. "A glass of water generously given has promise of reward in the annals of the Good Book."

"Do not mention such a trifle," answered the sweet girl.

"Thoughtful trifles for others are the golden lines in the chapter of life," said Lotus politely, as he lifted his chapeau and walked toward the gate. As he closed the gate, he glanced back at Clement St. John, lingering on the steps in futile dalliance, and he, too, had his instantaneous fit of green-eyed insanity.

"A sweeter draught from a fairer hand was never quaffed," he repeated, as he awaited the arrival of an approaching horse car.

Regenia Underwood, for this was the young girl's name, was the very embodiment of vivacious, budding womanhood.

Dressed in some kind of soft white goods, draped loosely and clasped at the waist with a rosette of cream ribbon, she made a picture seldom seen among the women of our country.

Too fair for a brunette, she was a shade too dark for a blonde. Her complexion was a cream, into which some fairy's hand had deftly mixed the first rays of the morning's sun, throwing into her color a soft, rich, radiance, indescribably elusive. Of medium height, her form was the perfection of symmetry. Her face, of classic mold, was almost severe in its hauteur, yet about the well curved red lips and large brown eyes, swimming in their liquid depths, played constantly the faint suspicion of a smile. A wealth of dark brown hair hung in natural ringlets above her oval forehead. In the company of such a girl, a plain man like Clement St. John might be excused if he tarried on the steps, manufacturing topics of conversation in order to prolong the interview. When, after an awkward pause, he detected Regenia, peering at the car, on the steps of which stood his friend, he hastily bade the ladies good day and ran to catch the car for Recreation Park.

"Well, well! Did you ever see anything like that?" he asked as soon as he could get his breath.

"You made a good run for an amateur, but I have seen sprinters in my time that could out-wind you," answered Lotus, ignoring Clement's meaning.

"Run? Out wind who? What are you talking about, anyway? Who said I wanted to be entered as a sprinter? What are you trying to give me?" These questions were fired at Lotus in a breath. "You can be obtuse when you are so disposed," he continued. "Are you stone in reality as well as in name? Does a few years in Washington affect a man that way?"

"Hold, hold!" cried Lotus. "You are drowning me in a sea of interrogations."

"Can you put your hand in the bosom of your waist-coat and say, honor bright, that you have not seen something unusual in the last half hour? If you can, I am 'dummed,'" he concluded.

"What are you driving at any way?" said Lotus, laughing.

"Do you mean it," asked Clement excitedly. "If you do I have nothing more to say."

"Well, I do not mean it," replied Lotus.

"You are talking now—like a man that has been dismissed from the asylum. Say, did you ever see anything half so beautiful?"

"Why do the heathen rage and the people imagine a vain thing?"

"Beautiful she certainly is, but from such beauty you and I are forever disqualified," he sneeringly replied.

"I am not half so hopeless as I was a few days since," remarked Clement. "There is compensation for all of us while the race has such women as that one. Why one look into her eyes would banish the 'blues' for a century."

"The more you talk the more I am mystified. What possible consolation to me did those eyes you are raving over contain?"

"I can't say what influence they exercised over you," replied Clement, indifferently, "but the Lord knows His own and so does your unworthy servant. That girl belongs to the unnamed race or I never wrote an editorial."

"What new wild goose chase are you on now? It is preposterous. She has not a grain of African pigment beneath her pretty cuticle."

"Call it a wild goose chase if the phrase suits your caprice, but mind if you are not on the same chase before another day. I may be a narrow, self-opinionated news-gatherer, but I find out thing—I do not mope and sigh and run after the impossible. I did not serve my apprenticeship on the 'Times' without learning a thing or two," said Clement proudly.

"Recreation Park," called the conductor. The two friends left the car and rapidly bent their steps toward the main pavilion. Lotus was silent and thoughtful. Clement St. John, with one hand on his friend's shoulder, and gesturing wildly, often awkwardly, with the other, talked incessantly until they passed into the crowd and were lost from view.

THE PRIZE CONTEST.

Chapter III.

Everything was bustle and excitement as Lotus and Clement entered Recreation Park. Covered with dust and reeking with perspiration, the Knights look anything but the gay gallants that rendezvoused at the city building a few hours before. Hunger and fatigue had robbed them of their soldierly bearing, but not even these could sully their good sprits. The Afro-American is proverbially cheerful. He banishes sorrow as an evanescent dream. Lotus Stone had been taking an introspective inventory as he listened to the laudatory exuberance of his friend. He paid but little heed to the impression that Clement declared the nymph of the "Elms" had made upon himself. He knew that Clement's intoxication would subside as rapidly as it had arisen. Lotus Stone saw in Regenia Underwood a possible future—a future in which he might play an important part. A consummate dilettante in the social world of Washington, he had made no embarrassing advancements. After floating for three years upon the vortex of that enticing whirlpool, society, he was as free, heart and hand, as when he entered its enchanting delirium. It was, therefore, with no longing for another "dangling" triumph that as he listened to Clement's somewhat extravagant praise, he resolved to know more of the pretty occupant of the "Elms."

Clement St. John, on the contrary, was interested in Regenia as a new type—somebody to talk about and rave over. His loquacity, at all times, was unbounded. He thought, he often said, by talking. He called this proceeding "thinking audibly." It was after his usual manner, he went into verbal hysterics concerning the adventure related in the previous chapter. As they approached the grand pavilion, at the top of the incline, an officer, who hurried them off to dinner, said, "Not a moment to lose; grand review at 2 o'clock sharp."

"I will be on time," said Lotus, seating himself in the nearest vacant chair. While Lotus and Clement are enjoying themselves at dinner let us take a look at Recreation Park, a recent addition to the pleasure resorts of Mt. Clare.

For years these grounds were the private belongings of Mr. G. N. Tolbert, an Afro-American, and but lately had fallen into the hands of their present owners. Located about two miles from the city, the rapid growth of population in that direction induced the street railway company to make the park the terminus of their road. They tried for years to purchase the grounds, but the owner, being a man of pronounced religious sentiments, refused to sell, fearing that the place would be converted into a beer-garden. Under a special stipulation that no intoxicating liquors should ever be sold in the park, he was finally induced to part with his interest. Tolbert Park was from that time known as Recreation Park. The corporation, as far as it could be done without destroying the natural beauties, had modernized the place. There was a shallow ravine between the entrance and the main part of the park. On each side of the carriage way, which was elevated so as to make the drive from the gates to the foot of the hill almost level, the ravine had been converted into artificial lakes. Covering the water almost completely, broad, green-leafed water lilies grew in picturesque profusion. The drive up the hill, called "lovers' lane," was canopied by the overhanging branches of the deep-rooted elms. Mr. Tolbert was a tree fancier, and every tree that could be induced to sprout in the region of Mt. Clare, he planted in his park. The great oaks, which were by all odds in the majority, lifted their proud heads like giant sentinels above their neighbors of a less hardy growth. On the east side of the park, the hill sloped gently toward the lake. At the foot of this incline the street railway company had fitted up a base ball park. This was to be the scene of the prize drill. Scattered about the grounds were rustic seats, sylvan bowers and every other device to charm and hold the pleasure seeker.

Promptly at 2 o'clock the staccato notes of the bugle sounded, warning the commanders to get their men in line for the "Grand Review." At the second call of the bugle, the Grand Officers took their places on a platform, erected for the purpose, in the centre of the park. To the thrill of inspiring music, each company, swords at a "present," passed in review and formed in a double line, facing the Grand Officers. The line having been formed the Grand Generalissimo advanced to the front of the of the platform and in clear ring tones, heard by every Knight in line, commands: "Attention, Sir Knights!" Then follows the sword manual. Apparently satisfied with the proficiency which the Knights have exhibited, he faces about and reports to the Eminent Grand Commander. The announcement is made that the prize contest will take place immediately at the Ball park, on the east side of the grounds. The contestants march to the place appointed, the others break ranks and hurry away to secure a comfortable point to observe the drill. The Grand Review being an event of the past, Lotus immediately instituted a vain search for Clement. Disappointed at not finding his friend, he threw himself upon the green sward, in the midst of a number of Knights, to watch the corps manoeuvre.

The grounds were so spacious that no one was jostled for want of room. The day was perfect. Seated upon the grass or reclining on one elbow, the crowed chatted merrily, while the "crack" commandery, heralded by the famous "Big Six Band," marched upon the field. A ripple of applause, swelling into a gushing outburst, greeted them, as with unity of step and elbow to elbow they presented swords to the judges. As each new picturesque evolution dissolved into another equally new and decidedly more intricate, the enthusiasm of the spectators was unbounded. In advance of the judges, the delighted observers, pronounced the movements perfect. Amid clapping of hands waving of handkerchiefs and ringing cheers, the first contestants marched from the field. One fact, however, was apparent to the initiated—much of the enthusiasm was started by a Knight in fatigue uniform who, surrounded by a half dozen others, reclined beneath the banner of the commandery first upon the field. Lotus, tired of reclining thought he would stand up and rest himself by a change of position. He noticed, as he glanced toward the right, a gentleman frantically waving his hat. He looked again, but as the waving had ceased, he gave the incident no further attention but turned to observe the second company, which, with great eclat, was marching upon the field. A slight tap on the shoulder and the familiar, "Well, old man," from Clement, standing behind him, left no doubt of whose hat he saw so imperatively waving but a short time since.

"I have been wearing my good right arm to a withered shadow of its former size trying to attract your attention," said Clement.

"I saw you," said Lotus, apologetically, "but in such a multitude, how could you expect a near-sighted man to determine whether the hat waved for him or someone else."

"Silence!" said Clement, in a mock commanding tone, "follow your leader and ask no questions."

Lotus obeyed orders. They had not gone far before they came to a number of ladies and gentlemen seated upon the grass, among whom were Regenia Underwood, Lucile Malone and Mrs. Levitt. The latter was Regenia's foster mother. With little ceremony, Clement introduced his friend to the ladies.

"I believe you have met my friend, Mr. Stone, Miss Underwood," remarked Clement, as he presented Lotus.

"In face and form he is familiar, but this is my first acquaintance with his name," said Regenia pleasantly.

"You were determined that Mr. St. John's implied quotation should be literally fulfilled. Your offer came at a time most needed; I was nearly famishing for a drink of water," Lotus hastened to reply.

"It was too bad that you should come for water just as the well had run dry," answered Regenia.

"Not as it ended. We have been thanking our good angel ever since that we did wait until the first supply had been exhausted," said Clement, who stood listening to the conversation.

Clement had Lucile Malone to thank for his introduction to Regenia. Lucile was a stenographer in the office of the "Times," and through her he had often heard of Miss Underwood. Lucile and Regenia had been friends for years. In company with Regenia was her chaperone. Mrs. Levitt had attended Regenia's mother in her last illness, and held her hand when she died. For more than two years after the death of Regenia's mother, Mrs. Levitt had cared for the child. She considered Regenia too precious to ever stray very far from her foster mother's sight. At eighteen, Regenia was as much of a child to Mrs. Levitt as she was at two. Wherever the young child went Mrs. Levitt was at her side, and where Mrs. Levitt was not acceptable, Regenia was rarely seen.

Lotus addressed his conversation more to Mrs. Levitt than to the fair girl who sat beside her. He talked of the Knights, their hopes and aims, regretting incidentally that he was obliged to see so little of the commandery to which he belonged.

This led Mrs. Levitt to inquire why he was so frequently absent from his commandery and Lotus to disclose his occupation at Washington.

To this conversation Regenia lent an ear not altogether free from curiosity.

"Is it your intention to make Washington your permanent abode?" she asked, unable longer to hide the interest which Mr. Stone's pleasing talk had created.

"No," said Lotus, "it has not been absolutely decreed that our party will always remain in power, and if I had permanent employment," he hastened to add, "I have determined to lead a life far removed from the delights of Washington."

"Would it be considered inquisitive if I should ask what profession you will follow?"

"Why a profession?" asked Lotus with a quizzical smile.

"I am sure I do not know, unless it is that you have a professional air," answered Regenia.

"There are professions and professions," said Clement St. John. "My idea of a profession—" he continued.

"Is publishing a tri-weekly newspaper," chimed in Lucile. "Let me warn you in time, ladies, Mr. St. John would write up the undertaker at his own wife's funeral, if he thought he could get the article in the columns of a leading 'daily.'"

"Not so fast, my fair little friend. I am not a benedict, and if you do not soon give me a more business-like answer, I shall be obliged to cast my eye in another direction," said Clement, with good natured raillery.

"You did not tell us what profession you are to follow, Mr. Stone," said Regenia, blushing as she pronounced the name of Lotus for the first time.

"Saw-bones," said Clement.

A rousing cheer from the crowd attracted attention to the drill.

"I like it immensely," said Lucile, "but the more I see of it the more complicated it appears."

"You would make an excellent judge," said Clement. "It is a pity that the sphere of woman is so circumscribed. The judges will award the prize to the commandery receiving the most applause. A knowledge and correct execution of military tactics have 'nothing to do with the case.'"

"Is that the way the victors are chosen?" asked Regenia with much surprise.

"Do not regard all Mr. St. John says to be sober earnest," observed Lotus.

"Do not take anything he says as sober earnest, and you will be nearer the truth," said Lucile, laughingly.

"Well, you would make a judge, and that, at least, is spoken in sober earnest. I am certainly sober, whether I meet the approval of Miss Malone in other respects or not, modesty alone deters me from saying," answered Clement, with a knowing smile at Lucile.

"You do not meet my approval," said Lucile, moving away from Mr. St. John.

"If you are not fire and tow for a half grown girl, I am mistaken," continued Clement, tantalizingly.

"I am not overgrown," she retorted, "that is some consolation." At this witty sally, the laugh is at Clement's expense.

Looking down at his large, knotty hands with a questionable smile, he said, "You are more than half right. I could take a slice or two from these hands and then have enough left for every practical purpose. "If your right hand offend you, why cut some of it off." As he said this he held up his hands, laughing as he put them together to show that one was much larger than the other.

"A hand to wield the pen or the sword with equal dexterity," remarked Regenia, sympathetically. She was unused to Clement and Lucile's badinage.

"Thank you. And although I do not appear in the ranks of these play soldiers, if Miss Underwood ever needs the services of a real knight she will find me at this address," he said, passing her his card, with a stage bow.

Regenia, discerning the mischievous twinkle in Clement's eye, accepted the card with the same theatrical dignity with which it was presented, little dreaming that the time would come when the playful promise would be redeemed.

Lucile smiled, but in her heart she wondered if Regenia knew that Clement would be as good as his word if any exigency ever put it to the test.

"Do you mean it?" asked Lotus. "If you do then I have nothing more to say."

Clement recognized the words he had used on the way to the park, and burst into a hearty laugh. The girls exchanged significant glances.

"Mr. St. John and I have a mutual sorrow, the memory of which has led us on a wild goose chase," Lotus remarked, by way of explanation.

"The game is at bay," said Clement, gleefully.

"You shall know all about it one of these days," said Lotus, smiling at the girls' evident perplexity. "It is a secret that, like wine, will improve with age."

"Tell us before it is old enough to walk," said Lucile, sarcastically. "When it reaches the talking age, it may tell on you."

"Do you girls know that the drill is over?" asked Mrs. Levitt.

"No, we do not; and the gentlemen are no better informed than we are. Mr. St. John you should have told us that the end was approaching. You know how we hate not to be in at the death."

"You were talking so entertainingly that after a hasty glance at the field I decided that your conversation was more interesting than the antics of those sunshine soldiers," said Clement with an apologizing smile at Lotus.

"Oh, thank you, if you really mean it," said Lucile laughing derisively.

"Half in jest, the other half in earnest. The jest for you, the sincerity for Miss Underwood," Clement replied, showing his teeth at Lucile, and bowing as gracefully as he could to Regenia.

"Listen!" said Mr. St. John, craning his neck toward the judges, who were announcing their decision.

"You ought to be there taking notes. You are a very satisfied newsgatherer, I think," remarked Lucile in a whisper.

"My paper is a weekly. I supposed you knew that," replied Clement.

"What has that to do with your neglecting to get all the facts concerning this affair?" she asked.

"Why write up matter that will be given in detail to-morrow. I can get my choice from the 'dailies.' When you go into the newspaper business you will learn a thing or two," he said, taking Lucile by the shoulders and turning her around.

"What is a flambeau drill?" asked Regenia.

"A flambeau drill is a flambeau—Come out tonight and see the Red Cross commandery," he said.

The announcement that the prizes would be awarded the victorious contestants from the balcony of the "White Elephant," immediately after the exhibition drill of the Flambeau Club occasioned Regenia's question.

Lotus and Clement escorted the ladies to their carriage. As the carriage threaded its way through the crowd along the drive to the exit, the two young men walked beside it as a kind of self-appointed body guard. As the carriage passed through the gate, Lotus tipped his chapeau and said, "Your presence at the flambeau drill will add much to its effectiveness, I assure you."

Lucile Malone, who had arrived a few hours before the parade, had accepted Regenia's invitation to spend the conclave week at the "Elms."

The girls had been fast friends in their school days, before Lucile had gone to Minton to study stenography and typewriting. By a streak of good fortune, she had obtained a position in the office of the "Times" the very day her course was finished. Lucile was plain, but extremely clever; poor, but independent, she went to Minton against the advice of every one of her friends, Regenia excepted.

"What is the use," they had said, "for a colored girl to study stenography? No business man will employ her. Thousands of white girls, just as clever, and in many other ways more acceptable, fail to get positions. It is a wanton waste of time and money," they said, "for Lucile to take a course of that kind."

To all of these croakers, Lucile gave but one answer: "I'll be convinced when I fail." She did not fail; such pluck seldom does.

When Lucile went to the "Times" office, Clement St. John was one of the local editors on the paper. To him she was indebted for many delicate hints, which counted in her success against the odds to be surmounted.

He considered her his special charge, and while Lucile was not the kind of girl that needed any special protection, it pleased Clement to imagine that some one, at some time, would attempt to impose upon her, and in the event of such an occurrence he would take no uncertain hand in her defense.

Lucile's perception was not long in noting the well-meant solicitation exhibited by Mr. St. John; and, although at first she mentally resented it, she had not been many weeks in the office of the "Times" before she began to rely upon Clement's guardianship and secretly take comfort in it. He assumed the role of protector because he thought Lucile a brave girl trying to make her way against untold difficulties. He had seen much of the sin and crime that dogged the steps of innocent womanhood. He opined that if these temptations were strong against womanhood in general, they were herculean when that womanhood had a dark complexion. He believed Lucile Malone proof against every temptation that might assail her; and, believing this, it would have been dangerous for any man to dally with her womanhood.

On her way from the office to her home, on dark winter nights, Clement either escorted her or kept near enough to brain any "masher" that made himself obnoxious. It was this appearance of espionage which Lucile at first resented. But when she learned that not fear that she would do wrong, but fear that she would be wronged, prompted his actions, the feeling of resentment gave way to one of gratitude. Gratitude ripened into esteem, esteem grew into love.

As they drove along, Regenia remarked mischievously, "I can understand now why your work is so lovely."

Lucile, coloring slightly, asked: "What has been the means of your recent discovery?"

"Mr. St. John is a very pleasant office boy," said Regenia.

"He is not in our office," protested Lucile. "He is awfully selfish. Do you know that sometimes I don't see that man one day in ten?"

"I suspect the knowledge that he is lingering near at night makes your work so 'awfully lovely,' as you always write me," added Regenia with provoking merriment.

"Well, he is kind," said Lucile, earnestly, wondering if Regenia did know that Clement lingered around. "At first I did not like him. His looks are against him, you know; but he has such a delicate sense of what one needs to know, and such a sweet little way of making you believe you do know it, when, in fact, he is telling you all the time, that—that—" coloring violently, "he is real interesting after all," she blurted out.

Regenia had found out more than she suspected; Lucile had disclosed more than she intended.

"Never mind his looks," said Mrs. Levitt, filling the awkward pause. "It is not the looks but the heart that makes the man."

"My dear, wise mamma!" said Regenia. "You always say the right thing. As far as his looks are concerned, I think he is handsome."

"Don't mention it," said Lucile, "He is the very paragon of ugliness. Do not praise Mr. St. John to please me. You can hardly say worse things about his looks than he says himself."

"He don't mean it, my dear. He is well looking enough, and you can depend upon his having sufficient conceit to think so. Men are seldom wanting in conceit. Disparaging reference to one's appearance as often arises from self-love as self-abasement," said Mrs. Levitt, wisely.

"You are always right, dear Mrs. Levitt, replied Lucile. "I have frequently suspected when Mr. St. John was descanting about his looks in his heart he believed himself not so bad as he delights to make others think he is."

"A glance into his secret soul, some fine Sunday morning, when in his best clothing, he gives himself the parting touch before his mirror, would be the only way to ascertain his real opinion of his looks," said Mrs. Levitt, with a satisfied smile.

Regenia put great store in Mrs. Levitt's common sense. Mrs. Levitt was about as well satisfied that Regenia was not far wrong in her opinion of her foster mother as Regenia was herself.

The carriage stopped at the "Elms" just as the street car, on the steps of which, Clement St. John stood smoking, passed. "Talk about the angels and you hear the rustle of their wings," said Lucile. "If you are looking for Mr. St. John," she continued, "he is standing on the steps."

"I am not looking for anyone," answered Regenia, blushing, as if she had been caught in the unmaidenly act of thinking of Lotus Stone.

"He has the advantage of being handsome," said Lucile, as she alighted from the carriage.

"Who are you talking of, pray? You grow more provoking every hour," said Regenia, with well feigned ignorance.

"'The pleasure of your company at the flambeau drill will add much to its effectiveness,'" said Lucile, imitating Lotus Stone.

The girls both laughed, and arm-in-arm they tripped gently up the walk to the house.

MRS. UNDERWOOD'S CHARGE.

Chapter IV.

REGENIA UNDERWOOD could scarcely remember when she did not live at the Elms. She was born in Canada. Around her life hung a mystery, as impenetrable as Egyptian darkness, to the curious, but perfectly clear to those who knew the history of Judge Underwood's family. Mrs. Underwood had cared for Regenia from childhood. Little by little, as the child as able to understand it, Mrs. Underwood had related to Regenia the story of her birth. The good woman, wisely determined to circumvent future heart rendings, by leaving no sad revelations, certain to creep out when most to be regretted, to mar the life and hopes of the sweet girl that day by day more closely entwined around her heart. Some things concerning the child's mother, discretion bade her withhold, but all that was necessary to acquaint Regenia with her lineage and race was duly disclosed.

There was a note of sorrow discernible in Mrs. Underwood's voice when speaking of Regenia. No one who saw the beautiful girl with Mrs. Underwood would have suspected that she was an Afro-American. Regenia knew it; but gave the fact no more thought than any other child does who is aware that it is of German, Irish or French descent. She never understood the soft, sad tone which Mrs. Underwood assumed, unintentionally, perhaps, when she spoke of Afro-Americans.

If Regenia's associates knew of the romance of her birth, they were too well bred to make the fact a cause for insult. She grew to womanhood feeling and acting not unlike the other children of her age, little dreaming of the sad awakening she was destined some day to experience. Regenia's mother was Mrs. Underwood's only child. Judge Underwood, a man of pronounced views on every subject, was an ardent disciple of Wendell Phillips. A lover of freedom, his home was the centre of the abolition movement in his county. A man of wealth and influence, a hater of every form of oppression, the cause of the slave appealed with unusual force to his keen sense of justice. His house was a station of the underground railroad, a peculiar method of assisting runaway slaves to Canada, conducted for years by the most courageous and daring lovers of personal liberty that ever graced American soil.

One dark, rainy night, a few years previous to the great political upheaval which swept away slavery and its attendant evils, a fugitive slave was spirited into Judge Underwood's barn. The slave slept that night in a cave on the premises, the sleuth hounds of oppression being hard on his track. The judge was away on his circuit; but his wife, who, though born in the south, sympathized with her husband's views of slavery, was severely taxed to invent some means of shielding the half-starved, hunted wretch, until opportunity occurred to forward him to Canada. The laws of the land made harboring fugitive slaves a crime that entailed upon those who disregarded them the most severe punishment. How to feed this poor slave, when every movement about the house was watched, became to Mrs. Underwood a question of grave concern. To go to the cave or to send anyone there would attract suspicion in that direction. All the next day, the poor fugitive, half wild from hunger and fear, awaited the coming of succor. Before the sun went down Mrs. Underwood had solved the vexatious problem. She made two long, wide bags, filled them with bread and meat, and pinning them securely to the dress of Ethel, her daughter, she bade her put on her apron and bonnet and drive home the cows.

"When you approach the cave," said Mrs. Underwood, "look carefully about you, and, if no one is near, go into the cave, unpin the bags and leave them for the poor man, who must be almost starved by this time."

Ethel was an intelligent child and quickly comprehended the nature of her mission. Fired with sympathy for the poor slave, she executed her mother's wish in a remarkably short time. In this cave, Ethel first met Regenia's father. George Stewart, a mulatto, with a shock of black hair and dark brown, dreamy eyes, was still in his teens. The southern man-hunters were thrown off the scent and George remained at Judge Underwood's as a servant.

Ethel was always fond of the young man; but her indulgent parents never suspected that her childish admiration might some day ripen into a liking more serious. During each winter George was sent to a seminary near his home, and, being naturally bright, soon became quite well informed. With little change in the friendship between the judge's protégé and his daughter, Ethel grew into womanhood. To George Stewart's credit, be it said, he was not aware that his fondness for the sweet girl whose hand first ministered to his wants in direst need, would bring the blush of shame to the cheeks of his kind benefactors.

The sentiments which Judge Underwood and his wife cherished for the final liberation of God's oppressed, took deeper root in Ethel's young heart than either of them supposed. With Ethel, sorrow grew into sympathy, sympathy deepened into affection, and at eighteen Ethel was in love with George Stewart. Mrs. Underwood first divined the girl's feelings toward the recent fugitive, and trembling with fear related her suspicions to the judge.

With Judge Underwood, to suspect was to act. He accordingly hastened to sound his daughter upon the state of her feelings toward his servant. She frankly admitted her love for George, and entrenching herself behind her father's oft-repeated arguments of the equality of men, the fatherhood of God and the brotherhood of all God's children, completely silenced him. George was questioned, but denied entertaining for Ethel any feelings other than those of kindness and esteem. The judge was thoroughly alarmed.

After a family council, it was decided to send George on to Canada and Ethel away to boarding school. In this way they hoped to end the unfortunate affair.

Ethel Underwood was a very determined young woman. With such a spirit, a change of place by no means argues a change of sentiment. She did not consider the objections offered by her father of sufficient weight to deter her from consummating the plans that were surging through her overwrought brain, concerning the object of her affections. She loved George Stewart; if she believed this before she was sent away, she knew it afterward. She regarded her father's determination to separate her from her lover as a species of the same sort of persecution she had heard him vehemently denounce. Ethel Underwood was not more determined than romantic. Reared in an atmosphere of high pressure sentimentalism, she would have willingly suffered martyrdom for the man she loved. She pictured poor George, driven out upon the charities of a pitiless world, because of his love for her, and linking with this the sad nemesis which had pursued him until shelter and sustenance could only be found in the caves of the earth, she resolved to follow him, and comfort him and make his life happy, whatever the cost.

Poor, misguided sentimental young woman; she never thought once how unhappy she might render two other lives, whose claim upon her love and obedience were more imperative than the much cherished fugitive's. Three weeks after entering the boarding school, she left to seek George Stewart. She found him sick and friendless in a strange land. She nursed him back to life and soon afterward they were married.

It was a pretty romance, this beautiful heiress following the hapless fugitive into exile, and giving up home, friends and luxury, all for love. A pretty sentiment, indeed, but a sad misfortune for the ill-advised child of indulgence who acts upon such sentiment.

Ethel's parents were speechless with horror when the news of their daughter's eccentricity came to their ears. Nor was this blow to fall singly upon the heads of these two life long friends of human rights. The news of Ethel's wilful misconduct had hardly been related when they were stricken with another calamity not less appalling. Judge Underwood was arrested for assisting runaway slaves, and hurried to prison to await the day of trial. It was then that the poor mother, doubly bereaved, longed for the solace of her child.

Ethel, buried in a little inland town in Canada, knew nothing of the awful afflictions through which her parents were passing. In the meantime, war came on, and through that the judge was released from confinement. He left immediately for Europe and did not return for three or four years.

During Judge Underwood's absence, George Steward died. In the arms of his devoted wife, never more devoted than during his last illness, the fugitive slave passed beyond the bay of blood hounds and the fear of the slave catcher. A few months after his death, Regenia came.

Poor, discouraged and alone, Ethel wrote to her parents, but received no answer. Grieving over her sad fate, she grew weaker day by day, until broken hearted and forgotten, she died.

One friend had remained steadfast during all her sorrows—Mrs. Levitt. Under her roof, the fair bride and hapless husband had eaten their wedding dinner. And proud, indeed, had she been that her hands were permitted to care for the sweet young woman who could give up all for her love. After the death of Regenia's mother, Mrs. Levitt took the child to her heart and cared for her as if she had been her own. On the return of the judge and his wife from Europe, they found the letter from her daughter. The judge came on and took little Regenia to Mt. Clare, where they had concluded to settle. Mrs. Levitt could not endure to be separated from the child, and in a few months followed her to Mt. Clare and took up her abode at the "Elms." About two years previous to the events of this story, Judge Underwood, broken in health from the misfortunes through which he had passed, suddenly died. At the death of Mrs. Underwood, Regenia will be sole heiress to the Underwood estates. Every day Mrs. Underwood discovered some new resemblance to her mother in Regenia. She had often intended to tell her of the fortune she would some day inherit, but from one cause or another she had neglected to do so.

After supper, on the evening of the day we last saw Regenia and Lucile tripping up the walk to the "Elms," they passed an hour sitting on the steps of the piazza, recounting interesting experiences.

"I am sure I never could have held out against the united opposition of all my friends, had it not been for you," said Lucile. "I believed that I could succeed, but what does the opinion of one poor, little, silly girl amount to against the conjoined disapproval of an entire community," she continued.

"Yet the one little girl had her way, and demonstrated, beyond our most sanguine expectations, the wisdom of her conclusions," answered Regenia, lightly.

"If one and God be a majority, then the girl with one faithful, sincere friend, as I had, was the largest number after all," said Lucile, laughing heartily at her own wisdom.

"Did you meet with many discouragements? But of course you did, although you were too 'plucky' to mention them in your letters," said Regenia, answering her own question.

"Not half as many as I had nerved myself to endure. Men overlook you, perhaps step on you in their haste, but once it is decided that you are a fixture, they mostly leave you to yourself."

"A fixture?" replied Regenia, "pray, what is that?"

"I only mean that they understand you have come to stay. It is wonderful how opposition ceases when people find out that in spite of them you will hold on your course."

"And Mr. St. John, was he of so much assistance?" asked Regenia innocently.

"He made many suggestions for which, I fear, I was not sufficiently thankful at first, but later on I learned to be secretly grateful for them. His help, however, was moral, rather than physical. His presence seems to breathe new life in one—that is," she said a little confused, "haven't you seen people before now whose very company seemed to drive dull care away?"

"I suppose I have," said Regenia, laughingly, "but I do not recall any of them just at this moment."

"Now, dear, please don't," said Lucile, pleadingly, "you must know what I mean."

"Oh, certainly, I have an idea, but of course there is a meaning that is too deep for sighs that I know nothing about yet, but I am beginning to live with the hope that the day will come."

"If you young ladies are going to see the fireworks, you would better be getting ready," called Mrs. Levitt, as she hurried up stairs to her room.

"Shall we go?" asked Regenia.

"'The pleasure of your company will add to its effectiveness,'" said Lucile, as she slipped her arm around Regenia's waist and pulled her through the open door.

THE FLAMBEAU DRILL.

Chapter V.

Not only the visitors, but apparently the entire population of Mt. Clare had preceded the carriage in which Regenia, Lucile, Mrs. Levitt and Mrs. Underwood were seated, to the square where the flambeau drill was to be conducted. Strung to the highest pitch of expectation, the nervous crowd, with frequent signs of impatience, awaited the advent of the "Flambeau Club."

Two squares from the balcony of the "White Elephant," the carriage was obliged to stop. The people, a solid mass of perspiring humanity, filled the street from curb to curb.

"We shall never be able to see anything in this out of the way place," said Lucile, with evident disappointment.

"It would not be advisable to drive nearer," answered Mrs. Underwood.

"No, indeed. Even the horses do not take kindly to the common herd," said Regenia, calling attention to the restlessness of the handsome span of black thoroughbreds, who movements required the driver's constant attention.

"As democratic as I am," said Mrs. Underwood, smiling faintly, "I am obliged to confess that I share their dislike."

"I like a crowd well enough, ordinarily, but we did not come to see the crowd. A flambeau drill can not be seen for the asking. I shall die of disappointment if I miss seeing it," said Lucile, her excitement increasing as she contemplated the bare possibility of such a probability.

"Your chances for living hang on a hair, if missing this drill will bring your existence to a period," said Regenia, smiling at Lucile's extravagance.

"The people ought to be kept back. Look! They have blockaded the streets completely," said Lucile, bristling with anger.

"I see you have been carried by the excitement into the very heart of the maddened crowd," said a pleasant voice beside the carriage.

The ladies turned in the direction of the sound, to see a physical entity of the vocal exponent, in the person of Clement St. John, standing, hat in hand, bowing and smiling.

"We are here, 'tis true, but from the outlook, we shall have only our experience for our pains," said Lucile, after the other occupants of the vehicle had exchanged greetings with Mr. St. John.

"The prospect is not the most inviting," said Clement, looking around to discover some means of exit. "If you will allow me, I think I can find a more suitable point of observation for you," he continued.

"We do not wish to discommode you, Mr. St. John," replied Regenia.

"Discommode me, indeed," thought Clement. He said: "I am only too happy to make myself useful, I assure you."

"We'll go and be glad to seize the opportunity," said Lucile, speaking the mind of the entire party. "How shall we ever extricate ourselves from this knotted skein of human beings?" she added.

"I have seats among the 'press gang' on the balcony," said Clement. "We can drive around the square to the 'ladies' entrance,' and in that way avoid the annoyance we should be sure to meet should we attempt to force our way though this 'tangled skein of human beings,'" he said smiling at Lucile.

To this proposition, Mrs. Underwood readily consented. Mounting to a seat beside the driver, Clement gave Mrs. Underwood's orders to drive to the hotel. Arriving there, they push their way through the crowded halls, ascend the stairs and emerge upon the balcony just as the street lights are being lowered to give the torches of the exhibitors the very best effect. Writing at a long table in the center of the balcony, sat a number of local and special correspondents. They nodded toward Clement as he seated his party, and a few who knew him well indicated their pleasure that Clement's card to the courtesies extended to the press enabled him to serve his friends in such a satisfactory manner.

Mr. St. John, on the principle before enumerated, did not deign to take notes. With a knowing smile, as he met Lucile's glance, he remarked loud enough to be heard by some of the reporters near him, "you will perceive, ladies, that these gentlemen serve me."

"Mr. St. John regards the seventh commandment very lightly," remarked his vis-a-vis. The ladies laughed.

"I am sorry to admit that my acquaintance with the commandments, numerically, is insufficient to grasp, without reflection, your reference, Miss Malone," he replied, with a well feigned look of embarrassment.

"Ignorance of the law is no excuse for crime," retorted Lucile, with assumed severity.

"Who speaks of ignorance, crime and justice in a breath and emphasizes her pharisaical condemnation with a piercing look in this direction?" said Clement, with a burst of merriment.

"Shake not thy bloody locks ignorantly committed?" asked Clement as he doffed his hat to expose his mop of red hair.

"Plagiarism," answered Lucile, solemnly.

"Plagiarism is good, but I always give credit when I steal. Quotations from the leading journals have more weight than anything I could write over my own signature. I write general accounts with the mucilage brush, but I reserve the right to comment editorially," said Clement.

After this manner the conversation rippled on, here and there taking a precipitous flight as it leaped from the sublime to the ridiculous.

Mrs. Levitt, who had not said one word since the party left the carriage, signalized her presence by saying with a sigh, "Well, I guess it is coming at last."

The others, who amid the constant flow of airy talk, had almost forgotten the event which was accountable for their presence looked in the direction indicated.

Away down the avenue, marching to a quick step, could be seen the approaching torches of the Flambeau Club. The sky was crimson from the reflection of "red fire." On they come, whizzing sky rockets and bursting roman candles, forming over their heads an arch of prismatic colors. Their glittering helmets, white uniforms and brass buttons beneath the flare of torch and red fire give to the scene a weird and melancholy beauty. The vast army of sight-seers herald their approach with one continuous shout of pleasure. As they arrive at the hotel, they wheel into line and salute the Eminent Grant Commander and ladies upon the balcony. The drill was beautiful. The combinations were formed more for picturesque display than for military correctness. Among the many notable effects produced by the flambeau drill, the serpentine movements were perhaps the most enjoyed by the observers.

To discuss each manoeuvre would be a needless repetition, as unprofitable to the reader as unnecessary to the ends of this story. At the conclusion of the exhibition, Mrs. Underwood, unused to the night air, expressed her readiness to return to the "Elms." The girls hung back, alleging as an excuse for their desire to remain, their wish to see the prizes presented to the victors of the afternoon. Mrs. Levitt, divining the real cause, suggested that Mrs. Underwood drive home and leave the girls in the care of Mr. St. John. Mrs. Underwood agreed to this, and, in company with Mrs. Levitt, left the hotel. As she passed through the door opening off the balcony, a young man approached her and entered into conversation. Now Clement St. John, from his position on the balcony, had detected that same young man observing him narrowly, more than once during the evening.

"Who is he?" thought Clement, "and why has he stared at me so rudely for the last two hours?"

As these questions pass through the mind of Clement, he overhears Regenia remark to Lucile: "That is Dr. Frank Leighton, Mrs. Underwood's nephew."

Regenia rarely spoke of her grandmother by any term more endearing than "Mrs. Underwood." She had kept her eyes on Lotus Stone during the entire drill. She thought, as she sat there watching him, for she only had eyes for the column in which he was a conspicuous part, "He is handsomer to-night than ever." Once, when the company faced the balcony for a moment, the electric lights were turned on, and Lotus instinctively looked up. His eyes met Regenia's for an instant only, but in that moment each felt the thrill of mutual admiration.

Clement said as Regenia turned from Lotus to him: "He is remarkably handsome, and the very finest gentleman I ever met."

Regenia, blushing hotly, made no answer.

The presentation speeches were half over when Lotus Stone, with a low bow, greeted his friends on the balcony. He had hastened to his room, as soon as the drill was ended, and exchanged his white duck uniform for a suit less conspicuous.

"Accept my congratulations, old man. Your people did themselves proud to-night. Who would not be a soldier and go on dress parade?" said Clement heartily, as Lotus came up.

The two young ladies offered congratulations when Mr. St. John had finished. "I think it was awfully lovely, Mr. Stone, and you were the very best of all," said Lucile, earnestly.

"Hear that!" ejaculated Mr. St. John. "'Who would not be a soldier and go on dress parade?'" he began singing, in a low key.

"And did you like it, Miss Underwood?" asked Lotus.

"Although I do not understand your movements, I think the flambeau drill the most beautiful sight I ever saw," replied Regenia.

"That is something like it," said Clement, mischievously, "but giving all the praise to one man is too much."

"Lucile does not think more highly of Mr. Stone's part in the evening's entertainment than I do," answered Regenia, with an arch look at Mr. St. John.

"What would I not give to be a member of the Flambeau Club," said Clement, with mock dejection. "There is nothing left for the rest of us but to seek the charitable seclusion of the grave, 'unwept, unhonored, an unsung.'"

"It is not that bad, I hope," said Lotus, smiling at the rare good spirits that possessed his friend.

"The drill was indeed lovely, Mr. St. John, but we are indebted to your generosity entirely that we were permitted to enjoy such an excellent view of it. We shall not forget your kindness, if we do praise the Knights of the Red Cross so enthusiastically," said Regenia in her sweet, earnest way.

"Mr. St. John knows how much we thank him," said Lucile. "Don't mind what he says, dear. When you know him as well as I do, you will read his talk between the lines."

"The idea of reading audible expressions between the lines! To thy finger board, Miss Typewriter. The copyist sees everything in violet ink. You see between the lines better than you see the lines sometimes, I suspect," said Clement, lightly.

"He is through at last," said Regenia, referring to the speech of presentation, just finished.

"How much of it did you hear?" asked Lotus.

"Not a great deal, I admit. 'Ladies and Gentlemen,' and perhaps 'I add no more,'" she replied, smiling at her questioner.

"I did not hear that much," he said, lowering his voice. "There was other music that I much preferred to hear."

"I suppose so," she answered. "The notes of praise sounded in your ears have not been confined to this balcony, I conjecture."

"With me," said Lotus, "it is not the song, but the singer; not the high key of mechanical training, but the sweet old songs that reach the heart. Not the applauding multitude, but the admiring few."

"I agree with you," she answered, dropping her bantering tone. "It is earnestness in everything that makes anything worth while."

"Suppose we go," said Lucile, rising. "They will think at home that we are lost, Regenia."

"Mr. St. John will be held responsible; he seems to be our scape goat," answered Regenia.

"Yes; scape goat, pack mule or anything else, so I may be permitted to bask in your smiles, Miss Underwood," said Clement, leading the way to the stairs.

"How do you get along with Mr. St. John?" asked Regenia, laughingly, as, clinging to Mr. Stone's arm, they pushed their way through the crowded corridor toward the ladies' exit.

"Clement is extremely well pleased to-night," said Lotus.

"When he is happiest he is most provoking," answered her escort. "We have always known each other," he continued, "and I do not know whether I came to the conclave for anything more serious than to see Clement St. John."

"I thought you enjoyed the wild applause of the gaping multitude. Oh, no," she made haste to say, "you did inform me differently."

"Speaking of Mr. St. John," he said, "there is not a more seriously earnest man of my acquaintance, notwithstanding his apparent lightness."

"I should think him anything but serious," answered Regenia, with much surprise.

"In that respect, you agree with everyone who has only seen the crude exterior. At heart, Clement St. John is an unusually thoughtful, level-headed man. His gaiety is often assumed. He makes the sufferings of his race a hobby and takes their aggregated wrongs as so many personal affronts.

Keenly alive to their multifarious grievances, with tongue or pen, he is ever ready to do battle in behalf of the cause he loves. I sometimes think that his opponents are only the conjurations of his over-active imagination," said Lotus. "Did you ever read his paper?"

"No, I have not," she answered.

"I would be pleased to send you a copy, if you would like to read it."

"Certainly if—if—"

"If what? You seem to hesitate."

"If you like," she added. She wondered if on such short acquaintance it would not be bad taste to accept his offer. He did not think so, or he would not have made such a tender, she finally concluded. After knowing him a day, Regenia found herself trusting this stranger in a way that almost frightened her. With a shiver, she glanced over her shoulder for Lucile and Mr. St. John. He noticed the tremor in the hand that held his arm, and instantly remarked: "You are not cold, Miss Underwood?"

"No," she said. "I fear I have not been confining my thoughts entirely to the subject of our conversation."

As they sauntered home in the moonlight, Lotus told her of his life in Washington; how he longed to go out in the world and make a name; of his intention to resign as soon as he had finished his medical course.

"Where will you practice?" she interrupted, with more interest than she was aware of.

"I have not decided, but most likely in the south," he answered. "The south offers the most flattering inducements to a young man who has no political aspirations," he continued. "I have had enough of politics," he continued, more to himself than to his companion.

She knew but little of politics and was therefore discreetly silent. Why he had enough of politics she neither knew nor was she particularly interested.

"Why do you prefer the south with its discriminations and difficulties to the north?" she finally asked.

"For many reasons, the first of which is, there are more of our people in the south than in the north." Regenia noted his emphasis upon "our" people. The expression was new to her.

"Second, the natural antipathy existing between the races in the south, makes the professional service rendered to the Afro-American grudgingly indifferent. The physician is a missionary. His work presupposes a double duty, healing the body and comforting the mind."

"I think that duty can be done in one place as well as another," replied Regenia, holding to her unexpressed wish.

"Perhaps so," said Lotus. "But in a city like this, say, a man could not get the patronage of his own race. The north is the best place to prepare for war, but an Afro-American must go south to practice it."

"Are you two so interested in each other that you do not know where to stop?" called Lucile.

"We are at home," said Regenia, blushing. By that time Clement and Lucile had reached the gate.

"Shall we see you safe within the door?" said Clement, opening the gate.

"You are responsible," answered Regenia.

"How would it do to let Mr. Stone share some of this responsibility? The load is getting too heavy for my shoulders."

"I am only too willing to share any responsibility that these ladies may see fit to put upon me," said Lotus gallantly.

"They may, is good; but suppose I wish to do some unloading, in that case is your gallantry unflinching?" asked Clement.

"Oh, certainly," said Lotus.

As they walked up the gravel way, Clement suggested that they march by fours.

"How about to-morrow?" asked Clement, as the girls bade them good-night.

"You arrange with Mr. Stone. I'll be responsible for Regenia," Lucile replied.

"If it is a conspiracy," said Lotus, "I only hope that in the intrigue you may contrive to capture me."

Arm-in-arm as in the days of old, Clement and Lotus walked back to the "White Elephant." Neither spoke until the "Elms" was left sleeping in the hazy distance. Clement as usual broke the silence.

"I might as well confess that I am hit hard. That bewitching little woman rivets her chains more securely every time I see her. 'She is all the world to me,'" he began to sing.

"A charming companion, indeed," said Lotus, "and best of all she believes in you."

"As if that was such a devil of a job," said Clement, laughingly.

"You are rather hard to find," Lotus replied, "but that mischievous little woman has found your heart, and more than that she believes in you, sees between the lines, and you know it and she knows you know."

"You are more right than wrong," said Clement. "How about our beauty at the 'Elms?'"

Lotus winced. He did not like Clement's familiar way of speaking about Regenia.

"She is yours, Lotus, if you follow up your impressions," he continued, misinterpreting his friend's silence.

"She is a noble, high-souled woman—such a woman as any man might wish to win; but wishing and winning are two things," replied Lotus thoughtfully.

"What a woman like Miss Underwood needs is some awful calamity to amuse her dormant affections. If she could be led to believe that she was making some great sacrifice for you, or you were being hated and maligned for her, either would answer, she would give up her life for you. Say, I have it. Suppose you hire some one to 'slug' you gently and do the unconscious act, and let me send post haste for Miss Underwood—why old man, what is the matter? You are not losing your temper?"

Lotus came dangerously near losing it at the nonsensical proposition Clement was making.

They walked on in silence until the lights of the "White Elephant" loomed up in the next block.

"Excuse me, old friend," Lotus said, stopping. "I believe I am hit harder than I thought."

"Don't mention it. Haven't I received, right between the eyes, a 'knock-out' blow?" said Clement.

At this they both laughed and Lotus, extending his hand, said, as Clement grasped it; "What fools we mortals be."

FROM LAKE TO LAKE.

Chapter VI.

The last day of the conclave had come. It was the intention of the committee to make the festivities of the day equal, if they did not surpass, the pleasure of the preceding one. An excursion up the river to an island, located in a not distant lake, and the banquet at night were to round out the closing hours of the conclave in blaze of glory. In order to accommodate the large number of excursionists, two palatial lake steamers were lashed together. The brass band, stationed upon an improvised platform built well to the front and between the two boats, discoursed sweet music for the occupants of both steamers. The removal of a part of the guard rails from the upper and lower decks of the steamers, and the substitution of a plank gang-ways, flanked on either side by ropes, virtually converted the two boats into one. The day was delightful. A gentle breeze sweeping down from the lake gave to the occasion an exhilarating zest, unfolded the flags which hung from the jack-staffs of the boats and fluttered into uncontrolled gaiety the tri-colored bunting which everywhere bespoke the patriotism of the promoters.

The scene at the landing was interesting in the extreme. The ticket agents, their satchels hung over their shoulders, pushed back and forth through the surging mass, apparently trying to accommodate everyone who wanted a ticket at the same time.

Clement and Lotus were there in time to see the excited crowd, elbowing each other right and left, excitingly securing tickets and hurrying aboard the boats.

"Nobody seems to be going," said Clement.

"My, what a crowd! Where do the people come from?" Lotus replied.

And it was a crowd. The fat woman was there, boisterous and self-assertive; the lean woman was there, spiteful and sarcastic; the refined woman, sad and disgusted; and the jolly woman, jostled, crushed, but delighted. Every size, class, cast and color of the Afro-American woman was on that quay, each knowing her rights, and, if belligerent looks are any indication, ready to maintain them. It was virtually a war between women, and with tongue and eyes was it bitterly waged. Nor was this scene void of other amusing incidents. More than one old lady, with a son or daughter taller than herself, labored in vain to jew the perplexed ticket agent from full fare to half that amount. So great was the rush that many in hasty disgust despaired of ever being able to get a ticket, and accordingly returned to their lodging places. These last were principally married women, whose husbands' slothfulness had rendered the pleasures of the trip "stale, flat and unprofitable," when compared with the future prospect of reminding these poor men of the disappointment their execrable conduct had occasioned. Some of the gay gallants halted between two opinions, undecided whether to go on the excursion or attend the banquet. Many could not attend both for financial reasons. It had begun to dawn slowly upon many of the young men and a few of the old, who had been living like princes for the past three days, that an awful financial catastrophe was staring them in the face. Others, as they hesitated, wondered who in all that knightly band would lend them the price of admittance to the banquet, provided they hazarded their last available penny on a trip up the river. Among the last to come aboard the boats were Regenia and Lucile; in fact the last warning tap of the bell had sounded before they pushed through the crowd and ascended the stairs. Mrs. Levitt and Mrs. Underwood waved a fond adieu as the two steamers backed away from the landing and slowly swung out into the river. Dr. Frank Leighton, a victim of curiosity, sat on the upper deck dreamily smoking a cigar.

It was a mixed multitude. A vast number of citizens, piqued by curiosity or from motives more friendly, grouped in little knots, seemed to be enjoying the prospect of a pleasant trip, quite as much as the Afro-Americans. The boats were fairly under way before Clement and Lotus were able to get in anything like speaking distance of Lucile and Regenia. The girls were comfortably seated in the after recess of the cabin. The young men had tried in vain to catch the eyes of the girls as they swerved back and forth through the talking, gesturing throng.

"At last!" said Clement, as he and Lotus approached the girls. "Do you know we have been trying every second the last half hour to reach this promised land, surrounded on all sides by water."

"Where have you been?" asked Lucile, with her usual impetuosity. "We thought you were left."

"We have been trying to find you, I believe I just informed you," answered Clement, smiling. "We have been in sight of the delectable spot for some time, but how to reach it without climbing over the head of some one who is here on equal terms with ourselves has kept us impatiently waiting until this blessed moment."

"And, Mr. Stone," said Lucile, who had been addressing Clement, "are you in good spirits after the severe test of yesterday?"

"A little the worse for so much marching," said Lotus, "but an excess of that sort of thing is so infrequent that the change is as beneficial as discipline."

"I prefer my discipline in broken doses," said Clement.

"Mr. St. John has a predilection for homeopathic treatment in this particular," said Regenia.

"I am regular," replied Lotus, divining Regenia's implied question.

"Oh, that's your school, is it? I am gaining information for which I did not ask," she replied naively.

The young men, dressed a la negligee, leaning against the guard rail, the girls, in their jaunty outing suits, made a picture that few of the moving mass passed without a second look.

Regenia introduced the young men to Dr. Leighton, who, after a few haughty words, went back to his chair a little distance away, whence he watched the group with eyes of jealousy, if not hatred. Dr. Frank Leighton's feeling toward Regenia, alternated between desperate love and blind hatred. Sometimes he has wished her out of his life and would have gladly stood by her open grave and dropped on her lowering bier, a tear of mingled joy and regret.

Regenia alone stood between Dr. Leighton and the Underwood estates. Cherishing such feelings toward Regenia, he was possessed with a spasm of hate as he saw her actually enjoying the company of Lotus and Clement.

When in Regenia's presence, her gentle manner and sweet face, almost persuaded Dr. Leighton to marry her, and end his agony; but when he thought of his social position and the pride of his relations he abandoned the idea and heartily wished her dead. To-day, as he sat there observing every move and mood of Regenia, he was a prey to the tortures of conflicting emotions. While the party in which we are most interested are conversing as light hearted, high-spirited young people will do, they have not noticed that the chairs are being moved back, and one or two sets are preparing to engage in dancing. Clement St. John and Lucile, after looking on for a while, joined in the in the merriment.

"As I shall be too busy to dance to-night, will indulge to-day," he remarked to Lucile.

She readily consented and they were soon whirling in the dizzy waltz, the gayest of the gay.

Regenia declined to accept Mr. Stone's invitation to participate. "I rarely dance," she said, "and when I do, it is not in public."

Lotus was an inveterate lover of dancing, and when, after a half hour of looking on, Clement, insisted that he and Regenia should make the final couple in a set of the Lanciers, he persuaded Regenia to forego her scruples and yield to the wishes of her friends. Regenia enjoyed the sparkling conversation of Mr. Stone much more than she did the dancing. She was not quite clear upon the propriety of dancing in public; from a moral standpoint she did not object, but found herself to-day, as on the evening before, wondering if it was good form to pass the time so freely with a man whose acquaintance she had so recently made. She greeted the last figure of the dance with secret delight.

When the girls were again comfortably seated, the young men proposed a lemon ice. The girls are requested to remain where they are, and Clement and Lotus started, edging their ways through the crowd intent upon their errand. The refreshments were upon the lower deck of the boat. The dancers, in their enjoyment, had not observed a dark cloud gathering toward the northeast, and that since the steamers had struck the open lake they did not move so smoothly. The young men noticed, as they pushed through the crowd, that the loud laugh had sobered somewhat and that here and there groups of wiser heads stood earnestly talking. Intent upon the business of the moment, they pushed on, shouldering right and left, and then, standing still until some one changed position. At last they succeeded in making the gang way leading to the other boat. Here the same process of inching to the stairway, stopping and waiting and creeping down had to be repeated.

"Well," said Clement, as he stood mopping his forehead, "we have at last reached the goal, but it seems longer since we started than it took Columbus to find a new world."

"What will you have?" sharply asked the woman selling ices for their weight in silver.

"Anything, so it is cold," answered Clement, good naturedly.

"How we shall ever carry a lemon ice back, through that crowd, it what knocks me," said Lotus, turning from the table with the precious aliment in hand.

"If those young ladies imagined what straits we are being put to in order to cater to their palates, they would worship us while they lived, and dying remember us in their wills," said Clement, laughingly.

"The average young lady gives herself but little worry about our sufferings when her pleasure is concerned," answered Lotus, ruefully.

As they stood there talking, the spray from a wave that dashed against the boat awakened them to a sense of their danger. Glancing toward the cabin of the opposite boat, they beheld a scene of greatest commotion. Hastening to the stairway, they try in vain to mount to the upper cabin. The steamer trembles and lurches and now and then a scream of terror shakes the multitude like an aspen leaf.

"What is the matter up there?" cried Clement to those above, but received no answer.

"We have struck the lake and are meeting a little heavier seas," remarked Lotus, noting the water dashing against the side of the vessel and breaking over the guards.

To stand there unable to lift his hand in Lucile's behalf, fills Clement St. John with a wild desire to be at her side or die in the attempt. Again he tries to mount the stairs; he throws himself against the wedged-in mass of men and women, but his efforts are in vain; he might as well kick against the rock of Gibraltar, so far as any visible impression is made. He vented his disappointment upon the inoffensive head of a nervous old man who sat at the foot of the stairs, weeping as if his heart would break.

"Lord have mercy on us! Mister, are we all going to be drowned?" queried the old man in a piteously piping tone, as he noticed the water dashing over the guards.

"That's the way it looks," said Clement.

"Oh, my Lord, oh my Lord!" cried the old man.

"If you don't shut up I'll pitch you into the lake. I'd put you there anyway," he said, his good nature getting the better of his anger, "if I did not have so much respect for the fish. They would need a dentist down there, sure, after one or two attacks on your tough hide."

"Oh Lord! Oh Lord!" cried the old man, as he dropped a piece of lemon pie which he was eating, and with big hot tears chasing each other down his wrinkled cheeks, and the remains of the pie clinging to the corners of his mouth, he fell on his knees and began to pray lustily.

Lotus, too, was baffled and out of humor, but he could not suppress the smile which Clement's droll remark called up.

"There, now," he said, kindly to the old man. "You are all right, no danger if you just keep quiet."

He had hardly ceased speaking to the old man when he heard an officer's voice above the roar of the wind and dash of the waves: "Stand back! That cable is going to part." He could hear the shuffling of feet above, and then like the report of a musket, the rope holding the boats together in front, snapped.

He could feel the boats swinging away from each other. His heart sank within him as he thought of Regenia. The tremor of the boats as they swing away from each other and alternately return, causes the passengers crowding the stairs to move a little; with the agility of a cat Lotus springs into the opening, and snatching the man above him backward, rushes into his place. He serves the man above him in the same way and in an incredibly shot time has gained the cabin. As he reached the cabin, to his infinite horror, he sees the boats gradually swinging apart. He starts for the gang-way, climbing over those in his way, being cursed, struck down, thrown back only to begin again with redoubled determination. As he pushes his way against tremendous odds to the guards, he sees the stage planks between the boats inching nearer and nearer toward the edge—he hears the platform fall and for a moment despairs. Looking across the abyss, what a sight meets his eyes! Regenia, pushed on by the force behind her, clings to one of the uprights of the guard, on the verge of the opening which made the passage between the boats. One of her feet hangs over the side, and the treacherous gang plank, one end of which has fallen to the deck of the boat on which Lotus is standing, while the other end is on the upper deck of the other boat, within a foot of Regenia. A motion of the boat will throw that plank forward, in falling it will crush the girl, break her hold on the upright and the cruel waves or more cruel wheel will hide her sweet face forever. All of this passes through Lotus Stone's mind in a moment. Glancing toward the stern of the boat he saw that the cables were being unloosed. This would separate the boats. Setting his teeth and tightening every muscle in his wiry body and whispering "God help me," he sprang forward. Throwing those in his way to the deck and walking over them, he mounted the guard rail just as the boats began to separate. Balancing himself for a moment, he sprang across the yawning, ever-widening chasm, and, catching the upright to which Regenia clung, he dropped upon the deck beside her. Throwing himself between Regenia and the slowly approaching stage plank, while he held to the upright with one hand, it was but the work of a moment to catch the stage plank with the other. Bending forward with almost superhuman strength, he threw the heavy plank into the foaming lake.

This done, he waved back the crowd and led the exhausted girl beyond the fear of danger. For a moment the people on both steamers forgot their fears and sent up a wild cheer that fairly rent the sky. The enthusiasm which the heroic deed created drowned for a time the mad plash of the waters and the moan of the threatening wind.

As Lotus glanced over his shoulder, he saw Dr. Frank Leighton, standing on the opposite side of the open guard rail, nonchalantly twisting the ends of his mustache—a disappointed sneer on his handsome face—an angry consuming fire burning in his black eyes. The eyes of the two men met but for a moment, but each read in the soul of the other that hatred which the other felt and gloried in the feeling. Lotus could not express the contempt he felt for the man who by the slightest effort could have rescued Regenia from the fate he must have seen so certainly pending, if that deadly stage plank but moved six inches more. Dr. Leighton, as usual, being doubtful whether to be glad or sorry at the rescue of his fair cousin, nevertheless hated Lotus Stone for saving her.

As the crowd gave way, Lotus helped Regenia to a chair. She had swooned. In the act of seating her, he unintentionally lowered his left arm allowing her head for a moment to drop toward the floor. The movement was fortunate, as the blood, at the command of gravity, rushed back to her brain, thus reviving her.

When Regenia opened her eyes for a moment, she was at a loss to know what had happened. But seeing Lotus, it all came back to her. "Oh, thank you, thank you," was all she could say.

But that was enough for Lotus. For such a look as she gave him, he would have willingly made a second leap.

The boats were separated, but not before Clement St. John had pushed his way to the rear end of the boat, and, crossing with less danger than Lotus had incurred, found Lucile. The boats having separated, slowly steamed back to Mt. Clare. On the way back Regenia had ample time to thank Mr. Stone for his timely help. Lotus protested that he had done nothing to be thanked for. When they were again safe on land, Clement and Lucile joined them.

"Where is Dr. Leighton?" said Regenia. "He made one of our party and ought to return with us."

"I do not see him," said Clement, "but I dare say he will put in an appearance when he is neither wanted nor expected."

"Why Mr. St. John," said Lucile, "you ought not to speak with so much asperity of one you have known so short a time.

"I only met him to-day, it is true, but I am as well acquainted with him as if I had been seeing him an age. Some people we know at a glance, others we never know," said Clement, dryly.

"To which of these classes does Dr. Leighton belong?" asked Regenia.

"To both of them," answered Clement. "One knows enough of Dr. Leighton to thoroughly detest him the first time he sees him; he would not know more if he made him the study of a lifetime."

"You are bitter," said Regenia. "The doctor has his faults, perhaps, but perhaps the rest of us are not faultless. Some of us are better than we seem," she added.

Clement was bitter. He was standing where he could look into Dr. Leighton's face when Lotus saved Regenia, and Clement declared to Lotus afterward that Dr. Leighton bit his lips with suppressed rage when, in the nick of time, his cousin was rescued.

It was five o'clock when the party arrived at the "Elms." Before they left, however, they had persuaded the girls to attend the grand finale at Fraternity Hall.

THE FETE TERPSICHOREAN.

Chapter VII.

FRATERNITY HALL WAS A STUDY on the evening of the banquet. As carriage after carriage drove up and their occupants alighted and tripped into the hall, they looked, and without doubt were, the equals in appointments and bearing of any Americans. The ladies were attired in evening costume; the men wore the conventional black. Here was to be seen the Afro-American at his best. The absence of flashy dress and cheap, showy jewelry, so often attributed to the Negro as a necessity on all public occasions, was nowhere to be seen. This is evidently not the class from which the usual American writer draws his characters, when moralizing upon the peculiarities of the Afro-American. The unprejudiced observer would have seen nothing in the appearance of the happy assembly congregated in Fraternity Hall, complexion excepted, to indicate that he was among a strange people. The banquet, in style and arrangements, was model of the highest rather than the lowest class of American affairs.

The average Afro-American has little inclination to copy the pace of those of his own financial class, but at heart he is an aristocrat and imitates the bluest blood of the land.

The ladies were there in all their glory, and as they promenade or whirl through the figures of the dance, what a picture for cosmopoly! Women as fair as the lily cling to the arms of their ebony Othello's with an air of entire satisfaction. Here is seen in happy association the union of every family of men—an ocular demonstration of the fact that from one blood God hath made all the nations of the earth. The social standards adopted by these people and the link that holds together a race so varied in appearance and origin, is character. The mind, not the man; the heart, not the features. Nor does this distinction argue that all social lines in Afro-America are obliterated. Among these people, as elsewhere, the marks of class difference are severely drawn; but worth, not complexion, forms the barrier of demarcation. It is from the point of public observation that writers like W. D. Howells and others fall into excusable error.

As all classes of Afro-Americans seem to mingle indiscriminately at public functions, it is often concluded that no line of separation exists. The initiated know better. It was noticeable on this occasion, as it is in all public gatherings, that the same persons made up a given set after each interval of the dance. There was indeed a change of partners, but no change of the company. Frequently one or two sets, by especial arrangement, interchanged partners. This then, is the fine shading of distinction unostentatiously made, that is entirely unnoticed by the casual observer. Each company of dancers form in themselves a social world undoubtedly satisfactory to themselves, but as free from invasion from without as if the dance was being conducted in a private parlor. Nothing is done or said which would lead a looker-on to suppose that a whit's difference existed between any one of these sets and the score of others that surrounded them; but should someone beyond the pale of the social world attempt to inflict his company upon them, the dancers would become promenaders, and the dancing in that part of the hall become a thing of the past.

The merrymakers were in the full tide of enjoyment when Lucile and Regenia, chaperoned by Mrs. Levitt, arrived at the hall. Clement St. John, seated in the balcony, for the first time during the conclave, was taking notes of the occasion. Notices of the banquet could not be copied from other papers. The racy descriptions of costumes and those who wore them required the skill of someone who not only viewed the proceedings, but enjoyed a personal acquaintance with the tastes and peculiarities of the persons described. He was well aware that the patrons of his paper would be more interested in a detailed account of the doings of the last evening than in all that preceded it. Lotus Stone, as if to make up for the time lost in the afternoon, was determined not to miss a number. After looking in vain for Lucile and Regenia, who were to come, by preference, under the care of Mrs. Levitt, Lotus had concluded that they would not be present, and giving wings to his longings entered heartily into the pleasures of the evening. Clement, also, had despaired of the appearance of his much-expected friends and busily observing a gentleman, from his dress, a representative of the cloth, he failed to see the party from the "Elms" come in and seat themselves immediately behind the quill-driver. It was evident to Clement that the man wanted to talk, so, closing his note book, he concluded to engage him.

"I suppose you are enjoying this sight, Elder, in common with the rest of us Philistines," said Clement, smiling quizzically.

"I am here, but I cannot say I enjoy anything so foolish as dancing," rejoined the Elder, in his deepest chest tones.

"If you do not enjoy it, why are you here?" asked Clement, still smiling.

"I am here, sir, for the banquet. What I think is this: there should be no dancing until the supper is over, so that those to whom dancing is insulting, sir, yes, I repeat it, insulting, sir," he said as Clement raised his eyebrows slightly, "could go about their business and leave Ephraim to his idols," he concluded with a snort.

"Did you not know that there would be dancing to-night?" asked Clement.

"What puzzles me," said Clement slowly, "is why you ministers accept complimentary tickets to affairs of this kind, well knowing that your feelings will be outraged, and then have the impoliteness to come here and mar the pleasure of everyone who comes in contact with you by your caustic criticism of the management. If you are opposed to this sort of thing, why trifle with your conscience by coming, and then raise the devil after you get here because you did come?"

"Young man, your observations are insulting—insulting, sir, in the extreme," said the elder, rising.

"They are true, all the same," said Clement, "and you are under no compulsion to hear more of them."

"I am cognizant of that," replied the now exasperated elder, as he beat a hasty retreat to repeat his tale of woe to more sympathizing ears.

"You are very severe," said Lucile, leaning over his shoulder.

"Ah, ladies," said Mr. St. John, now the very pink of politeness, "I did not know that such distinguished auditors graced my little tilt with the elder."

"Your directness left no doubt of your meaning. The elder could not accuse you of a want of clearness," said Regenia, laughing at the picture which the Rev. Mr. Foggs made as he left Clement in high disgust.

"Well, I was, perhaps, a trifle too outspoken, but I hate hypocrisy in any garb. If ministers will pervade what they are pleased to style the precincts of Satan, they must accept the courtesies which obtain there. I hold if a man accepts an invitation to attend a social gathering, he is under obligations to conduct himself in keeping with the laws of good form. He need not participate in what passes if his conscience or inclination forbids, but he ought either to contribute to the good cheer of those who invited him, or stay at home. Impoliteness is as sinful as dancing."

"Is dancing a sin?" asked Regenia.

"That is a question for theologians, not newspaper men; I refer you to Elder Foggs," said Clement, smiling at his own wit.

"Are you not a believer, Mr. St. John?" asked Mrs. Levitt, with considerable warmth.

"I should be sorry if I were not, Mrs. Levitt. If there is nothing beyond this world, life at its best is a disappointing farce. But I am from an authority upon matters of the soul," he added lightly.

"The good elder would agree with you, I dare say, upon your last proposition," said Regenia.

"Mr. Stone has forgotten that is was partly through his solicitations that we are here to-night. 'Out of sight, out of mind,' is the motto of your men the world over," said Lucile.

"Do you mean me, or is present company the honorable exception?" Clement asked.

"Are you a man?" she asked, laughingly.

"I pose for one on election day," replied Clement.

"Mr. Stone is enjoying himself, and he is right. We do not have a banquet every evening," observed Regenia.

"Lotus is a devoted dancer, but I fear he would lose his fondness if he knew how fortunate and happy I am, stowed away beyond the sullying influence of the maddened multitude."

"You many be happy, but by the way you glance down at your unfinished notes, you do not have that appearance," laughed Lucile.

"Mr. St. John must finish his notes when he has more leisure; for the present he is our captive and although we may bore him, we are determined to appropriate him for the rest of the evening," said Regenia with more boldness than usual.

"Was ever man a more willing captive? You are only to demand, I await your pleasure," said Clement. "What will you have me do? Only suggest something sufficient difficult to make my efforts equal the labors of Hercules."

"Little things well done, give to life its spice," said Regenia.

"First tell Regenia who the petite beauty is, with whom Mr. Stone is dancing so entrancingly?" queried Lucile, with a provoking smile at Regenia.

"You are to satisfy Lucile's curiosity, I have no interest in the matter," said Regenia.

"Oh, yes you have, dear. You can not dream of the awful looks you have been casting in that direction for the last five minutes. Tell her, Mr. St. John, she is dying to know."

"Lucile is more anxious than I am. Tell her and I will admit that I am not at all averse to listening," said Regenia blushing.

Clement informed them of the person in question, and also of the other ladies in the circle of which Lotus Stone formed the central figure, throwing in such scraps of personal knowledge as he knew or could invent. As he chatted away in his interesting way, the music suddenly ceased, and from the stir among the lookers on, it was evident that the procession was about to be formed to make a raid upon the supper room.

With serious misgivings that he had forgotten entirely the ladies from the "Elms," Clement glanced wistfully over the hall for Lotus.

"Shall we go down," he at last asked. "I think we would better if we wish to even see the tables."

"I do not care for the supper, but I should liked to have seen the tables," said Regenia, her very tone indicating her disappointment.

"If I had Lotus, I think I could teach him some sense," Clement thought. He said: "Why not go down? The sight of four hundred guests is worth seeing, because so rare."

Mrs. Levitt signifies her intention of remaining where she is. "I have eaten one supper, and do not care to eat again," she said.

"Pardon me," Clement heard in the low tones of Lotus, as he turned for a last look for his friend. "I know I do not deserve your forgiveness, but have you been here long?"

"Only about two hours," said Clement, with a visible touch of irony.

"So long?" asked Lotus. "Come let us get our places in the ranks and I will explain my seeming perfidy as we march," he remarked to Regenia, nothing abash.

The officers of the Grand Commandery and their ladies, placed according to rank, preceded the procession. Clement, representing the press, came just behind them. He did not, therefore hear what explanation Lotus made of his apparent neglect, but before the doors of the supper room were opened, he noticed Regenia talking as gaily as if the affair, of which he was ready to make a cause of war, had never happened.

After marching and countermarching several times around the room, the procession is at last formed. The Eminent Grand Commander, escorting the mayor, leads the way. As they approach the banquet hall, the doors are thrown open and the guests pass in, seating themselves at the long tables, the Grand Commander at the head of the first table, the mayor of Mt. Clare at his right. At a given signal, a tall white-haired man, in the uniform of the Knights, eloquently gives thanks. Regenia was delighted. She had never seen so many Afro-Americans under similar circumstances and, judging from the sparkle of her eyes and the tinge of her cheeks, the introduction was at least pleasing. Mr. Stone, keenly cognizant of an apparent want of gallantry, exerted himself to make amends. It was well for Regenia that her first contact with Afro-American society was under circumstances so felicitous. It was a rare combination of sparkling wit, brilliant humor and biting sarcasm which sat that night about the Eminent Grand Commander's end of the table. Gallant Sir Knights all, they were men of influence known and respected throughout the land.

She is yet to see the other side where ignorance is as pronounced as absence of it was conspicuous in the gay circle which surrounded her.

As everything comes to an end, so the feasting was at last finished. The toast master, taking his station, began to read the toasts of the evening.

They were such as are customary upon such occasions. The responses, with a few noteworthy exceptions, were listened to with indifference, if not to say impatience.

Mr. St. John spoke for the press. His effort was happily conceived, uniquely delivered and well received.

Lotus Stone made an ideal post-prandial address. "The ladies, God bless them," was the toast. Regenia sat throughout the address in a maze of happy surprises. Such a torrent of mellifluous rhapsodies flowed from the lips of Mr. Stone that the audience interrupting, burst forth time and again in uproarious applause. He closed with a glowing burst of eloquence, complimentary to the noble, self-sacrificing women of his race, in such pleasing contrast to the airy nothingness strung out on such occasions, that every woman listening left thankful for his earnest advocacy of their cause. Mr. Stone was surrounded by the ladies as he made his way back to the ball room. Congratulations greeted him on every side. Regenia alone seemed to have lost her tongue. From the moment Lotus Stone charmed and delighted that audience, compelled attention where older and more experienced men had signally failed, the world contained for Regenia Underwood but one man, and that fortunate creature, if he could only have known it, was the hero of the hour.

Soon after supper the party from the "Elms" returned home. Lotus and Clement escorted them to their carriage. As the carriage whirled around the corner, shutting out forever the glow of electric lights, streaming from the hall, Regenia softly sighed. It occurred to her that years would come and go before the streets of Mt. Clare would again echo with the tramp of marching knights. As they drove homeward, an unaccountable silence seemed to settle over them all. Even Lucile was quieter.

Was it a premonition of the future, looking backward and infringing its shadow upon the present?

SEVEN CORNERS.

Chapter VIII.

THE OFFICE OF DR. FRANK LEIGHTON was called "Hub of Seven Corners." Four streets converged to form the circle, in the centre of which stood his office, like the hub of a wheel. The drugstore on one corner ended the square like the apex of a triangle. Each of the other three blocks was in the form of a trapezoid, whose lesser base faced the circle.

Although a physician, Dr. Leighton did not practice medicine as the ordinary acceptation of the term implies. He was a specialist—a specialist of symptoms.

Five friends graduated from an eastern medical college eight years previous to the events which we are transcribing. One evening near the close of their medical course, the friends met to engage in a farewell supper. As each talked of his intentions and hopes, one of them was inclined to take a discouraging view of the whole subject. He expatiated upon the barren results which usually attended the administration of medicine to the cure of diseases. He made a singular proposal, and thereon hangs a tale. He said that as medicine had been almost vivisected by the introduction of specialties, why not end the agony and make one that would cover all of them? He proposed to divide the followers of Aesculapius into two general divisions; the first to devote their entire time to the diagnosis of diseases, the second to their treatment. The work of the first class to end, when the condition of the patient was ascertained; the second class to cure the derangement, if it be not beyond the reach of science.

The five doctors, being men of means, decided to go to Europe and take a post-graduate course. They subsequently put this decision into practice by spending three years abroad; two of them bending their energies to the causes and symptoms of diseases; the other three to the cure of ailments. It was a part of the plan to give to difficult surgical operations the united wisdom of the five. When these doctors returned to their native land, Mt. Clare was chosen as the best site to begin the new departure. The size of the place had much to do with the selection. The city was divided into three districts, with an office of a specialist of cures in each. The Hub of Seven Corners was the location of the office of the specialists of symptoms. The system, which at first would seem unwieldy and expensive, was offset by the superior skill of the practitioners. At the time of our story the specialists of symptoms had gained an enviable reputation by their unerring correctness in diagnosis; nor was their success more pronounced than their brother specialists, who had reaped a rich harvest from the increase of patients their skill had secured. The resident physicians had at first ridiculed the scheme as the invention of quacks, but failing in their attempt to laugh the specialists out of the city, had finally combined in a similar arrangement. Dr. Frank Leighton was the mouthpiece and inspiration of the new fraternity. A handsome, well born Southern gentleman, he gained and held an enviable reputation. It has been previously mentioned that he was a nephew of Mrs. Underwood and, Regenia excepted, the only direct heir to her property. This fact had due weight in the choice of Mt. Clare as the place best suited to introduce his much cherished innovation in the field of medical reform. Having determined to cultivate the good graces of his aunt, his suavity had early installed him as a prime favorite in her affections. Hardly a day passed that he did not find time to drive out to the "Elms." His movements had long since ceased to be a matter of concern to the family, so thoroughly did he ingratiate himself. Mrs. Underwood sought his advice in nearly every change she made in the management of her affairs.

Regenia liked him, also. He was frank and jovial with her in that degree men of experience find it so easy to be with girls of her years. As he sat in his office on the morning after the boat ride, Dr. Leighton was in any other than an amiable mood. He had a well-bred man's feelings after a night's reflection upon the fact that he has behaved badly. He wondered if Regenia had observed what must have been so manifest to her new found friends.

"Her friends," he repeated with a haughty smile. "What right have these impertinent, ill-born dogs to be her friends?" he asked himself. Then it occurred to him, if their friendship had been as cold, as his actions had been contemptible, where would have been the sweet girl to-day, who white and fearful yesterday, stood in such imminent danger? The very thought increased his hatred of Lotus Stone. In his heart he knew Lotus had performed an act of bravery for Regenia at the risk of his own life, which alone saved the girl from a premature death; but what right had he to meddle anyway? What right had this spawn of an outcast race to cross the path and thwart the purposes of his betters? Inwardly cursing himself for his own meanness, but despising Lotus for virtues the doctor did not possess, he arose, and taking his hat from the rack, entered the phaeton standing at the door and drove slowly out to the "Elms."

His distemper was not to be improved by a visit to his aunt. Before he reached his destination, he heard with rankling detestation the merry laughter which the witty sallies of Clement St. John were provoking, as, with the young girls and Lotus Stone, he lounged lazily beneath the inviting shade. The tender mouth of his horse felt the hate which the doctor could not otherwise express, as with a sudden jerk he stopped the faithful animal in front of Mrs. Underwood's gate.

He greeted the party under the trees with a slight inclination of the head and angrily stalked into the house. He went directly to the library, where Mrs. Underwood usually passed the morning hours. After greeting her, he said, in his light and airy way: "I see our friends still remain. They must enjoy the unaccustomed hospitality of their lately found acquaintances."

"I suppose so," answered Mrs. Underwood, with a smile.

"I presume the surroundings are a trifle more luxurious than they habitually find. One ought to forgive them for making the most of their opportunities," he said a little bitterly, as he glanced out of the window where our friends, all unconscious of the hatred their free and easy ways were kindling in the bosom of the master of the "Hub," passed the hours in innocent conversation.

"Regenia is happy," said Mrs. Underwood. "It is her first real contact with the world she must some day know."

Dr. Leighton inwardly winced, but wisely held his tongue.

"As I see how she delights in the company of her race, I feel a thrill of satisfaction that I kept nothing hid from her. She knows who she is and seems to gravitate toward the inevitable with the instinct of destiny."

"I should be sorry to think, dear aunt, that the destiny of Regenia pointed in the direction you indicate," he answered with a toss of his head toward the lawn.

"And why not?" she asked, somewhat piqued by the doctor's reply.

"What do any of us know of these men? Would you have been as free to allow your own," he checked himself, "your own dear friends to drift into an intimate acquaintance with people utter strangers to you until the last few days? Are you less solicitous for Regenia's future than you would be for any other young woman, similarly situated?"

"Do not go too far, doctor," said Mrs. Underwood, noticeably aroused by his insinuations. "I fear you forget yourself. Regenia and Lucile have been friends from infancy. Lucile introduced her friend Mr. St. John, and he, in turn, introduced his friend, Mr. Stone. I do not think it necessary in this case to demand a certificate of character."

"Very true; but I enjoy a more extensive acquaintance with that class of people than you do. I have lived among them all my life. I know that only about one every ten thousand is trustworthy. You must excuse my solicitude for the child," he said, assuming an injured look.

"Oh, well, we differ upon that subject, and as you are settled in your opinion, discussion would be worse than useless. You estimate people by your prejudice. I do not: I have no fears for Regenia's immediate safety. I think her fully capable of taking care of herself."

"And her mother was not," said the doctor, excitedly.

"Wrong with her mother is right with her," said Mrs. Underwood, rising with an evident effort to maintain her self-control. As she excused herself and left the room, the doctor had no doubt that he had indeed gone too far. Not a little chagrined at Mrs. Underwood's failure to accept his advice, he could not resist the inclination to stop awhile under the shade of the elms and make one of the company pleasantly conversing there. He surmised that his presence would be no particular pleasure to Clement and Lotus, but that fact only served to whet his curiosity. His hatred was a sufficient incentive to nerve his resolution.

"I need hardly ask if you are finding sufficient amusement to drive dull care away," said Dr. Leighton, accepting a camp-stool offered him by Regenia, and resting his hat on the grass, as he sat down in the midst of the merrimakers.

"Mr. St. John has been delighting us with some of his droll experiences," said Regenia, laughing heartily as she recalled the story just related by Mr. St. John.

"I am sorry that I am too late to laugh with you," said the doctor.

"Tell Dr. Leighton about the bootblack who found your report of a wedding, Mr. St. John," said Regenia.

"I have too much respect for the doctor's age and experience to repeat a stale story for his amusement; I can not bear to tell a story unless I am certain it will amuse. I do not doubt the doctor's sense of the ridiculous, but my ability to reach it," said Clement dryly.

"Repeat the story and I promise to laugh whether it be droll or dry," said the doctor.

"That would be insincerity. I would not tempt you to act a part," Clement replied.

"The world is a stage and all of us are actors. You have been cast for light comedy to-day. Act well your part, there all the honor lies," replied the doctor.

"Comedy and tragedy, daily rehearsed, make the annals of all our lives. To-day it is comedy; yesterday, almost tragedy. I am happy to-day whenever I compare it with yesterday. Was not that the most marvelous escape, doctor?" Clement asked.

"Very, indeed," the doctor answered, rising. "I fear you are not going to tell me the story. It must have been rich, or at least Miss Underwood seemed to think so." As he said this he turned on his heel and hastened to his phaeton. As he drove away, he registered a vow in his heart that those impertinent "cusses" should never spend another day at the "Elms." The place, some day, will have a different master, and then, none of that class, emphasizing "that" with a contemptuous sneer, shall ever stretch their legs under those trees.

Clement St. John smiled triumphantly as the last glimpse of Dr. Leighton disappeared from view. Regenia wondered why the doctor had addressed her as Miss Underwood.

Lotus was the first to break the silence. "Doctor Leighton is a relation of Mrs. Underwood's, I believe?" said Lotus.

"Her nephew," answered Regenia.

"Is he always so consequential?" Clement enquired.

"Why did you not tell him the story?" Regenia asked, ignoring his question.

"I reserve my stories for those who wish to hear them. I never pretend what I do not feel. Dr. Leighton had no desire to hear anything I had to say. He is your friend, perhaps, but worship of you would never make me even respect him."

"Dr. Leighton was politeness itself this morning, I am sure," interrupted Lucile.

"Say patronizing. It fits the condition better when you speak of Dr. Leighton. Dr. Leighton's politeness is from above downward, as the lord is to his footman, but never as an equal is to an equal. It is hard to be other than one's self and retain one's respect for himself," said Clement, apologetically.

"Time flies," said Lotus. "We leave on the evening boat and have ever so much to attend to before we shall be ready to start. I must therefore beseech Mr. St. John to cut short his homily and hope at some time more opportune, he may have leisure to finish it," said Lotus pleasantly.

"You have hours and hours before the night steamer leaves for Minton, but I suppose you have other places to call," said Regenia.

To this implied question Lotus made no reply.

He held out his hand, first to Lucile, with the remark, "For the present I must say good-bye."

"Say your farewells to Mrs. Underwood and Mrs. Levitt," said Lucile. "We expect to be at the boat. We want to see the last of everybody," she added with a merry laugh.

"Good-byes twice said are harbingers of happy meetings in the near future," said Lotus.

"It is to be hoped in this case," said Lucile, with a mischievous look at Regenia.

"And I say amen from the depth of my heart," chimed in Clement.

After they had bade the other members of the family adieu, the young men took their leave, the girls accompanying them to the gate. As Lotus held in his own the pretty hand of Regenia, he could not help wishing that some day, under circumstances more binding, he might claim it as his own.

HOMEWARD BOUND.

Chapter IX.

Our two friends were among the last detachment of Knights to leave Mt. Clare. The great multitude had returned on the "Carrier Pigeon" at an early hour that morning. The grand officers and a selected few of the other distinguished visitors, the majority of whom were from the far away south-land, had lingered until the last possible moment, drinking to its very dregs the delights of this, the happiest reunion of their knightly organization. Promptly at nine o'clock the beautiful "City of Athens" unloosed her cables and turned her prow toward the distant lake.

The night was perfect. The rays of the full moon touched with fairy fingers the sparkling waters in tints of purest silver. Streaming far in the wake of the steamer, the recently disturbed water glittered in the soft moonlight like a tremulous, phosphorescent sea. The party above referred to occupied chairs in the aft recess. Each filled with his own thoughts, conversation lagged.

Mr. St. John, as usual, broke the silence. "That is the last of Mt. Clare," he remarked, half to himself.

"I thought we had left Mt. Clare long enough ago," said Lotus Stone.

"No, I have been sitting here watching the last light as it grew smaller, until, just before I spoke, it closed its weary eye like a sleepy child and sank to rest beyond my visual horizon."

"I was watching the same light, but I missed it some time since," said Colonel Stanton. "Your eyes are younger than mine, St. John," he continued.

"A few years younger, I suppose, but yours, like the great George Washington's, have grown dim in the service of your country," said Clement, complimentary.

"Don't put such ideas into Colonel Stanton's head," said the Eminent Grand Commander, laughingly. "You will have him applying for an increase of pension. We have too many militia colonels on the pay roll of the government as it is."

At this witty thrust at the colonel's title, the coterie about the table burst into hilarious laughter.

"That's on me," said the colonel, dryly. "Come in and have something, gentlemen."

"No one can be dry when contemplating so much water," answered the Eminent Grand Commander.

"We don't drink overly much water in my state. We have a nameless void that yawns for Old Kentucky Bourbon," said Colonel Stanton.

"Colonel Stanton," said Clement, "you live in the South, and on business or pleasure you have spent a great deal of time in the North; from your standpoint, what is the difference between the two sections?"

"There are many sides to your question, young man," said the colonel, thoughtfully. "A conservative, intelligent, Afro-American will do well enough in either section. Nine times out of ten it is the man rather than the part of the country in which he happens to live that tells for his future."

"I agree with you in that statement, of course," said Clement, "but what differences, if any, do you observe between the North and South?"

"There is a marked difference, but to my way of thinking, it is from within rather than from without. Bear in mind I speak of the intelligent, conservative man. In the South, such a man knows he is a virtuous citizen, but feels that the majority of his fellow citizens doubt it. In the North such a citizen feels that he is a man, and that opinion is strengthened and encouraged by the knowledge that the majority of his fellow citizens take the same view of the subject."

"What other men, sinners like myself, think of my actions would have nothing to do with the case. The consciousness of a correct life is its own best reward," said Lotus Stone.

"We are not splitting ethical hairs, young man," said the colonel. "Virtue may be its own best reward, but to feel that every other man you meet regards you as an unhung villain, is not the most encouraging incentive to moral excellence. To feel than an unwritten presumption of guilt before the facts are known, constantly hangs above one's head, takes from the best of us that substantial aid which we all need to stem the current of temptations which we hourly meet."

"What our people need in the South and everywhere else is more independence. We are too docile, too subservient," said Lotus Stone.

"You speak well, but not by the card," said the colonel. "Their independence, in one respect, was their undoing. If, after freedom came, the former slave had sought the paternal care of his late owner, the master class would have defended him against the cruel indignities of the 'poor whites' to the last drop. Be it said, to the never dying credit of the Negro, that when the shackles fell from his limbs, he stepped forth in the power of his new found manhood to sink or swim by individual effort. He rightly chose the perils of freedom to the vassalage of a patron."

"More than fifty exchanges, edited by Afro-Americans, reach my office weekly," said Clement. "What I am at a loss to understand is why these papers so frequently deny or excuse the wrongs perpetrated against our people in the South. They often take me to task for flagellating American civilization in general and that part of it south of Mason and Dixon's line in particular. It cannot be that these journalists are not cognizant of the truth of my assertions."

"'Breathes there a man with soul so dead,
Who never to himself hath said,
This is my own, my native land?'"

said Colonel Stanton. "These Southern Afro-Americans are as indignant over the outrages occurring daily in their midst as their brothers in the North, but there is a note of patronizing pity in the tone of northern sympathy extremely exasperating to a southerner. One's country is his country however unkindly it may treat him. The Afro-American, south, loves his home notwithstanding its unjust discriminations. His state pride, indigenous to southern soil, often gets the better of his judgment," said the colonel laughingly.

"How an Afro-American of any intelligence can find anything in this country to be proud of is an enigma to me," said another member of the party. "I agree with one of our great leaders, that no negro should ever sing,

'My country, 'tis of thee,
Sweet land of Liberty,'

while a condition more revolting than slavery exists in the country."

"That is the purest nonsense," said Lotus excitedly. "The country in which a man is born is his country. If there are wrongs to redress, it is his duty to labor to right them. All the rights any other citizen can claim are not mine by special legislation, but by birthright. 'My country, 'tis of thee' I sing, and whether I sing it or not it is my country and there is no possible way to divorce myself from it, except I leave it and swear allegiance to another flag."

"Well, we can leave it; and the day will come when we shall turn to Africa, our native land, with eagerness," remarked the other gentleman.

"If anybody wants to go to Africa, let him go; but Africa as a native land for the American Negro is a myth. A great bishop may plant, and the colonization society may water, but the population of Africa will never be materially increased from the ranks of the Afro-American," said Lotus.

"Do you not believe that some day our people will return to Africa?"

"Yes; when every Jew goes back to the Jordan; when every Englishman returns to the Thames; when every Irishman goes back to the Shannon, every Frenchman to the Seine; every Italian to the Tiber and every German to the Rhine, then the Afro-American may sit down and seriously think of returning to the Congo."

"We shall never gain our fight for equal manhood by running off to Africa. But I admit that I grow discouraged and heart sick as I read of some fresh disregard for the commonest rights of men enacted with impunity, every day, in the South. It is a red letter day when some man, guilty or innocent, is not lynched. The most disgraceful side of the question is the equanimity with which the country receives the news of the most inhuman lynching. The press simply notes the fact as an item of news, with here and there an editor possessing the rare temerity to comment. The church is as dumb as an oyster upon the injustice practiced in our own country; but alive and able to hold indignation meetings and circulate petitions to the Czar of all the Russias for the alleviation of the condition of his subjects," said Clement, growing more indignant as he continued to talk.

"Lynch law is a foul blot upon the escutcheon of our civilization," said Colonel Stanton, slowly. "No enlightened European government would tolerate lynching."

"But can it be stopped until the moral character of the people rises above such illegal actions? Who can argue with a mob?" asked Lotus.

"Powder and lead," said Clement, rising and moving about to suppress his excitement. "Give them what they give—mob the mobbers."

"That is brave talk, considering your distance from the arena of daily disturbance, but just so long as the conscience of a people is so callous that it finds entertainment in seeing human beings roasted alive with all the eclat of a political barbecue, such people need missionaries rather than cold lead. The persecutors are more to be pitied than their victims," replied Lotus seriously.

"Christianity, wealth and education will some day lift a cultured American Negro to the status accorded an ignorant Italian," remarked the Eminent Grand Commander sarcastically.

"Christianity, wealth and education are great levelers," began Colonel Stanton, "but they have failed utterly to fill the requirements in this country. Christianity seldom rises above the masses that profess it. As a theory it is simply sublime. If those who claim to follow Christ acted upon the precepts he taught, then earth would be a paradise. Christianity, North and South, has done wonders for the Afro-American, but while the heathen rage and people imagine a vain thing, even the power of Christianity is unable to turn them from their purpose. Wealth is helping to beat down prejudice. The man who owns a home, however humble, is doing more to eliminate the unknown quantity that is necessary before the problem is solved, than the orator who delivers a vehement philippic. Education of the right kind is also an important factor. While it helps us it also deepens the hatred of the ignorant masses against us."

"I have always believed," said Clement, "that the solution of this perplexing question is not moral, material, nor intellectual; but the essence of the three—political. The palladium of equality in a republic is the ballot;

the badge of citizenship is the right to vote. It is the citizen's only protection; without it he becomes a political nondescript, at the mercy of every demagogue who bids for popular favor by preaching a crusade of prejudice. The non-voting citizen is the only person who can be maltreated with impunity. Men who vote elect judges, legislators, and governors, and if these officers forget the interests of their constituents, they receive a painful reminder when they again aspire for office. Would a legislature responsible to all the people, pass a separate coach law, sanction lynching, permit every kind of indignity to be put upon an inoffensive people? Not if the people knew their rights. The equality of citizenship, which is the foundation stone of our political fabric, promises to every native born freeman the same rights. By our laws, if a man is a citizen, he must be the equal of every other citizen, since our laws do not recognize the supremacy of one class above another, and therefore whatever right any other citizen enjoys is his by the common law of equals."

"How can an Afro-American vote when the constitutional amendments are null and void?" asked Lotus.

"What have the amendments to do with it anyway? The Afro-American's right to citizenship is not based upon amendments, but upon nativity and freedom. If a man is born in a country and is free, or ever afterward becomes free, that birthright entitles him to citizenship. The amendments were the officers that enabled us to get our rights, but our citizenship rights, are interwoven through the conception and structural erection of constitutional government," Clement concluded.

"That is at least a new presentation of an old subject. I must think it over," said Colonel Stanton rising. "You young men can settle this question between you," he added, "I believe I will retire."

All the company except Clement and Lotus followed the gay old colonel into the cabin.

The two young men sat there until far into the night discussing future plans, building air castles destined before many months or years to tumble about their heads. At last, as if at a loss for something more to say, or new to propose, they sought their state rooms to live again in a land of dreams, the experiences of the past week.

THE SHADOW OF A DREAM.

Chapter X.

It was late on the morning after the scene described in a previous chapter when Lucile and Regenia made their appearance at the breakfast table. The fierce rays of an August sun had been gilding the turrets and spires of the beautiful little city between the inland seas, for more than two hours. All night the rain had been falling and the evidences of holiday attire of which the city had not entirely disrobed herself, hung limp and unpicturesque from the wilting effects of the last night's down pour.

The reaction from nearly a week of continuous gaiety was plainly discernible, as the two young ladies seated themselves to partake of their morning's repast.

"Well, how do you feel the morning after?" said Mrs. Levitt, in her pleasant way.

"Very well, indeed," answered Lucile, "except perhaps a little duller and heavier than usual. An overdose of pleasure always leaves one with a sense of hollow pain. You see, Regenia, you are not quite up to this sort of thing and ought not to have been given such a lion's share at initiation."

"You would better take that admonition individually. If we except the late hours I was obliged to keep, my part has been anything else but lion-like," said Regenia.

"Do not look so solemn. You will ruin your digestion," said Lucile, with a merry laugh. "If you did not act the lion's part, you did duty as lamb very acceptably, being saved and taking the greatest pains to be rescued by the very nicest young man that attended the conclave," she continued in her tantalizing way.

"As I had to be rescued," said Regenia, catching some of Lucile's buoyant spirits, "Providence seemed to have chosen my savior with a singleness which I could not have improved upon had I personally supervised the list."

"Nor could a braver, more unselfish deed have been done. I shall love Mr. Stone all of my life for that one act of disinterested goodness," replied Lucile with one of her instant transfers from playful chaffing to sober earnestness.

"What would Mr. St. John think of that avowal, I wonder?" asked Mrs. Levitt, smiling with conscious satisfaction of her own depth.

"He would applaud that opinion. Mr. St. John never tires of praising the good qualities of his friend," said Lucile, trying to look uninterested, but feeling decidedly uncomfortable under Mrs. Levitt's knowing smile.

"And so would any other man or woman whose heart is in the right place. I am too grateful to Mr. Stone to know how to express my appreciation of his gallant conduct. But Mr. St. John would have been equally as noble," replied Regenia, as a kind of echo to the preceding thought.

"It is such a grand thing to be a man, anyway," said Lucile seriously. "A good man has unbounded opportunities to help everybody. Men are not hedged about with rules of conduct as women are. Our sphere of usefulness is so often circumscribed by the fact of sex."

"That is rather a strange admission to come from you, Lucile," said Regenia. "I thought you were inclined to be strong minded."

"And so I am in every respect that is womanly. I believe thoroughly in women preparing themselves for useful positions and filling them with the same skill as men; but I do not think a woman can ever be a man. When a woman attempts that she loses the graces of her own sex without attaining the powers of the sex to which she aspires," said Lucile rising.

Regenia made no answer, but motioning Lucile to follow, led the way to a hammock beneath the trees.

"Do you know," said Regenia, as she threw herself lazily into the hammock, "that I was haunted all night with premonitions of evil—and I had the strangest dream?"

"Tell me your dream. I have the gift of second sight," said Lucile, archly.

"I never pay any attention to dreams, nor do I think anything will come of this; but it seems to hang to me this morning with the persistency of fate," replied Regenia, soberly.

"I am waiting very patiently to hear your dream," said Lucile, "and when I do hear it I shall weave about it all the mysteries of the sibyl."

"Very well, put on the air impenetrable, take my hand as they do in all the story books, cross it twice, stare into vacancy and I will to you a tale unfold that will ruffle your spirits for the rest of the day," said Regenia, pleasantly.

"How is this?" said Lucile, as she assumed an attitude corresponding as nearly as possible with Regenia's suggestions.

"Excellent," said Regenia. "Now I will begin. I dreamed," she said, dropping into a low earnest key, "that Mr. St. John, you and I were standing in the Public Square, watching a sort of 'Wild West' parade. At Mr. St. John's suggestion, we started to move along with the crowd to the place where the exhibition was to be given, you and I arm-in-arm and Mr. St. John a few feet behind us, as a sort of rear guard to keep the crowd from jostling us. We had walked along in this way for some time when, looking around, Mr. St. John had disappeared and we were unable to stop to find him or to extricate ourselves from the mass of human beings who pushed us steadily onward. At last, in order to escape the crowd and if possible find our way back home, we stepped off the sidewalk into the street. Here, surrounded by Indians, buffaloes, dogs and ponies, we walked along as part of the pageant. We finally came to a dense woods and wandering forward we hoped to come to some place or meet some person we knew. Growing tired and hungry, we sat down on the body of a fallen oak and began to cry. We had been sitting there but a few moments when to our consternation we heard the most unearthly noise, accompanied by the splashing of water in the near distance.

"Looking in the direction from which the sounds came, we saw a long embankment, on the top of which ran a rail fence. Fearing some worse fate would befall us, I started in an opposite direction. With your usual fearlessness you urged me to go over to the embankment, and essayed to lead the way. Gaining courage from your boldness, I accompanied you to the bank, where, after numberless slips and falls, we reached the top. We climbed upon the fence, and there, sitting bolt upright between us, as we resume a vertical position, was Mr. Stone. He did not speak, but as he turned from you to me, in his sad eyes and despairing countenance were depicted a world of sorrow that smote me to the heart. He gazed out into the lake, flanked by the embankment, a picture of dejection. In the lake, as we followed his gaze, I saw a huge fish, with massive head, enormous jaws, and capacious mouth, snapping up the other inhabitants of the lake as they fled before him. The huge leviathan followed his destructive course until he came to the shore. On the shore by the side of the lake, grazing in unconscious security, were the animals belonging to the Wild West combination we had left in the woods, but the number had increased to a respectable menagerie. This fish, when he had reached the shore, assumed the form of a turtle, and rushing from the water crushed first one animal, then another until he came to a giraffe, which catching in his teeth, the huge beast began to make a circuit of the grounds. I could hear, amidst the wild cries of the terror-stricken animals, the grinding sound of the turtle's iron jaws, as he crushed the giraffe between them. Suddenly the beast stopped, turned toward the place where we were sitting, and dropping the lacerated giraffe from his bloody mouth, made toward us.

"In vain we entreated Mr. Stone to fly with us for his life, but leave he would not. He sat there sadly smiling into the open jaws of approaching death. Now in the woods near the embankment was a sawmill. An incline to carry the lumber down to the lake was between us and the approaching animal. I had jumped down from the fence, but unable to induce Mr. Stone to leave, had resumed my seat, fully resolved to die with him. As the turtle attempted to cross the track of the incline, a heavy car load of lumber caught him beneath its wheels and cut him into a thousand pieces, the animals on the shore, seeing this, burst into ghostly laugh, at the sound of which I awoke."

Lucile had long since dropped Regenia's hand in her excitement, and with wonderment portrayed in every line of her face, gave expression to her astonishment by injecting after every pause in the story, "How strange!" "Well, did you ever!" "I declare!" "I never heard anything like it!" etc., etc.

As she was about to ejaculate "How strange!" for the "steenth" time, Dr. Leighton, who had been listening to nearly every word of the story said in sepulchral tones, "And did you marry Mr. Stone and live happily ever after?"

The girls, thus taken by surprise, bounded from the hammock with a scream, and turning were half vexed to see who the unwarrantable intruder was.

Lucile quickly gained her composure sufficiently to say: "What a scare you gave us?"

"How long have you been here?" asked Regenia, trying hard to hide her vexation.

"Long enough to hear a most amusing story. Is it original, or was it rescued from Fairy-land?" said the doctor, with a good-natured laugh at Regenia's discomfiture.

"It was a dream," said Lucile, "and you managed to speak just in time to interrupt the grand finale." Lucile had either forgotten or preferred to ignore the fact the Regenia had signified the conclusion of the dream by saying "I awoke."

"Oh, it was a dream! I thought it was one of the good stories your friends seem to keep on ice for special occasions," remarked the doctor, a trifle sarcastically.

"It was one of my friend's good stories, and I am happy to know that I have more than one friend who can tell a good story," said Lucile, turning to Regenia with a smile, "Is it not true, dear?" she added.

"Mr. St. John seemed proof for the occasion yesterday, and I doubt not on better acquaintance he would be ample for all demands.

"Has Mr. St. John been shying his castor in more than one direction? I thought it was the silent fellow on the fence that you had sworn to never, never leave?" said the doctor, as he turned to Regenia with a look on his handsome face which would have done credit to the melancholy Dane, when contemplating whether "to be or not to be."

"It its certainly of no interest to you Dr. Leighton, which way Mr. St. John shies his castor, whatever that may mean. Better make sure that he never shies it in your direction—stranger things have happened," said Lucile with a proud toss of her head.

"A real gentleman would not seek to mischievously distort a conversation insidiously heard," said Regenia, rising, now unable to further conceal her anger.

"What a tempest!" said the doctor laughing heartily at the breeze he had unintentionally stirred up. "I leave you ladies, discomfited and virtually driven from the field," he added as he turned away, still laughing, and went into the house.

The girls sat for a time staring after Dr. Leighton, when Lucile remembered how irresistibly droll Dr. Leighton had looked when talking of the other fellow on the fence, burst into a fit of laughter. Regenia laughed also. Not that she divined the cause of Lucile's amusement, but because laughter in youth is contagious.

"Well it was too funny of the doctor to come in and spoil the strangest dream I ever heard," said Lucile, when she had ceased to laugh. "I am not in the spirit to interpret it now. A shadow has fallen between us."

"Perhaps the shadow has something to do with the unraveling of the mystery," added Regenia, thoughtfully.

"Perhaps it has. Who can say? Do you know I am becoming morbid? I shall begin to believe in dreams and ghosts and bogie men pretty soon?" said Lucile.

"Come, let us go for a long ride," said Regenia, starting toward the house, "and by the time we return we shall have driven away from the shadow of a dream."

As they passed by the gate a half hour later, Dr. Leighton, standing beneath the shade of the elms, twirling his cane, cried after them: "Mind you do not get lost in the woods before you return."

"If we do we shall expect you along in good time to find the 'Babes in the Woods,'" answered Regenia, with every vestige of her late anger dispelled.

"If you come to a high embankment with a rail fence upon it, you will find me sitting there waiting," he cried. As they drove away, they heard the silver laugh of Dr. Leighton ringing after them, the very index of the pleasure which he felt when contemplating the little war of words he had engaged in with the girls a half hour before.

LUCILE AND REGENIA.

Chapter XI.

"THAT IS THE FAMOUS SEVEN CORNERS," remarked Regenia, as they drove past Dr. Leighton's office. "Seven Corners is not a new place, but I refer to the office in the center of the circle."

"A Specialist of Symptoms," repeated Lucile, slowly. "Is that not an innovation?" she asked.

"Yes, I believe it originated with Dr. Frank or, at least, it is being given its first trial under his direction," Regenia replied.

"He is a singular man," said Lucile, thoughtfully, "perhaps he is not so singular either," she added apologetically, "but he is not like other people. I am at a loss to classify him. What do you think of your cousin, anyway?" she asked after a pause.

"I am not sure that I think of him at all. He is very fond of Mrs. Underwood and is so often at our house that his presence has ceased to arouse conjecture. He is very kind to me and I do not know that I find anything about him to especially dislike," Regenia replied.

"He is exceedingly polite, I admit, yet his very politeness causes me to mistrust him. His eyes always seem to be laughing at one," concluded Lucile.

"That is dear old Recreation Park," she cried, dropping Dr. Leighton and his peculiarities without another thought. "How forsaken it looks."

"Compare it to-day with the scenes transpiring there about this hour last Wednesday," said Regenia, regretfully.

"What stirring events animated the dreamy old place indeed. The vast multitude, the gallant Knights, the inspiring music, the competition drill and the numberless other happy incidents that are ineffaceably engraved upon my memory in vivid association with the thoughts of Recreation Park," said Lucile.

"One enjoys recalling happy incidents quite as much as experiencing them, I often think," added Regenia.

"I enjoy the recollection of them decidedly more; the unpleasant incidents which often precede our supremely happy moments can be eliminated or at least minimized during the serene hour that memory unbars her secret chamber for the reception of the joyous past," Lucile replied.

"How often," said Regenia, "do we make of our by gone pleasures an Elysian shrine, to which the mind in moments of sorrow fondly turns? Our golden era is ever behind us."

On a little eminence east of the park, Regenia drew rein and exclaimed: "See, over there among the trees is the very spot from which we observed the drill."

"And without a very great stretch of imagination, I can see Mr. St. John presenting his friend, whose easy manners made us feel, after an hour's acquaintance, we had known him for years," replied Lucile with a smile as they drove on, leaving the park and its romantic associations slumbering in the receding distance.

"We are not far from the river; are you going to Melton Inn?" she asked after a long pause, during which both of them had been busily thinking of the very recent past.

"No," answered Regenia. "We will drive down to the National pike, thence across to Shady Side and follow our old course to the city."

"All right," said Lucile. "I believe I will take the lines for the rest of the way."

"Most people wear gloves when driving," she remarked, as she deftly proceeded to strip hers off, "but I never could work in kids."

As she put her gloves on the cushion between them and took the lines, Regenia noticed for the first time, gleaming from the third finger of Lucile's left hand, a modest "solitaire."

"What a pretty ring!" she exclaimed with girlish enthusiasm. "How long have you worn it? Why did you not show it to me before this?"

"One question at a time, please," said Lucile, trying to speak with importance but to tell the truth, feeling very much confused.

"And it is a real diamond," said Regenia, holding Lucile's hand in a position to get a better light on the stone.

"I think it is ever so pretty," said Lucile, modestly.

"I think it is beautiful," Regenia said. "May I ask who gave it to you?"

"Certainly you may, but can you not guess?" asked Lucile.

"Mr. St. John?" Lucile nodded her assent.

"The darling," said Regenia, throwing her arms around Lucile's neck, and from some mysterious cause common to the sex, the girls dissolved this sweetest of all secrets in a flood of mutual tears.

The horse which drew the phaeton, either in dumb sympathy or from long acquaintance with the eccentricities of young women, stopped short in the middle of the road during this lachrymal performance.

"And when is it all to be?" asked Regenia, her curiosity getting the better of the shock Lucile's sudden revelation had occasioned. "No wonder you had so much faith in Mr. St. John," she added laughingly.

As they drove back home, Lucile unfolded her plans. They were to be married in October and thereafter the typewriter was to be transferred from the office in which she is employed at present, to a less pretentious building controlled by the proprietor of "The Events." To all of her plans Regenia gave her unqualified approval; not that she knew anything about them, but because they filled her friend's ideal of happiness. Regenia was in no mood to criticise any measure this independent, successful girl proposed.

When they returned to the "Elms" they found that dinner had been awaiting them for some time.

"You must have taken a long drive," said Mrs. Underwood, who met them at the door. "It is half past five—thirty minutes after the dinner hour, and you have not even been to luncheon. Lucile must be nearly famished. Regenia will starve you, dear. She seems to forget that her visitors might wish some times to stop listening to her talk and eat something."

"Lucile can eat any time, but she will not have another opportunity to talk to me again soon, so we are obliged to improve every moment," replied Regenia.

"No danger of starving in such a land of plenty," said Lucile, with a complaisant smile. "Your bread shall be given and your water shall be sure, we are taught. Is not that prophetic as well as proverbial, Regenia?"

"So Mr. St. John says, and of course there is nothing worthwhile knowing that he does not know," answered Regenia, as they sat down to dinner.

After dinner, and until a late hour that night, the girls passed the time out under the trees; Regenia asking questions concerning the coming wedding and Lucile gratifying her excusable curiosity by laying bare all of her intentions preparatory to this most important event. As it was Saturday evening, and Lucile must return to Minton the following night, the girls resolved to be up at an early hour the next morning in order to make the last day as long as possible. Agreeable to their resolution, they arose Sabbath morning long before Mrs. Levitt, who prided herself upon the fact that she awoke a little earlier upon God's day, as she called it, than on any other.

Lucile proposed that Regenia go with her to church, a proposal the latter accepted with eagerness. The Underwoods had always strictly adhered to the Episcopal church; Mrs. Levitt, reared as she was in Canada, was also a communicant of the Church of England. Regenia, therefore, had rarely attended any other service than those at St. Mark's, but a short distance from her own door.

If Lucile had belonged to the church toward which she was most inclined, she would have been an ardent church woman. She had often accompanied Regenia to St. Mark's and frequently regretted that her own people, as well as the majority of her friends, were satisfied with a less pretentious church and a simpler form of worship.

On this Sabbath morning, Regenia's anxiety to go was heightened by the incidents of the past week, and it will reveal no secret to suspect that thoughts of the future played no unimportant part. What woman lives who does not dream of some future in which an ideal man forms, at least a shadowy background?

The two friends were among the first to arrive at the place of worship. Although Regenia had been assured that services commenced a full half hour later than at St. Mark's, her constant fear of committing that most heinous breach of good form, tardiness at worship, caused her to quicken her pace sufficiently to be in her seat at the ringing of the first bell. Just as Regenia's patience was about exhausted, the organ voluntary, followed immediately by the minister taking his place in the pulpit, assured her that the service had begun. The music was simple, but Regenia thought it was sung with a pathetic sweetness unequaled in all her experience. After the reading, singing and prayer, the minister arose. He was tall and somewhat inclined to stoop. As black as ebony, his features were sharp and well proportioned, his hair as white as driven snow. Apparently old, judging from his white locks, his black eyes had lost none of their fire; his voice, none of its pathos. It was plain that nature had carved him for a ruler. His text was from the Psalms, his theme "God's Protecting Care." Regenia listened like one entranced. The minister stepping in front of the small stand, on which sat a glass of water beside the open Bible, spoke without notes. His voice, at first low, but wonderfully distinct, gained strength and power as the theme unfolded. He related incident after incident of God's protecting care. Regenia thought she could see his countenance soften, his eyes brighten and the very man himself gradually living through the scenes he so eloquently described. The auditors were wrapped in attention and it did not occur to her that an occasional "amen" from some of the older members marred the interest, but she felt rather thankful that someone had the forethought to express audibly that approval in which her heart so readily acquiesced. When the minister had concluded, Regenia found herself wondering where this man obtained his unusual wisdom and fluency of speech. How, she thought, could a people whose aspirations had been beaten down beneath the earth, in a few short years rise from their degraded condition to such rapturous flights of burning, convincing thought? "Whence this power?" she asked herself. She took refuge in the oft-repeated Scripture: "God's ways are not our ways, verily out of the mouths of babes and sucklings thou hast perfected praise." What a long, weary way, she thought, from the slave pen to this pulpit; and yet this white-haired angel of God was there, and a consummate master of his position. Thus she sat musing until awakened from her reverie by the congregation rising to sing the closing hymn. Again Regenia was fortunate in seeing the Afro-American at his best. She was delighted with the service. She was as delighted with its simplicity as Lucile was with the solemn grandeur of the Episcopal forms. After the service, Lucile, at Regenia's request, introduced her to the minister. As they walked home, Regenia talked of nothing but the morning's experience, and again and again expressed her intentions, in the future, to hear the same kind of inspiring truth from the same pulpit.

Lucile was silent; but she thought how often in going home from St. Mark's she had wished that fortune had permitted her to attend such a service every Sabbath. After all, is it only the unusual which attracts?

Lucile, with many regrets and after many a "locked embrace," left for Minton on the evening boat. That night, after Mrs. Levitt and Regenia returned from the landing, they sat on the steps of the veranda and talked for hours before going into the house. It was a glorious night. The moonlight fell through the trees with a soft but broken radiance upon Regenia, seated at the feet of her foster-mother, her beautiful head resting child-like in the old woman's lap.

"Are you tired, my dear?" asked Mrs. Levitt, at the same time turning her face up to her own. "My, my, how your favor your mother. If you did not have your father's sad brown eyes, I would think you were that poor child risen from the dead," she continued thoughtfully.

"Am I so much like my mother? How I wish I could remember her," said Regenia sadly. "I miss her now more than ever before. It seems to me that the older I grow the more I long for mother."

"Well do I remember her," said Mrs. Levitt, slowly. "She was but a child, you might say, when she came to my house, though older than you; she had grown up in an atmosphere widely different from the one she had entered, yet through it all I believe she was happy. How she loved your father, and how he petted and spoiled her. I cooked their wedding dinner and lived in sight of them until she—" Mrs. Levitt hesitated and then in a broken voice continued, "until they brought you here. Before your mother died she put you in my arms and after kissing you, oh, so fondly, whispered, 'Be a mother to my baby.' After I had promised to do as she requested, she closed her eyes and breathed her last," said the old lady, wiping away the tears that chased each other down her wrinkled cheeks.

"It has been my prayer day and night," she said, after a pause, "that you may some day be as good a woman as your mother."

Regenia buried her head in Mrs. Levitt's lap and they wept together over the memories of the past.

After awhile, Mrs. Levitt put her arm around the young girl and lifting her to her feet, said: "Come, dear, it is time to go to bed."

THE "EVENTS."

Chapter XII.

We left Lotus Stone and his friend dreaming sweet dreams on the bosom of the lake. In due time the next morning they reached Minton; Clement to look after his paper and Lotus to drift about for a few weeks in the further enjoyment of his vacation. Clement settled down to his work all the better for the few days' recreation he had taken. As we have said in a previous chapter, Clement entered the office of one of the great dailies in Minton soon after he had left school. He entered under the ban of a vigorous protest from men and boys, as poor and decidedly less prepared for the work in which they were engaged as he. For many months his life in that office was one continued day of martyrdom. No imposition was too groveling, no practical joke too severe to play upon this courageous boy. All that littleness of heart could contrive or meanness of soul could execute, was placed in the path of this honest lad, striving under difficult circumstances to win his daily bread. In the teeth of every discouragement, he succeeded in gaining the confidence of his employers, and, in time, the good will of those who at first so bitterly opposed him. Courage of the right kind seldom fails to win its way. There are some spirits that no disadvantage can daunt and to whom opposition is worse than useless. The errand boy who met the favor of his employer, gradually worked himself up to typesetter, despite protest after protest from the narrow and biased Union. The typesetter's wit and pleasant manners earned for him a position on the reportorial staff. Time and diligence finally associated his pungent paragraphs with the editorial page of the paper. For years he wrote the comments accredited to the editor. Being thoroughly acquainted with the newspaper business, he determined to set up for himself.

He did not leave the office in which he worked, however, but bought type, set up his paper at odd times, and had it printed on the Daily's press. His paper, "The Events," was from the beginning a free lance in the newspaper arena. He was slave to no party, and therefore did not spare the meanness and cupidity of either of them. In time his bristling fulminations attracted the attention and criticism of the great daily from whose press his paper was issued. The editor of the before-mentioned daily objected to the vigorous style of Clement's paper and advised him to be more conservative. But the little paper continued to attack the hateful attitude of the demagogues who ruled in both political parties, with the same trenchant force. A rupture between Clement and the proprietor of the daily necessarily followed. The paper dispensed with the services of Mr. St. John, and, of course, their press ceased to send forth his paper. For a few weeks, Mr. St. John could have been seen carrying his forms from one place to another, in constant danger of having an entire edition pied. But courage and perseverance won the day. Clement was at last successful in exciting the interest of a number of friends in his venture, and the result was an electric plant and press of sufficient capacity to answer all the ends of his paper, and also to attach a job office to his business. The demand for the paper gradually grew; those of the race who had first discouraged the enterprise came to its support when their help was no longer absolutely necessary to its success.

It is indeed a lamentable fact that the best educated and most able Afro-Americans find themselves possessed with a rare conservatism when any race enterprise bids for their support. It may arise from the belief that anything founded upon a strictly race basis is unAmerican and therefore trends toward isolation. The Afro-American press has done, and is destined to continue to do, great good for the people whose cause it advocates. Any independent venture, however short of our ideals, is a manly demonstration of an instinctive wish to rise. Under the management of Clement St. John, "The Events," was newsy and ably edited. It did not bid for distinction by catering to the native jealousy of the race. It recognized the common needs of all and manfully fought for them. While it did not fondle upon the rich, haughty and powerful, it also refused to incite against them the distrust of the ignorant and less fortunate. While the paper sought to commend the good, it did not scruple to attack the evil. A friend and believer in Christianity, the editor despised the shams and ignorant practices which have been interpolated into the church by half-hearted ministers, more desirous of a name for themselves than zealous for the purity of the church of God. "The Events" castigated pagan marches and spectacular side shows as disastrous to the spiritual growth of Christianity. The outspoken opinions of the paper made its career for a time one of uncertainty. Its refusal to fill its columns with uninteresting personals curtailed its popular sales. The personal happenings of general interest "The Events" willingly chronicled, but printer's ink was not wasted in glorifying every "dude" who bought a street car ticket from one ward of the city to another. The opinions of the editor met a varied reception. Now an Afro-American convention is lauding the editor to a place among the benefactors of mankind; now some influential minister is damning every stream of the paper's circulation; now a Grand Lodge is making it the spokesman of the Order; now a coterie of wounded politicians are advocating its suppression. In the midst of all these eulogies and animadversions, Mr. St. John steadily pursued his course. Little he recked with what direction the cat of public opinion jumped, for he knew full well that through all the changes public sentiment might pass, the right in the end would prevail. His methods savored more of reformation than sensation. If he ridiculed some breach of common sense suicidal to party success, if he impaled with burning sarcasm some pagan practice in the Christian church, if he expressed his utter contempt for the course of some political shyster, if he disconcerted some social heresy, through it all the intelligent reader saw the interest of the reformer rather than the spleen of the egotist. The progress of such a paper would necessarily be slow. Mr. St. John was not unaware that every step upward must be a measured one. On the whole, he preferred the solid march of merit to the wind-blown inflation that burst after a six weeks' voyage. The bounds of "The Events" had been carefully set. The editor knew that if he lived his paper must live too, for worth alone can stand the test of time. As the paper broadened in usefulness and deepened in solidity, its sunshine friends, who bought a copy every fortnight and claimed for that support a half a column to spread airy nothings, as uninteresting as silly, noticeably fell away. The influence of the paper at last began to be felt and its admonitions heeded.

Its editorials had united the race and brought a prejudiced candidate for Congress to his senses by first cutting him to death at the polls. Politicians learned to fear the "mad frothings" of "The Events," as they had formerly styled Clement's editorials. The paper was not only working out political reforms, but assisting the race in other ways. In time it added to its job office a book bindery; in its columns it welcomed meritorious poems from the rising literati of the race. The patent story now and then gave place to some tale written by an Afro-American. To do this the paper at first lost money, although the story writers and poets gained nothing but publicity by their efforts. Clement knew that the readers of stories and poems were numbered by the millions. These millions hungering for literary food or literary recreation must have their wants supplied. Could not this hoard of constant readers be at least partially supplied by the men and women of their own race? Is not a race literature just as necessary as a race church, club or school? He believed the probability worth acting upon and was therefore willing to give it a trial. All of this was within the bounds, Clement St. John had set for "The Events." At work, this man of unconquerable determination was thoroughly in earnest, but when he left the office and gave himself to his friends, he was amiable, jovial and companionable. He hardly knew Lucile Malone before the editor of "The Events" was the saucy little stenographer's slave. Nor did he waste time nor words in making her acquainted with the wishes of his heart. He saw in Lucile what he wanted in a wife—an actual helpmate. Lucile was taken aback at his proposal and could hardly believe that this acknowledged "prince of wits" was sincere in his attention to a penniless typewriter. Clement was unceasing in his suit. Her hesitancy only added fuel to the flame. His constancy finally won her consent.

The paper on a safe basis, Clement believed he could afford a wife. Lucile prevailed upon him, however, to make her one of the force in his office and thus she would still be able to earn her salary. He was in a mood to promise anything, if consenting would accelerate the desire of his heart.

So in the month of July, before the Conclave, they had decided to be quietly married when the leaves had fallen and the trees were cold and bare.

WEDDING BELLS.

Chapter XIII.

August and September have been numbered with the past since last we saw Regenia Underwood and Mrs. Levitt sitting on the steps of their home at the "Elms," dreaming over the gilded romance and stern realities of bygone days.

The leaves which at that season clothed the oaks and elms in nature's royal green, had grown sere and yellow and left their former associates in winter's rough undress. The crisp wind and biting frost of October had stripped bush and tree of their drooping foliage. The sweltering sun of sultry dog days, followed by the masterful touch of Autumn's artistic brush, had tinted all nature with cardinal and gold, and yet the hasty promises sown during Conclave week, had not ripened into garnered realities. Not a word had penetrated the seclusion of the "Elms" from the undoubted Knight and gallant, Lotus Stone.

If he had written, Regenia had not received the missive. It was not likely, Regenia said to herself, day after day, that a letter directed to the "Elms" could have been miscarried. To this innocent girl, firmly believing the sunshine promises of those she met, the silence of Mr. Stone presented a dilemma too complicated for her solution. Mr. Stone had obtained her permission to further pursue the agreeable acquaintance formed between them by a friendly correspondence. Regenia believed he meant what he said, but despite her faith, the long expected letter did not come.

It did not occur to Regenia that his letter might have been intercepted. The postman could have informed her differently. He could have told her of a polite friend who on several occasions kindly relieved him of the mail intended for the "Elms," and if she had received no letters, Dr. Leighton might account for their disappearance.

In truth, Lotus Stone had written more than once since he left Mt. Clare. His first duty after his return to Washington was to write to the woman to whose unknown keeping he had consigned his heart. He waited more than a month, but received no answer.

He resigned his position in the departmental service and decided to finish the last year of his medical course in one of the great schools of New York. Before leaving Washington, however, he addressed a second letter to Regenia, but that receiving the same fate as the first, he left for his new field of study a sadder but wiser man. For some reason he did not attempt through the medium of Clement St. John to solve the problem of Regenia's silence. Concealing his disappointment beneath the mantle of his pride, he entered upon the pursual of his course a more determined if a less happy man. He tried to shut Regenia out of his thoughts and efface the image of the sweet girl from his memory, but the effort was in vain. He wasted the nights that should have been given to rest and recuperation for the work before him in idly indulging his fancy in the most ridiculous conjectures. He would sometimes imagine himself dead, and from a martyr's heaven watching Regenia as she stood above his cold corpse weeping herself away in the remembrance of her disregard for his devotion. Again he would congratulate himself that he had succeeded in forgetting her; this stage of the case, however, would rarely last longer than a day. Whenever books and lectures left his mind to its own resources, Regenia Underwood, try as he might to banish her, occupied it to the exclusion of every other thought. He had arrived at that stage of self-deception, or he at least flattered himself that he had, when he believed women as inconstant as the wind. "What more is she to me than any other butterfly of a day's devotion?" he asked himself frequently, and as often answered, "Nothing;" but the response belied the facts. Did he grow thin and petulant worrying over the other butterflies that time and again had flitted into his horizon? In one resolution, however, he was persistent: he would never write again until she answered the letters already sent, nor would he ever manifest his disappointment to Clement. In this determination, however, he was not alone, Regenia had also resolved never to indicate her chagrin to Lucile. If this love-sick swain and innocent lass, hardening their hearts against each other, could have peeped into the secret drawer in a certain specialist's office in Mt. Claire, they would have lost no time in apologizing for a misunderstanding for which neither was to blame.

Dr. Frank Leighton smiled with fiendish delight as he observed the keen disappointment exhibited by Regenia when the postman passed day after day without even so much as a look toward the "Elms." He was not so lost to every trait of the gentleman, however, as to read the letters he had surreptitiously intercepted. He often half relented the tendency to meddle with matters which did not concern him, but whenever he thought of Lotus Stone, whom he bitterly detested, he strengthened his resolve to see to it that Regenia never heard a word from him. During the latter part of October, Lucile was to be married, and although the affair was to be a very quiet one, she had set her heart on having Regenia present.

Mrs. Levitt and Mrs. Underwood had also been invited. For weeks Regenia had been looking forward to this event with the greatest interest. It was her intention to go a week before the event and remain a week or two after the marriage had been duly solemnized. Mrs. Levitt evinced as much interest in the approaching nuptials as Regenia; she had entered into all of Regenia's plans with the delight of an actual participant and discussed the coming wedding, the gown Regenia was to wear, the present she intended to take Lucile, and everything else about it, to the young girl's unbounded satisfaction. A few days before the time fixed for Regenia to leave to Minton, Mrs. Underwood complained of illness. As her malady was nothing more alarming than a severe headache, the matter elicited but little comment. The day that Regenia and Mrs. Levitt were to start to Minton, Mrs. Underwood's symptoms assumed a more threatening aspect. It was finally thought best for Mrs. Levitt to remain at home, but both Mrs. Underwood and her housekeeper insisted that Regenia should go. She accordingly set off, Dr. Leighton kindly consenting to see her aboard the boat. Regenia was inclined at first to regret that she had not decided to remain at home. Although she so much wished to see her friends married. After hearing Dr. Leighton's opinion that Mrs. Underwood's sickness was nothing more than a passing ailment, consequent upon old age, she was contented to make the journey to Minton.

He adroitly directed the conversation from the illness of his aunt to Mrs. Levitt, and casually observed, "Your foster mother has known you from childhood; I suppose she seems nearer to you than my aunt."

"She is the very soul of kindness," replied Regenia. "I hardly know what would become of me if I did not have Mrs. Levitt's oversight."

"She knew both your mother and father," said Dr. Leighton. "Did she know them when your mother first made that wild goose chase to Canada," he asked.

"Do not say that," answered Regenia. "What my mother did is sacred to me."

"Oh, certainly," said the doctor, seeing he was setting a match to powder. "She acted up to her ideas, and who of us do more?" he added.

"Mrs. Levitt was present when my parents were married, and it was in her house that the wedding dinner was served. You ought to hear her tell about it; she related to me the entire story the night Lucile left for Minton."

"I expect she surrounds it with a romantic halo not justified by the facts," the doctor disparagingly answered.

"Oh, no. She was there, and you know poor mother died in Mrs. Levitt's arms," said Regenia sadly.

"She did?" was what Dr. Leighton said; he thought, however, "Mrs. Levitt knows more than is safe for her or good for me."

"Here we are," he remarked, after a long silence; "we are at the landing." He alighted and assisting Regenia from the phaeton, saw her safe aboard the boat.

The next morning Regenia was met at Minton by her friends and whisked away to Lucile's boarding house. During the days that followed, the girls were busily concerned with preparations for the momentous event. Lucile wondered why Regenia never spoke of Lotus Stone. Regenia wondered if Mr. Stone would be present at the marriage of her friend. To Regenia, the suspense was unendurable and at last she broke the silence. The day of the wedding but one she said to Lucile: "Have you told me of everyone you expect to-morrow?"

"Yes," she answered. "Mr. Stone could not come. We are just as cut up at the thought of his absence as you are," added the impetuous girl.

"Are you sure that he will not be here as you seem to be confident that I am expecting him?" asked Regenia, laughingly.

"Of course you know he will not be present. What was I thinking about anyway? But if he treats you as coldly as he does us," emphasizing the "us," "you are not too well informed of the eccentricities of Mr. Lotus Stone."

"It is not necessary that he should treat me at all. I have never received a line from him. Is he still in Washington?" asked Regenia, blushing at this confession.

"Well, do you tell me he has never written to you?" said Lucile, rising in her excitement. "What is the matter with that man? He seems to have forsaken all of his friends."

"Mr. St. John declares that something has come over Lotus beyond his ability to comprehend. You ought to have seen the stiff letter of regrets he sent in answer to our invitation. We thought you were the cause of his strange actions, but as you are as innocent of any knowledge of his malady as we are, I am at a loss to think what the matter is."

"Do not think at all. Mr. Stone has, perhaps, other interests that engage his attentions, to the exclusion of 'marriage and giving in marriage.'"

"Has he never written to you?" she asked again, ignoring Regenia's admonition. "I can not believe it. He has written and the big fish of your dream has snapped up the precious missive. He has written more than once, I am sure, but failing of an answer he has coiled himself up within himself and gone into a state of hibernation. He is not in Washington, but in New York, concluding his studies." This information, Lucile, in her haste to deliver, fairly threw at Regenia's head.

"I know nothing of Mr. Stone since I last saw him at Mt. Clare, and if he has ever written to me I have not received the letter. Who would be sufficiently interested in Mr. Stone to intercept his letters to me?" asked Regenia excitedly.

"Only one person on earth," answered Lucile slowly, "Dr. Frank Leighton."

"I cannot believe that Dr. Leighton, however much he may dislike Mr. Stone, would stoop to such a scurvy trick. What motive could induce a man of his respectability to commit such a palpable crime?" asked Regenia doubtingly.

"The same motive that induced the big fish to snap up the minnows, because he could and because he wanted to do so," replied Lucile, a little hurt at Regenia's lack of belief in her theory. No argument that Lucile might offer could have convinced Regenia that Dr. Leighton, whom she had never known to do a mean thing, would be guilty of such a crime. At this stage of the discussion Mr. St. John made his appearance and the subject was dropped. During the rest of the day the girls were too much occupied to revive it.

The next evening Lucile and Clement were made man and wife.

At the little stone church, in the presence of quite a few of their most intimate friends, the Episcopal rector read the beautiful ceremony, which forever afterward was to make the interests of Lucile Malone and Clement St. John, one. After the marriage a selected few drove to the snug little home Clement's frugality had provided, and discussed a modest supper.

At the height of the enjoyment, a sharp, potential ring called Mr. St. John to the door. It was a messenger boy, bearing a telegram for Regenia. Clement, with as little ado as possible called the trembling girl into the next room. If was from Mrs. Levitt: Regenia's grandmother was dead.

That night as the clock struck twelve, Regenia Underwood, her head resting on her hand, was a silent passenger on the west-bound train.

A COMPULSORY DESERTION.

Chapter XIV.

All the way from Minton to Mt. Clare Regenia sat with her head in her hands. Still wearing the gown in which she had gone to the wedding, she had not even divested herself of the flowers, which a few hours since were fresh and beautiful, but now as wilted and lifeless as her smitten heart. Dazed by the suddenness of the terrible information, she could not realize how sad was her bereavement.

The shock had come in such an unexpected moment. "If I had only known," she wailed over and over again, "it might have been so different."

Who is ever prepared for death? What boots it that we are in the very presence of the dying when Death insidiously approaches, we are as illy prepared to admit him and as unwilling to part from our loved ones as if he had entered without warning. Regenia was filled with remorse for leaving home at such a time, all forgetful that her departure had been at the earnest request of Mrs. Underwood. "Why was I not sent for sooner? Why was Mrs. Underwood left to die with no one but Mrs. Levitt or strangers to close her eyes?" Such questions crowded into her mind again and again during the long and tedious ride. At last the train reached Mt. Clare and Regenia hastened home. As she hurried up the gravel walk, the very quietness of the place filled her with a nameless dread. Softly she entered and made her way to the room where all that was mortal of her late benefactress lay. The room was empty. She silently closed the door and kneeling beside the bier, poured out the pent up sorrows which filled her lonely heart. Time and again she removed the cloth from the face of the departed and covered the placid brow with affectionate kisses. How she recalls now her poignant grief, the numberless times, alas! forever past, when with more than a mother's tenderness those kind eyes, now glazed and sightless, had dwelled with loving compassion upon the lonely child of a daughter's disobedience. How gently, yet how wisely, had she directed the straying steps of her often wayward little girl back to the path of right.

As Regenia stood there alone with her dead, all the high hopes and resolves of the past seemed to fly away on the sombre wings of her sorrow. Throwing herself across the body of the dead and vainly wishing that she too might die, she burst into a fit of passionate weeping.

Sob after sob, sad and heart-rending, reached the ears of Mrs. Levitt, who, tired out from watching, sat dozing away the morning hour in an adjoining room. She did not need to be told that it was Regenia weeping so bitterly in the other room. She waited until the girl had spent the first force of her poignant grief and then softly entering the room she lifted the young girl up and led her out from the presence of the dead.

Assisting Regenia upstairs she took her to her own room and sitting down took Regenia in her arms just as she had done a thousand times before and stroked her hair and kissed her forehead until wornout nature came to her relief. Then putting her charge on the bed, she knelt beside the sleeping girl and asked God's aid and guidance through the weary years to come. Mrs. Levitt had a premonition how often and how sadly in the future Regenia would sigh in vain for the return of that kind friend who had been more than a mother to her.

Regenia was not less surprised than the rest of her many friends at the suddenness of Mrs. Underwood's demise. The day she left for Minton as we had before noted, her grandmother complained of a severe headache. For a day or two after Regenia left, Mrs. Underwood commenced to be annoyed with her eyes. She finally concluded to call in Dr. Leighton, who for some reason had not been over to the house since the day he drove Regenia to the boat. The doctor, after a few minutes' examination of his aunt's eyes, hurriedly departed. He signified his intention, however, to return in a short time. When he came back he brought an ophthalmoscope and carefully re-examined the eyes of his aunt. Before he put down the instrument, Mrs. Levitt observed his hand shake and his face assume a deathly pallor. When the examination was concluded he turned to Mrs. Levitt, saying, "Do you know where the office of Dr. S——is?" Receiving an affirmative answer, he sat down, and drawing a prescription pad from his pocket, rapidly noted thereon Mrs. Underwood's symptoms. Tearing off the paper and carefully folding it, he gave it to Mrs. Levitt, and in tones slightly tremulous said: "Take this to Dr. S——. Ask him to return it with the medicine," he added after a moment's reflection.

The broken tone in which he spoke, in spite of his attempted self-control, somewhat alarmed Mrs. Underwood. "What is it, doctor?" she asked. "Is my condition worse than you expected?"

"Oh, no," he answered lightly, now thoroughly master of himself, "it is only a little stomach trouble. I think you will be all right in a day or two."

"We must go some time," continued Mrs. Underwood, quietly, "but if my time is drawing near I should like to be apprised of it for Regenia's sake."

"You are good for a great many years yet, auntie," he said. "When Mrs. Levitt comes, ask her to save the prescription for me, I wish to keep it for future reference."

Dr. Leighton left that house steeling himself against his conscience. He had enacted a deliberate lie. Well he knew that his aunt was not destined to live three days longer. While examining her eyes, he had made a discovery that curdled his blood and sent a tremor through every nerve. On the optic nerve he had seen signs of a ruptured blood vessel, and he knew full well if something was not done immediately to counteract the effect, Mrs. Underwood must die from paralysis of the brain.

Of this he was aware and knowing the awful consequences, had deliberately decided to permit the death of his aunt. The day after the examination, Mrs. Underwood was no better; the day following she died. Dr. Leighton had lost no time in preparing for the event. He did not want Regenia to know a fact more than that of which he was already in possession.

After Mrs. Underwood's death, this Specialist of Symptoms, who had indirectly led up to her demise, by indicating a false diagnosis, rummaged the library through and through in search of a will or any other papers of value he might secure to aid him in his design. In persual of his intentions, he went to Mrs. Levitt and asked her concerning Mrs. Underwood's papers. Mrs. Levitt quickly divined the purpose of his quest, and unhesitatingly denied any knowledge of Mrs. Underwood's private affairs. This she did with perfect truthfulness, although she might have told him of several sealed packages confided to her by the deceased the day before her death to be kept in trust for Regenia. These papers, Mrs. Levitt had thoughtfully concealed. Dr. Leighton, believing that Mrs. Levitt knew more than she was willing to tell, resolved to get her out of the way before his purpose was made manifest. The day after Mrs. Underwood was buried he again called at the "Elms," and being informed that Regenia was in her room, sent for Mrs. Levitt. After a polite good morning, he said: "My lawyer will probably be over here to-day to learn what you know of the papers my poor aunt left." This he said in order to frighten Mrs. Levitt into some kind of an admission which would assist him to determine his course toward her.

"Your lawyer or anybody else can come, but they will never succeed in drawing blood from a turnip."

"You must know something," said the doctor, exhibiting a pretended impatience. "Tell me you could live in confidential relations with my aunt all these years and never have heard her intimate in any way what disposition she intended to make of her property."

"I am not obliged to divulge everything I have heard during the years I have lived here. If I were, I might tell you something not very complimentary to you, Dr. Leighton," she replied with some heat.

"I do not care a cent what you have heard concerning me, but you know something of my aunt's private affairs, and I am going to get it out of you, cost what it may," said the doctor, unguardedly.

"Suppose you try it," said Mrs. Levitt in a towering rage. "What I know I know, and any trust Mrs. Underwood reposed in me I will be true to, if it cost me my life. I know what you are after," she cried as he stalked angrily out, "but you will never accomplish it while my head is hot."

He did not speak—he dared not. His blood was up. "Shall I be balked in my plans by this old negress? No! not if I have to kill her to attain my ends," he muttered to himself.

That night Dr. Leighton went to a low dive he had often frequented and concocted a plan to rid himself of this old woman, whom he had every reason to believe was all that stood between him and the consummation of his designs. He surmised that Mrs. Levitt carried Mrs. Underwood's last will and testament about with her, but in this he was mistaken. If he could get possession of the old woman, search her, abstract the papers and destroy them, he would be master of the wealth of the Underwood estate. The only way to do this was to kidnap her, but he hesitated to run this risk. To his credit, it might be said, that he also disliked to leave Regenia without a friend in the world.

He had fully resolved to rob her of her property, but he excused himself by saying that Regenia had no business to be born, anyway. It would be just punishment meted to the heir of his cousin, who had so far forgotten the pride of her birth as to make such a mésalliance.

After a week of cogitation, he could find no other way to dispose of Mrs. Levitt but to send her back to her native land, as he called Canada. Having once determined upon this plan he had no difficulty in securing dupes to carry out his designs.

He knew a drunken lighthouse keeper who lived in an unfrequented place far up among the hills near the light he tended. If this man would take care of Mrs. Levitt during her long visit in Canada it would be worth a pretty penny to him.

He visited the lighthouse keeper and had no trouble in arranging for Mrs. Levitt's detention. Accordingly one cold Sunday night in December, as Mrs. Levitt was returning from church alone, she was hailed by a cabman, who asked her some question sufficient to detain her. The carriage drove up to the curb, the driver alighted and while he engaged Mrs. Levitt in conversation a confederate stealthily appeared from out the darkness, and throwing a heavy shawl over her head, she was forced into the cab and rapidly driven toward the river. They crossed the ferry and pushed on until nearly daylight. At last the cab stopped. Not a word had been said from the time they started until Mrs. Levitt was lifted from the carriage, frozen almost stiff. They helped her up a hill to a cabin which contained but two rooms, into one of which she was ushered. The men tied her hands, after which a tall, gaunt woman came into the room and thoroughly searched her.

"One of them men says along, ahow that if you tell him where them papers is, how that he'll let you go," said the woman.

"Who said that?" asked Mrs. Levitt warily.

"Tell her she knows well enough who said it," cried a well-known voice.

"Tell him to hunt till he finds them," replied Mrs. Levitt.

"Keep her here and you shall be paid every month in advance," said the well-known voice.

He went out and slammed the door, but shortly Mrs. Levitt heard him return.

"Don't let the woman leave this room," he continued, "and should she ever attempt it, shoot her down like a dog."

Mrs. Levitt sat down on the bare floor and drawing her hymnal and common prayer, she opened the prayer book and by the light of the wood fire, repeated the forms in which Christians have found consolation for centuries.

DISINHERITED.

Chapter XV.

Regenia had retired earlier than usual the evening of Mrs. Levitt's mysterious disappearance, therefore she did not learn of her absence until the next morning at breakfast. She had felt some surprise before coming down to her morning's meal that she had not heard the usual rap upon her chamber door and the usual admonition, "It is time to rise, my dear." "Where is Mrs. Levitt?" she enquired of a servant, as she unfolded her napkin and prepared to eat breakfast.

"In her room, I suppose," answered the person addressed. "She has not been down—perhaps she is sick," suggested the servant. "Shall I go and see?"

"Never mind; I will go myself," replied Regenia, feeling that if anything had gone wrong with Mrs. Levitt, the matter required her immediate attention.

Pushing back her chair, she hastened to Mrs. Levitt's chamber, and after knocking, first gently, then more imperatively, she ventured to open the door. Not finding Mrs. Levitt, she rapidly retraced her steps to the dining-room, where she informed the astonished servant of the fruitlessness of her search.

"Were you awake when Mrs. Levitt returned from church?" she asked excitedly of the servant.

"I did not hear her come in," was the answer. "I remained up reading an interesting story until long after church was out."

"I wonder where she could have gone," said Regenia, tears slowly trickling down her cheeks. "Do you suppose anything has happened to her?" she asked, drying her eyes on the napkin.

"If she was at church, perhaps the rector knows something about her. I will run over there and find out if she was at church," she said, rising. Throwing a shawl around her shoulders and weeping as she went, with flying feet she started for the rectory. "Was Mrs. Levitt at church last night?" she asked the minister's wife as soon as the door was opened to admit the excited girl. The rector, hearing the question, also came to the door.

"Come in and compose yourself," he said kindly. "Mrs. Levitt was in her usual place last night, did she not return after services?"

"I do not know, but she is not at home this morning, and we are at a loss to account for her absence," Regenia replied, with increasing composure.

"She was certainly in church," remarked the rector's wife, "for I saw her turn down the street that leads to the 'Elms.'"

Mrs. Levitt was known to be interested in charity work, and the rector therefore suggested, "She may have gone to some sick friend's house and the nature of the case detained her during the night."

To this remark Regenia made no reply, but aimlessly rising, she prepared to go. Both the rector and his wife bade the broken-hearted girl to cheer up, at the same time assuring her that Mrs. Levitt would return in her own good time with the very best excuse for the scare she had unwittingly given them.

From the rectory, Regenia directed her steps toward "Seven Corners." She did not think Dr. Leighton knew anything of Mrs. Levitt, but it was perfectly natural that she should appeal to him in the hour of her great misfortune.

"Good morning," he cried in his cheery way, as Regenia entered. "What has brought my fair cousin out so early this inclement morning?" he asked. Then, as if having just discovered her swollen eyes and tear-stained face, "Why, what's the matter? You are not ill?" he exclaimed, as she sat down in one of the large office chairs.

Regenia told him what the reader already knows that Dr. Leighton was well aware of, striving as she repeated the story to retain her self-possession.

The doctor listened to her plaintive recital with well feigned surprise and when she had concluded questioned her carefully concerning Mrs.

Levitt's movements, her evening at the church, the rector's story and the general habits of her foster-mother.

When he had ascertained how much was known of Mrs. Levitt's movements on the previous evening, he sat for some time as if in contemplation of the best method to pursue to find the old lady and restore her to her friends.

"The rector is probably right," he said at last. "She must be detained somewhere on a pressing mission of mercy."

"The probability is hardly admissible," said Regenia thoughtfully. "It is so unlike Mrs. Levitt. If she were going to be absent all night, she would have come home first to tell me, however urgent the call. She knows too well what a fright her failure to return from church would occasion."

"Now that my poor aunt is no more," said Dr. Leighton, "it may be that Mrs. Levitt feels that she is not obliged to give such a strict account of her doings. The most trusted servants grow careless when the pressure from the parlor is removed."

"Mrs. Levitt was never a servant in our house," spiritedly objected Regenia. "She has never been obliged to give any account of her movements."

"If she was not a servant, what was she?" asked the doctor, unable to hide his annoyance. "I confess my inability to understand your fine distinctions. She lived with you and assisted in the direction of the affairs of the house. If she was not my aunt's equal she must have been an inferior; in other words, a servant. I mean no discredit to the old woman," he said in an apologizing way, as Regenia arose to leave.

"I do not know what you consider her, but she has been everything to me—mother, companion and friend, and on these terms she shall remain," replied Regenia.

"If we are able to find her," said the doctor laughingly. He bade her as she left the office, to try and compose herself. "If anything can be done to find Mrs. Levitt, you may depend upon me to do it." He promised to advertise in the evening paper, offering a reward for any information concerning Mrs. Levitt and to forthwith put detectives on the case, providing they suspected foul play.

With laggard steps and heavy heart, Regenia returned home from her bootless search. For the first time during her short life she realized what it is to be alone in the world. All that day she watched in vain, for Mrs. Levitt's return. Every footfall that reached her ears, she hoped marked the coming of her dear old friend. The day slowly wore away, and night came, but brought no news to Regenia of the much desired object of her solicitation. Dr. Leighton came over, early in the evening, only to inquire if the lost had been heard from. The rector's wife also came over to cheer the young girl and strive to revive her drooping spirits.

So the first night came and went and the next day and the next week, until poor Regenia, despairing, gave up all hope of ever again seeing her friend. With a grief that could not be consoled, she passed her days in waiting; her nights in weeping. From a bright, happy girl, in a few weeks she had grown prematurely settled. She looked years older than she did the day we first saw her standing on the steps of the "Elms" saucily allaying the thirst of Clement St. John and Lotus Stone.

One morning about two weeks after the search for Mrs. Levitt commenced, Dr. Leighton called. Regenia's heart beat high with swelling hope as she saw him enter the gate. A glance at his face assured her he was on no unimportant mission. She was certain he brought news of Mrs. Levitt's whereabouts.

"You have heard something from Mrs. Levitt," she said, as the doctor followed her into the library.

"I am sorry to say, that I have not," replied the Doctor, making no attempt to dissemble his annoyance, that the girl seemed to think of nothing but her old nurse. "I am here on business of quite a different nature."

Regenia interest immediately subsided. "If he knows nothing of Mrs. Levitt," she thought, "anything else he has to say is of no consequence."

"You do not ask the purpose of my business," he said, piqued at the awkward silence which followed his first affirmation.

"I am waiting," she said spiritlessly.

"Did it every occur to you that at sometime Mrs. Underwood's business would have to be settled and her last intentions concerning the distribution of her estates ascertained?" he asked sharply.

"I never gave the matter a moment's consideration. Grandmother had no child, but mother," she continued, lowering her voice, "and my mother none but me. I naturally supposed—" she hesitatingly added—"there was no one else to inherit what she left."

"Very true from your standpoint, and if things could be adjusted in that simple direct way, writing wills would be a waste of energy," replied the Doctor, with a forced laugh which made Regenia shudder and wish for Mrs. Levitt.

"Mrs. Levitt knew more of grandmother's wishes than anyone else; if she were only here," sighed the puzzled girl.

"Mrs. Levitt can not be found, it seems, but in her absence we may be able to find something more important. Where did my aunt keep her papers?" he said, at the same time rising and approaching a secretary in another part of the room.

"I do not know, but she often wrote at that desk," timidly replied Regenia.

Dr. Leighton opened the writing desk, and taking out the key proceeded to unlock and examine the contents of drawer after drawer. He at last drew forth a package, yellow with age, and, untying it, took out a paper, which, after looking over it a few moments, appeared to greatly agitate him.

"What is it?" said Regenia. "Have you found the will?"

"This seems to be it," said the doctor slowly, "but there seems to be some mistake. Look at it."

Regenia took up the document and had read but a short time before she dropped it with the exclamation: "Why this gives everything to you! Poor grandmother, how could she have felt so bitterly against me!"

"It was the expressed wish of Judge Underwood, she says here, and in keeping with a promise extracted from her by him on the day he died," said Dr. Leighton.

The severity of the conditions of the will did not dawn upon Regenia until Dr. Leighton said: "You need have no fears, I will always look after you. The will enjoins, as nothing could be left you directly, that I provide an allowance which is to be yours exclusively as long as you live."

"Mrs. Underwood had a right to leave my mother's portion to whoever she listed, but placing me on your bounty, Dr. Leighton, is beyond her power. If I am to be disinherited, I will not accept the verdict with recommendations to mercy."

"I willingly assume the responsibility," he said approaching and essaying to stroke her hair.

"I am not a child," she said, "and need no cajoling. I thank you very much for your generosity, but I do not feel that I can accept anything from you on the terms set forth in that will."

"You are entirely wrong, my dear," said the Doctor, attempting to take her hand. "I want to be a friend to you. Is it my fault that your mother made a wretched mistake?"

"Not another word," said Regenia. "Whatever my mother did, her child willingly accepts as right."

"But, my dear Regenia, you must let me explain," he said, throwing himself between the irate girl and the door through which she attempted to escape.

"Explanations are unnecessary," she said, waving him away. "I fear, Doctor, you will end by adding insult to injury."

"Don't be a fool," said he, losing his temper. "Do you persist in your refusal of my offer?"

"I do," she replied. He stood aside and she passed through the door and with measured steps made her way upstairs.

Dr. Leighton smiled as she left, thinking how easily his scheme had worked. There was a degree of dissatisfaction, however, in the girl's refusal to accept the offered allowance. "I'll bring her around," he thought, as he helped himself into his overcoat and prepared to leave the house.

"Now to have the will probated and I take possession—nine points in law," he chuckled.

Regenia went to her room no longer a girl. This last stroke of sorrow had made the girl a woman. To question the genuineness of the will Dr. Leighton had produced, never occurred to her. If an expert had examined it, he could have told her that its aged look was the work of a clever villain; that deft hands had forged the signature and that the very paper was placed in that drawer not a week previous to the day it was found. She had not been in her room five minutes before she had decided upon her course. Brushing away her tears, she began packing her trunk. If the property were Dr. Leighton's, she had no right to remain there another day. She must go away, but where? "I will go to Lucile," she said, half aloud.

She had a little money; she counted it over and found it was enough to pay her fare to Minton and a few dollars besides.

"When this is gone, what then?" she thought. "God will take care of me," she said devoutly.

Having packed her trunk she put on her wraps and prepared to leave. "An hour to train time," said she, consulting her watch. Before she left, she went into Mrs. Levitt's room, and kneeling there asked God's guidance and that the patient, loving disposition of Mrs. Levitt might fall upon her, and then, with streaming eyes, she left the house.

She ordered her trunks sent to the depot and in less than two hours after Dr. Leighton left her, she was flying toward Minton.

ALONE AND PENNILESS.

Chapter XVI.

The train on which Regenia Underwood was a passenger, had left in the distance many a mile post, before the excitement under which she labored had sufficiently subsided to permit her to take a sober inventory of the events which had transpired in the past few hours. She did not question the wisdom of leaving the "Elms" so hastily; this she had determined to do, be the action wise or foolish. She would not eat the crumbs of charity that fell from the table of Dr. Leighton. Her woman's intuition told her that all was not right. She did not suspect the forgery that had been so cleverly sprung by Dr. Leighton, but she suspected his intentions toward her, and rightly decided that her greatest safety lay in instant flight.

As the cars sped along her anxiety increased. She sat idly looking out of the coach window, counting the miles she must yet travel before reaching the end of her journey, and after the stop at each station consulting her traveling guide and timing the distance to the next stop. It seemed to Regenia that the space between Mt. Clare and Minton had lengthened since last she passed that way. The car was crowded, hot and poorly ventilated. She tried to while away the time by trying to surmise where so many people were going, what their mission, and who awaited their coming? Would sorrow or happiness crown the end of their journeys? "Some of them, perhaps, are going home," she mused. "Home!" she said to herself, and for the first time in her life she realized what it is to be without a home. Alas, she had no place she could call her home. No home—how the sad admission echoed through her young heart. "Perhaps everyone in this coach has a home, but me," she thought. "I have neither home nor friends." Dropping her young head into her hands, she began to picture to herself the miseries of a friendless, homeless life. How little she had ever thought of this before. She realizes now, how cold and perfunctory had been her sympathy for others similarly situated.

After what seemed to Regenia an unending journey, she welcomed the brakeman's nasal cry, "Minton." As the crowded surface car wended its way from the depot, Regenia noticed that nearly every passenger carried a package. It slowly dawned upon her that it was Christmas eve—"Christmas for all the world," she thought, "but how sad indeed it will be for me?"

Regenia was tired and thoroughly unhappy before the creeping car stopped at the corner of the street a few doors from her friend's house. She almost ran in her impatience to reach the door. She rushed up the steps of the house she had left but a few weeks before and rang the bell. She waited, but no answer; she rang again and after ages, it seemed to her, an upstairs shutter was slowly opened and a voice she knew and welcomed called out: "Who's there?"

"It is I," said Regenia. "Do you not know me?"

The window went down with a crash and flying feet were heard hastening down the stairs. Then the door flew wide open and the two friends threw themselves into each other's arms.

"Come right in," said Lucile. "What a surprise you gave me. I knew it was not Clement; he would have let himself in by his latchkey. Why did you not write? Did you want to give us a real surprise?"

Lucile did not expect these questions to be answered, but in her happy excitement she seized a woman's right to ask all the questions she chose.

Regenia, now that she was safe with Lucile, could not say a word, but with her arms around her friend's neck, she wept until she was calm enough to tell her story.

"Do not try to speak, my poor dear," said Lucile, after a time. "I do not care if you wait weeks to tell me all about it." Stroking the girl's hair and now and then affectionately kissing her, Regenia soon became composed enough to tell her all.

"We thought as much," she indignantly replied when she had heard Regenia's story. "Clement has been looking for just such a finale. I could not believe that Dr. Leighton could be such a doubly-dyed villain. But Clement was right about him, as he is about most people," she replied with pardonable pride. "You are just right in refusing to touch a cent of his blood-money."

Lucile has scarcely finished her sympathetic remarks before she heard Mr. St. John's key in the door. She hastened to meet him and said, "I have a great surprise for you."

"Maybe you are not alone with your surprises, my little woman, seeing this is Christmas eve," he said pleasantly.

"No but I have a real surprise, one in human flesh."

Mr. St. John surveyed his wife a second time saying, "Now that's a 'poser.'"

"You mean thing," said Lucile, slapping him fondly.

"Come in here," she continued at the same time opening the door.

"Why Regenia," he said, "this is a delight indeed that Lucile has brought as a Christmas gift."

Regenia hardly had time to respond to his royal welcome before Lucile, anticipating her, related the whole story.

"Why did you not write to us?" said Clement, a little hurt by Regenia's apparent reticence.

"I could get no reply to my letters, and naturally supposed that Lucile, happy in her new life, could not find time to devote to idle correspondence."

"I did answer your last letter, dear, and receiving no reply wrote a second time, with the same result," said Lucile.

"I have never received a line from you since I left your house the night of the wedding," replied Regenia with astonishment.

"Your mail has been intercepted; of this you may be assured," said Clement, hotly. "I more than suspect that is the reason you have not heard from another quarter."

"Just the very reason, dear, you have not heard from Mr. Stone. Poor Lotus!" continued the impetuous Lucile. "He has been eating his heart out with grief, I know."

In the mind of Mrs. St. John the matter was quite satisfactorily explained.

"I am inclined to think you have hit the mark this time, my little woman," said Clement, amused at his wife's rapid conclusions.

"Of course I am correct. Am I not always so?" asked Lucile.

"Yes, yes, certainly you are—and Mrs. Levitt, what has become of her?" inquired Clement turning to Regenia.

"Mysteriously disappeared. She went to church two weeks ago last Sunday night and has never returned. The doctor advertised and exhausted every means to find her without success," said Regenia, the tears chasing each other down her cheeks. "Dr. Leighton thinks she will be found, though," she added through her tears.

"He does?" said Clement, with a sneer. "I wonder if he does? Doctor seems to be a very hopeful man. Did Mrs. Levitt know anything about Mrs. Underwood's affairs?"

On receiving an affirmative reply, he continued, "She will never turn up if Dr. Leighton can prevent it."

For awhile the big awkward fellow sat looking into the fire thinking—thinking of the past summer and the transient nature of everything in this world.

His face took on a blacker look, his form assumed a more rigid tension, and gazing at Regenia sitting there so frail and sad, he said:

"In happier days, my little friend, I promised perhaps thoughtlessly, to be your knight. You took my card and very wisely call at my home for a redemption of former pledges. What I said then in playful pastime, I repeat now in terrible earnest. You know how welcome you are here with Lucile, just as welcome as if you were her sister. You have been wronged, the cause of the wronged innocent is my cause. Lucile is your sister, I am your friend. We'll make common warfare. Mrs. Levitt will be found and for every sorrow that white-livered villain has caused you and her to suffer, he shall suffer doubly."

The two girls sat looking at Clement, and each seem to see the rough hard face lose itself in the beautiful heroic man who sat before them, the personification of every holy virtue.

Lucile stole softly behind his chair and with her arms around his neck and her glowing cheek against his gnarled face, silently thanked God that heaven had sent her such a man. Regenia rose, also, and taking his hand, knelt beside him, covering the unshapely member with kisses; over this blissful scene the angels that surprised the lowly shepherds so many years before were chanting in seraphic harmony, "Peace on earth, good will to men."

Regenia first found her voice and in broken words stammered her thanks to Mr. St. John.

"I never thought of asking you to take up my cause. I did not come because I wanted you to trouble about me; but there was no one else to go to. I am alone and moneyless."

"There, there, not another word. Of course you would come to your Lucile. I should never have quite forgiven you if you had not. Let me take your things up to your room. Come with me," she said, slipping her arm around Regenia's waist in her old girl-like way. "Are you going to hang up your stocking? I am," she continued without awaiting a reply.

Lucile was not long in making Regenia feel at home. Clement sat by the fire, musing for sometime, then hearing Regenia's cheery laugh vibrate through the hall and musically ring in his ears, he arose with a complaisant smile on his earnest face and noiselessly stole into the street to make his stock of Christmas presents meet the demands of his recently increased family.

When he returned, the house was dark, but by the flickering glare of the dying embers he discovered on each side of the mantel, limp and black, the "sister's" stockings. With a happiness akin to bliss, for the first time in his life he played the part which Santa Claus is believed by all good children to fill so delightfully. This being done, he silently crept off to bed. It was late the next morning when he awoke. As he lay there turning over in his mind the events of the evening before, the voice of his wife ringing out a "Merry Christmas," was heard without the door.

When he descended to the sitting room, he found the two girls bubbling over with joy. Each had received or pretended to have received the very thing that she most desired. Clement did not go to the office that day, a holiday edition of "The Events," having been sent to its destination the day previous; he thought that he could well afford to make the day a happy one for his wife and her unexpected visitor. No references to the sorrows of yesterday were allowed to intrude themselves upon the unalloyed pleasures of the day. The consummate skill with which Lucile filled the duties of hostess, kept Regenia's mind too much occupied to prey upon itself. What, with a matinee in the afternoon, dinner at six, and a round of pleasant levees and receptions at night, excepting the nameless void, too deep for utterance, which filled Regenia's heart, she almost forgot her unhappiness.

The day passed all too soon, as happy days will pass, and Sunday following, she had time to brood over her misfortunes. She found it no easy thing to determine what course to pursue in her sad distress. Upon one thing she had early resolved, she would not sit in idleness an expense to her kind friends, a misery to herself. She would work if work could be found. During the afternoon she ventured to indicate to Mr. St. John her wish to find something to do as soon as possible. He counseled patience and promised, in the mean time, to keep a sharp lookout for a position.

"Try to content yourself here with Lucile," he said, kindly.

"I could live with her forever," she hastened to reply, "but now that I shall be obliged to look out for myself, the sooner I face the stern truth by actual experience, the better."

"What would you like to do? I understand," he continued, interpreting her look, "but while we are at it we might as well try to find something congenial. If that is not possible, why then we can try for the next best, and so on down to the end of the list," he said laughingly.

"Now you are laughing at me," said Regenia, a little discomfited.

"Oh, no, indeed; not at you, but rather at my own thoughts. I was thinking as I spoke how far down we should go before you cried, 'Hold, enough!' I was wondering if at the end of the list we found a laundry, how long it would take you to rub out both patience and muscle?"

"I have determined to do any kind of house work rather than eat the bread of idleness. Of course I have my preference, but no choice," she added with a sigh of resignation.

"How would you like to teach?"

"Better than anything else. You may put that at the head of the list. I love the little folks so dearly, that I cried when my six weeks in the 'School of Practice' were ended," she said eagerly.

He did not reply to her enthusiastic expression of preference, but arose and hastily left the room. He shortly returned bearing in his hand an open letter, which he silently passed to Regenia.

"Write that I will accept the position," she said, rising excitedly.

"You are not going now, are you?" he asked with a smile. "At least, you will say good-bye to Lucile," he continued, his smile now spreading into a broad grin.

She either did not hear or ignored his question. Sitting down, as if forgetful of where she was, she asked earnestly: "How far is it to Grandville?"

"Too far to walk to-night. Had you not better wait and take an early breakfast and a fresh start to-morrow morning?" said Clement.

"Oh, Mr. St. John, do not trifle with me, I am so much in earnest."

"So I observe," he replied.

"What is the matter?" said Lucile, coming in just as her husband was finishing his observations.

"Nothing, only I have just informed this young lady of a school away down in 'Dixie,' and she wants to start off walking before supper," replied Mr. St. John with a merry laugh.

Well he knew what heart drippings awaited this enthusiastic young woman in her eagerness to rush into an unknown world. His jolly laughter was only the cloak that disguised the pity which filled his big, loving heart.

"Of all things," said Lucile, "teaching is the last which I should wish to try. Why do you want to go down into that heathen country? It is bad enough for a man, let alone a little frail mite like you," she said, slipping her arm around Regenia's slender waist. "You stay here with me, I was just thinking a moment ago, Clement, it would be nice to teach Regenia stenography."

"I would rather teach," Regenia replied. "I believe it is my work. I have determined to accept this place and try it, anyway. If I do not like it, I will come back next summer and learn stenography."

So it was decided that Regenia would go South and take up the ferule and the pointer. Mr. St. John wrote immediately to the trustees of Grandville that he had secured a teacher, and on New Year's night, after much good advice and as many precautions as if Regenia were going among the cannibals of the South Sea Islands, Mr. St. John and Lucile kissed her good-bye and bade her God-speed.

AT WORK.

Chapter XVII.

It was with feelings of fear bordering on despair that Regenia Underwood alighted from the coach the second morning after leaving Minton. She had pierced through to the very heart of the South, an absolute stranger. Armed with a letter to Rev. Mr. Foggs, she set out, carrying her traveling bag, on a hunt for this much desired person. It was through this gentleman of some importance in the community where he lived, that Clement had obtained the position that Regenia so readily accepted. After some inquiry of the hangers-on, always about the station, she secured a hack and was driven to the parsonage. The parson was at breakfast and Regenia was received by his good wife, who, with true southern hospitality, invited the young girl out to breakfast.

Regenia wanted no second invitation. Her scanty lunch-box had been turned bottom side upward and thrown from the car window, long before the sun had closed his burning eye the evening before.

She was tired, hungry and sleepy, a trio of discomforts, which when added to loneliness, made a combination hard to outweigh in the scale of misfortunes. While Regenia is enjoying her much needed refreshment, let us take a little glimpse at the place in which she is to meet humanity in every form for next few months.

On a little knoll in the centre of clump of trees, near the outskirts of the city of Grandville, stands a neat white building. The school house has been recently erected. The knoll on which it stands slopes gently for some distance until it reaches the banks of a babbling brook whose clear waters laugh and frisk over its shallow bed. A rustic foot-log, hewed smooth on one side and made safe for passengers by a rude guard consisting of a hickory pole placed between the forks of two uprights nailed to the above-mentioned log, formed the approach to the school. The building had desk room and seating capacity for sixty, but was expected to accommodate more than twice that number. The school was new because the necessity for it was new also. A Northern syndicate had recently established in the vicinity of the school, a large steel plant. The workmen about this new enterprise were for the most part, Afro-American. The company, with far-seeing generosity, had almost immediately erected two churches and a school house; well aware that around these institutions, so highly prized by the Negro, could be best made permanent a happy and contented class of laborers.

The Afro-American, unlike any other people similarly circumstanced, believes in God and intelligence. Toward these two ideas he inclines with unerring instinct. He may be irreligious; he may be ignorant, but with all the strength of an over-enthusiastic heart, he believes in the church and the school. The shrewd Yankees knew this, and planned their campaign of cheap labor with gilded generosity, accordingly. It was the generosity that pays, the religion that brings shekels with its contentment. The children of the laborers at this new plant were to be the recipients of the syndicate's generosity. Regenia Underwood thenceforward would share with them their sorrows and misfortunes and through them hear more acutely the heart-throbs of this sin-burdened world than she would have heard in a century at Mt. Clare.

As Regenia entered the dining room, Rev. Foggs pushed his chair back from the table and walking around a number of little Foggs, made his way to Regenia, and grasping her hand with a warmth too genial for comfort, welcomed her to such hospitality as his table afforded.

"Make yourself at home," he said, re-seating himself and tucking his napkin under his chin, "you must be hungry after your long ride. How far have you come? I received Mr. St. John's telegram yesterday, but supposed you would not arrive until this afternoon. How did you find me, anyway?" he continued, not even deigning to await a reply to all of these questions. When he was at last satisfied that he had asked about all the questions he could think of, he paused for a reply.

Regenia answered his series of questions in a general way, which seemed to satisfy him until he could get time to cut another huge rasher of ham and fill his plate sufficiently to begin a new siege of stuffing and talking.

The breakfast being over, Mr. Foggs busied himself getting Regenia's things together, preparatory to escorting her to her boarding place.

"You will find Mrs. Landers a most excellent woman," he said, after Regenia had thanked the parson's wife for her kindness, bade the group of little Foggs good-bye, and started off with her new found clerical friend.

To this information Regenia very discreetly made no reply.

"I have known her for years," continued her escort, "and she has always been a consistent Christian. She is one of the leading members of my church and stands very high socially," he volunteered. "As soon as she heard you were coming, she sent over to tell me that she would take you," he continued.

He might have said, if he had been nice about little truthful expressions, that he was at Sister Landers' very hospitable home when Clement St. John's telegram reached him. In fact, if the truth must be told, when Rev. Mr. Foggs was not at home, it was safe to predict that he could be found at the house of this most excellent woman. Mrs. Landers kept a very excellent kind of brandy and soda, a decoction for which it is painful to relate, Rev. Mr. Foggs had a decided partiality.

"Does Mrs. Landers live near the school?" Regenia finally ventured to ask.

"No, not very near, but near enough to give you a good appetite after the walk," said Mr. Foggs, eyeing his companion narrowly.

"Mrs. Landers lives in the city," he continued, "but your school is out in the suburbs, in the vicinity of the steel plant. It is a little walk from here," he said, as he rang the door bell of a large sombre brick building. "But after you become accustomed to the journey, you will rather enjoy it than otherwise."

As he finished the last sentence, the door was partially opened and a pair of lynx-like black eyes peeped out at the two visitors. It was thrown wide open when Elder Foggs' bland voice cried out, "Good mornin' Sister Landers, this is Miss Underwood."

Mrs. Landers came forward, took both of Regenia's hands into her big brown palms, and said, "Welcome to Grandville, Miss Underwood."

The woman that Regenia saw standing before her was a thin, wiry individual, neither black nor brown, but a soft shading off between the two, a color not unknown among Afro-Americans, raven black hair, little sparkling watery black eyes, and an obsequious, overweening manner that was intended to inspire confidence, but had exactly the opposite effect upon our young heroine.

Mrs. Landers bade her visitors to be seated and after indulging in the ordinary commonplace, thought necessary on such occasions, she showed Regenia to her room. The poor child was glad at last to be alone. She lost no time in lowering the blinds and throwing her tired form across the bed, where she slept until called to dinner.

Mr. Foggs threw himself upon one of the large sofas in the room and with the contentment of one who is perfectly at home availed himself of the prerogative of his cloth to enjoy a tête-à-tête with Mrs. Landers.

It is well to mention at this juncture, that the Rev. Ananias Foggs was a powerful man in Grandville. His name was a tower of strength among the members of his faith and order. In appearance he was rather striking. Dressed always in full clerical attire, his vest buttoned to the throat, a white cravat, that reminded you that perhaps there had been a time when it was immaculate, but that time was in the grim and dizzy long ago; a shining black hat, sleek in spots, looking for all the world as if it had been treated with beeswax and tallow; black trousers, ornamented with tobacco juice and bulging slightly at the knees; rattling grey and white celluloid cuffs and collar; smoothly shaven saddle colored face, large gray eyes; of medium height, inclined to stoutness and a self-conscious, self-important air, will give an excellent mental photograph of Rev. Ananias Foggs. He always carried a book in his hand, in order, as he himself expressed it, "that I may seem deep."

Rev. Mr. Foggs was a very friendly man; in fact his friendliness was so fullsome, especially after a prolonged stay at that "most excellent woman's," Mrs. Landers, as to be tiresome. He was, of course, an educated man—educated from above downward. He had begun his intellectual structure at the cupola. He had commenced the study of theology when the third reader was a mazy dilemma. He was said to be an erudite Greek and Hebrew scholar, but judging from his pronunciation, English was to him a foreign language. He had a head full of other men's ideas, indiscriminately mixed. He was an adept in the theories and disputes of Augustine and Thomas Aquinas, but in the vast sea of independent generalization, he was without a helm, rudder or sail. His sermons were a combination of bluff, bluster and crocodile enthusiasm, and he had reached the highest pinnacle of pulpit oratory when he had hypnotised his hearers into a wild orgy of muscular gyrations—motion rather than emotion. A conscious hypocrite, he misled rather than directed the native devotiveness of an ignorant people. No sermon was complete that did not end in a shout, and to this end he regularly wound up his noisy diatribe with a pathetic description of the dead or dying, which, as he expressed it to those in his confidence, "was sho' to fetch 'em!"

With all of these defects, the character of Rev. Foggs was not without its redeeming qualities. He was generous and hospitable to a fault. No traveling brother in straightened circumstances ever left his home hungry, or wanted a bed to rest for the night, who could not find it for the asking at the open door of the humble parsonage. No night was so dark that he could not find his way to the rude homes of the sick and dying. He had a weakness for preaching funerals. His obituary efforts were noted for miles around. Judging other men's frailties by a knowledge of his own, he found it easy to throw over their indiscretions the mantle of charity and stretch to the point of breaking his rigorous creed, if need be, to assure their friends that the dead had passed the grim portal in perfect safety.

It has been previously stated that he was a regular caller at the boarding house or lodging house of Mrs. Landers. Mrs. Landers, as far as anybody knew, grew up with the town of Grandville. She had owned that large brick house and lived just as she was living the day Regenia entered her door, for so many years that the community had ceased to conjecture about her age and solved the tireless enigma by considering her a fixture. She did not look a day older than she had looked twenty-five years before. He hair was as black, her step as light and her ability to get on in the world as pronounced as it had been at anytime during all the years the community had known her. She was wonderfully fond of pretty young girls, and never seemed to be so thoroughly happy as when surrounded by them in her home. There were those who nodded their heads and smiled knowingly when Mrs. Landers' name was mentioned. Some even doubted her loud amens and moments of entranced happiness during Sunday services, but by regular contributions and a whispered suspicion that she carried under her black bonnet a knowledge of the frailties and mishaps of many of the leaders of the congregation, for a quarter of a century, enabled her, in spite of her enemies, to hold her state unchallenged in church and society.

Mrs. Landers enjoyed the friendship of many of the oldest white families of the city; what tie bound them was not disclosed, but it is certain that, some of them seem to come and go, night and day from her door; what their mission was, is not known, but no one seemed to question their propriety. Into such a home and among such people goes Regenia Underwood to make her maiden effort at bread winning.

When Mrs. Landers came down from Regenia's chamber, she invited Rev. Foggs into the dining room, where she set out a bottle filled with brandy, some sugar and water, and bade him enjoy himself while she busied herself with her morning's work. The Elder sat by the blazing fire, alternately snoozing and in his moments of wakefulness mixing with the deftness of a veteran his favorite drink.

After awhile he went out into the kitchen, "making himself at home," as he called it, and kept the widow company until dinner. He was very talkative during the meal and once or twice the shrewd Mrs. Landers felt it her duty to interpose, to keep Regenia from seeing in Rev. Foggs' rambling, hilarious conversation, something that might prejudice the young girl against him.

The dinner was at last ended, to the infinite relief of both Regenia and Mrs. Landers. Regenia was tired and longed for quiet and rest; Mrs. Landers had the good sense to see that every moment, the possibility of Elder Foggs' making a fool out of himself was measurably increasing.

After many promises to call around the next day and escort the new teacher to school and introduce her to the pupils, Regenia was permitted to slip away to her room and think over the incidents of the past few days and plans for the morrow. The shades of evening had fallen around the dimly lighted streets before Elder Foggs, his steps still unsteady, made his way back to the parsonage.

TEACHING THE YOUNG IDEA.

Chapter XVIII.

Too much praise cannot be awarded the brave-hearted girls who leave without a murmur their pleasant homes and agreeable companions and in answer to the call of duty or necessity, go forth alone into an untried world to take up the burdens and responsibilities of life. Friends at home never know what they suffer. If one real chapter from their lives, with all of its sorrows, temptations and unmentioned privations, could find its way to the happy firesides they have left, it would fill the doting parents' hearts with sadness. Regenia Underwood had few to regret her mishaps, or condole her sorrows. She was alone in the world, and a world, too, in which she was in many respects a stranger. Reared in an atmosphere of ease and refinement, she was illy prepared for the uncouth side of life she was so soon to enter. She was, of course, well educated. Without a thought of ever having any practical use for her education, she had finished the High and Normal school courses in the city of Mt. Clare. She never dreamed, when spending her six weeks in the "School of Practice," that stern necessity would some day demand an application of the knowledge attained. As she sat by the flickering wood fire, on the first night of her stay at Mrs. Landers,' she ransacked her brain to recall any little scrap of theory concerning the first day in a new school, she had heard with indifference, if not with actual impatience. In vain she wished for some of her old notebooks, packed away in some dark closet at Mt. Clare, perhaps to be remembered, but never again to play any part in the real work of life. At last, by dint of hard, constant thinking, she managed to recall a few facts which would serve as a beginning, contenting herself with her partial preparation and relying on circumstances for future developments, she went to bed, to dream of schools of fretful children, stern trustees, and duties but indifferently performed, till the loud rapping of Mrs. Landers the following morning awakened her to meet her fate.

Her breakfast was not more than half finished when the door bell rang and the cheery voice and loud laugh of Mr. Foggs was heard in the front parlor. True to his promise, he was on hand to escort the new teacher to her school. To Regenia, Mr. Foggs, with all his kindness, had grown to be a somebody that she must tolerate, but could not esteem. His want of modesty, his coarse, unintentional familiarity filled her with a nameless dread. His exhibition of himself the evening before, concealed as it was by Mrs. Landers, had not escaped her sharp eyes. She was unaware, it is true, of the cause that had so transformed the man who had assumed a virtue, if he had it not, on the morning she first met him, but it was evident to her inexperienced eyes that Mr. Foggs was no better than he should be, considering the sacred office that he filled. She had therefore resolved to pursue his friendship no further than necessity compelled.

When she came down to the parlor prepared for school, she found Mr. Foggs impatiently awaiting her. He was conscious that his behavior the evening before was not of a nature to increase the new teacher's good opinion of him, and, therefore, he attempted to repair the supposed injury that his dignity had suffered by a liberal dose of politeness.

"Ah, good morning," he said, advancing to meet her and rubbing his hands expressive of his delight, "I hope you rested well and that you are in prime condition to wield the rod," he said, taking Regenia's hand and giving it another of those vise-like contractions that almost made her scream with pain.

"I am very well," she said, wincing with pain and extracting the ring that had buried itself in her tender flesh during the bear grasp that Mr. Foggs called handshaking.

"It is a beautiful day," he said as he opened the door. "One of those rare winter days that you never see in your climate."

And it was a beautiful day. The warm rays of the Southern sun fairly penetrated Regenia's heart as she walked along. As she listened to the incessant flow of Mr. Foggs' wagging tongue, she felt for such a day in January she could really feel happy, even in the company of Mr. Foggs.

"You have never been South, Miss Regenia?" he queried, as they walked along.

"Never before," replied Regenia.

"Then you have missed half your life. You will find us a broad-hearted, kindly disposed people, entirely different from what we are represented to be; entirely different," he added, repeating himself without apparent satisfaction.

"I should be very much surprised to find you other than kind. Hospitality is considered one of the cardinal virtues of southerners," Regenia ventured to say.

"Your school is over there," said Mr. Foggs, pointing toward the knoll, where Regenia could see a white building nestling among a clump of trees.

"How beautiful," she exclaimed. "It is not so far, after all," she thought. So busy had been her own thoughts that she had not observed the distance passed over.

"There are the children," she said, as she saw a number of little girls, bolder and less patient than the others running down the hill and across the foot-log to be the first to meet her. They stopped half afraid to come forward and greet her.

Regenia's woman's instinct immediately mastered the situation. She called out a pleasant good morning and taking each of them by the hand, she thanked them for being so thoughtful as to bring their greetings. The children answered never a word but walked back to the school, the fortunate ones holding her hands, while the others, with wide-eyed admiration, followed along behind.

A strange procession they made, the rotund, smooth-faced Mr. Foggs, the slender, refined girl, dressed in deep mourning, and the accompaniment of girls, of every color, age and size. As they reached the school, others came forward, boys and girls, some leading their little brothers or sisters, who hung back in awe of the new teacher. As they entered the school, Regenia was surprised to find every desk appropriated and the children sitting there as orderly as if the master had just stepped out, leaving them on their honor. Long before time to ring for the opening hour, she divined the cause of their phenomenal behavior. There were more pupils than desk room, almost two for one, and happy indeed was the pupil who by dint early rising had got there in time to seize and hold a desk. The less fortunate ones stood around the walls or seated themselves on the platform at the teacher's feet. When the bell tapped for order, those that could not find seats, crowded into the seats already occupied, to the discomfort, not so say disgust of the first possessors. Regenia did not know what to do. She gave her own chair to a disappointed little one who had had a seat in the beginning, but had been hustled out by some of the more aggressive. She cast her eyes at the chair held down by Mr. Foggs and inwardly measured the time that would have to elapse before she could give that to some of the children.

As she read the Twenty-third Psalm and looked out on the motley crowd of waiting children, she never before felt how precious were those simple words: "The Lord is my shepherd." Asking the children to rise, she bade them repeat after her the Lord's prayer. Solemn as the moment was to Regenia, she could not help noting that hand in hand go the sublime and ridiculous. Some of the children, in rising for prayers, kept one hand on the seat they had vacated in constant fear that some less devoted pupil would steal into it during the solemn moment. Others knelt—knelt on their seats and even then opened their eyes occasionally to make certain that they still held their own.

After the opening, Mr. Foggs blew his horn, and while he plastered Regenia with florid compliments, he did not fail to make plain the fact that she was there through the energy and forethought of Rev. Mr. Foggs.

Having finished his remarks, principally complimentary to himself, he left, after offering to call that evening and see that Miss Regenia found her way back home, an offer which Miss Regenia modestly but firmly declined. The exit of Mr. Foggs was a relief in more ways than one. In the first place, Regenia was anxious to secure his chair to seat a bright-eyed little boy who had been crowded off the platform and was sitting, with his bow legs doubled up under him, on the floor, the very picture of forlorn disappointment. In the second place, she was growing rather restless under the continual stare of so many pairs of eyes and wanted to begin work, but was not desirous of any company more critical than the children.

What to do first, she scarcely knew. It was evident that so many things were necessary that she hesitated where to begin. Finally as a sort of compromise between discordant intentions, she asked those who could read to come forward. According about half of the school rose as one man and made a rush for place in front of the platform. There was crowding and pushing, and tears and angry looks among the children that came forward, while those that were seated on the platform, at the teacher's feet, mostly small children, rolled themselves up like a spring curtain to save their toes from being trampled. Regenia smiled at the picture. She found on examination that there were almost as many grades and as many different kinds of readers as there were children. She separated them as best she could, putting them in temporary classes, according to size, and then, after seating part of them, finally succeeding in bringing a kind of order out of the chaos.

The children were eager to learn, for the most part kind and obedient, and in many a rough exterior, the teacher was not long in ascertaining that an angel slumbered. Books were the greatest hindrance to progress. Whole families had come to school, carrying, by turns, one book, the sole possession of four or five. The one book was expected to serve them all, irregardless of gradation. One little boy, a stranger to the intricacies of the alphabet, brought a dog-eared edition of the Old Testament. Who gave it to him or what he was expected to do with such a book was not apparent, but that he prized it highly was evident from the great care he took in keeping it constantly near at hand. No rollicksome game on the play ground could induce him to surrender for a moment the guardianship of that book—a lesson from which older and wiser heads might profit.

The first day had not ended before Regenia discovered that the poetry of the situation was every moment growing more prosaic. She saw before her nearly one hundred of raw nature's children; children coming from all kinds of environment; children whose little hearts, perchance, were to be for the first time thrilled by a gentle word; children that were unlovable, because they had never been loved. In their crude existence, she was for the first time to send a loving influence that would change their ideals, soften and subdue their hard lots, aye, prove the very savior of life unto life to many of them.

It was with a heavy heart that Regenia closed her school that day and slowly took her way down the hill, across the foot-log and set her face resolutely toward home. She indeed wondered if from these sad-eyed boys and girls trudging along at her heels she would ever be able to accomplish any lasting good. Comparing her school with the well ordered schools of her childhood, she had her serious doubts. She could not see, for the future is veiled, that forth from those surroundings would issue an influence whose power for good would water the barren places of time and tell in eternity. She little thought that sitting at her feet that day were boys whose noble lives would tell on the future, that from the lofty pinnacle to which some of those very children would rise, they would tell of her influence and bless and glory in the fact that she was born.

She stopped a moment in her reverie, and turning her thoughts from the school and its future, looked down the valley toward which the little stream was making its way, toward the black smoke of the Steel Plant. Flanking it on all sides stood row after row of shacks, as they are called— one-story frame houses stripped on the outside, unplastered and forming a refinement of the old quarters famous in slavery days. Here lived the parents of the children she was to teach. The houses for the most part contain two rooms and a loft, where the children, by the help of a ladder, climbed to sleep. Some of these houses were occupied by two families and not infrequently contained a boarder or two besides. The workmen came from every part of the state where colored men had opportunity to engage in skilled labor. It is useless to say that such environments and such a place, especially in its formative period, is a very hot bed of ignorance and vice. Hardly a night passed that forth from the low dives that were everywhere prevalent, some human being was not ushered, shot or cut to death. Whisky never more certainly performed the work of its fell master, the devil, than among these hard working Negroes on the outskirts of Grandville.

Before she had been many weeks a teacher, the children insisted that Regenia accompany them to their homes and meet their parents, a proposal she readily accepted. She soon learned to move in and out among the rough crowds that stood about the doors of the shacks with as much confidence that she would be kindly received as if she had been at her own home. It was noticeable how the loud talk was subdued, and with what politeness the greatest swaggering bully about the furnace lifted his hat when Regenia passed by. In short her amiable disposition and unostentatious kindness soon made her the idol of the children's parents as well as of the children.

About a month after her arrival in Grandville, as she turned the corner on her way home from school one evening, she came face to face with Dr.

Leighton. She knew him instantly, but hoping he had not recognized her mumbled out an excuse and hurried on.

"I have been up to your boarding house, Regenia, and had started out to meet you," said the doctor pleasantly.

Regenia, being cleverly caught, turned and spoke to him. "What in the world ever brought you here, of all places?" he said, friendly extending his hand, which she pretended not to see.

"I am winning my way as a teacher. What are you doing?" she interrogated in sharp contrast with his friendly greeting.

"This is my old home. I came to see my folks and also to look after you," he said laughingly. "You dropped out of the world so suddenly last December that finding you again comes in the nature of a resurrection."

"I am contented and well employed, and while I thank you for your solicitation, I am in no pressing need of a guardian," she said, giving the door bell a sharp jerk.

Mrs. Landers, came hurriedly to the door to ascertain who rang so imperatively. Seeing it was only Regenia, she lifted her eyes indicative of surprise, but spying Dr. Leighton, remarked, "Oh, it is you, doctor, come in."

If Regenia had thought to escape Dr. Leighton by taking refuge in Mrs. Landers' boarding house she was not long in discovering her mistake. Frank Leighton was better acquainted with this "most excellent woman" than Regenia ever would be, if she spent the remainder of a long life in her company. The doctor, therefore, not in the least abashed, entered, closed the door, talked as long as he desired, and after signifying his intention to call often, took his departure.

AN OLD NEW FRIEND.

Chapter XIX.

It was with premonitions of dreaded contact with Dr. Leighton that Regenia left her home for the school room the morning after the meeting described in the previous chapter. Around every corner, as she hastened to and from school she expected to come face to face with him. During the morning and until the last tardy pupil had come trooping in, her nerves received a new shock at each opening of the door. Her fears were unnecessary. Dr. Leighton did not annoy her with his presence for many days. He had wisely surmised that his sudden meeting with his cousin had served to increase rather than to lessen her fear of him.

The dictation of a wise policy, therefore, kept him out of sight until the old dislike consequent upon his unexpected appearance, was somewhat allayed.

On one Saturday afternoon, allowing a few weeks to elapse, the doctor called at Regenia's boarding house. He found her in the parlor, idly running over some music she had recently purchased.

Regenia drew back as if to leave the room when he entered.

"You need not run, my dear cousin, I do not intend to eat you up doday. You are not in prime condition," he said with a laugh, referring to her attenuated appearance.

"The life of a school marm does not seem to agree with you," he continued, interrogatively.

Reginia, addressed in such a frank way, could not consistently withdraw.

"I have never been an Amazon," she said, laughing at the picture her words called up. "I have been flattering myself that I have grown stouter since I saw you last," a shade of sorrow instantly flitting across her face, at the remembrance of their last meeting at Mt. Clare.

Dr. Leighton immediately changed the trend of the conversation; it was verging toward a subject he feign would have blotted from the tablets of his mind.

"And do you really like your work?" he said, betraying an interest in her occupation he did not feel.

"Better than anything I ever did in my life," she enthusiastically replied.

"I can easily believe that," he said, laughing in his old way. "In what work or business did you engage previous to you entering upon the present fascinating pastime?"

"You understand what I mean," she said, laughing also. "I am truly fond of my work and love the children dearly. In fact, I never seemed to have lived or had any right to do so before. Now it is so different. I seem to be living with a purpose: living for one's self is not half so noble as living and laboring for others."

"A very excellent sentiment and wonderfully becoming to you my philanthropic little cousin, and one that would make the world happier, did everybody act upon it. The charity of the most of us, I fear, too often begins and ends in the same place—at home," he added.

"It would not begin and end there, I am sure," she said, "were it not that most people lack opportunity to have brought to their doors, through actual experience, the old heaven-sent truth, 'It is more blessed to give than to receive.'" Regenia, like most young people that have not been tainted by temptation and soiled by sin, refused to believe the world as sordid and self-centered as it is often portrayed.

"And yet, with all your faith in the ultimate good, that dwells native in the human heart, you pack up and run away from the only person whose right to look after you would pass unchallenged in any court in the world. How do you reconcile your faith with your actions?" he asked in an injured tone.

"Oh, I do not try to reconcile anything. I only know I could not have remained in Mt. Clare another day if I had been sure death awaited me only a few miles from the place. I was so bereaved, so thoroughly miserable with my double sorrow that death anywhere in the wide round world would have been preferable to life at the 'Elms.'"

"I can understand," he said kindly, "how you must have felt, but do you think I was happy? Two mysterious disappearances in so short a time unstrung me also. If you had only indicated that you wanted a change, I should have been glad to have offered any assistance consistent with my duty, as your guardian. But to have you leave as you did, with the ink that advertised the other lost one scarcely dry, put me in a whirlpool of crossed purposes, painful to relate," he said, covering his face with his hands, as if to banish the distracting remembrance. Dropping his voice and speaking as if struggling with his long pent up feelings, he continued: "I am at a loss even to surmise what designing wretch, playing upon the credulity engendered by your recent great sorrow, could have persuaded you to take a course so unnatural, so contrary to what would have been expected from a girl of such an open trustful disposition as I know you to have."

"I did what I thought was best then and what I have thanked God every day since that I had the courage to do. I sought advice from no one, I simply followed the promptings of my own heart. I am past the years when the law requires that I should have a guardian, yet I am grateful to you," she said, relenting a little, "that you offered to act in that capacity. As I had to make my own way, I resolved the sooner I set about it the better, so, taking counsel with my own sense of right, I could not be dependent upon any one for my subsistence. Through the help of very kind friends, I obtained an opportunity to come here. I came and have nothing to regret."

"You were left, a not very liberal allowance, I admit," the doctor replied, "but of course, you must have understood that I intended to supplement that sufficiently to permit you to live on just as you had been living all your life."

"Very true, and I so understood it, but changes come and I would have perhaps been obliged to take up the burden of life when less inclined to bear it, so it is the best for all concerned that things happened as they did. You meant well by me, and I may have acted unadvisedly, not to say unworthily, but as all is well that ends well, let us each take up the threads of our fallen shuttle and weave away, careless of the texture of the cloth, conscious that the great loom master will credit us for our diligence at the last."

As she said this, she rose, indicating that the interview had shaped itself to a finality.

Dr. Leighton rose also, and, extending his hand, said: "Now that we understand each other, I hope that we shall at least be friends."

"As you like it," said Regenia, taking his hand. "I have no wish to be unfriendly to you or to judge too harshly what was perhaps providential," she said, as the doctor bowed himself down the steps.

Dr. Leighton owned to himself as he lighted a cigar and sauntered aimlessly down the street, that he had not accomplished his purpose as easily as he had intended. "How the girl has changed," he muttered, "thoroughly self possessed and as beautiful as Venus."

She had changed. The weak, weeping girl that he had thought to make the plaything of his caprice, had passed through the school of adversity since the day she left him in the library of her deceased relative. Some girls are never women; others leap to that estate, by suffering, in a day.

The sands of time, ran on in their usual groove. The changeable winds of March, followed by the showers of April, had given place to the delightful days of May. Dr. Leighton came in now and then to pass an hour, spend an afternoon or listen during the long balmy evenings, to Regenia play, but oftener to bring some piece of new music to sing. These calls were not sufficiently frequent, nor so illy timed as to excite remark. The doctor had told Mrs. Landers frankly of the relation he bore to Regenia, and that discreet dame, pandering to an innate love for southern aristocracy, secretly rejoiced that she kept beneath her roof someone so nearly allied to this scion of "blue blood."

Regenia spent a great deal of her spare time among her pupils. No place was too humble, no home too sordid to daunt the missionary spirit of this sweet young woman. Like an angel of mercy, she moved in and out among the people, carrying the sunshine of a helpful sympathy wherever she went. If somebody was sick, some pupil detained to home, forth after nightfall sallied Regenia, to administer to the sick or look after the delinquent. She brought to the homes of the poor and neglected something more than the necessities of life. For while she administered, too often, it is to be feared, from her meager wages to their physical wants, she threw around them a subtle refinement, a gentleness of touch, a subdued sweetness more lasting than temporal blessings.

One evening as she passed out of one house into another just across the way, to make a last call, and spend a quiet hour with a sick scholar, whose convalescence seemed to depend upon her daily visits, she observed, as she entered the house, a buggy standing beside the board walk in front of the door. She turned the knob with gentle and continued pressure and glided like a sylph, unannounced, into the bed chamber of her little friend. Her intuition told her in a moment that a change for the worse had come over the patient. She heard the doctor and the mother of the child conversing in a low tone in the adjoining room. The little boy was groaning with pain and talking wildly. She knelt beside the bed, and stroking the sufferer's head, began to talk to him in that low, soothing key that the gracious Father has given only to the angel heart of woman. The doctor noted the cessation of hard breathing and with a motion toward the mother to quiet her fears, stepped lightly to the open door. As he started to the door, in his heart, he verily believed all was over. He stood a moment as if fixed to the spot. He rubbed his eyes and looked a second time. Kneeling at the bedside, her sad sweet face beside the little sufferer, her hat filled with loose roses, daily brought to comfort him, the child, under her magic touch had gone to sleep.

He motioned to the mother, who seeing Regenia, could not be restrained but pushing past the astonished doctor and clasping the girl in her big strong arms, lifted her to her feet, exclaiming: "God bless your dear life! You are an angel sent from heaven, I do believe!"

"He is sleeping now," said Regenia. "Oh I hope he'll be better by morning."

She had not noticed that a third party was an interested observer. Seeing the doctor, she gave a little start, then instantly gaining her self-control she faced the stranger, whom in the dim light she failed to recognize.

Reaching out his hand, he said: "Do you not know me, Miss Underwood?"

"Dr. Stone!" she said, unable to hide her astonishment.

They stood there for some moments holding each other's hand, both too full of the thoughts of other days for utterance.

"This is indeed a doubly fortunate meeting—fortunate for the child, whose life not my medicine but your influence has saved, and fortunate for me. I never thought when I hurried out here tonight that my visit would be fraught with so much happiness."

"Nor did I think of seeing you," she replied.

"What a change from the scenes that surrounded us when last we met," said he, trying to divine if she too recurred to those happy days with regret.

"Pleasure then, but an hour of this is worth a lifetime of that," she replied, thinking of how little idle hours of fickle folly are to be compared with earnest sacrifice for the good of others.

"It depends upon the value of the standard we use a unit of comparison," he replied, thinking how readily he would exchange a month of the half-payed responsibilities of his thankless lot for about an hour of that blessed, care-free conclave week.

"I did not know you were in the South," he continued. "How long have you been here and what mad notion of self-sacrifice has driven you from the delights of Mt. Clare and the 'Elms' to try conclusions with the world in this hamlet of sin and vice?" In his heart he disliked the very idea of Regenia, the sweet Regenia of his dreams, living and laboring among such surroundings.

"To answer your first question," she said, "I have been here since last January, and while it will despoil my mission of half its poetic glamour to confess it, candor compels me to say that not fanatic notions of self sacrifice, but stern necessity, if not a harder, a more exacting master, brought me here to win my bread by teaching."

"You here and a teacher!" exclaimed the doctor, not knowing whether he was more astonished or delighted at the news his ears were hearing. "Where are you stopping?"

Regenia named the street.

"Oh, you are up in town. I drive past there. You will let me give you a lift?" he said, drawing on his gloves and hastily giving a few final instructions to the mother of the sick child.

After promising to return the next morning on her way to school, Regenia bade the grateful mother a cheery good night and was handed into Dr. Lotus Stone's buggy, where, as they drove along, never faster than a walk, the moon's broken reflections fell on a new life for them both.

THE CLOSE OF SCHOOL.

Chapter XX.

When Lotus Stone graduated from the College of Physicians and Surgeons, he was for weeks undecided where he would begin the practice of his profession. He certainly did not intend to settle in Grandville. From the very first he had, however, turned his eyes southward. Why he preferred the South has been previously mentioned. Weighing the advantages of two places, toward which his mind had inclined, he wrote to his old school fellow at Minton for an opinion upon the relative advantages of the places selected. In this letter to Clement, he stated at large, his view of the probabilities and drawbacks that might attend the beginning of his professional life in either place. To this friendly renewal of the confidence which had been somewhat shattered in the months that had elapsed since their conclave experience, Clement made an immediate reply. He did not, however, favor either of the places, between which Lotus was inclined to make choice, but recommended instead the flourishing city of Grandville. He pointed out the advantages of the new industrial life the place had taken on, and demonstrated the fine opening for surgical practice that would be sure to come to him through the daily accidents occurring about a plant of this description.

Clement was too well acquainted with the unreasonable pride of his friend, however, to give the reason uppermost in his mind. Dr. Lotus Stone went South, confident that he was leaving Regenia Underwood and his heart under the waving elms of Mt. Clare. What his feelings were the night he found the angelic apparition pursuing her deeds of mercy among the shacks on the outskirts of Grandville is left for the reader to conjecture.

As they drove along through night, beneath the moon-lit, southern sky, a sense of serene contentment which had never before experienced stole into the heart of the young doctor.

"What an unexpected delight," he said. "I cannot realize that it is not an evanescent dream. Miss Underwood at Grandville! The thought is too preposterous to be true."

"And yet you are here. Can you not reconcile yourself to my presence as well as account for your own?" she replied lightly.

"I cannot say I can. My intention from the first was to come to the South. If you remember, your ideas were decidedly against it."

"'Circumstances alter cases,' says a wise old saw, and I am as enthusiastically in favor of the South as the place for work and race development tonight as I was opposed to it when we discussed the subject last," she said.

"Where are Mrs. Underwood and Mrs. Levitt? How I have lived over the few bright days spent in Mt. Clare. That conclave, to me, I have often thought since, was the one glimpse of paradise given a man at rare intervals on this earth of sad regrets and bitter disappointments," he said, lost in the afterthought which his mention of Mrs. Underwood and Mrs. Levitt's names recalled.

"The first is dead," replied Regenia with as much calmness as she could command. "Mrs. Levitt, poor, poor dear, no one knows what has become of her."

"I did not know that," he said apologetically. "Pardon me, if, in my ignorance, I have given you pain."

"Apologies are unnecessary," she said. "Ask me what you will. It seems ages since I heard from kindly lips the mention of those two names. Your reference to them is rather in the nature of a blessing than otherwise. Grandmother died the night Lucile and Mr. St. John were married," she hastened to say. "I was not at home and know but little of the cause of her sudden demise. Mrs. Levitt left home to go to church a few Sunday nights following and has never been heard of since. Dr. Leighton advertised and employed detectives to search for her, but the only evidence of her existence ever disclosed was her shawl, left near the ferry landing, at the foot of Scranton street.

"And left alone," he repeated slowly, "your property in the hands of Dr. Leighton, you came South seeking bread? Oh, the burning shame of it, that Dr. Leighton could permit anything so revolting!"

"No, you do the doctor an unintentional injustice. He possesses the property and offered to take care of me, but I refused to accept his offer and came forth into the world of my own volition to support myself."

"Brave little girl," said the doctor, attempting to take her hand. Regenia drew back. He instantly saw his mistake and hurriedly asked, "Does St. John know of all this?" He asked this in a half resentful mood, not knowing whether to spend his chagrin on the inoffensive head of his old friend or apologize for the thoughtless familiarity his sympathy had betrayed him into.

"Oh, yes, I told Lucile and Mr. St. John everything. Mr. St. John is my best friend. Through his kindness I came south."

For the first time it occurred to Lotus why Clement had sent him to Grandville, and if he had ever felt angry with his big-hearted friend, the remembrance of the service he had done him in directing his footsteps to Grandville made ample amends.

"Have you heard from Mr. St. John lately?" she asked archly.

Lotus was on his guard in a moment. He divined that she was trying to ascertain whether the knowledge that she was in Grandville had not figured largely in sending him there.

"Clement and I have not corresponded regularly since I left Washington. I am ashamed to confess the fault lay at my door, however. I am a poor letter writer."

"So I have observed," she said reproachfully. She would have given a great deal to take those four words back. "What must he think of me?" she thought.

"He thinks you an angel," is what he would have answered if he could have listened to the murmuring of your mental graphophone.

He said: "And are you a better correspondent? It seems to me that you some times fail in that respect as well as myself."

"Promptness in letter writing is my one virtue. I never received a letter that I did not answer."

"Did you never receive a letter from me?" he asked excitedly.

"Never," she replied.

"Then we have an enemy, that will not scruple at anything to—to make us unfriendly. I wrote to you from Washington as soon as I reached that city. I also wrote you twice from New York. I concluded that you did not care to pursue my acquaintance further."

Regenia listened to what he was saying as if stupefied. The old question recurred, "Who is my enemy?" The old answer was on her lips—the accusation which she had mentally made a thousand times, but ties of consanguinity restrained her.

They were nearing the house. As the buggy turned the corner into Fourth street, Dr. Leighton, leaning against a tree on the sidewalk, beheld a sight which made his heart stand still. Dr. Lotus Stone and Regenia drove up to Mrs. Landers.' The doctor alighted and assisted Regenia to the curb, stood there until the door opened, then entering his buggy, drove rapidly past Dr. Leighton a second time, in the direction of the Steel Plant. Dr. Leighton watched the buggy until it was lost in the darkness, then uttering a terrible oath, crossed the street and entered a near-by saloon.

As Regenia bade Dr. Stone good-night, she invited him politely to come and see her some time.

The words sang in his ears as he drove along in the moonlight. "Come and see me some time," he said over and over, now in a whisper, now half audibly. "Come and see me some time," as if he would not, he thought. Come and see you, I would if every window pane in that old brick house was darkened with a siege gun. Faster and faster he drove until the red light of the furnace was only a reflection in the distance. The unspoken yearning of his heart filled him with a wild desire to drive on and on until day should come and with it one more sight of the woman he loved. How he loved her he had not realized until chance again brought them face to face. He thought of Clement, and, reining his horse, turned toward Grandville and drove back home to write to Clement, beg his forgiveness for the negligence of the past, and tell, above all things, about Regenia.

The next day seemed so long Dr. Stone could not endure the wait until evening, but drove out to see the sick child he had visited the night before. He excused himself to the mother by saying that he was called out there anyway, and to save two trips came to her in the afternoon. He said the same thing to Regenia. He was called to see a patient and dropped up to look in on her olive branches incidentally. He remained, however, until school closed and drove Regenia home.

Dr. Stone had not been in Regenia's company a second time until he saw what Dr. Leighton had discovered, the Regenia of Mt. Clare and the "Elms" was not the self-possessed young lady whose shadow he was preparing himself to follow about the city of Grandville. If he booked upon the former friendship between himself and Regenia, he was soon made aware of his mistake. Throwing the past to the winds, he commenced anew to study the object of his intended conquest. Madly in love, from the very first, the doctor was unable to hide the face from the sharp eyes of Regenia. She received his visits however on the same footing which any other young man of the city came. With native cleverness, she succeeded in hiding her own feelings from the blind eyes of the enamored doctor. He knew he loved her to distraction and only wanted an opportunity to declare his love. This opportunity Regenia always managed to elude. On the brink of a declaration, she would suddenly leave the room, if out driving she would naively call his attention to some sight or scene that tended to drift the conversation in an opposite direction. In this way matters stood at the close of her school. Schools closed the last of May. It was indeed a trying time to Regenia; days of exacting labor and sleepless nights of nervous headache. She had more than once declared to Dr. Stone that she did not believe she could hold out if school closed the last of June, as it does for the most part throughout the North. The children were as excited and anxious about the last day as their teacher. To them it was a day fraught with momentous import. At last the day came and with it such a crowd of proud mothers and doting indulgent fathers as the building could not have contained if it had been twice or three times its present size. Both the teacher and school had in some way gained a notoriety beyond the confines of the Steel Plant and the city on whose outskirts it stood. Many persons from the city and even trustees of country schools from the neighboring districts, had made it a point to ride or drive in to the city to be present at the closing exercises of Regenia's school. Dr. Lotus Stone, of course, was present; also Dr. Frank Leighton. These two gentlemen, together with a number of the clergymen, of large and small fry, were there to give dignity to the occasion. Chief among the latter class was the Rev. Ananias Foggs, his vest buttoned to the throat and wearing a new white cravat probably not more than five or six months old. Those who could not pack in the house, hung in the windows, and made life in that room anything but pleasant. The examination, as it was called, but to the initiated it was only a rehearsal, was pronounced to be a tremendous success. The work was indeed commendable to the intelligence and painstaking labor of the teacher. Near the door on a table were displayed specimens of the pupils' writing. These specimens, together with the copy-books, were put into the hands of a committee to decide which was the best and awarded the prize to the successful competitor. Dr. Stone, Dr. Leighton, and one of the ministers were chosen by Regenia to perform this important function. While the committee was making its decision, the time of all times to the Afro-American, was spent in telling the children how they (the speakers) would have improved this chance if it had only been offered them, a statement, however, which must be swallowed with due caution, judging from the way some of them have improved their time. The committee finally reported and Dr. Leighton was asked to present the prize. This he did in such a pleasing way that not only Regenia and her visitors were delighted, but Dr. Stone was obliged to relent some of the hard things he had been thinking of his professional brother. The trustees held a meeting at the close of the exercises, elected Regenia to take charge of the school during the year next ensuing and also made arrangements for an assistant. Regenia was highly pleased with the complimentary things which both Dr. Stone and her cousin poured out without restraint.

She drove home with Dr. Stone. The next day Regenia was to leave Grandville for the North. Dr. Stone sought in vain that evening to draw her aside and declare his love, but she adroitly avoided every intrusion of sentiment.

When the doctor left that evening he held out his hand to say good-bye.

"Not good-bye but adieu. Will you not see me at the station?"

"No," he said. "I will send the buggy around. I am engaged at the very hour your train leaves," he replied, holding her hand.

"Then I shall not see you again?" she said, evincing no little disappointment.

"Not until you return." His grasp tightened. He thought he felt a return of the pressure.

"Will you not let me say just one word?" he pleaded. "Will you not at least hear my confession? Do you not love me, just a little?"

Her head lowered, and turning she said, "Now good-bye, and oh, I shall thank you and think of you ever so much when I get away from here."

The next day the doctor's buggy drove Regenia to the station, but Dr. Stone had to forego a pleasure that was hard to bear, but what could he not bear when the happiness of the women he loved was at stake.

MRS. LEVITT.

Chapter XXI.

Standing at the one window of the room where we left her six months ago, prematurely old and gray beyond recognition, looking out at the grim lighthouse and watching the glinting rays of the setting sun as their reflections fall aslant the restless waters, is Mrs. Levitt. Sometimes praying, oftener singing and talking to herself, she passes her days within the enclosure of those four walls. Believing herself forgotten by the world, she begins to wear the look of stolid indifference characteristic of the hopeless.

Several times in the last few months, almost crazed by the gnawings of hunger and the bitter cold, she has been on the verge of betraying her trust and for the sake of freedom, disclosing her knowledge of Mrs. Underwood's last wishes. At such times, however, she would think of Regenia and what an opportunity it would give Dr. Leighton to wrong her and bearing her misfortunes she had resolved to hold out a little longer. Escape she has long since despaired of. The lighthouse-keeper's wife had on several occasions showed that only fear of the cruel brute she had promised to love and obey kept her from treating Mrs. Levitt with the leniency her age and sex demanded. If Dr. Leighton had searched the world over he could not have found a man more thoroughly devoid of human qualities than this drunken lighthouse-keeper. A human vulture would have been an angel of sweetness and light beside this man. He had answered a heart-rending plea of Mrs. Levitt's, during the coldest night of that long severe winter, to be allowed to come out and warm, by a most unmerciful beating. The wretch kicked and bruised the helpless old woman until fearing he had killed her, he slunk off to the lighthouse and remained all night.

When his wife drew Mrs. Levitt out to the fire and bathed her bruises, she was more dead than alive.

"Why did he not kill me?" the old lady gasped. "I should much prefer death to the life I am living."

"I am so sorry, but he's in his cups, and when he's a drinkin' there's no doin' ner livin' fer 'im. If I'd said a word he'd like as not pitched onto me."

Mrs. Levitt was not long in detecting the note of true sympathy in the woman's voice.

"What do they intend to do with me any-how? I am nothing but an old woman, of little account to myself and of less service to anybody else."

"Dear me, dogged 'fi know what they mean. Laws-a-me! That man wouldn't tell me nothin' fi's a dyin.'"

"How can you live with such a brute?" said Mrs. Levitt indignantly.

"He's my man. An' I s'ppose if fi didn't live with him, plenty others would."

"May be so," replied Mrs. Levitt, growing sleepy under the influence of the warm fire. "Let me sleep here before the fire to-night, won't you? If I was to die in this house from ill treatment there would be no living here afterward."

"Why, ye wouldn't come back, would ye?" queried the woman, shivering with fear at the very thought of such a probability.

"Of course! My spirit would hover around that lighthouse and in this room as long as they stayed here," said Mrs. Levitt, now fully awakened to the fact that by playing upon the woman's superstitious fears, she might obtain, at least, a little more humane treatment.

At that moment a gust of wind blew the door open, and the light which flickered and sputtered in a pan of swimming fat, went out.

By the dim glare of the wood fire, burning low, the shadows of the waving trees fell in weird and grotesque figures on the walls of the room. The coincidence was providential. The woman stealthily walked to the door and pushed it shut. She came back to the fire and stood stretching out her long, lean fingers, while she narrowly watched Mrs. Levitt.

Finally, lighting the tallow dip, she said: "I've often heern kullard folks could conjure. Kin you do that?"

"Don't trouble me now," said Mrs. Levitt, "I am sleepy."

The woman pulled Mrs. Levitt's bed in before the fire, helped her into it, blew out the candle and went to bed herself. From that time forward, she secretly connived at many little privileges Mrs. Levitt took.

The only incident concerning this story necessary to relate is the plan Mrs. Levitt devised to communicate with her friends. As the summer came on she was sometimes allowed to sit in the door while the woman, who was for the most part her guard, worked in the garden or about the house. This was a coveted privilege. Mrs. Levitt's rheumatism made escape impossible.

One day, seeing some hunters come by and knowing that they would probably pass that way again on their return to the city, she racked her brain for some device to send a message by them. At last she fell upon this plan: she procured a strip of brown paper and with a piece of charred wood sharpened to a point scratched these words:

"I am a prisoner at Lighthouse, N. W. of Mt. Clare, on road crossing Scranton street Ferry. MRS. LEVITT."

She did not believe that Regenia was still at the Elms, and as she could think of no other address, she turned the paper over and scrawled on the back: Mr. Lotus Stone, Washington, D. C.

This she concealed about her clothing and watched for the return of the hunters. A few days afterward she succeeded, by dint of bribing and playing upon the superstitious fears of the lighthouse-keeper's wife, to smuggle the note into the hands of one of the hunters and get his promise to properly address and mail it.

About this time Dr. Stone was beginning to reap golden opinions in the practice of his profession. Regenia was with Clement and Lucile and Dr. Frank Leighton, secure in his possessions, had begun to congratulate himself that "All is well that ends well."

* * * * * * * *

Let us look in on Dr. Lotus Stone, who seated by the window on this June evening, is reading his first letter from Regenia. There is a look of disappointment on his face as if the contents of the letter were not to his liking. He reads it over and over again, vainly trying to extract some meaning from between the lines that he is morally certain is not there and ought not to be there, and no one would have been more surprised than he if it had been there. Yet he is looking for it. The letter is frank and informal to a remarkable degree for a first letter. She tells him all about Clement and Lucile and the kind friends in the North and how they were all talking of him the evening she wrote, and at last one little word that a less obtuse man than Lotus Stone would have seized upon and hugged the flattering unction to his heart. This was the sentence: "I have not forgiven you for not coming to the station to see the last of me."

As he sat there musing over the letter, Dr. Leighton came in. The doctor had called several times since the incident at the closing of Regenia's school. Lotus was not only pleased to talk with a physician of Dr. Leighton's experience and well known celebrity, but flattered to have him call. Lotus Stone was neither vindictive nor suspicious. The pleasing manner and apparent interest which Dr. Leighton evinced in the success of the young physician was not long in winning, to a limited extent, his confidence. This evening he brought some book of rare value to the profession and asked Lotus to keep it and read it. This kind of treatment is not at all unusual in the South. The educated professional men of all classes are rarely unkind to their brothers in black. It is to be doubted if in the North there is half the courtesy between professional men of opposite races as there exists in the South. In this way Dr. Leighton and Dr. Stone often spent an evening investigating some subject or discussing some disputed point in which the older man's wide experience and thorough scholarship gave to his opinions on some subjects the weight on an authority.

"Hello! reading a letter from your girl," he said cheerily, as he entered. "I have brought you the book I was telling you about."

Lotus folded the letter, placed it in his pocket, and picking up the book, remarked: "Thank you. I'll look over it when I have time." And while he turned to the index of the book to look up a subject on which he wished to compare the assertions of the author with one of the well known opinions of one of his favorites, Dr. Leighton picked up the envelope, glanced at the postmark, and said: "From Regenia. How is my fair cousin?"

"All O. K.," said Lotus.

"Where is she? She promised to write to me, but I suppose she naturally thinks of you first."

"She is at Minton at St. John's," Lotus replied.

"I remember him. Wonder you wouldn't marry Regenia, Doctor?"

"I wonder if I wouldn't if I could get her over to my way of thinking. She don't seem to go in for that sort of thing much," said Dr. Stone, laughingly.

"You don't use the right kind of bait. Ask her again. Any woman will marry you, if you are persistent enough."

"It has not gone that far. I would not ask a woman to be my wife unless I had more assurance of making her a comfortable living than I have found in my present locality," said Dr. Stone.

He changed the subject and the two men sat there smoking and talking until far into the night. When Dr. Leighton left Dr. Stone's office, he swore by all the stars never to go there again on any pretext. He knew in part now what he had every reason to believe before. Lotus Stone wanted, and ultimately would, marry Regenia. So far his suit was not successful. Regenia has Leighton enough in her blood not to "show her hand until she is ready to play her cards," he said aloud. At heart, he rather liked Lotus Stone. But having taken so many chances in the desperate game he was playing, should he let professional courtesy keep him from separating these two people? If he did not fear Dr. Stone's superior intelligence would ferret out the real reason why Mrs. Levitt disappeared, he might go further and do more—produce Mrs. Levitt herself—and thus balk entirely the game that up to the present, he had played without an error.

Lighting a cigar and drifting into a saloon, he found a worthless spittoon cleaner, sitting there nursing a broken leg.

"Hello, Abe, what's the matter?"

"Down wid broken laig, doctah."

"Why didn't you come around and let me fix it up for you?"

"I had that new fellow to fix it up for me, but I don't believe he knowed what he was doin,' 'pears to me its worse now than it was at first."

The doctor examined the leg and found it had been set once and before the fracture healed it had been broken again in the same place.

"Who did you say reduced this fracture?" asked the doctor.

"What you say, Massa Leighton?"

"Who set the bone for you?" repeated the doctor.

"Oh, that new doctah—What's his name? Oh, yes, that's it! Dr. Stone!" repeating after Dr. Leighton.

Taking the half-drunken, wholly profligate old negro into a back room, the doctor reset the broken limb and ordered him home, to remain until his leg was better.

sentiment to enter, would have been disgraceful to use for cattle. The air was thick with every odor that burning tobacco could produce. Ribald stories went the round and bad whiskey played no minor part in the hilarity of the crowd.

The girls sat all that long night with their faces out of the windows, trying in vain to get a pure breath of air. We need not linger over the sickening details of this unhappy journey. What they suffered that night would be harrowing to relate. At daylight, to the intense relief of two passengers, at least, the train reached Grandville. The girls dragged themselves from the coach and hurried to Regenia's boarding house.

Still smarting from the refusal of Dr. Stone to see her off when she left in June, it was with feelings akin to resentment she went down to meet him on the night of her arrival. After the usual greetings, she introduced her friend, who came with her.

Miss Wilson, for that was the girl's name, immediately launched into an unreserved denunciation of the treatment received on their way to Grandville.

"You must look for that sort of thing here, but do not denounce too severely the employee, as he said, he was only obeying orders," remarked Dr. Stone.

"No orders could ever make a real gentleman rude to a lady," answered Miss Wilson hotly. "I never wished I were a man before yesterday. If the men of our race had half the courage of the women, they would stand by their rights to the bitter death."

"That would be about the size of it," said Lotus coolly.

"What would be the size of it?"

"Death, that's all," said Lotus lightly.

"Well, one has but one time to die. I would rather a thousand times die in defense of my rights than live a cowardly poltroon, the scorn of every self-respecting man on earth. Is life so sweet or existence teeming with so many awaiting pleasures that to hold on to a few more uncertain days of it, we must suffer any indignity if we may only be allowed to live?" asked the angry girl.

"All you say is true enough, but it is hard to get discreet men to act upon your advice. We all like to live, I hardly know why unless it is because we are built that way," said Lotus, laughing, "but to be serious, it is probably the hope of a better day that restrains men from flying into the face of fate and heroically surrendering their all to let the world stop long enough to sigh: 'One more unfortunate.'"

"Is it getting better, Doctor, or worse?" asked Regenia. "As one by one the old safeguards once thought necessary are being removed, I confess my faith in a better day is growing weaker."

"The better day is coming, if, in the language of an old friend of mine, 'It's away off.' Just as the asperities that once existed between the North and South are gradually melting away and the old fraternal ties are being more endurably welded, so, against all reason, perhaps, I believe that the real heart of the South is measurably softening toward us. The reign of the poor whites has reached that point where it is a stench in the nostrils of the better classes everywhere. We must not lose faith," he said, nodding toward Regenia. "We must look into the frowning face of blackest night of the rosy hues of coming morning, have faith to believe that though the gathering clouds of social and political despair will break the glorious sunlight of a new emancipation."

"It is helpful to listen to the avowal of such faith, but in the fierce light of the past day's experience I am unable to agree with you," said Miss Wilson.

"Our greatest hope lies in the noble women of our race," said the doctor, politely.

"Our greatest hindrance, perhaps, in our cowardly, lecherous men," said Miss Wilson. With this parting shot, she excused herself and left the room.

"I suppose it is patent to you why I did not accompany you to the station?" said the doctor, as the door closed after Miss Wilson.

"Not exactly," said Regenia.

"If you had not been accompanied on your return, the second trip South would have been as barren of annoyance as the first. If I had escorted you to the station in any other capacity than servant, you would have left Grandville in a smoking car. Under those circumstances you would not have returned. For ten minutes' pleasure I would have sacrificed many happy hours," he said, laughing.

"I should have preferred my friends to accompany me to the station, if a smoking car did loom up as the result," said Regenia.

"Certainly you would," said Lotus, "and for that very reason none of your friends would unnecessarily subject you, through their thoughtlessness to that indignity. It is glorious to have the power of a king, but it is tyrannical to use it. Your unselfishness is proverbial; should I be less unselfish? You would risk all for your friends, but he would be a selfish man indeed who would permit you to do so when threading the perils of a lone woman on a southern railway car."

The doctor soon departed. As Regenia lowered the gas and started to her room, she nearly collided with Mr. Foggs, as he hove from the dining room, breathing like a freight engine going up grade, and pulling about as heavy a load, considering the difference in horse power.

"Ah, Miss Underwood, come and shake hands with me, I haven't laid these two eyes on you since your return. Mrs. Landers informed me this evening that you were back among us," he said, trying to stand still.

"I am very glad to be back," said Regenia politely.

"Come and give me a kiss, won't you?" said the Reverend, bracing himself and starting toward her.

Regenia moved further away, but was evidently speechless with indignation and astonishment. As she attempted to escape him and pass through the door, he caught her by the hand and attempted to embrace her.

"What do you mean?" she said.

"Don't get angry. I don't mean no harm. You do not make so much fuss, I lay you, when that white doctor tries to kiss you," he said with a satanic grin.

Regenia's anger knew no bounds. She unloosed his grasp and before she thought had given the lecherous, drunken old hypocrite such a slap in the face that the impact awakened Mrs. Landers from her doze in the kitchen. The sudden belligerency put forth by Regenia, by its very energy, frightened her from the field.

It sobered old Foggs sufficiently to make an untruthful explanation to Mrs. Landers, and present Regenia's side of the case in a most uncomplimentary light. Regenia had not heard the last of that foul slander repeated by Mr. Foggs. From that night, whenever the young girl's name is mentioned, he will, with many expressions of unbelief, repeat the story connecting it with Dr. Leighton's.

Thus it is ever: the cormorants of society, whenever their familiarities are rebuffed, wreak their vengeance upon the innocent by sly insinuations intended to ruin the character of those who defend their honor.

BEHIND PRISON BARS.

Chapter XXIII.

When Regenia awakened the next morning the sun was high in the heavens. The accusation made by Mr. Foggs, together with his coarse familiarity, had served to keep her sleeplessly tossing from one side of the bed to the other the most of the night. She came down to a late breakfast still nervous and excited. For the first time during her short life she felt the poisonous sting of slander. Conscious of her innocence, she knew how impossible it is to defend a pure life against the insidious touches of that hidden serpent—a lie. She knew too well that error traveled like the hare; while truth took the gait of the tortoise.

Mrs. Landers observed the forlorn look in Regenia's face as she left the table, her breakfast untouched. She could not eat. The cankerous lie had already robbed her of her roses. She returned to her room, locked the door and throwing herself across the bed gave way to a fit of passionate weeping. Again and again did Miss Wilson tap at the door, only to receive no reply. She could hear Regenia's bitter heart-rending sobs, but was powerless to take her that comfort which she knew her companion needed. Regenia had gone directly to her own room the night before, and consequently Miss Wilson was in blissful ignorance of the cause of her trouble.

In the afternoon Dr. Leighton called. He sent up his card, but Regenia refused to make any answer to Mrs. Landers' repeated raps at her door. Mrs. Landers was for awhile non-plussed, but finally succeeded in opening the door. Regenia eyes and hair awry, was sitting on the bed when she entered.

"Why did you not open the door?" demanded Mrs. Landers, in a peremptory way.

"Because I did not wish to be disturbed," said Regenia.

"Dr. Leighton is in the parlor and wishes to see you," said Mrs. Landers, a triumphant smile lurking about the corners of her mouth.

"Tell him I am indisposed," said Regenia, her color heightening in spite of herself.

Mrs. Landers descended to the parlor and shortly returned with Dr. Leighton's message.

"Dr. Leighton wishes to come up and see you if you are ill," she said.

"I have no malady he can cure. Now please go away. I am sick and tired of everybody."

"You certainly do not object to seeing Dr. Leighton after striking Mr. Foggs for the mere mention of his name," said Mrs. Landers, spitefully.

"That's my affair," said Regenia, "and I am under no compulsion to make any explanation to you about it."

"You are under obligations to treat people with common politeness as long as you stay in my house," said Mrs. Landers, hotly.

"I try always to be polite," answered Regenia, "but if your company is as ill bred as that swaggering, familiar old inebriate, Foggs, I wish to be delivered from any contact with them in any way."

"You need not put on any of your high-toned airs," she replied. "Sally Landers knows a thing or two and can call the turn on Miss Regenia Underwood, as well as a good many other high steppers in this town if she is a mind to." She fairly hissed these words out as she left the room, slamming the door after her.

Regenia had risen from the bed, where she had been sitting. She stood there like a statue for some time after Mrs. Landers, in a towering rage, had left the room. What to do she hardly knew. She was not long in reaching a decision. Necessity is a great "encourager of hesitancy." She washed her face, put on her hat and went over to Miss Wilson's room. She told her the cause of her trouble.

There was one other person to whom Regenia lost no time in relating her story and asking his advice. Rev. Simon Thomas was one of the ministers who lived and labored among the people surrounding the steel plant, because he saw in administering to the poor an exemplification of his humble Master. With him, sacrifice for the Master was a labor of love. In the midst of temptations and crime, he led the life of a saint. His sermons were a simple and free from ostentation as his life was pure and humble. He met every requirement of Goldsmith's ideal preacher:

"Who pointed to heaven,
And led the way."

His wife, "Mother Thomas," as she was familiarly called, was a fitting companion for such a husband. In her works of charity she had met Regenia and learned to love her. It was therefore into sympathetic ears Regenia poured her tale of mistreatment. When she had finished, Mrs. Thomas said to her husband, "Simon, go out and get an express and send it over to Mrs. Landers' to get Miss Underwood's trunk."

Then turning to Regenia and putting her arm around the young girl's shoulders, she said: "You will stay here with us, dear. We understand you."

How often had Regenia heard almost the same loving words when she had gone with some of her troubles to Mrs. Levitt. It all came back now as her troubled head lay upon Mother Thomas's shoulder, and the load of pain and anguish floated away with the tide of grateful tears that chased each other down her cheeks. After a while the good woman said: "Come to your room, dear, and lie down until supper. By that time Simon will have your trunk sent up."

As Rev. Simon Thomas was an ideal minister so his home was an ideal home. His house, the only two-story frame about the steel plant, had been the dwelling of the original owner of the land from whom the syndicate had purchased the site for their new enterprise. In time, Regenia was thoroughly domesticated, not as a boarder, but as a member of the family.

Monday came and with it the re-opening of school. The division of the work and the new classification necessary, kept Regenia so fully occupied that she had hardly time to think of the sorrow that overshadowed her. Weeks ran rapidly into a month before Regenia was reminded of that most pleasant of all days to a teacher—pay day.

Dr. Leighton had tried every way to see Regenia, but for a month had signally failed. At last he went to the school. Regenia received him as she would have received any other visitor, but went on with her work as if he was not present. He remained until school closed, hoping in this way to have word with her. If he hoped to force Regenia to recognize him, he was not long in learning his mistake. Having dismissed school she called two of her girls, and taking them by the hand, she walked to her home. Dr. Leighton could scarcely hide his chagrin.

Dr. Stone hardly allowed a day to pass that he did not manage to see Regenia. His fertility in manufacturing new excuses for visiting the parsonage, was as amusing as ingenious. Regenia was an enigma to Dr. Stone. He had made a dozen futile attempts to declare his never-dying love for her, but on every occasion some trivial occurrence, real or imaginary, had served to divert her from the burning issue. She had neither encouraged his attentions nor had she discouraged them. He had given her numberless opportunities to say yes, but she had not accepted them. She had also had an equal number of chances to say no, but she had not availed herself of them. Her apparent serenity in the face of his evident devotion he could not understand.

One evening in November the doctor had driven over to Irondale, as the steel plant was beginning to be called, to see a patient, and as usual stopped at the parsonage. For some reason he was low spirited and on that account was rather a grewsome visitor. Regenia was in high spirits.

"What has gone wrong?" she asked. "You are as melancholy as the oft depicted Dane."

"Nothing is wrong that is not usually so," he answered. "Am I such a dull companion that my room to-night would be more cheerful than my presence?" he asked petulantly.

"Oh, no," Regenia answered lightly. "Any kind of company is preferable to being alone. I am alone to-night."

"And as you are alone, you can even endure me!" he said ruefully.

"Don't talk like that. You must know now glad I am always to have you come," she said kindly. "Come, let us have some music. That will charm back your spirits and drive the 'blue devils' away, as poor Mrs. Levitt used to say."

"What shall I sing?" she asked, as she seated herself at the piano and began, in a dreamy way, to play. She chose something light and airy, and as she sung, Lotus sat listening and watching her nimble fingers dance over the keys.

"Now," she said, when the song was ended, "I have sung for you. Come and sing for me."

He walked over to the music rack and having selected a simple ballad, placed it upon the piano, saying, "I will sing this."

"As you like it," she said, as she ran over the prelude. Regenia thought, as she listened to the song, that never in her life had she heard such a world of subdued pathos.

"Adieu! When next our pathways meet,
When down life's stream our boats
A little space have flown
Will you forget our converse sweet,
The past, the happy past, unknown?

"Will you forget
Perchance regret
The nights ambrosial,
Days of idle dreaming;
The songs we sung
When love was young
And earth a paradise was seeming

"When the days shall lengthen into years,
And seared and yellow
Life itself has grown;
Will you resentful,
Or with grateful tears
Seal the past, the happy past, unknown?

"Will you forget
Perchance regret
The night ambrosial,
Days of idle dreaming;
The songs we sung
When love was young
And earth a paradise was seeming."

When the last note of the song ceased, Regenia arose and walked over to the window, unable to keep back the tears. Lotus followed her, and taking her hand, said: "I have waited so long, dear heart, you must hear me, for somehow, I am unable to stifle the belief that something dreadful that will separate us for years is about to transpire."

"You must not feel that way. You are only morbid, and the song has served to intensify that feeling," replied Regenia.

"Regenia, darling, I cannot live without you. You must know I worship, I adore you. Will you promise to love me, just a little?" he pleaded.

"Oh, how can you ask me such a question?" she said, her voice falling almost to a whisper.

"How can I help asking?" he replied, his faint heart sinking.

"Do you not know I love you?" she said, at the same time bursting into happy tears.

For a moment it seemed to Lotus Stone that the low ceiling of that dingy parlor was lifted into a vaulted dome and a ray of light from heaven gilded it with celestial brightness.

Pressing the drooping head to his bosom, he covered Regenia's face with passionate kisses.

"My love, my life, and are you at last my very own?" As he uttered these words, steps were heard on the porch, and a sudden noise at the window made the two loving hearts stand still. The door was opened and Mr. Thomas and his wife came in from prayer meeting.

After the untimely interruption Lotus was in no mood to prolong his stay. Regenia, making an excuse to run over to a neighbor's, accompanied her lover to the corner, where his horse was tied.

The night was beautiful. The full moon, playing hide-and-seek with the clouds, hid her face just often enough to make the night an ideal one for lovers.

Lotus insisted that Regenia go with him for a drive, but she did not accept his urgent invitation. She stood for a moment watching him, as he slowly drove away, half inclined to come back and go with him. The buggy turned a corner and she walked slowly in the opposite direction, performed the duty which she had set out to accomplish, and in a brown study was returning to her home, when just as she was entering the back gate she came face to face with Dr. Leighton. His back against the gate, standing under the shade of a giant tree, whose abundant foliage hid him completely from view, he smoked his favorite Havana with no apparent intention of moving to give her entrance.

Regenia screamed with fright, as she nearly ran into the smoking statue.

"Hush!" he said. "There is no occasion for fear." His words served to reassure her.

"Dr. Leighton, how you scared me! What are you doing here?"

"I might ask the same of you," he answered with cool assurance.

"I live here," she replied. "I fail to see the impropriety of entering my own house."

"The impropriety preceded your attempt to enter, perhaps," he said tauntingly.

"Let me pass. I will not stand here and listen to your implied insults."

"Don't be in a rush. I have had a word to whisper in your ear for sometime, but untoward circumstances robbed me of the opportunity. It is a case of now or never and I have decided to take the bit between my teeth irregardless of consequences," he said in a cold, villainous tone. She turned to retrace her steps, but he caught her by the wrist and prevented her.

"Stay, Regenia, I have something to relate that concerns your friend." Instantly she was all attention. "You might as well hear me calmly," he continued with provoking deliberation, "to make a scene and awaken the neighborhood would only injure you. You are not in Mt. Clare."

She knew too well how truthfully he spoke.

"What have you to say that concerns my friend?" she asked, her excitement having vanished at the very mention of Dr. Stone's name.

"Not so fast. We are in no hurry. What I have to say about your friend, the doctor, will keep. To return to the first question, What are you doing away from your home at such an hour?"

"I consider such a question the height of impertinence. Your are neither my guardian nor father confessor," she said sharply.

"Suppose I was both, or either, what account of your warbling lover would you give?"

"Such a supposition is preposterous, since I have passed the age when I need the first, and you are too wicked to assume the role of the second—especially with me."

"I hope you will live long enough to verify that opinion," he answered ironically.

"Oh, as to that, I have lived more than long enough to know that Dr. Leighton is not the friend he pretends to be," answered Regenia disdainfully.

"Dr. Stone comes up to your ideal I hope, judging from a painful discovery I made to-night. His theatrical platitudes were useless, however. He did well to make the most of his chances—this was his last," laughed the doctor scornfully.

"What do you mean?" said Regenia, now thoroughly alarmed for the safety of Lotus.

"He is arrested. He sleeps to-night behind prison bars," he coolly averred.

"This is some of your work. It is in keeping with what I already know of you."

"Have a care, young lady, you are in my power," he answered angrily.

"What do I care for you or your power?" retorted Regenia.

"You had better care," he answered under his breath.

"Oh, I do not fear you, coward, forger, thief, villain," she hissed.

"Shut up," he said, "or by the gods, I'll throttle you," hissed Dr. Leighton, assuming a threatening attitude.

"Do it. It will be a fitting climax to the other crimes you have committed—forged a will, spirited away, perhaps murdered, an innocent old woman, killed your own aunt, and now you are planning the murder of a man toward whom you have been masquerading as a friend. The sum of your villainies would be incomplete without my life. Take it, but remember, Dr. Leighton, there is a day of terrible retribution, awaiting you. A day when the black page of your checked career will be made manifest."

"Stop," he cried, "you minx, I will strangle you." Throwing himself upon the girl, his fingers on her throat tightened; she tried to release herself, but it was of no use.

"I'll shut your mouth you indiscreet little fool," he muttered as the girl writhed and twisted beneath his iron grip. Slowly she sank toward the earth; her muscles began to relax; she had given up to die, when a black hand from out of the darkness closed about the neck of Dr. Frank Leighton with the power of a vise. He slowly unclasped his hands from Regenia's neck, and as his face slowly turned up to the moonlight he looked into the flashing eyes of a black hero, already marked for death. The giant lifted the would-be murderer from the ground, tightening his hold until the victim's face took on the hue of his antagonist's. Walking across the road that followed the creek bank in its tortuous route, he dropped Dr. Leighton, more dead than alive, into the sand below. Then coming back, he picked up the unconscious girl and carried her into the house. He cautioned the inmates to keep the matter quiet and await developments.

THE LYNCHING BEE.

Chapter XXIV.

A SHIVER OF HORROR CREPT over Dr. Stone as he raised himself heavily from the iron bed upon which he had passed the night, on the morning after we last saw him slowly driving away from the parsonage, self admitted "the happiest man in the world." The events of that night the reader has been led to anticipate from the words which escaped Dr. Leighton in his conversation with Regenia. Dr. Stone drove home, put away his horse for the night, and had just time enough to settle himself comfortably in his chair, light a cigar and open a letter which he was about to read, when an imperative knock called him to the door. Two officers stepped inside and presenting cocked revolvers at his head, said: "Not a word; you are our prisoner."

"Permit me to get my hat, gentlemen," the doctor said coolly. "I will accompany you without protest."

Slipping a pair of nippers about his wrists, they led him away to prison. As the officers handed him over to the jailer the doctor said: "Now that I am here, you will be kind enough to inform me of the nature of my offense."

"You will find that out soon enough," the officer addressed replied, significantly. "Your crime is not a killing one," he said, relenting a little as the jailor led the crest-fallen young man away to his cell.

As the doctor raised himself on his elbow and looked around, he saw, standing at the barred window, across the room, gazing for the last time upon the rising sun, a man. His face was black, his features sharp, his form symmetrical, and the doctor noted as the man turned slowly toward him that his eyes flashed with a dangerous daring. He also discerned that the stranger wore the badge and uniform of the Grand Army of the Republic.

"Good morning," said Lotus, as the man slowly moved over toward him and sat down on the bed by his side.

"Good morning, Doctor," he replied. "I did not know I had such good company."

It was Harvey Meeks. He had been arrested a few hours before and surreptitiously incarcerated.

"You are about as much surprised to find me here as both of us are to find ourselves in such a predicament," said the doctor huskily.

"Your company is indeed an unlooked for sorrow, but I have been expecting something of the sort since yesterday," Mr. Meeks calmly answered.

"I am in ignorance of my offense," said the doctor. "Of what have they accused you?"

"Defending a helpless child, I suppose," said Mr. Meeks. "It was this way: Yesterday two boys, one white, the other black, engaged in a youthful setto in front of my grocery. A crowd was attracted before I went out to see what was the matter. The black boy being the most hardy, came off first best in the melee. I stopped the fight and thought that would be the last of the trouble. The crowd continued to hang about the store and in an hour or two had been largely augmented by a number of 'roughs.' I noticed the colored boy sitting in the store, but busy with making out my bills, to-morrow being pay day at the mill, had entirely forgotten the incident, when I was rudely awakened to the danger of the situation by hearing loud, angry voices calling the boy to come out. I went to the door, tried to persuade the crowd to leave, told them that it was only a boyish encounter and it was too trivial for men to pay any attention to. I turned to go back into the store when one of the half-drunken wretches called after me: 'You are trying to shield the little nigger, and you need a dressing down as well as the boy. You are too saucy anyhow, since you got into your new store, Harvey Meeks.' I might say here that I noticed in the crowd a rival groceryman, busily circulating among the men, and from his air and frequent gestures, knew that he was urging the excited men to loot my store. To make a long story short, the crowd seeing that they could not pick a quarrel with me, avowed their intention to come in and take the boy out. They made a rush for the door, pushed in, and advanced to take the child. The little fellow ran to me and clinging to my coat skirts, pleaded for protection. I ordered the crowd back and when they continued to advance, seized an ax-handle from the counter and engaged with them. Several bullets whizzed past my head, but in my anger I did not mind them. I whipped out of my store the whole cowardly crew, closed the door, locked it and fled to the woods. I went home last night, hoping against hope that the matter would blow over. As I left my house about four o'clock to again seek a hiding place, I was arrested. I saved the child, though," he added proudly.

Lotus sat there for sometime holding the big manly fellow's hand, and in the tears that chased each other down the cheeks of both, a sympathy which neither could have expressed in words sealed the tender compact of brotherly love so soon to be sundered by the hand of death.

"If the mob that fled before the strokes of that ax-handle finds out that I am in this jail, all the law in the state will not keep breath in my body twenty-four hours," said Mr. Meeks, sadly.

"Surely the authorities will protect you," said Lotus reassuringly.

"The sheriff holds his office by the will of that mob. I am a citizen and a soldier, but belong to the class that can be maltreated with impunity. We have no vote. Such a citizen is a non descript, a waif, a plaything at the mercy of every counter current in the sea of hate."

"Do not look at it in such a funereal way. While there is life there is hope," replied Dr. Stone.

"If it ends as I feel it will and you escape death as I hope and pray you may," he went on, ignoring Dr. Stone's words of consolation, "make me one promise, doctor. I have a wife and son. The woman can take care of herself; see that the boy is sent north and educated."

"If I live," said Lotus, "I promise to carry out your wishes."

"I did you a service last night. I saved Miss Underwood from the clutches of Dr. Leighton. I left him more dead than alive—another point in favor of my hanging," he added.

He related to Lotus the incident with which the reader is already acquainted.

"Dr. Leighton is at the bottom of my trouble," said Lotus. "He has been too friendly with me recently to pass without suspicion."

Dr. Stone was silent. As he sat there thinking over the events of the previous night he wondered in his heart if ever again those scenes would be repeated. The jailor came in with breakfast, but neither of the prisoners had the appetite to touch it. The day wore away. As the scenes of night closed in upon them, Lotus noticed that his companion grew restless; his step more quick and nervous, the lines of his face tightened as the hours dragged their slow length along.

At last as if impatient, he turned to Lotus with a look he will never forget, and said, "It must be nearly midnight. I have only a few hours to live."

He knelt by the side of the iron couch and in a low, but steady voice, thanked God for the blessings of the past, asked in childlike simplicity Providential care of his soon to be widowed wife. His voice trembled a little as he prayed for his boy. Lotus was not forgotten. He prayed for him also, and then, as if all the hopes of his life had centred around him, he pleaded again for heaven's blessings and guidance for the child of his love. Then, "Into thy hand, Father, I commit my soul. All my life I have trusted Thee, sustain me now."

Never before had Lotus Stone heard such a prayer. If through the days of his college course a doubt of the realities of Christianity had ever darkened his thoughts, that prayer had driven that doubt away forever. He rose from his knees with a look of triumph in his eyes.

"They are coming. My hour is at hand," he said resignedly. His keen ears had detected the tramp, tramp of approaching death long before Lotus was aware of its insidious approach.

"This is the cell," Lotus heard someone say without. There was a moment of deathlike stillness; then the thud of a huge half of a telephone post, told to the silent watchers within that the mob was at its work. One tremendous thud, and the huge hinges break from their fastenings—the door, followed by the telephone post, falls to the floor with a deafening crash. They enter.

Rushing along the corridors, their torches casting weird and ghostly shadows on the dingy walls of the prison, they come at last to the cell where the two men are incarcerated.

"There he is," someone cried. A wild yell, like the roar of a horde of hungry, ferocious brutes, greets this information. Lotus instinctively turned toward Harvey Meeks. He stood there, his arms folded, his head erect, the very personification of chivalrous manhood, "without fear and without reproach." The door opening into the cell was battered down and "the best citizens," as the cowardly ruffians are called, dragged Harvey Meeks from the prison. To call this vile, low born trash best citizen, is to promulgate a libel upon decency that true Southern manhood, in the name of honor, should refute.

The mob moved along the street. Harvey Meeks, the rope already around his neck, was pulled after them to the place of execution. The bystanders hurled vile epithets at him as he passed, and little boys wantonly stuck their knives into his quivering flesh. Several times, as the blood from these numberless wounds ran into his shoes and spurting out marked the trail of the serpent to the bridge where he was to die, did the victim piteously beg that he be killed outright.

"Do not cut me up by inches. Kill me like a man," he entreated.

No heed was paid to his prayer, save to increase the torture which he was receiving. At the bridge the mob tightened the rope and then ordered him to get upon the rail and jump over.

This he refused to do. "I will not kill myself," he said.

"Stand back!" said two stalwart fellows. "We'll throw the d—d old scoundrel over."

They picked him up, lifted him upon the railing and then shoved him over. As he fell he caught hold of the side of the bridge. "Let go!" they cried. Harvey, like a drowning man clinging to a straw, tightened his grip.

"Here, I'll make him let go," someone said, and drawing out a long knife, he reached down and cutting off the victim's fingers one by one, passed them to the jeering crowd, as mementoes of the occasion.

At last the dying man, for want of fingers, loosed his hold and dropped with a dull thud over the side of the bridge. As his body writhed and twisted in the air, a hundred revolvers, more merciful than man's torture, filled the swaying body full of holes, putting the struggling soul beyond the reach of misery. The blood of that martyred Christian, spilt by the relentless cruelty of white heathens, ran red in the muddy waters of the eddying river. The evidences of guilt were carried on to the father of waters, the Mississippi bore them to the restless ocean, and the accusing winds gathered them into their friendly arms and wafted them up to the courts of heaven.

Not satisfied with his bloody deeds the man who cut off Harvey Meeks' fingers, returned with some of his companions and drawing the body up, decapitated it. Attaching the rope under the arms of the corpse, he swung the ghastly, headless body over the bridge, to hang there over Sunday. Taking the head over to a neighboring saloon, the crowd pushed through the glazed doors in high glee. Two of the men, staggered up to the bar and stood there, while one of them said, "Give us three whiskies; one for me, one for Jack, and one," he said, as they lifted up by the ears the amputated head to the counter, "for old Harvey."

Dr. Leighton, throwing his cigar from his fingers, left the room. He had seen enough for one night. Of the best families of Grandville, this spotted scion of a highly respected ancestry was the solitary representative.

AT THE TRIBUNE OF JUSTICE.

Chapter XXV.

When the mob which murdered poor Harvey Meeks left the jail, the night of the lynching, Lotus Stone was so shocked at the fate of his friend that it never occurred to him to walk out of the open doors and make his escape. For two hours the egress from his place of confinement was unguarded. The sheriff, the jailor and everybody else were having a two hours' respite. They had gone to see the hanging, which if they had not aided openly, in their hearts they had connived at the work the mob had so easily accomplished.

In the early hours of the morning the jailor returned. He visited the cell inhabited by Dr. Stone and having satisfied himself that the prisoner had not taken "French leave," fastened up the main entrance as securely as he could and went to bed. Lotus Stone did not sleep a wink that night. Whenever he closed his eyes he could hear the wild yells of the infuriated mob ringing in his ears and see the firm, resigned face of Harvey Meeks calmly awaiting the worst.

All through the weary hours of that long night he sat on his iron couch, his head buried in his hands, fearfully, if impatiently, awaiting the dawn of the morrow. What a change a few hours can make in the life of a human being! Verily, existence is as the days of a hireling; life is but a tale that is told. One short day and the self-admitted "happiest man in the world" is as ready to confess that Misery claims him for her own.

When the first red rays of the rising sun fell through the iron lattice of the only window in the room, Dr. Lotus Stone was hardly less unwilling to believe, than had been his sad companion the morning before, that perhaps it would never again rise in all its glory to shine for him. One thought alone beat in upon the discouraged condition of Lotus with the certainty of fate: "Whatever the accusation against him, Regenia would never believe it true." His faith in her love was an impregnable barrier against the dashing waves of despair. Let all the world be false, Regenia, at least, would be as true as gold. It remains to be seen whether the faith, which he believed on that morning to be as fixed as the eternal certitudes, will be shaken by the trials awaiting him.

There was a marked difference between the man that the officer led out to the preliminary trial and the one he brought to jail two evenings previous. Haggard, his eyes sunken, his face bristling with a beard of two days' growth, halting steps, untidy in appearance, the elegant Dr. Stone staggered into the presence of the justice and took his seat on the prisoner's bench. The accusation was read and the hearing was begun. Lotus looked around for his accuser. He was not left long in ignorance.

Abe Johnsing, whose acquaintance the reader has made in another chapter, seated himself in the witnesses' chair. This indolent rascal, who by a strange mischance, had broken his leg instead of his worthless neck, brought suit for mal-practice. He told his story, a web of well-woven lies, concocted of course, by the chicanery of Dr. Leighton. Abe Johnsing would never have dreamed of prosecuting Dr. Stone had not the blandishment of Dr. Leighton excited his cupidity. Dr. Leighton knew that Lotus Stone had no money to pay damages, but he persuaded Abe Johnsing that he had, well knowing that with a few dollars in sight the ignorant loafer could be induced to swear away the life of his own sister. Abe Johnsing was one of those traitorous Afro-Americans who for a few paltry dollars and the deceptive smiles of such as Dr. Leighton, would sell the fee simple of their soul's salvation. "May their tribe wither and die under the righteous hate of all true men."

Dr. Leighton followed Abe Johnsing. While professing the greatest esteem for Dr. Stone, candor and professional pride compelled him to make an unbiased statement of the case of the case of Abe Johnsing as he found it.

The justice stopped him. "The court," he said, "has already heard testimony enough to hold the prisoner."

Dr. Stone asked to make a statement.

"It is entirely unnecessary," was the reply. "You are bound over to court without bail. Take the prisoner back to jail," he said to the officer. "Bring on the next case," Lotus heard the unjust judge cry out, as the officer led him back to his dingy cell.

Lotus was surprised the first day of his arrest that Regenia did not come to condole with him in his misfortune, but when two, three, four days, and finally a week had passed, he settled down to the conclusion that Regenia was no better than the other sunshine friends who had flitted about him in prosperity, only to disappear when clouds arose.

The Grand Jury sat a week after the preliminary hearing noted above; and a "true bill" was found, an indictment alleged, and Dr. Lotus Stone was ordered to appear in court and show cause why he should not be punished in consequence of mal-practice inflicted upon Abe Johnsing. It was evident to Lotus after the rank partiality evinced at the first trial, that he need not expect a shadow of justice from the stultified court of Grandville. He was given counsel, as a matter of course, but counsel without heart or sympathy injures rather than assists. He had no witnesses. Not a friend showed his face to give comfort or offer assistance, from the time of his incarceration to the day of his trial. True, he was not well known. He was a man that made friends slowly. He went to Grandville to stay, and therefore did not waste his time fawning upon the necks of half the city that thrift might follow fawning. He wisely concluded that time and merit, with close attention to his exacting profession, would bring him both friends and success. What friends he had were intimidated by the lynching of Harvey Meeks and consulting discretion, left Dr. Stone to his fate.

The day for trial arrived. The evidence was a repetition of that given in the preliminary hearing. Dr. Stone's testimony in his own behalf would have convinced an unprejudiced jury of his innocence. He clearly showed that against his admonitions Abe Johnsing had made his crooked leg more crooked, by breaking it a second time in a drunken debauch.

Why weary the reader over the details of this one-sided trial? When the evidence was all in, the judge, to the surprise of everyone, instructed the jury to bring in a verdict of guilty. It need hardly be recorded that the jury followed the judge's instructions.

The next day sentence was passed. When asked if he had anything to say in his own defense, why sentence should not be passed, Dr. Stone arose. There was a hush in the crowded court; all eyes were turned toward the prisoner whose manly bearing excited admiration, if his words could not change the intention of the court. In a few clear, well formed sentences Lotus dissected the trumped-up evidence presented by the plaintiff and then turning to the judge, he upbraided him for his rank unfairness. As he proceeded to pour out a torrent of invectives, the crowd began to cry out "Lynch him, lynch him," and pushing by the sheriff, started toward Lotus to carry out their intention.

The judge and sheriff, by dint of threats and admonition, finally succeeded in mollifying the irate citizens. Sentence was pronounced and Lotus Stone was ordered to spend three years in the convict mines and to pay a fine of two hundred and fifty dollars. He was accordingly ordered to be ready to start for the mines that night. His horse, buggy and other savings of a lifetime were seized to answer the demands of justice. He waited and hoped till the last minute that Regenia would come to say good-bye and strengthen his courage to bear up under the living death which he felt awaited him. He looked in vain. Handcuffed, he was marched off to the station. Only one soul in all that city showed him a single mark of kindness.

As he neared a corner where a crowd jeered at him as he passed, the little boy who was his patient the night he had first met Regenia, heedless of the guying by-standers, pushed out and gave him a flower. The tears flowed down his cheeks at this grateful remembrance of happier days. When the train pulled from the station, the hapless doctor still held as if a most precious antidote, the flower, a fading reminder of life's yesterday and to-day.

Where was Regenia Underwood, that she thus neglected her friend—her avowed and accepted lover? Wild with delirium in the parsonage in Irondale. The shock she had received at the hands of Dr. Leighton had left her unconscious for two days. When consciousness returned, brain fever set in and for weeks after Lotus Stone was an inmate of the convict camp, she lingered between life and death. When she finally began to convalesce, her good nurses were put to their wit's end to hide from her the facts of Dr. Stone's conviction. She finally worried so over his failure to come and see her, that the doctor feared that keeping the truth from her longer would be more deleterious than telling the whole story. The knowledge that her lover had suffered so much and was still suffering, and not a friend had been near to protest his innocence or cheer his sad heart to bear up misfortunes, affected Regenia deeply; but her physician had timed so well his revelation, and proceeded with so much tact, that the evil effects feared were warded off.

Regenia wrote to Clement St. John as soon as she was strong enough and asked him to advise her what steps to pursue to have Lotus pardoned.

She did not begin work till after the Christmas vacation. Her work no longer filled the nameless void, which widened and deepened as the days went by. With Lotus a martyr to the machinations of Doctor Leighton, life was robbed of half its charm; her school of all its interest. She grew listless, her step lost its elasticity, her eyes their sparkle, her life its elixir. The world said she was ill, her work was too taxing, and advised rest and change. Mother Thomas could have told a different story—a story of sleepless nights, tear-bedewed pillows and a heart slowly breaking with piteous sorrow for the man she loved.

THE CONVICT MINES.

Chapter XXVI.

In the midst of a dense woods, flanked on the east by a broken chain of low-lying hills, stood a convict mining camp, operated by a millionaire senator, wined and dined as a social magnate in the capital of the nation. Here, before man came to curse it with his cruelties, Nature exulted in surroundings the most picturesque and beautiful. All day long the pure mountain stream, gushing forth from a perennial spring in the solitudes of the forest, pitched over miniature Niagaras, dodged and frisked between sharp upturned rocks, grew thoughtful and sedate, as it paused for a moment of recreation, in the deep quiet waters shadowed by overhanging oaks and elms. The morning sun as he chased the shadows of night from this sequestered bower, surprised nature in a rude undress more entrancing than any clothing the facile pen or the artist's brush can depict. Here unmolested, the partridge built her nest, the squirrel cracked nuts and saucily licked his paws, while the timid deer lapped water from the laughing brook and lead through the devious pathways of the unbroken forest her brown-eyed young. Into this natural paradise, like the serpent into Eden, came man. He broke through the forest, tunneled the mountains, bridged and vitiated the stream, killed the game and in place of the song of the bird and the murmur of the stream, brought the whistle of the engine and the weird murmurs of sadness and despair. On the banks of this stream in midwinter, years before the beginning of our story, about forty wretches, handcuffed two and two, with a chain passing through links on the chain that coupled them, were driven from the railway to the spot where they were to form the nucleus of a convict's camp. The neighboring hills were seamed with a vein of excellent coal and these men were brought to open and work in the new mines. They built a "cell house" first and afterward a number of other outbuildings for the deposit of such stores as are needed about a mine.

The "cell house" was built of logs. It was a long, low structure, covered with brush, without windows and having but a single door.

In this the prisoners ate and slept. Two platforms, one above the other, gently sloping toward the centre of the building, were erected on either side. When the work of the day was over, the prisoners, men and women, were driven into the cell house; made to take the places assigned them, and after eating required to lie down. Half way between the upper and lower platforms, a chain was stretched, fastening on the outside of the cell house. This chain, called the "building chain," passing through a link on the end of the "waist chain" of each of the convicts, made escape almost impossible. Suspended from wires, throughout the building, were pine knots. These, when lighted, gave to the strange scene within a grotesque appearance. The front of the cell house was not fastened up as the other sides, but between the logs were spaces, across which strips of wood were nailed perpendicularly, through which the guard that stood without, could always command an excellent view of the interior. The building was surrounded by a palisade.

The sanitary conditions of such a place necessarily beggars description. The prisoners, with scarcely clothing enough to cover their nakedness, had no change until the clothes they wore fell apart by their own weight. Working in mud and water fifteen hours a day, with scarcely food enough to keep soul and body from divorcement, sleeping in an atmosphere thick with noxious exhalations, fetid with filth and teeming with vermin, death itself was a welcome relief. Nor was there any distinction of age or sex. Women and men, boys and girls, lived in this foul prison pen utterly regardless of the laws of morality.

The guards under a condition where no one was responsible, were cruel and vindictive. No report was given nor was any required. When a new batch of prisoners were driven in they changed their citizen clothes for the convict's stripes, were numbered and immediately set to work. Each morning the convicts were awakened at four o'clock, treated to a breakfast of salt pork and corn bread hurriedly prepared, and handcuffed in pairs, a squad chain running through links in the chain that bound them together, they were driven on a trot to the mines. Arriving at the mines they were separated into groups of ten or a dozen and hurried to the rooms or entries in which they were to work. Here from five o'clock until eight they worked without respite, not even stopping to eat. The day's work being done they were chained together as before and driven back to the cell house. The guards were armed with muskets, fitted with bayonets, and if any poor wretch too weak and hungry to keep up, chanced to fall, he was prodded with the bayonet as the squad dragged him along. The mortality was fearful. Hardly a morning's sun looked upon this scene, once a delectable garden of the gods, that did not behold a squad of "trusties" carrying some fortunate victim to his last resting place. The dead were buried in long shallow trenches. It was no rare thing to see scattered about the woods a grinning skull or a bleaching shin bone disinterred by dogs or other domestic animals.

There was scarcely any hospital arrangements. In fact, the haggard, starved victims of this cruel system rarely ever had any use for a hospital. A rude shanty covered with brush and filled with damp straw and vermin was appropriated to serve in that capacity. An accident in the mines often brought this building into use, but the convicts were worked until they were so near dead that death usually relieved them in the cell-house. It was no uncommon occurrence to a man to find when roused in the morning, that he had been sleeping all night beside a corpse. The prisoners for the most part were Afro-Americans.

The question would naturally be asked if, from a pecuniary standpoint alone, it would not have been better to treat these poor convicts more humanely? The only object the lessee had was to get every hour's work out of these men possible while breath was in their bodies. The state was glad to dispose of the expense of keeping them, whatever the consequence. And it was frequently mooted among those who knew, that whenever by reason of death hands were scarce at the mines, agents trumped up petty accusations against able bodied Negroes and secured long time sentences to the shame of justice, in the convict mines. More than one man has received a ten years' sentence for stealing a chicken, and that after the most shameful prostitution of every form of law.

Dr. Lotus Stone had not arrived at the camp before he beheld a scene that made his blood run cold and served to prepare him for what he was soon to see so often as to scarcely occasion a passing notice. When the squad of which he formed a part alighted from the train, they were taken to the commissary department, clothed in stripes and numbered. On their way to the camp they came upon a man hanging by the thumbs. The poor fellow had been there some time and writhed in mortal agony. It is customary when administering this punishment, after a short time, to lower the culprit. In this case the guard, wishing to make an example of a troublesome disobedient convict, left him hanging an hour or two beyond the usual time. He ceased to move as the squad with which Lotus came passed. They cut him down soon after—he had received his last punishment. His face seamed, his muscles knotted with excruciating pain, the haggard, half-starved wretch had passed through to that bourn from which no traveler ever returns.

"99," as Dr. Stone was numbered on the prison roll, entered the cell house that day as a man condemned to die enters murderers' row to await the day of execution. He knew after glancing around the room that unless kind heaven or the crack of doom interposed, he would never leave that place alive. The attendants about the prison regarded every new man with suspicion. He must be "broken in," as they express it.

"99" was therefore put in the first couple the morning after arriving, and when the gate of the palisade flew open, led the squad on a run for the mines. Lotus Stone had never before entered a coal mine. He had no more notion of the work he was expected to do than a man reared in a balloon. As he hurried down the incline that morning he resolved to do the best he could. He would not give up to die was long as there was an ounce of active muscle unused in his body. When the worst comes, as it surely will, "I will sink out of sight without a complaint," he said to himself.

He had hardly worked all that long day in the mud, under the constant drip from the black roof above him, before, hungry and tired, he wished for death. His room-mate, a tall raw-boned man, showed him every kindness. Taught him the art of "bearing in" and using the drill, in a way not so expensive to nerve and sinew. At the close of the first day, stiff, hungry and uncomfortable, Lotus dragged himself to the main entry and in the lead, as before, started on a trot for the camp. He kept this up the first two or three hundred yards and then endurance could bear it no longer. His head swam, his muscles relaxed and he fell prostrate. The men behind him stumbled over his prostrate form and the squad, rolling over each other, amid prods from the guard's bayonet and the terrible execrations on the head of the man who caused the accident, the prisoners scrambled to their feet. Poor Lotus tried in vain to rise, but so weak was he from hunger and overwork that try as he might he could not get up. The guard, after kicking him and sticking with his bayonet the poor tired shoulders, unfastened the squad chain and placing the first couple in the rear, ordered the men forward. In this manner, poor Lotus, more dead than alive, was dragged into camp. Shivering in every limb, he stretched himself upon his hard bed, too miserable and exhausted to attempt to eat.

The next morning when ordered out he could not rise. He attempted it but fell back in his place. "I know what you need," said the guard, "You are one them high-toned city niggers, but I'll take the shine out of you." So saying he dragged Lotus from the platform and taking him into the yard made him get down on his hands and knees. Stripping his shirt down, he applied the rawhide to his back until the blood oozed out and ran to the ground in streams. Then washing the gaping wounds with salt and water, he ordered him to rise and start on a trot for the mines.

If Lotus was too ill to go when first ordered to do so, it would seem that after this he would have been utterly incapacitated. But not so; the human will, when wrought upon by fear of death, exercises a tremendous influence over the body. After two or three desperate efforts, Lotus rose, and although verily believing every step would be his last, at the prod of the bayonet and the storm of abuse that followed him, he staggered off to the mines. He worked that day and for weeks afterward, believing each night as he lay down on his hard bed, that before the morrow death would come to his relief. Days rolled into months and still Lotus bore up under the severe trials through which he was passing. His only solace was his working mate. Often he would have given up, or brooding over this injustice of his lot would have taken his own life, but for the hope his partner, No. "47," breathed into his ear.

At last one morning after No. "99" had been in the camp about five months, when ordered out he was unable to rise. Aching all over he tried in vain to sit up and go through the farce of dressing. When breakfast had been served and the guard was going through a process called "chain search," No. "99" was not in rank.

With a muttered oath, the guard went into the "cell-house," and catching "99" by the collar, snatched him down into the middle of the room. "You lazy devil," he cried, in towering rage, "get out there in your place or I'll brain you."

Poor Lotus tried to rise. He pulled himself up by the assistance of the platform, but when he attempted to walk, staggered and fell into the guard's arms. Kicking him off with an oath, "Don't try your fits and starts on me, you miserable nigger. I'll beat your face into a jelly!" So saying, he struck Lotus in the face, felling him to the earth.

"Can't you see that man is sick?" said Lotus's partner.

He had hardly got the question out of his mouth before the guard struck him down with a pine knot that lay on the floor. "Get up, you rascal—now open your mouth again and I'll send you to hell."

The man staggered to his feet the blood streaming from the wound the jagged pine knot had left.

"Are you going?" he said, turning to Lotus, "or will I have to kill you to conquer your obstinacy?"

"I would go if I could, indeed I would. I can't stand up. Can't you see I am sick? Have you no heart, no pity?"

"Shut up your whining or you'll be sicker than you are now before I get done with you."

He called another guard to take the men to the mines; then turning on Lotus, who still lay on the floor, having tried time and again to sit up, but try as he might, each time Mother Earth would snatch him to her cold bosom, said: "I'll see if watering won't help you. If you are sick, a little washing out will do you good."

Lotus by this time was too sick to know or care what became of him. The man soon returned with a wooden pail filled with water. He lifted Lotus up and sat him against the platform. "Open your mouth," he said.

Lotus mechanically obeyed. He then began that most cruel of all the punishments practiced by the Spanish Inquisition, pouring water down a victim's throat through a funnel until the stomach distends, and pushing up against the heart and other vital organs, produces a pain not less severe than death itself. This the villainous guard continued until the head of the tortured man fell over, his arms relaxed, then became rigid, and the pallor on Lotus' face made him remove the funnel and drop the cup with fright. Rolling the poor fellow over on his face, the guard, in his excitement, did unwitting the only thing that could have saved his victim. The water spurted out of his mouth in a stream, and after some time Lotus opened his eyes.

"Where am I?" he said. "Oh, Clement, my boy, I knew you would come to see me."

The guard lifted the slender body back on the platform and with the wild talk of Lotus ringing in his ears, left him to his fate. By night Lotus was raging with an attack of fever. The guard, conscious that his last punishment had hastened the attack, begged the captain to have the man placed in the hospital. The request was granted. Here Lotus was carried and all night and for many nights afterward, his life hung on the turning of a hair. To the guard who in his ignorance and meanness had treated Lotus so illy is due the fact that he finally recovered. His chain partner was allowed to sleep at the hospital and administer what comfort his presence would afford. Hospital men were usually allowed more privileges than those in the "cell house." The habitues of the hospital were, as I have said before, men who had been severely injured in the mines and would not as a general thing have escaped if opportunity offered.

When Lotus had been in the hospital about three weeks and was beginning to sit up a little every day, his partner was brought in one night, when the squad returned, dangerously injured.

"FORTY-SEVEN."

Chapter XXVII.

Two events which occurred on the night that "47" was injured served to make the day memorial: the escape of two convicts and the wounding of the guards that attempted their capture. "47" was buried under a fall of slate about noon, and although his sad plight was discovered soon after the accident, no effort was made to ascertain his condition until late in the afternoon. When he was finally extricated from the living death he had been enduring for hours, he was simply laid upon a slack pile until the men, after the hour work ceased, would have time to carry him out.

He lay there suffering inexpressible pain until nearly eight o'clock. At that hour a squad of men placed his broken body on a board, in which plight he was conveyed to the main entry. Arriving there, he was placed upon a car of loaded coal and driven to the shaft and hoisted to the surface.

The men went up the incline, climbed the steps to the tipple and placing the body upon a skid, two squads of them, bearing the skid with their free hands, thus conveyed it to the camp.

As the men entered the tipple, it was observed that there were ten men in one squad and only six in the other. In order that the number in each might be the same, the guard released two of them from the larger squad and essayed to attach them to the smaller. In doing this he thoughtlessly set his gun against the wall.

The two men released, jumped between the guard and the gun, opened the tipple door, rushed down the steps and slunk away in the darkness. The guard fired several shots in the direction he thought they had taken, and hastened to camp to make the affair known. The blood hounds were released and taken to the tipple, where they were put upon the trail of the men.

The men in the meantime had secured a good lead, making straight for the Welsh mining camp a few miles across the hills. By the help of the hounds the guards tracked them to their place of concealment and demanded their surrender. The men had gone to the principal loafing place in the little town and poured their tale of suffering into the ears of sympathetic listeners. They had related the story of "47's" accident and the criminal neglect which had followed, the unusual and cruel methods of punishment practiced by the heartless guards, the long hours of labor, the starvation rations. They stripped off their shirts and displayed the scars which the bayonets had left. They ended all by begging if it was the intention to again deliver them to the clutches of these fiends incarnate to season justice with mercy and kill them on the spot. They said they had no idea that escape was possible, for even now the blood hounds were baying upon their tracks, but hoping that the world might be enlightened upon the condition of the poor helpless victims whose case was worse than death, they had tempted fate and came forth to give to the world some idea of their condition.

The miners were touched by their story—who with hearts would not have been? Hiding the convicts, they secreted themselves and awaited results. In due time the blood hounds, closely followed by their attendants, tracked the convicts to their lair. The miners shot the dogs and after overpowering the guards, beat them severely and sent them back to camp. There was not an honest heart in the entire vicinity of that convict mine that did not throb with pent-up hatred toward it.

The stories of heartlessness which found their way to the homes of the people living near the camp, engendered a hatred for those who conducted it more deeply seated than the proverbial dislike of His Satanic Majesty for disinterested goodness. The miners had many additional reasons for hating the system as well as the men. First, it degraded labor by coming into competition with it. Second, the convicts fill places that were the just due of free labor. Third, convict coal could be put on the market cheaper than that dug by free labor, and hence the owners of mines operated by convicts regulated the wages of those conducted by them. Fourth, a deep seated hatred, native in the human heart, against systematic cruelty.

From the above observations, the reader will gather the causes that led up to the events which follow.

The assaulted guards went back to the camp and spread the news of their adventure and after consultation, the captain, with a dozen guards on horseback and armed cap-a-pie, rode over to the mining town.

While they are riding over to the Welsh town, let us go back to the hospital and look upon the scene transpiring there. The evening "47" was brought in, crushed beyond recognition, Lotus had sat up a short time. He had taken his milk, which constituted his diet since he had been able to eat anything, and dozed off in a restless sleep, when he was awakened by the men bringing in his old partner. They deposited the poor fellow on the straw and were marched off to the "cell house."

Lotus called a guard to him and asked: "May I not try to dress his wounds?"

"You would better attend to your own ills," said the guard, laughing.

"No, but I am a doctor and perhaps," said Lotus with an invisible blush, "I can relieve the poor fellow."

"You can give me instructions," said the guard. "I'll do it."

The face of the injured man is washed, splints are secured and under Lotus' instructions the bones are set and bandaged and "47" made as comfortable as possible for the night.

The old man did not regain consciousness until about the turn of the night. About this time Lotus thought he heard someone speak and raising himself on his elbow, he listened, then he heard: "Ninety-nine, where are you ninety-nine?"

"Here I am," said Lotus, crawling over to him. He motioned to his parched lips. Lotus called the guard and asked him to bring "47" a drink of water. The guard complied.

After he had moistened his lips he said: "Ninety-nine, I have but a short time to live, and I am glad of it. I dreamed of you just now. You'll live to get out of this place. Don't lose heart," he said huskily.

Lotus moistened his lips and said: "What did you dream?"

"My dreams always come true—you'll live to get out of here and the knowledge of that fact makes death a happy release."

"How long have you been here?" said Lotus. He had never asked "47" even his name. Fearing that reference to his past might call up unpleasant reminiscences, Lotus had purposely refrained from asking the old man anything about himself.

"Ten year as nearly as I can reckon it," he said, with a far away look in his eyes, as if trying to bridge the awful space of ten years in a convict mine.

"My life has been a hard one," he continued, without further questioning. "I lived the slave to a cruel master until after the war. When I became my own master, the first thing I did was to get married. I worked on the farm year after year, sometimes coming out a little behind at the end of the year and at rare periods coming out a little ahead. We had no children. We never cared much whether we had money or not: we tried to lay up our riches," he said, raising his eyes impressively heavenward, "Where moth and rust doth not corrupt, nor thieves break through and steal."

"What a wealth of faith these old people have and how they apply what few passages of Holy Writ they know to the salvage of every wound of life," thought Lotus, as he moistened the old man's lips again. Breathing with difficulty, he continued.

"The last year me and the old woman spent together, after the year's crop was gathered and sold, the boss figured us in debt to him. I ventured to protest, when he drove us away from the place. On our way to find a new patch for the next year, we passed by a field where cabbage had been growing. We had some bacon and bread and stopped in a fence corner to cook our dinner. The field had been reaped. Standing in the field I saw a collard which was not considered worth cutting up when the cabbage had been cut. I went over and pulled it up, and boiling it with my little piece of bacon, it served to help our dinner greatly. This was my undoing. We were arrested for stealing and I was sent up for fifteen years—she for ten as my accomplice. She died of a broken heart a few months after her arrival. She could not endure this place. I used to wish I could die. I finally settled down to trust in God and stay until he called me."

Seeing the tears in Lotus' eyes, he said: "Don't cry, ninety-nine, forty-seven will soon be better off."

His voice grew weaker and Lotus could see what an effort it was for him to talk. "Don't try to talk," said Lotus.

"Take my hand, take my hand, ninety—ninety-nine—the pine knot is growing dim, it is nearly day."

For a long time Lotus lay there, holding the lean hand in his, and now and then exploring the wrist for the pulse. About four o'clock Lotus heard him say: "Night is breaking, the day is dawning—" then raising himself up in bed he lifted his hands heavenward exclaiming, "I'm coming now—I'm coming now!" and falling back on his couch of straw, the eyes of "47" closed on the sights of the world. May we hope that he saw in the beckoning distance angels awaiting him in a heavenly rest.

As he expired a gust of wind blew out the pine knot that had flickered and glared all night over the couch of the dying. The clouds rolled back and through the broken roof, a flood of moonlight fell on the bed of the dead man, shrouding it in a sheen of silver.

Lotus was roused from the reverie which the circumstances produced, by hearing gunshot after gunshot, and the far away sound of galloping horses hastily approaching the camp.

CLEMENT ST. JOHN.

Chapter XXVIII.

The trip made by the captain of the convict mines and his troop of horsemen to Welshtown proved to be an event pregnant with thrilling experiences. The air of conscious superiority, which the company had worn, when riding away from the camp was changed to the crestfallen look of the vanquished, before it returned. The arm of the law was not only challenged, but an appeal was made to the higher, if unwritten statute, which makes right more potent than might. The captain and his guard rode through the little mining town with all the haughty hilarity of a victorious army entering a conquered city. When they approached the house, where the two convicts were supposed to be in hiding, their progress was somewhat impeded. The entire male population of the usually quiet little place, had sallied forth from their homes and assembled about the point of disturbance.

The captain, nothing daunted, drew rein before the house and demanded the surrender of the convicts.

"They are not here," said one of the convicts, "and if they were, we'd see you in hell before we'd send them back to the charnel-house you keep down there in which to beat and starve men to death."

"They are our prisoners, put into our hands by the authority of the state, and Welshtown has widened its corporate limits considerably, if it is bigger than the whole state," said the captain cooly.

"We do not give a continental who put them into your care. A wolf couldn't be more gentle with a lamb than you are with your charge," the miner replied.

"If they are in that house we expect to have them. The law sanctions our right and I call upon all good citizens to assist me in the prosecution of my duty," said the captain, dismounting.

"There is a higher law—a law that existed previous to the legislature that legalized this damnable tool of cheap labor. We refuse by the law of common humanity, by the statutes of self preservation, to allow these men, to the detriment of our wives and children, to longer compete with us in the struggle of existence. If we had no hearts, if our sympathies did not go out to the poor, ill-treated, half-starved wretches, an enlightened self interest would no longer permit oppressive capitalists to use these victims of a misdirected and ruinous state economy, to glut the markets with their cheap products to the injury of free labor. This convict system is a piece of short-sighted retrenchment; it may be a saving to the state, but it means poor work at starvation wages for the miners," ("Hear, Hear,"cried the men, crowding about their leader).

"You have those men in there and we intend to bring them out," said the captain. "I know nothing about the policy of the state and less about the condition of the miners. My duty is plain. Those men have been sent to me by the proper authorities; your quarrel is with them. Until some other arrangement is made to support the men under my charge, I shall continue to work them in the mines. Give them up peaceably and settle your dispute about prices with someone that has use for your labor."

"You had better come and take them," cried a miner.

"That is just what I intend to do—peaceably if I can, forcibly if I must," replied the captain firmly.

As he said this he gave the reins of his horse to one of the guards and approached the fence. The guards quickly brought their horses into line and detaching their Winchesters, prepared to attack the crowd. As the captain advanced he was ordered to halt, but fearlessly disregarded the command.

"Halt, I say!" rang out on the still mountain air. "If you advance another step, I'll shoot you dead."

The guard, hearing this, awaited no further orders, but commenced firing into the crowd. The miners were at first disconcerted, but rallying, returned the fire from the shelter of the house, well-frame and windows. Two of the guards were shot.

The captain, discerning that they were outnumbered ten to one, hastened to his horse, mounted and ordered a retreat. The miners fired a volley after them and then a company of the bravest sallied forth in pursuit. The horses being obliged to keep to the roads, the miners, by short cuts over the hills, were able now and then to come in range of the flying guards and pour into them a deadly fire. Thus they follow them into camp.

Flushed with the success of their easy victory, the pursuers did not halt until they had crossed the creek and attacked the convict camp. For awhile the guards were able to check the impetus of their antagonists, but the miners, dividing their forces, began to pour in upon the beleagured camp a destructive cross-fire, which sent the defenders in hasty retreat, leaving the camp and the convicts in the hands of the triumphant mountaineers.

They proceeded to despoil the camp. They broke open the palisade gate, made a prisoner of the now thoroughly scared custodian of the door of the cell-house and walked into the presence of the convicts. They unfastened the building chain and freeing the captives, ordered them to take to their heels if they valued their liberty. The prisoners needed no second invitation. The convicts having vacated the cell house, the enraged miners set fire to it. They broke into the commissary, destroyed the stores and threw the clothing and other supplies about the building. Not thoroughly satisfied with their work they went over to the mines and completed the destruction. The tipple was fired, the mine flooded, the air chamber closed and hundred of empty coal cars piled up and made a bonfire of. They did not disturb the hospital. When they had fully satisfied the pent-up hatred which years had engendered toward this foul blot on the fair name of the state, they marched to the top of the hill, and turning looked back upon the scene of their late victory, their leader lifted his cap and said, "Give three cheers for the capture of Camp Hell Fire."

The men obeyed orders with three rousing cheers and a tiger. Long before the victors got back to their homes, the gray dawn had gathered about her the skirts of night and the east had changed her robe of blue, dotted with stars, for the rosy hue of coming morn.

The captain and his vanquished guard had ridden on to the telegraph station beyond the convict camp and dispatched to the governor for troops to uphold the arm of the law.

On the very morning that the bulletin boards were telling the story of the assault upon the convict mines, Clement St. John was walking up from the station of Grandville, having just arrived from Minton. He saw the crowds gathered about the corner upon which the Western Union telegraph office was located, and curiosity impelled him to cross over and ascertain the cause of excitement.

He eagerly read the news—"Perhaps Lotus has escaped," he said half audibly. "If he has, he will probably need some assistance to stay escaped," he mused laughingly.

He set down his traveling bag, took a card from his vest pocket, tore it into as many tiny pieces as possible, then as if satisfied that with the tools at had the card could not be further divided, he flung the pieces into the street, and picking up his carpet bag, retraced his steps to the station.

"It's risky business," he said to himself, "but Lotus would chance it for me."

The first train was leaving for the convict camp when he rushed out and mounted the last coach. He had just time enough to leave his satchel in the baggage room, get a ticket and catch the train. Clement St. John, more to please Regenia than to demonstrate any faith he had in its ultimate success, came to Grandville to try and secure a pardon for Lotus. The injustice exhibited at the trial, the severe sentence for such an offense, both argued eloquently against the hope of seeing his friend the recipient of executive clemency. Nevertheless, at the continued beseeching of Regenia, and urgent wish of his wife, who ceased not day nor night since first hearing of Dr. Stone's sentence, to insist that something should be done. What that something was she never explained, but the burden of her song was "Can't something be done?"

Clement, knowing how powerless he was to change the course of law, was made to feel that he had lost interest in his old friend by the constant contentions of Lucile that "something should be done." He had at last concluded that if he valued his peace of mind he would better do something or pretend to do something. Either case, he hoped, would serve to satisfy his wife of the futility of his attempt.

He arrived at what a few hours before had been the camp, about noon. He walked in and out through the smoldering embers and felt that he had come on a fool's errand. He came by accident up to the door of the hospital. He thought he heard some one groan. He took a step forward and looked again. He discovered the outline of a human being, wrapped in a dirty blanket, but motionless.

"What have we here, pray?" he said, approaching the bundle and pushing away to straw from the half-buried form.

"A dead man?" he exclaimed, starting back. The seeing another form covered entirely with straw, "Great Caesar! This must be a dead house," he said so loud that one of the figures heard the noise and stirred.

Now Clement St. John was anything but a superstitious man, but the straw shaking over what to all appearances was a corpse, filled him with an uncanny feeling akin to fear. The straw shook again, this time more pronounced than the first. Clement, throwing his fears to the wind, went over to the figure and clearing away the straw, saw it was a man.

The supposed dead man sat up, rubbed his eyes and looked at Clement for a long time. Observing the eyes of the sick man to fill with tears, Clement asked, "What's the matter, are you wounded?"

"Yes," said the man.

"Where?" asked Clement, kneeling by his side.

"Here," he replied, placing his thin hand over his heart.

As he spoke the last time, Clement raised his eyes. "My God! Lotus, is it you?"

"Don't you know me? Have I changed so much?"

"Have you changed?" thought Clement. "Even your voice is not the same."

Clement could say no more. He grasped the almost transparent hand of his friend and, shocked almost beyond the power of utterance, sat down beside him on the heap of straw.

"Have I changed so much?" said Lotus, breaking the silence.

"Not so much," he said, "but I was so dumbfounded at seeing what I supposed to be a dead man come to life, that it dazed me"

Worn to a shadow through sickness and constant labor, covered with filth and grime until his color and features were undiscernable, his hair uncombed, a shaggy beard covering his face, who that knew the elegant Dr. Stone a few months ago, could have recognized in the dim light of that log pen, the man who masqueraded as his shadow.

"What brings you here?" said Lotus.

"I came to help you to escape," said Clement. "Get up and come away."

As Clement essayed to rise, he put his hand out to assist himself. It fell upon the cold face of a dead man, and he recoiled with a shiver.

"Don't they bury their dead here?" asked Clement.

"He died last night," said Lotus, "and there has been nobody here since. The Welshtown miners assaulted the camp last night and everybody but me has taken French leave.

"You must go immediately. What on earth are you hanging on to?" said Clement, as Lotus shook his head.

"I am hanging on to life. I am just recovering from the fever and could not walk a step if I were to be pardoned for it," he replied.

"Well, I'll have to carry you, for I do not intend to leave this place without you. So you might as well dress and mount my back."

"I have nothing to dress in but stripes and you would not get very far with your load before some officer would capture us. Then the mines would have two convicts instead of one. I cannot allow you to do that, my friend. You have a wife. I have no one—" he said dropping his voice—"it don't matter so much about me."

"I'll soon get clothes enough," said Clement, leaving Lotus staring after him as he hurriedly quit the room.

He returned shortly with the very suit of clothes Lotus had worn, when he came to the mines.

"Here we are," he said cheerfully. "I'll put you back in your old suit."

He had hardly commenced to dress Lotus when looking up he saw a guard standing in the door, his musket leveled at him.

"What are you doing there?" asked the guard.

"Don't you see?" said Clement, with cool assurance. "I am trying to make this sick man a little more comfortable."

"What are you taking those stripes off for?" asked the guard.

"I think these will look better and besides, the old ones are filthy."

"Who are you?" said the guard.

"Only the governor's private secretary," said Clement, continuing to dress Lotus.

The gun dropped and the guard came forward, offering his assistance.

"The soldiers and perhaps thousands of citizens will be down on that next train and it will be as well for all of us, that this single sick man looks as if we were not as black as we are painted."

"You go and get some water and wash this man up a bit. If the governor's secretary is not afraid of him, I guess he won't bite you. When you have done that, get some clean straw or a cot, if you have one, and put this man on it. Have this dead man buried," he continued as the guard started for the water. Clement cried after him, "Where is the captain?" The guard answered and went on a trot for the water.

Clement had taken care to keep his head down and profit by the darkness of the place. As soon as the guard left, Clement said to Lotus, "I must leave you, but I'll be back and take you North with me, or die in the attempt."

"Tell the guard I have gone out to see the captain and will be in again shortly. I expect the governor himself will be down with the soldiers."

As he walked rapidly through the woods to the station, true to the newsgatherer's instinct, it occurred to him that being first on the ground, he might make a "scoop" and add a turn of business to his little adventure. He stopped in the dense forest, donned a black wig to cover his red stiff hair, drew a pair of nose glasses from his pocket and adjusted them, then hurried on toward the station. On his way he met a guard coming in with a convict. He hailed him, represented himself to be a correspondent for a well known administration paper, and stated his mission to be to get a correct report of the affair before it was misconstrued by the opposition papers. Producing his note-book, he rapidly noted the guard's explanation of the affair. He thanked him and walked on to the station.

Arriving there he learned that it would be two hours before train time. He concluded to walk over to Welshtown and board the train for Grandville at that place. Fortune favored him. He chanced to meet up with a countryman jogging along in a wagon, from whom he got a lift to Welshtown. At Welshtown he succeeded in getting an account of the affair from the other side.

He went to a hotel and wrote up the matter. In his excellent report he deftly worked a description of the solitary convict. Pictured him as stating that having been unjustly imprisoned he refused to go away with the rest and thus be hunted up and down the earth, never to be free from the ghost of the convict mines. He incidentally hinted that the case ought to be looked into. Evidentially, he added, the case appeared to be one for executive clemency. He reviewed the case of Dr. Stone, spoke of him as being a victim to insatiate hate of Abe Johnsing, whose character alone ought to belie his sworn allegation.

Boarding the afternoon train, he took advantage of a thirty-minute stop at the only place where his article could be put on the wires and sent the message to the evening papers at Grandville. He met six companies of militia about 40 miles from Grandville enroute to the supposed scene of the disturbance.

On every corner, as he walked toward the parsonage in Irondale, he heard the newsboys crying: "Latest news from the convict mines."

EXECUTIVE CLEMENCY.

Chapter XXIX.

By the smoldering wood fire, the evening paper having fallen from her slender hands, her eyes closed, her head resting on the back of the big arm chair, sits Regenia Underwood, thinking of the past. She has just finished reading Clement St. John's stirring report of the events at the mines. Through all the long weary months which have elapsed since Lotus was snatched away, he has been the center of her thoughts by day, the object of her prayers by night. She is recalling a moonlit night in the long ago; reflecting upon the loving words, remembered now with a thrill of passionate sadness. How vividly the picture comes back. How she hears over and over again the pathetic refrain:

"Will you forget
Perchance regret
The nights ambrosial,
Days of idle dreaming;
The songs we sung
When love was young,
And earth a paradise was seeming?"

She had striven to forget the song, but tonight thoughts of the past rise unbidden like a dream, and through the dreary isolation of her starved and broken heart, ring anew in a minor chord of sadness. "Can I forget?" she murmurs through her tears. "How can I forget the nights ambrosial, days of idle dreaming?"

She covered her face with her hands, while sob after sob resounded through the quiet room.

Mrs. Thomas had come in and sat down by her side, bringing that comfort she knew so well how to administer. While the two women sat there holding each other's hands, someone opened the gate. The steps approached the door. Regenia was thinking of Lotus, Mrs. Thomas was wondering when Simon had left the house. There was a ring, Mrs. Thomas busied herself making a light. Another ring, this time a little louder than before.

Regenia, after drying her eyes on her apron, opened the door. It was Clement St. John.

"Well, Miss Underwood, are you not glad to see me?"

Regenia was disappointed. She was hoping it was Lotus. Being thus addressed she made haste to give Clement a hardy welcome.

"You know how glad I am to see you. And Lucile, is she well?"

"Quite well when I left home. I have not heard from her since my arrival."

"Of course not," said Regenia, smiling. "How long have you been here?"

"I came this morning," he answered.

"And have you been all this time finding us?" she asked with evident surprise.

"No, I have been down to find Lotus," he said carelessly.

"How is he? Is the report in the paper true? Have you read it? Here it is," she said in a breath.

"No, I have not read it," he said with a quizzical smile.

She handed him the paper, pointing out the glaring head lines.

"I do not care to read any fake newspaper report," he said, waving the paper away.

"Do read it," she said. "It is so kind to my—" she colored violently—"to Dr. Stone," she added.

"Some other time," he said laughing. Then noting the tears gathering in her eyes, he said, "There, dear, don't look like that. I do not care to read my own scribbling. I wrote the account."

"You dear, good Clement," she said, calling him by his first name, "how Lucile must love you." Getting up from her chair, she walked over to the big, kind-hearted, red-headed, homely fellow and gave him a kiss.

"That's from Lucile," she said.

"I accept it for the Doctor," he replied laughingly. "If I had known such pay was awaiting me at this end of my journey, I would have doubled the length of my article with the hope of receiving double pay," he said with a knowing look at Mrs. Thomas.

By this time, Rev. Simon Thomas, who had been in the library, making final preparations for his Sunday sermon, came into the room. He was introduced to Clement, whom both he and his wife felt they already knew from hearing Regenia speak of him so frequently.

The trio gathered about Mr. St. John and listened with breathless interest while he related the experiences of the day. He touched lightly upon the condition of Dr. Stone, softened into a minimum the sufferings and deprivations through which Lotus had passed and ended with a glowing description of the heroic fortitude exhibited by Lotus in bearing uncomplainingly his unjust sentence.

Regenia's eyes expressed the thanks she could not find words to express. "Your account in the paper is very different from the version you give to us," she said, fearing that Mr. St. John had been more influenced by what his auditors wished to hear than by a strict adherence to the actual facts.

"I plead guilty to the soft impeachment," said Clement, his face assuming a questionable smile, "but the first account was to influence the public; the second," he added laughingly, "is for private consumption only. I was in duty bound to present the affair in the way best calculated to forward the ends I wished to attain—the delivery of my friend from the unjust imprisonment he is undergoing. That may not be in keeping with your code of morals, Reverend," he said, glancing at Mr. Thomas and vainly trying to ascertain that gentleman's opinion of the course pursued, "but this is one of the cases where the ends justify the means." In his heart he was thinking "What a dilemma I have got into by my twice told tale, and neither of them will stand the test of the ten commandments."

"Do you think there is any hope of Dr. Stone being pardoned?" asked Mrs. Thomas.

"You angel," thought Clement. "Anything is better than a continuancy of the explanation of why I told two tales." He said: "That depends upon how much influence we can bring to bear upon the governor. If we strike the iron while it is hot, I have every reason to believe we can secure his release."

"The account in the paper ought to awaken an interest in his favor," Mr. Thomas answered.

Clement had no wish to revert to the paper or anything it contained; having got safely away from that subject, he was determined to give it a wide berth the rest of the evening.

"If we can get the signatures of some of your influential citizens and bring their prestige to bear upon the governor, we may succeed beyond our expectations. I have been thinking we might see what we can do to-morrow," said Clement, looking at Regenia.

"Why not go to-night?" she said. "If his pardon depends upon our energy, I am ready to begin work now. I do not think I shall sleep a wink to-night, anyway, and lying awake idle will be such a loss of time, " she added, unable to suppress her excitement.

"Not to-night," said Clement kindly, "to-morrow will be early enough. Go to sleep and get all the rest you can; it will stand you in excellent heed during the work of the next few days."

It was decided that the next day Regenia, accompanied by Mr. Thomas and Clement, should take the initiatory steps toward securing a pardon for Dr. Stone.

When the sun rose the next morning and fell in golden beams through the half-open shutters of Regenia Underwood's room, it disclosed the anxious girl sitting by the window, her chin resting on her hand, impatiently awaiting the hour to begin her work. She had not been to bed. Unmindful of Clement's admonition, she knew that there would be no sleep for her eyes until at least an effort had been made to bring her lover back to her side. Mr. Thomas, too, was up by times. Indeed an air of restlessness pervaded the whole house.

Breakfast over, the three friends started upon their mission, fraught with so much interest to the sick convict, fretting his life away at the mines. The prosecuting attorney was first visited and his name secured to head the paper. Then followed the manager of the Steel Plant, and before the day was done, a long list of signatures representing the solid citizens of Grandville were added to the paper. Indeed few could listen to the sad story so touchingly related by the attenuated petitioner and withhold their signatures. Rev. Simon Thomas was also a tower of strength. He had numberless friends among the best people of Grandville, as what upright Afro-American has not? The men who signed the petition were not politicians. They had long since become disgusted with the methods pursued by this gentry and withdrew from their blighting influence, such men are the real leaven of the state. Their names attached to a paper gave it the weight of a worthy cause.

The next day the petition was carried to the governor. He listened with interest to Regenia's story, and taking the petition glanced down the list, nodding his head as some name of particular interest met his eyes. Calling Regenia to him when he had gone over the list he said kindly: "Your matter shall have my attention at the very earliest convenience."

Regenia thanked him and the three bowed themselves out of the great man's presence.

The worry and loss of sleep consequent upon Regenia's anxiety, left her in a very debilitated state. Clement insisted, her doctor joining him in the opinion, that Regenia should resign her work and go home. He wished to have her leave Grandville before the issue of the petition was disclosed. He believed, whether the issue was favorable or otherwise, it would be alike injurious to Regenia. Day after day she searched the papers for notice of the governor's action upon the cause nearest her heart. When a week had passed away and nothing had been done, she began to evince symptoms of the return of her old malady.

One day, nearly a week after the petition had been presented, Clement came to the parsonage with word from the governor that action would be taken the next day. Before Regenia, however, he read to her a letter from his wife, bemoaning the loneliness of her state and beseeching Regenia to come home and keep her company. Clement, seeing he had touched a tender chord in Regenia's nature, put on the wind harp stop and in half suppressed tones, eloquently supplemented his wife's request. Regenia was convinced and accordingly the next day left for Minton.

As the train left the depot, Clement called after her, "I will be home soon and bring the doctor with me."

The day following he left for the mines, bearing the governor's permit to remove Lotus to a neighboring house and attend him until he was well enough to move. He did not grant the pardon, but Clement considered this a good omen.

CLOUDS LIFTING.

Chapter XXX.

Armed with the governor's permit, the morning after Regenia left for Minton, Clement bade farewell to his kind friends at the parsonage and made his way a second time to the convict mines. His arrival was indeed opportune. Lotus, grown restless on account of the constant tumult kept up by the drunken citizen soldiers, had given away to a fretful impatience that had materially lessened his chances of recovery. Otherwise his condition was decidedly improved. The filthy straw in which Clement found him immured on the occasion of his first visit, had given way to a neat clear cot, and the dingy walls, whose dampness had emitted a stifling stench, were brightened and sweetened by a coat of whitewash. Clement noted with satisfaction that the orders of the self appointed governor's private secretary had been obeyed with a startling celerity. Clement knew that the first step necessary to his friend's complete convalescence was to get him away from the din of that camp. Once away from the memories of his condition, recovery would be only a matter of time.

As soon as he had arrived in the camp and made his presence known to Lotus, he repaired to the captain and presented the permit for the removal of Dr. Stone. The captain consented readily. His inhuman treatment of the convicts had received such a notorious airing that he was glad of an opportunity to show his clemency. He was under the watchful eye of the omnipresent press and knew full well that any lack of courtesy would be sent on the snowy wings of the morning news to every village and hamlet in the country.

Accordingly Clement hastened to a farm house near the camp and arranged with its Afro-American tenant to bring his friend there. With the help of an ambulance, Lotus was conveyed to his new abode with little discomfort. The house and its location were all that could have been desired. A two story building made of hewed logs, and smooth floors, strangers alike to dirt and carpets. Lotus was domesticated in a large airy room upstairs. The first thing Clement did after seeing his friend comfortably situated was to send to town for a box of books and arrange to have the daily papers thrown from the cars at a point near the house.

Here, perched in a big old-fashioned split-bottom chair, you might have seen him day after day reading to Lotus, preparing his medicine or relating some droll story or incident calculated to interest or amuse the patient. Under such favorable circumstances and in the hands of such a nurse, it would have been strange if the improvement of the patient had not been marked. Clement had not been at the farm a week, before he received a letter from his wife informing him of Regenia's arrival and the shocking condition of her health. The doctor had advised a trip to the sea shore and insisted upon her accompanying Regenia. Clement sat down and wrote to his wife to go by all means. He said nothing to Lotus about this letter. He did not wish his friend's nerves disturbed by the additional foreboding.

In a week Lotus as so far recovered as to be able to sit up for hours each day. Clement was growing restless with anxiety at the delay of the pardon. He had kept his fears to himself, however, but Lotus could see that something was wrong.

On one thing Clement St. John had decided: Lotus Stone should never return to that convict camp. He would take him from the fires of that slow consuming hell, or lose his life in the attempt.

About two weeks after Clement left Grandville, the long-expected pardon came. Clement ran every step of the way from the station to the farm house. He burst in upon the astonished farmer and his wife, waving the precious paper over his head. "It has come at last," he exclaimed as soon as he could get breath enough to force the words through his lips.

"What's the matter down there?" a weak voice cried from the room above.

Clement cleared the steps three at a bound a rushing into the room, the big fellow nearly smothered Lotus in the mad exuberance of his expressions of joy. He took the emaciated doctor in his arms and pointing to the pardon in his hand, wept with uncontrolled joy. His feelings had been strung to such a high pitch in the weeks and weeks of hoping and waiting that when the object of his labor had culminated successfully, he could not refrain from weeping.

Dr. Stone wept with his friend. Men weeping! Yes, under the circumstances, who will say that in the expression of such joy as they felt it was unmanly to give vent to it in any way.

All that day the two friends talked over plans for the future. Lotus was first inclined to go back to Grandville and take up his work where he had so suddenly left off. Clement discouraged this. He had his reasons, but he wisely refrained from expressing them.

"As soon as you are well enough," said Clement, "we'll go over to the mines and bid farewell to the scenes which will no doubt linger with you all through life."

"No, thank you," said Lotus. "I think I have had those scenes engraved upon the tablets of my memory indelibly. I never want to look in that direction again, if I can help it."

"Now that you are free from its terrors, I would fancy you possessed with a morbid curiosity to study the subject from a different point of view," said Clement.

"I have gone through an experience in the past six months, my friend, from the effects of which I doubt that I shall ever thoroughly be free. The world has no conception of the suffering attending the poor unfortunates driven to death in those mines. I have seen sights and experienced degrees of depravity that beggars my vocabulary to describe. I believe in total depravity. The men who goad, whip and starve the helpless wretches under them in that earthly hell, are totally depraved."

"Yet it is the law; it is so nominated in the bond," said Clement.

"I have read the lucid descriptions of George Kennan," said Lotus slowly; "I have studied the tortures of the Spanish Inquisition, but I unhesitatingly declare that the Convict Lease System, as practiced in our own land, is the most cruel, heartless and tyrannical the world has ever seen.

"Every system of punishment contemplates however remotely, the reformation of the culprit; this reckons only upon his death. How many more days can he stand before it kills him, enters into the cool calculation of those who perpetrate this villainous system."

"The system has received a breath of air from without in the last few days and I think the flood of light that will fall through the rent already made will be sufficient to institute an inquiry that must result in good," replied Clement.

"I signed a petition once, circulated among the students at college, praying the Czar of all the Russians to take steps for the amelioration of the condition of his prisoners in the convict mines of Siberia. How often since, as I rolled on the hard boards, laden with chains, in the 'cell-house' at the mines, have I contemplated the grim irony of that petition. Physician heal thyself. We could give Russia points on convict tyranny her lictors never dreamed of. Ah!" he said, as if weary of the subject, "I have always been a conservative believer in the final triumph of liberty, an intense sympathizer with the oppressed of every land. When autocratic Russia confines in Siberia's dreary mines her noblest hearts, my heart in sorrow pities them. When haughty Britain grinds beneath her iron heel, the evicted tenants of conquered but not subjected Ireland, I feel with them the iron enter my own soul; but when America, our own native, God-blessed land, enters the list of oppressors and confines men in a hell more torturing than Siberia, more despotic than Turkey, more cruel than the grave, I weep for the sad degeneration of my own countrymen."

Clement, observing that his patient was growing more and more dispirited as his mind contemplated the scope of his wrongs, sought to divert the course of his thoughts by changing the conversation. "I have a letter to answer," he said, and as Lotus seemed indifferent to the implied question, he continued, "Why do you not ask to whom I am about to indite my epistle."

"You write so much that another letter, more or less, scarcely excites any special interest," Lotus replied.

"Well, I am going to write to Lucile. Shall I send her your love?"

"Just as much of it as you can get inside of an envelope," replied Lotus.

"She is at Breeze Nook, spending a few months," he explained.

"At Breeze Nook, by the sad, sad sea? What could have taken her so far from home?" asked Lotus in some surprise.

"She went with Miss Underwood," Clement answered carelessly, at the same time narrowly observing the effect the information would have upon his friend.

Lotus was visibly affected at every mention of Regenia's name. He made no reply, but Clement discerned his color change and his face twitch in spite of his efforts at self-control. From considerations best known to himself, Clement had not told Lotus the part Regenia had played in securing executive clemency for him. Nor had he related how the young woman had day after day worn away to a shadow in sympathy with her lover.

Dr. Stone still believed her cold and unsympathizing. The fact that she was off to the seaside forgetful of his sorrows, confirmed him in the belief that she was entirely heartless. He was too proud to make a single inquiry of the cause of her leaving the South, and Clement decided that having opened the way to induce his friend to talk of the subject nearest to his heart, he must either show a desire for more knowledge or wait until circumstances pushed him in the right direction. Circumstances might kindly direct him in the right direction, but it is certain Lotus could not be led to evince an interest in one he thought lost to every proper womanly feeling.

Clement had not lost anything by his trip South. He had filled his paper, "The Events," with the freshest news from the seat of disturbance, while at the same time he had kept a glowing column of special correspondence in several daily papers, which had made his stay very remunerative.

Shortly after the pardon came, Clement concluded that his patient was so far advanced in the path of health that it would not be unsafe to remove him. About a month after his first visit, he turned his back on the convict mines forever. The threatened trouble had cleared away, the soldiers, after costing the state a large sum, had returned, and as most of the escaped convicts had been recaptured, the camp, with a few outward reforms, had dropped into its accustomed routine. The Convict Lease System, however, had been given a blow from which it would not soon recover. The illumination it had received had served to array against it a class of agitators who, it is hoped, in time will erase the foul blot from the escutcheon of civilization.

Rev. Simon Thomas and his wife gave a royal welcome to Lotus on his return from the mines. Many of his sunshine friends who had hid behind the clouds in the day of his trouble, fell over each other in their efforts to express their delight at his pardon. Their intense interest, months after it was needed, produced in the mind of Lotus an inexpressible weariness. He smiled as he remarked to Clement: "Having escaped from the water, is it not remarkable how many of your friends are waiting on the shore to save you?"

They left Grandville after a few days for Minton. Lotus had nothing to say about the car in which he was obliged to ride; the worst fare on earth was grateful after what he had just left.

It was near the middle of May, and as the two men sat in their shirt sleeves, Lotus noticed tangled in the lining of his coat a letter. He turned the coat up and took it out. It was the letter he had placed in his pocket unread the evening of his arrest. It had slipped down between the lining and cloth and remained there unnoticed for all these months. "It is from Mrs. Levitt," he said.

"You are jesting," said Clement.

"No; look for yourself." The letter was sent to Washington to the department and forwarded.

"Well, well, written on brown paper with charcoal."

"Read the explanation," said Lotus, passing that to Clement. The explanation disclosed the fact that the letter had been received the previous June, and being placed in the gentleman's hunting coat, had escaped his attention until the day it had been mailed. He had hung up his coat and had never thought of the letter until he needed the hunting jacket. He asked pardon for the delay and hoped the information would yet arrive in time to serve the end wished.

"What do you think of that? Why, it is providential," said Clement.

"I expect she is dead before this," said Lotus, thinking of his own fortunate delivery from a premature grave.

"No, never." She must be somewhere in Canada. We'll make it our first duty to find out," looking at Lotus, he continued, "I'll make it my first duty, you will hardly be strong enough to undertake such business."

"When you go I'll go with you. We need not go for a few days. By that time I shall be strong enough to accompany you."

When the two friends arrived at Minton, Lotus was surprised to see the Red Cross Commandery drawn up in line at the depot, to receive him. Clement had wired to his friends the day to expect them, and the notoriety that the case of Lotus had received through the papers, served to bring to the station hundreds of people curious to see the man who had escaped from the jaws of that living hell. Lotus was pushed into a carriage to escape the enthusiasm of his friends. The horses were taken from the carriage and escorted by the Red Cross Commandery, he was drawn to the home of Clement St. John. Nor was the brave editor of "The Events" forgotten. He came in for a large share of the glory that surrounded Lotus. Already popular, his conduct had served to make him an idol among the people he loved so well.

HEARTS OF GOLD.

Chapter XXXI.

Dr. Stone was the lion of the hour for the next few weeks in Minton. The social world was at his feet. No lawn fete, private picnic or excursion was thought complete without his presence. Doting mothers courted his favor and men of high and low degree vied with each other in expressions of respect for him. If Lotus had not been unusually well balanced, so much patronage would have turned his head. To his credit it can be said that through it all he was wise enough to see the morbid curiosity that prompted the most of the attentions paid him. The young girls like to look at his hands, callous from toil; to hear him tell again and again some indignity he was made to suffer. He grew tired of recounting his experiences and fain would have stolen away from the prying eyes of the curious crowds, but where and how? He could not refuse the invitations sent him, for whatever the motive he was grateful for the consideration and intended kindness everywhere showered upon him.

Clement at last came to his rescue. "When are you going to be strong enough to make the trip to Mt. Clare?" he asked one day as he and Lotus were sitting in the office of "The Events."

"Strong enough?" said Lotus, laughing. "A man who can endure the round of picnics, balls and receptions I have been forced to attend for the past few weeks, can be trusted to take a voyage around the world and steer his own yacht."

"I have been waiting for somebody to declare a flag of truce," said Clement, "and during the armistice I thought we might slip away to Mt. Clare."

"Anything or anywhere to deliver me from the gentle hands of my friends," replied Lotus.

"Mt. Clare and the road to the lighthouse will be sufficiently exciting to create at least a healthy reaction from the too much joy business you have been indulging to distraction for some time past," Clement replied.

"I can be ready for the night boat," said Lotus. "You know I am a gentleman of leisure these days."

"Suppose we say to-morrow evening," said Clement. "By that time the weekly edition will be off and I shall be more at liberty."

"You shall be the judge. I have been so long under orders that I find it somewhat novel to decide for myself."

The evening following found the two friends seated in the recess of the cabin of one of the splendid lake steamers, which ply between Minton and Mt. Clare.

"I am willing to wager that I can indicate your mental processes for the past five minutes," said Clement, after they had been sitting for some time watching the lights of Minton one by one disappear.

"Doughnuts to dollars that you cannot," responded Lotus.

"As I have neither, I am safe in taking the wager," said Clement.

"Well, what was I thinking," asked Lotus.

"First, of a night two years ago when you and I and a number of friends sat whiling the hours away enroute from Mt. Clare to Minton. Second, of Mt. Clare. Third, of Regenia Underwood."

"You must be a mind reader. The doughnuts are yours. I was thinking a little of that night, less of Mt. Clare, and a great deal of Miss Underwood," said Lotus.

"Do you know," said Clement, "it has puzzled me to understand why you have always been so reticent, when Miss Underwood's name was mentioned. I have studiously managed to speak of her as infrequently as possible, gathering from your manner in the few times I did speak of her that the subject was painful to you. I am at loss to account for your indifference, possessing as I do such undoubted proofs of her devotion to you."

"Yes, rather devoted. A girl who could heartlessly desert a man because he was in trouble, refuse to come near him because he was under the ban of dishonor, hurry off to the seashore to flirt to her heart's content when the man she pretended to love is lingering between life and death in a convict mine. I know that a convict has no claim on the affections of such a woman, but a decent show of belief in my innocence—"

"Don't you say another word, Lotus. If you do I'll think you unworthy of the noble little woman whose pleading secured your pardon. I did not get that pardon, she went from office to office and from mansion to the governor's chamber, rehearsing, as only a loving heart could portray, the story of your wrongs. She was unconscious for days after your arrest from a shock received at the hands of Dr. Leighton the night before. You were imprisoned for weeks before the doctor would allow her to know of your condition, and when she did learn the truth, did she sit down and weep and wring her hands? Not she. She wrote letter after letter, begging me to come and try to secure your release. At last, broken in health and fearing for her reason, her friends persuaded her, through a ruse, to go to Lucile. She was taken to the seashore and has only been kept there through the most gigantic fabrications, for which may heaven forgive me."

"I am unworthy of her," said Lotus now thoroughly repentant. "Why have you not told me all of this before?" he asked sorrowfully.

"Simply because you did not deserve to know it. Your high blown pride had nearly brought me to the resolution never to tell you and to let you lose the only woman in the world you care for. But I could not bring myself to do it, old man," he said laughing heartily as he thought how rapidly he had taken the wind from Lotus' inflated sails.

"You would have served me right," said Lotus. "I had gone on hardening my heart against Regenia, notwithstanding I was morally certain, that there must be some extenuating circumstances. What I could not make out was why she went to Breeze Nook."

"You expected her to be sitting at the depot day after day awaiting your arrival, I suppose," said Clement sarcastically. "The display made over you here in Minton has turned your head, I suspect." He did not think so, but as he had Lotus eating humble pie, it was with a kind of fiendish delight he tried to keep him at the table.

"You do not think that, do you, Clement?" asked Lotus, somewhat dejected.

"Not exactly. But I warn you if you ever say an unkind word, nay think an unkind thought of that little angel who kissed me for you when in Grandville—you didn't know that either, did you? Well, Lucile does and she thinks Regenia never displayed such good taste before in her life."

"When she kissed you for me," said Lotus with a merry twinkle.

"She left me to draw my own conclusions. I did not take your view of it," said Clement.

They arrived at Mt. Clare the next morning and went out to the "Elms." They found the place looking much as it did the summer of the conclave. The servants were still there and Dr. Leighton spent a month or two during the year, looking after the estate. No time was lost dreaming of the past under the elms; but securing a two seated carriage, they drove down to the ferry, took the left hand road, keeping a sharp lookout for the lighthouse.

"We can drive on all night," said Clement, "and if we see no signs of the light house, why to-morrow we can drive back."

The lingering twilight had gone and the shades of evening closed in upon them before they saw in the distance the welcome rays emitted from the lighthouse windows. They drove their horses into the woods below the house and thought best to reconnoitre before approaching and demanding the release of Mrs. Levitt. Following a ravine which led them near the back part of the house, they stopped to listen.

From an open window in Mrs. Levitt's part they could hear the old woman talking to herself. She was calling: "Regenia, Regenia, will that child never come," she said. "I have been standing here night after night calling and waiting." She came to the open window and stood gazing at the moon.

"How she has changed!" said Lotus.

"She talks rather wildly," said his companion.

"Hush!" said Lotus. "I thought I heard footsteps approaching."

Mrs. Levitt began to sing in a low, crooning tone some old plantation hymn. As she continued, someone within yelled "Stop that. I can't bear to hear it."

The old woman sang on, repeating the same words. "Do you hear what I say? If you don't come away from that window and shut your old mouth, I'll come in there to you," repeated the hoarse voice.

The singing stopped and then the old woman began again to call, "Regenia, Regenia, oh Regenia! Where is that child? I've been standing by this window calling her, but she seems to never come." Having repeated this several times, she commenced to sing the same weird song with the same repetitions. From their watching place they saw a man come to the window and snatch the old woman away, uttering oath after oath as he covered her with blows.

Lotus, setting his teeth, would have rushed to the rescue, but the cooler head beside him counseled patience. "Not yet, not yet," whispered Clement. "He will leave for the lighthouse pretty soon and then we can seize our prize without bloodshed."

For an hour they lay there awaiting events. Finally the man left the cabin for the lighthouse. On his way he heard a horse neigh and following the ravine, came upon Clement and Lotus. He started on a run for the house, but Clement, divining his purpose, beat him to the door and turning closed with him. They had been scuffling but a moment when the door flew open and the lighthouse keeper's wife, gun in hand, came to her husband's rescue. Lotus covered her with his revolver and demanded that she drop the gun.

By this time Clement had brought the man to the earth and tying his hands behind him, forbade him at the risk of his life to move. While Lotus stood guard, Clement went into the house and led Mrs. Levitt out. The woman did not seem sorry to see Mrs. Levitt get her liberty.

They put her in the carriage and drove rapidly to Mt. Clare. As the sun scattered the fog that gathered over river and lake the next morning, the two friends and Mrs. Levitt were alighting from the carriage at the gate of the "Elms."

Mrs. Levitt was taken into the house, but did not recognize the old servants, nor did she know Lotus or Clement.

The young men took their horses to the stable and as they had eaten nothing since the morning before, they were in prime condition for eating without being coaxed. After breakfast they returned to the "Elms" to find Mrs. Levitt washed and dressed and apparently in her right mind. The old servant said she had wandered about the house calling Regenia and apparently demented until she went upstairs and by chance walked into Regenia's old room. Stopping before a large painting, she gazed upon it wildly for awhile and then, bursting into tears, for the first time she was conscious of her surroundings.

Sitting in the parlor, surrounded by the old servants, Mr. St. John and Lotus, she related the story of her stay in the home of the lighthouse tender.

She did not spare Dr. Leighton. "He wanted this property, but I never intended that my child should be swindled out of it."

"He got it anyway, you know, he found the will," said Clement.

"He did?" said the old lady, bounding out of her chair and leaving the room.

They followed her, thinking she was again losing her mind. She went up into the garret and with a hatchet pried off the mantle and taking out a brick or two, she drew from the chimney a tin box and bore it in triumph to the parlor.

The box contained the deeds and securities for the Underwood estates and the lost will. Mr. St. John took the papers and put them into the hands of old Judge Underwood's former law partner, and Mrs. Levitt swore out a warrant against Dr. Leighton for kidnapping. That night Lotus and Clement left for Minton, taking Mrs. Levitt with them.

BY THE RESTLESS SEA.

Chapter XXXII.

Regenia and Lucile were cosily situated at Breeze Nook. The freedom from care, together with the salt-laden sea breeze, had not been long in bringing the roses back to Regenia's cheeks. Lucile, too, had been benefited by her sojourn at Breeze Nook.

Clement had kept them in touch with the affair which was nearest Regenia's heart. The successful termination of Dr. Stone's stay in the convict camp, contributed in no small way to the robust health the Regenia had lately regained. Peace of mind is always conducive to a well ordered physical condition. The young women had lived much in the open air. They had paid little heed to the effect this change was producing in their complexions. What did they care if they were as brown as berries, so they ate heartily and slept soundly? Every morning they walked on the beach and more than a score of times had seen the ruddy face of Phoebus dripping with golden perspiration, rise like a fire king from beneath the ever restless waves. At eleven they took their daily plunge in the foaming surf, in the evening they walked on the beach, sat down in the white sand, and through all this programme they talked of Lotus and Clement. They did not join in the busy whirl everywhere buzzing around them. While the social world of Breeze Nook feasted and danced, these two friends in pursuit of health (how commonplace) simply slept.

Breeze Nook was the place to meet fashionable Afro-America. Here gathered the departmental clerk from Washington, frittering away that part of this thirty days' vacation not already used; the solid man from the city in pursuit of health or long-delayed pleasure; school teachers from the far away South or West; the porter of the flat with the dress and airs of a millionaire; the "dude" and "dudess" from nowhere in particular but everywhere in general; the minister whose congregation has granted him a well earned vacation; the editor seeking a rest from the arduous duties of hunting his subscription money; the student seeking work to help him through college; all kinds, all classes of men and women of high and low degree flock to Breeze Nook for at least a day or two during the "heated term." It was amusing to Regenia and Lucile to observe these people in their efforts to assume airs of importance. Want of sociability is rare in Afro-America. Breeze Nook in this respect was an exception. It seemed to our friends that Miss "A," fearful that a little courtesy would in the estimation of Miss "B," detract from Miss "A's" social standing, made Miss "A," who at home was a friendly somebody, at Breezy Nook a disgusting little snob.

Regenia and Lucile, having no particular social standard to keep up, were content to act abroad as they did at home, with becoming consideration for all they chanced to meet. They did not think it necessary to act the lady, they found it far simpler to be ladies. Their unassuming ways made them liked by all.

The day Mrs. Levitt was brought back to Mt. Clare, Clement had telegraphed the good news to Lucile. Regenia had been down to the beach alone that morning, and when she returned Lucile met her at the gate. "Guess what has happened?" she said slipping her arm around Regenia's waist.

"I never was good at guessing, tell me," said Regenia.

"I received a letter from Clement," said Lucile with tantalizing deliberation.

"Are they coming down?"

"Yes, all three of them."

"Three," exclaimed Regenia, "and who is the third one, pray?"

"The third is a woman."

Regenia stopped a moment, and looking into Lucile's eyes, said: "Have they found her?"

Lucile nodded, "Yes, and I have just sent them a telegram to repair at once to Breeze Nook."

"Where did they find her? Did the telegram say how she was?"

"Now, do you know what you are saying? What do you want anyway in twenty-five cents' worth of electricity? I think they will be here by Friday or Saturday. Let me see—this is Thursday—yes, they ought to get here by Saturday, anyway. Until then, have patience," she said, as she tripped lightly up the steps to the house.

True to the prediction of Mrs. St. John, Saturday brought Clement, Mrs. Levitt and Lotus. Regenia and Lucile were seated on the broad veranda when the cab drove up. The driver had hardly opened the carriage door and assisted Mrs. Levitt to alight, before Regenia had bounded down the steps and with her arms around Mrs. Levitt's neck, was covering her face with kisses.

"You dear old mamma, you, how glad I am to see you again." Careless of the lookers-on, forgetful of Lotus and Mr. St. John, Regenia clung to her foster mother as if she expected every moment some unkind fate would spring up to separate them.

"How I have missed you," she continued.

"And I have missed you, too, dear," said Mrs. Levitt speaking through her tears.

Lucile had kissed her husband and given Mr. Stone a rousing welcome, and stood waiting for Regenia to give Mrs. Levitt a moment's cessation, so she could speak to her.

Clement at last broke the awkward silence. "I suppose you are not going to share your greeting with us less important folks."

Regenia, blushing with confusion, as she greeting Clement, said: "Oh, yes I am. I was so glad to see dear old mamma that for a moment I forgot my other dear friends. And you, Dr. Stone," she said, "are you quite as well as you were when I saw you last?"

"Yes, thanks to you and Clement, and you too, Mrs. St. John," he said, as she cast a saucy glance at him.

"I thought you were not going to leave me out. I was not in the forefront of battle, but I was a powerful reserve."

"Never fear, I would sooner leave myself out than to detract one jot or tittle from the obligation I feel toward all my friends."

"None of that Lotus. You are under no obligation to anybody," said Clement. "You can feel just as thankful as you please, but keep it to yourself. We were only too glad to be of service."

"Yes, indeed, and if you had not got out of that den as soon as you did, I fear it would have been the death of all of us," she said, laughing and looking at Regenia, who at that moment was busily talking to Mrs. Levitt.

That night and the next day were spent in hearing the experiences which each had passed through since last they were all together.

Monday at eleven they went bathing. Here, as everywhere else, discrimination exists. The Afro-Americans had their separate bath houses, and special part of the beach for bathing. Clement St. John found this arrangement something to be thankful for. He remarked to Lotus as they came out of the water, "My suit would make a good life preserver. It has been 'shingled' so often," referring to the numerous patches it contained, "I do not believe a fellow could sink in it if he tried."

Dr. Stone did not know whether to consider himself on the same terms with Regenia as when they had last met, or to commence over again. He was not long in determining, however. The evening after the day just spoken of, he invited Regenia to take a walk on the beach. By degrees he led up to the days at Grandville and the months of suffering which had passed for them both. They walked on in the moonlight, talking over the pleasures and sorrows.

"We had better turn back," said Regenia, "we have walked a long way."

They stopped and Lotus, taking her hand, said:

"Can you forget,
Perchance regret?"

"No," she said, "I can not forget, I will not regret."

"It is all so different now. I am a convict and you an heiress."

"Have you changed? Is your heart the same as it was that happy night, followed so soon by months of sorrow?"

"My heart is the same, but what was admissible then, might be presumptuous now," he replied.

"If you were suddenly made rich," she said, "would you cease to love me?"

"I could not cease to love you, no matter what changes came," replied Lotus feelingly.

"Do you think me less constant than yourself? Do you think I would ever enjoy a penny of that money without you? Never call yourself a convict again. You are a nobleman upon whom fortune for a little while frowned. What is the money worth when compared with the service you rendered me? Saved my life. I have never forgotten that, and more, you offered me your love and I accepted it and returned it."

The rough rocks roared as the mad waves dash against them, the laughing whitecaps trembled and shook with suppressed merriment; the moon glimmered again and again from behind the cloud, but Lotus and Regenia recked them not as Cupid led them captive back to the cottage.

They sat on the veranda in the moonlight and talked it all over as lovers will. Regenia at last arose to go in, he still held her hands and sought to see once more in her big brown eyes, swimming in their liquid depths, that truth so sweet to know: "I love you."

As he leaned against the porch, still holding her hands, there was a scuffle, a scream and the report of a revolver.

Clement St. John came round the corner of the house holding his revolver in his hand. "Nothing to be afraid of, only my carelessness. I was changing this revolver from one hand to the other and it went off," he explained.

For once his story was not believed by Regenia. She had seen Dr. Leighton, as he raised his revolver, and in that awful moment had seen Clement brush it aside from its mark.

Dr. Leighton had deliberately attempted to murder Lotus, but Clement had saved him in the nick of time. It had only been the work of a moment to wrench the revolver from the would-be assassin's hand, and his first thought was to shoot him, but as Dr. Leighton leaped over the back fence, Clement lowered the smoking revolver and through the awful stillness he could hear "Thou shalt not kill."

Everybody about the house condemned Mr. St. John for his carelessness but Regenia. She alone knew the truth. Even Lotus was unaware how near he had been to eternity.

The morning paper described an accident which forever freed Regenia from the fear of Dr. Leighton. As he bounded over the fence that night and slunk away under cover of the darkness, he had to cross a dozen railroad tracks directly behind the cottage from which he was fleeing. Running out of the way of one engine he did not see another which passed over him, mangling his body beyond recognition. A card in his pocket told who he was.

Lucile remarked on hearing the account read aloud on the veranda the next morning, "And this is the reality of your dream, Regenia. Do you remember the big fish and incline car that mashed it into a thousand pieces?"

They gathered around while Lucile related the dream.

THE CONVOCATION.

Chapter XXXIII.

FOUR YEARS HAVE PASSED since we last saw Dr. Lotus Stone and Regenia Underwood renewing their vows of undying affection at Breeze Nook. During the following summer they were quietly married and took up life's joys and sorrows at Mt. Clare. Nothing particularly noteworthy has occurred since their marriage to distinguish them from the thousand and one happy families that pass unnoticed day by day.

The doctor has unostentatiously followed his profession; while his loving wife has spent much of her time in relieving the wants of the poor, carrying the sunshine of Christian sympathy where it is oftener needed than received. One child, a boy, has come to bless their home. He bears the name of Dr. Stone's best friend, Clement.

Clement and Lucile still live at Minton. Mr. St. John, in the midst of an unusually busy life, finds time to pull himself away from his paper and his politics each year, to steal away to Mt. Clare and spend two or three weeks at the "Elms."

As we finish our story, Lucile and Clement are at the "Elms," Mt. Clare again echoes to the tread of marching men. This time it is the "Convocation" instead of the "Conclave;" the Patriarchie instead of the Knights Templars. Clement and Lucile, with their little girl, Regenia, in company with Dr. Stone and family, have just returned from Recreation Park.

Again they have lived over the events of a summer long ago and sitting on the spacious veranda, are interested observers, as company after company of the tired Patriarchies alight from the cars in front of the "Elms" and make their way to the city.

Mrs. Levitt, a pleasant smile on her broad, loving face, is sitting on the steps. Regenia, as much of a child as ever when in the company of her foster mother, sits at her feet, Lucile, with her arm around Regenia's waist, sits beside her, talking incessantly. Clement and Lotus are standing on the porch, while little Regenia St. John and Clement Stone, hand in hand, are observing from the yard, with wild-eyed delight, the soldiers who from high private, to self important captain, wear the sword and uniform of an officer.

As the happy friends sit talking, the last rays of the sun slowly setting, falls in trembling reflections through the waving branches overhead, softening and retouching the picture with tints of purest gold. Clement and Lotus, inspired by the sight, instinctively turn toward each other. Lotus said: "After the clouds, sunshine, after the darkness, light, after sorrow, joy."

"I was just thinking that the sight of such contentment is ample pay for all of the struggles and sorrows of the past," responded Clement.

The two men stood for some time silently contemplating the picture before them, as they looked at the children hand in hand, Lotus turned to Clement and taking the hand of his friend said:

"May the Lord be between me and thee and between mine and thine forever."

THE END.

APPENDICES

APPENDIX A

In 1896, the West Virginia Republican Party invited Jones to give a speech seconding the nomination of George W. Atkinson as the Republican candidate for governor in July 1896. The speech was published in the July 31, 1896 Wheeling Daily Intelligencer.

AN ELOQUENT ADDRESS.

THE SPEECH OF JAMES MCHENRY JONES, WHEELING'S MAGNET COLORED ORATOR, SECONDING THE NOMINATION OF GEORGE W. ATKINSON FOR GOVERNOR, AT PARKERSBURG.

Following is the eloquent speech of Professor J. McHenry Jones, seconding Mr. Atkinson's nomination in the state Republican convention at Parkersburg. It created great enthusiasm and is published by general request. Professor Jones said:

ON THE FIELD OF GETTYSBURG, IT IS SAID, that the soldiers wearing the blue and the gray, were buried after the battle in long trenches, one upon another. A traveler who passed over that immortal battle ground a few days afterward, declared that the earth over which these soldiers so gloriously died and under which they were so ignominious covered, swayed up and down. This may be fact or fiction, but he who observes the signs of the times must be cognizant of the tremors from an irresistible groundswell which began at St. Louis and will not cease until it rolls incompetent Democracy out of the White House.[1]

I misinterpret the spirit and intelligence of the American people, if by their permission, that herd of wild-eyed fanatics which broke loose at Chicago, ever heads toward the national capital.[2]

The Republican party is confronted to-day, as it has been in the past, with wild speculations and untenable theories; but true to its traditions, it fearlessly faces the blatant slogan of error with the gleaming torch of demonstrated truth.

The history of our party is simply a record of the triumphs of right. We were right in 1856, at the birth of Republicanism. Right in 1860, under the leadership of the immortal Lincoln, right in '61, when it was determined that one flag should wave over an undivided country and liberty should not perish from the face of the earth. Doubly right in 1863, when it was finally concluded that the life of the nation demanded the freedom of the slave. Right under the peerless leadership of that matchless soldier, Grant; right in the resumption of specie payment under Hayes, right under Garfield, right under Harrison, eternally right when under James G. Blaine and William McKinley, were welded in a common chain of protection and reciprocity.[3]

We are right to-day, when against the tumult and above the roar of the babel of populism, we re-assert our intention to defend to the last ditch the national honor, and preserve inviolate and untarnished the institutions transmitted to us from our forefathers. And the grand old party will be right in November when it wrings from the red mouth of populistic Democracy, the black, the hissing tongue of anarchy.[4]

West Virginia is naturally Republican. The candidate named was born within her borders. It will not be necessary to look into the misty record of the forgotten past, to extract his name from the cobwebs of oblivion. He is known from where the rugged Alleghenies lift their giant shoulders up into the trackless blue, to where the fretful Kanawha unites with the muddy Ohio, on her restless mission to the sea, from the eastern pan-handle to the southern extremity of the state, the name of and fame of George W. Atkinson is a by-word in the mouths of an admiring people.

The logical candidate, his is a fitting name with which to close the century. The nineteenth century grows apace. Already the fading glow of approaching twilight throws its lengthening shadows around us. Soon the rosy morn of a new century, fresh fallen from the finger tips of God, will dawn upon a waiting world. As the purple curtain of the new born century is slowly lifted, and the God of day, his ruddy face dripping with golden perspiration, sends his first fierce gleam athwart the oceans of time, may he discover the union's fleet of states, after a three years' battle with contending forces, moving steadily, majestically forward. The flagship of McKinley, the harbinger, the advance agent of a better day, far in the lead. The twin relics of free trade and free silver deeply buried beneath the rolling wave.[5] Confidence after four years wandering in the dismal swamp of Democratic delusion, returned to fill her accustomed place in the company of her friends, while Hope, her sister, dips her golden pencil in the rainbow hues of heaven and writes upon the emblazoned, the imperishable records of the republic—prosperity, protection and patriotism.

The good ship West Virginia cut loose from Democratic moorings, must be directed by a helmsman trained to the sea, a pilot with a cool head, discerning eye, pure life, strong arm, open hand and patriotic heart.

Ohio County believes that these qualifications are transcendently developed in the superb statesman, erudite scholar, far seeing party leader and Christian gentleman, the Hon. George Wesley Atkinson.

Therefore, in the name of the Republicans of Ohio County, whose idol he is, in the name of the unconditional Republicans of West Virginia, who love him as their friend, I heartily second the nomination of the next governor of West Virginia.

Notes

1 For the 1896 presidential election campaign, the Republican Convention was held in St. Louis.

2 The Democratic Convention for the 1896 campaign was held in Chicago.

3 Jones refers to various historical events—including the founding of the Republican Party, Lincoln's election as president, the beginning of the Civil War in 1861, and the Emancipation Proclamation of 1863. He refers as well to various Republican leaders, including presidents Ulysses S. Grant, Rutherford B. Hayes, and James Garfield, as well as presidential candidate (elected in 1896) William McKinley and James G. Blaine, the unsuccessful Republican nominee for president in the 1884 election.

4 William Jennings Bryan, the Democratic nominee for president in 1896, also had the support of the Populist Party.

5 Free trade and free silver were defining issues in the 1896 election. McKinley had long supported tariffs, or taxes on imported goods, and so opposed free trade. The free silver issue had to do with whether the U.S. Mint should purchase silver and whether gold or silver (or both) would back U.S. currency.

APPENDIX B

Jones's speech to the British Grand United Order of Odd Fellows 1897 Annual Conference was published in pamphlet form by Tillotson and Son of Bolton. The text below is drawn from the copy in the Library of Congress's Daniel A. P. Murray Collection and bears the notation "Extract from The Bolton Journal *of Saturday, June 12th, 1897." British spelling has been retained, although paragraphing has been added for readability. The speech appears on pages five through eight of the eight-page pamphlet, and page three bears a striking image of Jones in full evening dress.*

BRO. MAJOR [RICHARD] HILL-MALE, who had seen something of the working of the Order in America,[1] had undertaken to introduce Bro. [J. McHenry] Jones. Major Hill-Male thereupon retired, and in a few minutes reappeared with Bro. Jones on his arm, their entry into the hall being the signal for loud applause, which was renewed with redoubled vigour when they appeared upon the platform. Bro. Major RR. Hill-Male then introduced Bro. McHenry Jones to the G[rand]. M[aster]., and through him to the Order. He congratulated Bro. Jones upon his safe arrival amongst them. At an informal meeting the previous evening Bro. Jones told them that in his explanation to some of their brethren in America as to his visit to England that he thought his presence amongst them would add colour to their meeting. (Laughter.) He assured Bro. Jones that the Order welcomed him as representing the great American branch of the small tree in the United Kingdom. (Applause.)

Referring to his own visit to America as Grand Master he [Hill-Male] acknowledged his splendid and fraternal reception, and he was sure nothing could happen between the two nations but goodwill, brotherly love, relief, and truth. They could not give Bro. Jones the same reception that he had in America, but he could assure him of equal feelings of friendship which were felt towards him in this country. He hoped that meeting would be the means of cementing and binding together with iron links that friendship which had subsisted for so many years, and be the means of laying the foundation of such a Grand United Order that might face the Opposition of the Whole World.[2]

The Grand Master [William Elliff] also added a welcome, remarking with satisfaction that it was the proud boast of their Order that it fixed no distinctions narrower than those fixed by the Great Father of all. (Hear, hear.) On rising to respond Bro. Jones had a cordial reception, the delegates rising and cheering lustily.

He said:

Brethren, your brothers from beyond the deep and rolling ocean, plighting their vows at the same sacred altar, drinking from the same perennial stream at the fountain of Friendship, warmed by the influences emanating from the glowing coals on the altar of Loved, and worshipping at the Shrine of Truth, with increasing affection send fraternal greetings and goodwill to the mother Grand Lodge in England. (Hear, hear.)

Having for years attempted to make known through correspondence, the love and gratitude Order in America cherishes toward you, I have been sent to emphasize and in measure give voice to the enduring nature of those sentiments. It is now more than a half-century since a few noble men of my race despised, outlawed, and virtually expatriated, turned their discouraged faces toward this God-blessed land. It was with feelings of mingled hope and fear that these determined, righteous men made their appeal to the Grand United Order of Oddfellows.

Repulsed at home, their petition treated with contempt, their aspirations, ridiculed[,] their right to brotherhood peremptorily refused, is it strange that day by day, awaiting the return of their chosen messenger, their hope in the final triumph of their cause grew dimmer, and their faith in the justice of the world was on the eve of going out for ever? Lashed by misfortune, strangers in the land of their nativity, without political standing and under the ban of social ostracism, waifs upon Time's heartless ocean, they longed for a resting place among the brotherhood. Keenly sensitive to the isolation of their condition, they sought through Peter Ogden, a member of Victoria Lodge, admission into the temple of Fraternity, and rising above the littleness of caste, too great to be mean, the Grand United Order of Oddfellows welcomed our fathers into the family of mankind.[3] (Applause)

Holding aloft the gleaming torch of Truth, the Order in England declared: "Fraternity is an ocean which washes the shores of every country, and its influence can only be bounded by the jutting crags to Eternity." [On behalf] of the widows and orphans of our brotherhood[,] I came to thank you that his story was believed. He came bearing the petition of the oppressed; I come to offer the homage of the free. Over him hung the raven-wing of doubt, above me expands the rainbow of eternal promise. (Applause) He came from the night in search of the dawn; I come clothed with the morning, expecting the noonday. Like a dove, bearing olive branch, Peter Ogden returned to the long neglected ark, beneath whose roof our fathers impatiently waited.

I bring back the much cherished emblem of peace, and with a full heart and open hands, present the greetings of 160,000 Black Oddfellows,[4] whose lives have been inspired and manhood strengthened by its significant teachings. It would not be amiss on this auspicious occasion, to turn on their golden hinges the gilded leaves of the past and take an inventory of the historic foot-prints left by progress on the years that have flown. "Tis greatly wise to talk with your past hours. And ask them what reports they have borne to heaven, and how they might have borne more welcome news."[5] What a change has come over the world since our fathers gathered first around the scared alter, and pledged their fidelity to the principles of our Order! What a breath of years, measured by the events which have crowded into history since that of which must endear their memories to their race! The world has lived a thousand years since then, so rapidly has progress trodden upon the heels of time. In 1843 Bismarck was unknown; Gladstone, the grand old English gentleman, winning his spurs as a statesman; Lincoln, a name sufficiently glorious to illuminate any age, was a country lawyer; Grant was at West Point, at the foot of his class. It was the darkest hour for my people in American history. Every device that the hate could concoct, brain contrive, or oppression execute, fell, unchecked, upon the bowed back of the poor forsaken Negro.

The return of Peter Odgen, therefore, triumphantly bearing the charter of English recognition, was like a ray of light from a midnight sky. In 1843, without property, without the moral support of the community, without anything save our faith in God and hope for a better day, we organised the first Lodge. A decade after the institution of the Order in America, our number had grown to 1,482. We now number nearly 160,000. We expended for sick dues during the past year 198,423.82 dollars, paid to widows and widows and orphans 40,360.72 dollars; paid for funerals 96,400 dollars, and after the expenditure of this large sum, aggregating 335,183.54 dollars, we still have invested in funds and securities 1,867.597 dollars. We have subordinate Lodges in thirty-nine States, four Territories, the District of Columbia, West Indies, Canada, Hayti, South America, and Africa. Our Past Grand Masters' Counsils number 182.

Our women, also, have joined with us in pushing forward the victories of our most humane institution. Experience has fully demonstrated that the union of man's strength and vigour with woman's faith and sympathy in a friendly society is an act of the highest wisdom. Nowhere has this fact been more satisfactorily exemplified than in the organization of the Household of Ruth.[6] Side by side with the brethren our sisters, 30,000 strong, are dedicating their services to the scared cause of practical charity. Nor are they satisfied to move along in the beaten path, but with a more enlighten[ed] conception of their needs they are proposing and organising new departments in keeping with the progressive lines of their development. The last B.M.C. [annual national meeting]; stamped with its approval the organization of Juvenile Lodges, to be controlled by the Household of Ruth. Through this new organization our God-fearing mothers, wives, and sisters will strive to inculcate lessons of virtue, economy, and sobriety in the hearts of the children. Too much credit cannot be given to the women of our race. The world has but one new woman—the Afro-American women. In the face of the most cruel conditions that ever Blighted and Outraged Womankind, our mothers—God bless them—conquering fate, have outlived the past, and are rearing and educating manly sons and virtuous daughters to fill places of trust and profit in the Great Republic.

Our military division—the Patriarchie, like the Household of Ruth, is an innovation unknown in England, but filling an actual need in our work. The highest branch in the Order, it seeks to weave into an endless chain the teachings and experiences of the subordinate Lodge and Past

Grand Masters' Council, and with heart to heart and hand to hand render inseparable the moral lessons of Oddfellowship. We have laboured to conserve in their pristine purity the principles and mysteries entrusted to our fathers in the days of other years. We teach the Fatherhood of God, and thus postulate the brotherhood of men. The Grand United Order are at one with Christianity in promulgating the universal truth. "From one blood hath God created all the nations of the earth."[7] We believe in the absolute equality of men. Before liberty, equality, and fraternity became the rallying cry of oppressed humanity, it was taught and widely practised among Oddfellows. Justice and charity, friendship and truth bear the same interpretation, and kindle the same enthusiasm in America as in England. Liberty founded upon justice, charity tempered with fraternity, equality based upon merit, shares a large place in the teachings of our Order.

It would not be un-interesting perhaps to notice in passing the character and progress of the people among whom the seeds of Oddfellowship have been planted in America. Much been said of us at home and abroad; much, the out-growth of ignorance or prejudice; much a combination of both ignorance and prejudice. We are too often judged by our worst, rather than our best performances. Who would visit Whitechapel to find an average Englishman, or the Tenderloin district in New York in search of a representative American?[8] We judge a people by their statesmen, artists, scholars, artisans, in short, by the industrious producers of all classes. We are too frequently measured from beneath, from our criminals, our worst elements. The indolent, vicious and improvident are pointed out as a proof of our worthlessness, while the toiling, industrious millions scarcely merit a moment's notice. Our fault[s] are hunted down and exaggerated, our virtues overlooked or minimised.

Our Order represents the high-water mark among the masses of our people. Young men of the best social standing, cultivation and worth, as well as their white-haired sires, the solid men among us, have linked in their fortunes with our brotherhood. The progress of the American negro during the last generation finds no parallel in the history of the world. Whatever our enemies may say, facts are more convincing than theories, and truth is stranger than fiction. At the close of the war of the Rebellion the freedmen were the poorest people on the face of the earth. We had no home, no roof to shelter us from the inhospitable storm, nothing save the blue sky and friendly sunshine by day, the unsympathising stars by night. We were houseless, homeless wanderers upon the face of the earth. The Negro had no family to strengthen and encourage him, family ties were largely denied him by the circumstances of his most unhappy past. He was void of household gods or sacred memories to hold him in a steady course. We had nothing but willing hands and unshaken trust in God. Under such circumstances, to have established a home and gathered under a common family tree, in a generation his wife and family would have been one of the most remarkable accomplishments of history.

To our credit we have done more. In a generation we have accumulated and pay taxes on $400,000,000 worth of real estate. We own and operate a street car railway in Arkansas. We own $630,000 worth of shipping, $102,000 worth of wharfage; fine banks with capital of $3,000,000; 200 daily and weekly newspapers. In one State alone we own 800,000 acres of land. Small, indeed, are these figures when compared with the aggregate wealth of our great country, but worthy of consideration when it is remembered that under circumstances not the most favourable, we have accomplished so much in so short a time.

Our material prosperity is by no means our proudest monument. Our mental advancement has surpassed our material advancement. In a quarter of a century over 3,000,000 of our race have learned to read and write. We have acquired and control 18 colleges, 34 academies, 51 high schools and seminaries. We have more than 30,000 teachers in the public schools, 33 painters of merited reputation, 16 sculptors, 2,000 physicians, 295 dentists, 3,000 lawyers, 1,800 B.D. ministers, 540 telegraph operators, 1,466 engineers, 1,600 captains and pilots of vessels, 3,970 book-keepers and stenographers and 30,000 skilled workmen of all sorts and conditions. The work of educating and uplifting the masses has been largely done by our own people.

Circumstances have compelled us to uplift ourselves. Where in the annals of mankind can be found another example of a race rising to the sublime status of intellectual manhood and womanhood by its own power? We have been largely our own teachers. We would not detract from the help given us by the church, nor the noble self-sacrificing men and women who have suffered ostracism and contempt in order that they might devote their energies to the cause of the despised, but the fact remains, the great force used in elevating our people has come from within. We have made bricks, gathering our own straw. We do not complain, the exertion has been helpful rather than enervating. Circumstances have taught us self-reliance. We only beg for our schools and churches—bread for the mind, bread for the soul.

I am telling you of these things now, for it may be 50 years before representatives of the two countries again meet like this. ("No, no.") It would, however, be a grand thing if an International Congress of representatives of our great Order could be held in Philadelphia next year. (Applause.) There might be brought together English speaking races the world over, and we could proclaim the great fact that in accepting coloured races the Grand United Order stands alone as being world wide. But I will proceed.

The Marks of Past Sorrows are not altogether obliterated; still our star of manhood continues to ascend. Reformations go not backward. If the race has left the first apathy of ignorance, when it longs to shake off the darkness of the past, then are we in the whirl of advancing time, and keeping step with the music of progression. Trained in a school of misfortune, we hopefully, fearlessly face the future. Our past sorrows were providential. Through the fiery cloud of suffering can be dimly outlined the puissant hand of God. These facts may be prosaic, but they lead to a broad generalisation. If the Order has been able to grow under circumstances so forbidding, what must be the future under brighter skies and more inviting prospects? It is a pleasure to report that the night is passing, and faint streaks of the coming light soften the threatening sky with prophecies of a better day. Here and there as the gray dawn steals noiselessly upon us a flickering bon-fire, or an illegal lynching flashes out, proof that error dies hard. By the heart throbs that beat in unison, by the mutual sorrows of the past, by the frequent touches of nature that make the whole world kin, we are nearing a better understanding. It is coming by the way of the schoolhouse, scattering enlightenment, by the way of the churches disseminating a purer conception of the holy Christ. Just as the hatred engendered between the two sections of our country by war is disappearing as distance from it recedes, so we believe that the asperities between races must yield to the better influences which time alone will produce. (Hear hear.)

We have faith to look into the frowning face of blackest night for the rosy hues of coming morning: faith to believe that through the threatening clouds that so long have overshadowed us, will break the golden light of a new emancipation. Next to our own happiness we pray for the prosperity of England. Our people to a man, hope that the friendly feeling, so long existing between England and the United States, may continue to strengthen as the year roll by. We cherish the hope that never again shall the two nations bound by a common tongue, heirs to a common literature, seeking the same high destiny, the nestors and promulgators of civil and religious liberty, we hope, nay, we demand, that nations so united by a community of interests shall always find some means to settle their difficulties, without an appeal to arms. (Applause.)

We join with you in saying "God save the Queen." (Hear, hear.) Who can estimate the blessings which have unceasingly flowed from the simple act of justice toward our fathers granted by the Grand United Order of Oddfellows? What tears has it wiped from the eyes of the lonely widow, the poverty stricken, and fatherless? What hearts smitten by the heavy hand of discouragement it has caused to beat with the hope of a better day? How many lives it has cheered, and how often scattered the flowers of charity along the thorny pathway of the forgotten poor? Time cannot measure the far-reaching influence of this Deed of Disinterested Goodness.

Eternity alone can fully unfold its unalloyed blessings. Taking courage from the success of the past, we are enlarging our sphere of usefulness, spreading the boundaries of charity, engrafting into our scheme homes for our orphans and endowment for the relic's of our brotherhood. Side by side with the church we are doing the practical work of Christianity, preaching economy and frugality to a people by nature prodigal, and thus giving true religion an onward impetus. We are only on the border of the wave of fraternity which must ultimately sweep our land. We increased our membership 13,000 during the last year, and still there are more to follow. (Applause.)

The principles which we teach and practice are destined to live for ever. No clime nor country can limit their influence. Whenever sorrow lifts its mournful head or want unbidden lurks there the influence of our noble

Order will make its appearance. And when our weak efforts are forgotten, and those that follow us shall have suffered our fate, when the flags of England and America, twin sisters in the fore-front of destiny, shall have fallen for want of defenders, the principles which we teach will live on, breathed upon new tongues, articulated under new lies, until the Great Father of the universe shall [?] the chapter of time, "Mid the wrecks of matter and crush of worlds."[9] (Applause.)

In the name of the S.C. of America, in the name of the B.M.C., and in the name of the black host of Oddfellows in America. I extend to you fraternal greetings. (Loud applause.)

Bro. Curnow expressed his great appreciation of the address, and proposed that it be printed in pamphlet form, adding that such a speech should be sent throughout Europe. Bro. Thornley (Burton-on-Trent) seconded, and the resolution was carried. It was further agreed that the Grand Master's speech should also be published in the same pamphlet.

Bro. Jones next presented an illuminated address from the Order in America to adorn the offices in Manchester.

The Grand Master asked if their fathers did right 50 years ago in admitting the race to which their brother, who had just spoken, belonged? He answered unhesitatingly they did. (Hear, hear.) With the single exception of the Church of Christ no organisation had done so much for their American friends as the Grand United Order of Oddfellows. Their success with the coloured race had been a lesson to the whole of civilized humanity. Their Order had done much in lifting up their American brethren, and he thought they ought to be proud of what they had accomplished. For 54 years there had been constant correspondence between the American and English offices, and the American Order had always been loyal to them.

It was impossible fittingly to reply to the address given by Bro. Jones, and he moved that a small committee be appointed consisting of five Past Grand Masters and the Grand Editor to draw up a suitable address in reply, to be submitted to the Conference for approval, to be signed by the Grand Master, the Deputy Grand Master, and the Grand Secretary, and presented to Bro. Jones for him to take back with him to America (Applause).[10] The Deputy Grand Master said he had pleasure in seconding the resolution. He (the speaker) stood before them as the son of a father who had assisted in the granting of the first dispensation to America, which had borne such good fruit, and the wonderful progress of which was evidenced by the eloquent address of Bro. Jones. Many societies claimed the privilege of having introduced Oddfellowship to America, but none could dispute his word when he asserted that the Grand United Order was the first to do it, being led on by Peter Ogden (Hear, hear). The proposition was then put and carried.

NOTES

1 Then-Grand Master Richard Hill-Male toured the U. S. in 1894. He was feted by African American Odd Fellows from New York—where he visited the first Black Odd Fellows Lodge—to Chicago and from Boston to Richmond, Virginia. He also met with several prominent whites including, reportedly, the President of the United States. See Charles H. Brooks, *The Official History and Manual of the Grand Order of Odd Fellows in America* (1902, rpt. Freeport, New York: Books for Libraries Press, 1971), 270.

2 Jones's visit did set in motion a small trickle of black Odd Fellows visiting British Annual Conferences over the next decade.

3 David M. Fahey offers a brief summary of the events leading to Ogden's securing permission for a chapter in New York City in "Grand United Order of Odd Fellows," in *Organizing Black America*, ed. Nina Mjagkij (New York: Taylor and Francis, 2001).

4 Jones's numbers are likely quite accurate, as the black Odd Fellows were the largest such organization at the end of the nineteenth century.

5 Drawn from Edward Young's *Night Thoughts* (part II, line 376) and a staple of *Bartlett's Quotations*.

6 The female auxiliary of the Black Odd Fellows.

7 A variation of Acts 17:26, a verse regularly cited by black clergy of the period.

8 Both Whitechapel and the Tenderloin had long-held reputations as dangerous and stunningly poor neighborhoods.

9 A variation of a line from Joseph Addison's *Cato* (5.1.31).

10 While the address Elliff gave prior to Jones's speech is included in the pamphlet, no response to Jones's speech has yet been located.

APPENDIX C

This advertisement appeared in the Charleston Advocate *on April 18, 1907 and May 2, 1907. Given that Jones addresses the abuses central to the coal industry in* Hearts of Gold, *his endorsement of this call for black laborers is interesting. According to historian Ronald L. Lewis, "although leasing convicts to private contractors was common in the South, it became prevalent in the coalfields of Georgia, Tennessee, and Alabama. Other southern states with significant coal reserves did not use prison labor in mining."*[1] *This advertisement suggests that Jones was ready to believe that conditions were significantly different in West Virginia.*

OPPORTUNITY

OPPORTUNITY===========================OPPORTUNITY

TWO THOUSAND COLORED MEN WITH OR WITHOUT FAMILIES WANTED FOR PERMANENT EMPLOYMENT AND RESIDENCE IN WEST VIRGINIA

THE MINE OWNERS in the rich and rapidly developing coal fields of West Virginia are anxious to secure two thousand colored men to work in the coal mines of the state.

Men are not wanted for a few months work nor to take the place of strikers, but they are wanted for permanent work and permanent residence.

This is not a new field but one that has been in operation for twenty years. There are thousands of colored men in these fields who came here years ago with their families and they have educated their children, saved their money, bought property and are now among the state's most respected citizens.

The state of West Virginia welcomes respected colored people within her borders and gives them opportunities and advantages which can be obtained in no other Southern State.

In West Virginia there is no discrimination in the public school laws. The colored schools have the same length of term that the white schools have and the colored teachers are paid the same salaries that white teachers are paid. At present there are only 50,000 colored people in the state, for those the state maintains three state schools. One in the center, one in the southern and one in the northern part of the state. At these schools, collegiate, academic, military and industrial education can be had. In addition to this, the state supports a colored orphans' home, reform school for girls and colored people are admitted to all the Humane Institutions.

In West Virginia, there are no Jim Crow cars, disfranchisement laws and other discriminations so common in southern states. Every man can vote his sentiments and is guaranteed every right and protection given by the Constitution of the United States.

At each works, good houses at reasonable rent, school houses and chuches are provided by the Companies in nearly every locality, Pythian, Masonic, Odd Fellows and other lodges will be found and the Companies furnish Halls for same.

Men are wanted as miners, drivers, engineers, carpenters, skilled and common laborers. From $2.00 to $5.00 per day can be earned. It takes only a few weeks for a man to learn the trade of mining. All wages are paid in cash every two weeks. No one is compelled to deal at Company stores, as is usually the case on public works.

This is an opportunity of a life time for colored men who want to better their condition, earn good wages, educate their children and enjoy the same privileges that others enjoy.

WE WANT TWO THOUSAND MEN. WE WILL PAY TRANSPORTATION FROM ANY PLACE IN THE UNITED STATES.

Good men are wanted and we are willing to give these inducements. If you are interested, let me hear from you at once.

J. M. HAZELWOOD, Agent, 22 Capitol Street, Charleston, W.Va.

REFERENCES

Hon. W. M. O. Dawson, Governor of West Virginia, Charleston, W.Va.
S. W. Starks, Supreme Chancellor, Knights of Pythias, Charleston, W.Va.
J. McHenry Jones, Ex. Grand Master, Grand United Order Odd Fellows, Institute, W.Va.
Kanawha Banking & Trust Company, Charleston, W.Va.

NOTES

1 Ronald L. Lewis, "African American Convicts in the Coal Mines of Southern Appalachia," in John C. Inscoe, ed., *Appalachians and Race: The Mountain South from Slavery to Segregation* (Lexington: The University Press of Kentucky, 2001), 259.

APPENDIX D

The following, Jones's overview of the mission and success of the West Virginia Colored Institute, appeared in "The History of Education in West Virginia," revised edition (Charleston, WV: Tribune Printing, 1907), 100–103.

THE WEST VIRGINIA COLORED INSTITUTE

By President J. McHenry Jones

The problem of negro education is by no means a simple one. How to lift an ignorant and long neglected race to the plane of the twentieth century requirements, fitting it for the complicated economic and moral duties of life, giving it the fibre to contend patiently for place amid the maddening competition of the business world; to lay bare the mistakes and follies of the first intoxication of long prayed for freedom and inspire with the spirit of real liberty and true citizenship millions of unfortunate but native born Americans, challenges the sacrifice of the deepest thought and the truest patriotism.

In studying the question we must not eliminate from our calculation the fact that we are dealing with the children of a race scarcely a generation removed from slavery and around whom still cling many of the sad results of their parents' unfortunate past. In the minds of most of these children education and labor are distinct and opposite concepts. Education is associated with luxury and idleness, labor with ignorance and drudgery. To teach the nobility of labor and that the greatest usefulness and highest happiness are the handmaids of diligence is the mission of our school. In this work we must make haste slowly. We must guard against unfair standards of comparison and observe that the educational progress of a race cannot always be measured by a progress of things. Buildings and apparatus measure largely the progress of things, but time is a very important element in ascertaining definitely what has been the ultimate progress of hand and mind.

The West Virginia Colored Institute, like the other agricultural and mechanical schools for the colored race, is a child of the Morrill Bill. This bill was approved by Congress August 30, 1890, and entitled "An act to apply a portion of the proceeds of the public lands to the more complete endowment and support of the colleges for the benefit of agriculture and the mechanic arts established under the provisions of an act of Congress approved July 2, 1862."

By this act West Virginia was apportioned eighteen thousand dollars and by act of the Legislature, session of 1891, fifteen thousand dollars was given to the West Virginia University, and three thousand to the West Virginia Colored Institute, established by the same act. By the conditions of the act these sums were to be augmented until the University should receive twenty thousand dollars and the Institute five thousand dollars annually, which sums would be the maximum.

Mr. J. Edwin Campbell, the first principal of the West Virginia Colored Institute, gives the following account of its establishment: "An appropriation of ten thousand dollars was made by the Legislature with which to purchase a farm of not more than fifty acres and to build a suitable building for such an institution. As the act provided that the institution should be located in Kanawha County, it was first thought best to purchase the property known as "Shelton College," situated on the lofty hill overlooking the village of St. Albans. But the committee appointed, after investigation, reported adversely. It was then decided to erect a building at some suitable location.

Finally, thirty acres of level bottom land was purchased from Mrs. Elijah Hurt, near "Farm," on the Great Kanawha River. This land is a part of the estate left by Samuel Cabell, deceased. Upon this farm the Board of the School Fund erected a building.

Ground was broken August 25, 1891, and the corner stone laid Sunday, October 11, of the same year. The building was completed about the 1st of April, 1892, and was received by the Board of the School Fund on April 20th.

BUILDINGS.

The main or academic building, Fleming Hall, which was the first erected, cost in round numbers about ten thousand dollars. It was carefully designed and planned to meet the needs of modern education. Since its erection, the building has been considerably enlarged, and is now eighty-three feet long, seventy-six feet wide, and is in every way modern in its appointments. Besides an additional purchase of thirty-eight acres of land, a modern barn and seven other buildings have been erected upon the Institute grounds. Five of these are built of stone and brick; the others are frame buildings.

MacCorkle Hall is a large and beautiful building, one hundred and six feet long and fifty feet wide and accommodates a hundred girls. Atkinson Hall, the young men's dormitory, rivals MacCorkle Hall in convenience and beauty. The A.B. White Trade School, the most commodious and by far the largest building connected with the school, being two hundred and forty-four feet in its greatest width, with ornamentations of stone and roofed with slate, would be a credit to any institution. This building, erected at a cost of thirty-five thousand dollars and finished by the students of the school, is intended to contain all of the industries for boys. If we except the Armstrong-Slater Trades School at Tuskegee, this is the largest building of its kind in the United States, and without exception the best lighted and most convenient. Dawson Hall, the building for Domestic Arts and Sciences, now in course of erection, when finished, will be the most beautiful building on the campus. This hall, built of brick and stone, will contain all the girls' industries, and the third story will be utilized as a Senior Girls' Home. These buildings, together with West Hall, a large frame building, containing the library and the departments of agriculture and cooking, and with the principal's home, a large and convenient frame building, constitute the buildings of the institution. All of them are heated by steam and lighted with electricity.

ALUMNI.

It is a well-known fact that the worth of an institution is generally measured by the character of its graduates. The West Virginia Colored Institute has a pardonable pride in the work of the Alumni who have issued from its walls. In all one hundred and sixty-one students have graduated from the school since 1896; of these eighty-five are engaged in teaching, three are successful pastors, two are machinists, one an attorney-at-law, sixteen are carpenters, six blacksmiths, and twelve are dressmakers. The remainder are leading useful lives. A casual glance at the above figures reveals the fact that by far the larger half of the graduates from our school have devoted their energies to teaching. This is true of the first graduates from nearly all institutions for normal and industrial training for the negroes. It grows out of the great demand among us for trained teachers. Many of these teachers, however, follow their trades during vacation from school duties.

THE COURSE OF STUDY.

The course of study in the West Virginia Colored Institute is the same as that which is pursued in the other normal schools of the State. In addition to the bookwork, every student is required to learn some useful trade before graduation. To do this, it is necessary to divide the six grades of the school into equal divisions, one-half pursuing book-work in the morning, while the other half are in the shops and in the various departments. In the afternoon the first half go to the shops, while those who work in the morning have book work in the afternoon. In this way the pupils are given equal opportunities for mental and manual training.

DEPARTMENTS.

The school has six well equipped departments under the direction of twenty-two teachers, viz.: Normal, Agricultural, Mechanical, Domestic, Commercial, and Musical. The Normal Department has been previously discussed. In the Mechanical Department, Smithing, Wheelwrighting, Steamfitting, Carpentry, Woodwork, Brick Laying, Plastering, Printing, and Mechanical Drawing are taught.

The Agricultural Department, besides giving a good course in scientific farming, also offers to students entering it practical opportunities in dairying, poultry raising, stock judging, and general farm work.

The Department of Domestic Arts teaches Plain Sewing, Dressmaking, Millinery, Cooking, Laundering, and Housekeeping.

The Commercial Course—designed to give the student a knowledge of business forms—besides giving a short course in Bookkeeping, has an excellent course in Shorthand and Typewriting.

The Musical Department, besides giving instruction in Sight-Reading, Voice Culture, and Ear Training, offers an excellent opportunity for instruction on the Pianoforte. Pupils pursue the course of study in this school at a very small cost and with no extra charges for the use of a piano for practice.

MILITARY DEPARTMENT.

Besides the well organized departments above mentioned, the State provides for the appointment of sixty cadets, who receive their uniforms, room rent, books and stationery free of charge. The course in this department is both theoretical and practical; the first includes recitations in drill regulations, supplemented by lectures on minor tactics; army organization, administration and discipline; small arms, firing regulations, and other military subjects.

The practical course includes military drill and gymnastics, target practice, military signaling, marching, and castrametation.

NUMBERS.

The school at present has an enrollment of two hundred and twenty-five students, which is the largest in its history. This number fills the present dormitories too full for comfort. Students are in attendance here from eight states; as we have said before, one hundred and sixty-one graduates have gone forth from the institution, to say nothing of the large number who have gone into the field of life without finishing the prescribed course.

INCOME.

The income of the school is derived from two sources: First, an annual amount of $5,000 received from the Morrill Fund; second, Legislative appropriation. The money received from the United States Government can be applied only to instruction in agriculture, the mechanic arts, English language, and the various branches of mathematical, physical, natural and economic science, with special reference to their application in the industries of life, and to the facilities for such instruction. The State has dealt very generously with the West Virginia Colored Institute, as the following list of appropriations will show:

1891	$10,000
1893	14,000
1895	16,000
1897	29,000
1899	39,000
1901	66,000
1903	54,000
1905	64,705
Total	$352,70

The idea which has dominated the school from its beginning has been that thrift, education and religion were necessary to lift the negro to the full enjoyment of modern civilization, and following out that original conception, the school aims to teach the hands to work, the mind to think and the heart to love.

APPENDIX E

The following, J. McHenry Jones's eulogy for Samuel W. Starks, was published in the April 11, 1908 Advocate.

BIOGRAPHICAL S-KETCH OF S. W. STARKS

Prepared and Delivered at the Funeral Exercises by President J. McHenry Jones, of the State College

Hon. Samuel W. Starks was born in this city, March 10th, 1865, and died Friday, April 3rd, 1908. He was therefore 43 years and 24 days of age. He is survived by his wife, mother, and one sister.

Sam Starks as a boy attended the public schools of Charleston, and obtained a common school education. During his school years he was a cooper apprentice, working in the shops beyond Elk. After leaving school he followed the copper's trade for a short time, but becoming dissatisfied obtained a place in the office of the K. & M. railway.

As he went in and out about his work, the constant clicking of the telegraph apparatus filled him with a nameless longing to know its language, to interpret for himself, the stories of danger, daring and adventure it daily told. In company with a fellow-workman he bought the necessary apparatus, set up a miniature telegraph wire, hired the operator during the idle hours to give him a little help, and by dint of constant effort became a successful operator. Knowing how, he was ever ready to oblige the operator to take his place when absent, to indulge him when he was inclined to be inactive, but all the time glad of the opportunity to familiarize himself with the real work of the office. Col. Sharp soon took note of this young janitor, who had also become an operator, and gave him employment with him in Columbus, at a salary scarcely sufficient to pay his board and washing, and so hard put for money was he, that in going to and from the colonel's house on an errand he would run every step of the way there and back in order to save the street car fare given him. He stuck it out in prayer and penury, hoping for a better day. At last it came.

Operator in Charge of Charleston Office.

First as both janitor and operator and then in charge of the Charleston office, he won by patience and sacrifice (in spite of his color) the confidence of his employers.

From Charleston he was transferred to Corning, Ohio, (then, as now, an important point on the K. & M. system). Becoming dissatisfied that he was not promoted as fast as he thought he deserved, and believing that he was discriminated against on account of his color, he resigned. He entered the school of Bryant & Stratton in Chicago, completing the courses of bookkeeping and stenography. This led him to Denver, Colorado, where, after a short stay, he returned home. Here he organized a company and went into the grocery business, which he successfully conducted until appointed state librarian by Governor A. B. White, March 4th, 1901. He was reappointed by Governor Dawson four years ago, and continued in that position until the day of his death.

His Highest Work.

It was not as a telegrapher, stenographer, bookkeeper or librarian that the name of Samuel W. Starks will be best remembered, but as leader in the order of the Knights of Pythias. He was one of the charter members of Capitol City lodge, No. 1, and from that day until he passed to the great beyond, he has been virtually the main spring of Pythianism in this state. He was the state's first Grand Chancellor, and has served in that office 16 consecutive years. He saw the order in the state grow from one castle to more than 100. In a state sparsely populated with men of his own race, he has made Pythianism the most virulent and helpful influence among us. He put into every thing he touched brains and energy, compelling by the force of his intelligence and genius success, where to less masterful men success seemed impossible. His management of our state fraternal insurance department has made it one of the safest and most reliable in the entire jurisdiction.

His Work in West Virginia.

The Pythian Mutual Investment Company is a child of his fertile brain. He conceived the idea that the dimes thoughtlessly thrown away by our people, if wisely invested, would aid in building a monument of beauty and usefulness. This idea in the concrete stands on the corner of Dickerson and Washington streets, facing the state capitol, a monument to Negro thrift when wisely directed. The first success accomplished, Mr. Starks turned to Huntington and purchased the Herald building, an investment equally wise and profitable. It was his fixed purpose to dot the state with beautiful castles, and if the sands of time had run on a few years more he would have coined his wishes into realities. His accumulations of wealth and affluence is an example of his own teachings. He saw his race on the ragged edge of the world begging a place to meet socially, and he determined that this should not be, and he used the things within his reach to better their condition.

Elected as Supreme Chancellor.

In the fall of 1899, after serving several terms as Supreme Vice Chancellor he was elected Supreme Chancellor of the Pythian world. Entertaining the office he found the business of the organization in a chaotic condition, the treasury depleted, the order split in twain, and failure and ruin of the beloved order staring him in the face. Nothing discouraged, he began with indomitable courage and sleepless energy to right the ship, patch up the rents and begin anew to put the craft out on the open sea. In 1900 the order had less than 20,000 members; as Supreme Chancellor Starks turns over the ship to other hands there are more than 160,000 members. In less than 10 years, under his progressive leadership, he has increased the membership seven times. When he began, the order could not pay the expenses of its Supreme representatives to a biennial convocation, today it owns a temple on State street, Chicago, worth $160,000, and only a few months ago purchased a sanitarium for sick fraters at Hot Springs, Arkansas. The order is in excellent financial condition, having thousands of dollars in the banks of this and other cities.

Converted in the church, S. W. Starks has led a Christian life from his youth until the day of his death.

Well has the *Daily Mail* said:--

"Starting as a poor cooper's lad, he worked himself up in half of the allotted span of life, to a position which made him not merely a man of local prominence, but one whose reputation was world wide, and whose example will be a guide to generations of his race yet unborn."

We have watched him, friends, in every step of his career. At his rise we have rejoiced. We have been proud to call him our leader, and prouder still to know in our hearts that with all of his worldwide fame he was still the same, simple, loving friend that he was before his elevation. He did not get above us as the world called him higher and higher, but all of his thoughts were of us, and how he might lift his brothers as he climbed. He might have left us as he climbed, but the poorest and the most humble had his ear in their sorrows and his help in their need.

He Loved His Race.

He loved his race and never wanted for himself any privilege that it could not share. When injustice and prejudice bore hard on his race, his heart felt the blow, and those of us who were near him have seen him shed bitter tears over race oppressions that he could not cure.

He believed in our future and longed for new paths up the hill of difficulties, over which he might lead the way to higher grounds. He believed that much of our troubles grew out of the fact of our poverty, and urged thrift as a cure for part of our ills. He gained success as a leader of men, because he put right always before might. He never attempted to gain a point by double dealing, for after all he often said: "Only by doing right can we obtain permanent success."

The soil of West Virginia never grew a better or a bigger soul than filled the body of S. W. Starks, and the Negro race never had a kindlier nor a more beloved leader.

He never lost a friend, nor knowingly made an enemy. When the chapter of his life closed last Friday morning the sun rose on a world poorer for his departure. His life was sweet and full of sympathy, and the tracks he left on the sands of time will be revered by his friends and their children's children to remote generations.

The clock has struck, the light has flickered and gone out forever. In the shadows as we wait and weep. If on his grave could fall a flower from every man and woman to whom his work has brought friendship, charity and benevolence, he would rest tonight beneath a wilderness of roses.

Ah! my brothers and sisters, we must take up the work of life tomorrow bravely, if bitterly, without his help. The days and nights must come and go, until we are called to follow him; but many glimpses of the moon will look upon our sorrows before we see his like again. The world will be lonelier for us without Samuel W. Starks.

But speak no more of his renown,
Lay his works and honors down,
And in the silent churchyard leave him,
God accept him, Christ receive him.[1]

NOTES

1 Jones here quotes the closing lines of Alfred Lord Tennyson's "Ode on the Death of the Duke of Wellington" (1852).

APPENDIX F

The following are extracts from Jones's July 8, 1909 speech on "The Epworth League and the Enthronement of Christ" presented at the Eighth International Convention of the Epworth League at Seattle, Washington. These extracts are drawn from John L. Jones's History of the Jones Family.

THE QUESTION SEEMS TO BE, in what way can the Epworth League by its service, contribute to the Enthronement of the Christ? It is not enough that we be called and equipped but that we give ourselves to the work of making the teachings of the Master the supreme force in the direction of the world's affairs.

During his sojourn among men the Master Himself said, "And I, if I be lifted up from the earth will draw all men unto myself."[1]

It, therefore, appears that the chief work of all Christians is to lift high the Christ, bring His life into fuller view, make His work more manifest until the great heart of the universe throbs with adoration at the sound of His name. As the sun gives light and warmth and life to our physical world, so Christ gives light and life to the mortal world for He is the light of the world.

The great problems, challenging the profoundest thought; questions of state that have unsettled the foundation stones of national life and embittered the stream of international relationship; social disorders which threaten the existence of the present compact, all find a simple solution when subjected to the light emanating from the glowing words of the lowly Nazarene. It is only through the predominance of the Christ idea that the circle of brotherhood will continue to increase, and justice and equality, the dream of the ages, reach universal application.

Men need a saving sight of the Master, they must be induced to look and live in order that they be transformed into His likeness. We unconsciously become like those we most admire. If by observing the serene expression of the Great Stone face from youth to old age the good man finally resembled it, how much more will looking into the benign countenance of the Christ, living in close proximity, imitating his life and inculcating his character, make men like Him.

In the first place, no service can be fully acceptable that does not begin right. The empire of our King is an invisible one. The Kingdom of Heaven is in you. His rule is void of the ordinary trappings and insignia of earthly powers. His servants, therefore, must enter the army by the sanction of heaven, they must be regenerated or born from above. They must have on their foreheads the kiss of the Holy Ghost, if they would have on their service the blessings of God.

The Enthronement of Christ, fellow Leaguers, depends upon our wisdom to win souls for His cause. Men must humbly, but cheerfully acknowledge His way and lovingly bend under His yoke. Take my yoke and learn of me. See how I do.

A man's world consists of the number of persons and objects in which he is interested. While we all live on the same globe, we do not necessarily live in the same world. The cause which thrills every fiber of my being, may appeal but indifferently to your heart, and, so, the underlying thought which is the mainspring of your ambition may have but little influence on my life. Your struggle and mine, while one in purpose, may be as different as night and day. We must each labor to overcome our own little world, to bring the life and light of an Enthroned Savior to act imperatively in our sphere of influence. "We must work in our own appointed sphere and wish it none other than it is." I must carry the story of a Savior, to the backward, the hated, the discouraged. I must struggle to make them forget their complaints in the thought that earth has no sorrow, that Heaven cannot cure. I must make them see that the powerful hand that made the world is so gentle that the bruised reed it will not break and the smoking flax it will not quench.

Each Epworthian must feel that he is divinely called and sent to forward the Enthronement of the Christ. It helps in the midst of the heat and burden of the day, to feel that I am on the King's business, I have royal authority for my action. He sent them into the vineyard.[2] If we would enthrone the King we must give ourselves unreservedly to his cause. We must not waste effort thinking of ourselves, for selfishness is often the cloud that hides from us the Sun of Righteousness. Knowing our authority and certain of our equipment there is but little reason that we should go limping to the battlefield. We have orders to contend for the coronation of our King, to fight in our part of the field. "For it is ours not to reason why, ours but to do and die."[3] Earnest men care little for sacrifice, not even for death.

The service is, to produce, through Christ, men and women of perfect character. "Character is a unity and all of the virtues must grow in harmony."[4] This harmonious development of the completely fashioned will must be aided by the Spirit of God. All that there is in the Bible, all that there is in the world, is simply an exposition of character of the God who created them. To teach men to keep the soul in adjustment with the Eternal, to supply the conditions necessary to produce character, is the heart of the service.

Methods must change with the demands of the age. What would reach men in the sixteenth century may not reach them today. Religion does not change but the manner of appeal to men must vary with the nature of the people and the character of the age. We are appealing to our young people to be something, "to be rather than to seem."[5] Not simply copies of their neighbors, but conforming to their neighbors' higher ideals so long as those ideals conform to the law and spirit of right.

Neither Saxon Christianity nor Saxon civilization can make of my race a simple reflex in ebony of itself. Race ideals and race distinction must not be ignored. The excellent work of Secretary I. Garland Penn,[6] could not have been accomplished if the church had not granted him the largest liberty in the methods to be pursued. He must use the means best adapted to reach the people. He must use his own weapons in his contention for the King. The service with us is to urge not only the necessity to be something, but also to do something useful. The Master has no use in heaven or earth for a lazy do-less people. A man's religion is often more evident in the way he weeds the garden than in the way he sings a psalm. Religion is a life, and what we do measures our devotion to God. The service is not only to be something and do something but to have something. The old notion that we are especially loved of Heaven because we are poor, has given place to the better notion that God loves us because we are pure. We are not teaching a religion devoid of proper emotion, a soulless materialism, but we are striving to eliminate emotion, the muscular product and to properly care for the blessings God puts into our hands. We do not agree with the demand to stop singing, "You may have all the world, give me Jesus."[7] We are saying as long as there is an unfed human being in the world, to waste is sin. We are coming to see that a farmer is often of as much use to the world as a reformer and that conscientiously plowing a straight furrow forwards the Enthronement of Christ.

The service is the regeneration of the masses. The route is from the college to the crowd. The man with the hoe must be reached and enlightened. The body of death that hangs around the neck of respectability in my race must be called back to life, must be quickened and saved by introducing Caliban to Cadmus. . . .[8]

Jesus Christ saved men by coming in touch with them. He did not sweep like an angel of light away from the crowded streets where men struggled and sinned, away from the hovels where men suffered for bread, away from the seamy side of life and bid us behold Him in all His glory, but down in the midst of the crowd where men sweated blood, in hearing of the groans of the oppressed and dying, He made His way, too busy doing good to think of the grime that might cling to His garments.

We are often so good that we are really worthless, so constantly on guard at our own door that we are of no possible use to the rest of the army.

The cloister has its uses but true warfare is upon the firing line. Our powers must be daily renewed in the closet but the practice is gained in the market place, in the business center, in contact with men.

NOTES

1 John 12:32.

2 An allusion to Matthew 20:1–16.

3 Drawn from Tennyson's "Charge of the Light Brigade," a poem that would have been deeply familiar to his listeners.

4 A variation of a line from Henry Drummond, included in collections like his *Beautiful Thoughts*.

5 From Cicero's Latin "esse quam videri" in his text "On Friendship."

6 On Penn, see Jennifer R. Thomas, "Penn, Irvine Garland," *African American National Biography, Volume* 6, ed. Henry Louis Gates Jr. and Evelyn Brooks Higginbotham (Oxford: Oxford University Press, 2008), 302–303, as well as the introduction to this volume. Penn actively engaged with the Epworth League during these years.

7 Drawn from the African American spiritual "Give Me Jesus."

8 Caliban was the wild antithesis to civilization in Shakespeare's *The Tempest*; Cadmus was credited in Greek myth with sharing the Phoenician alphabet and thus aiding the Greeks in becoming a literate culture.

ABOUT THE EDITORS

John Ernest, the Eberly Family Distinguished Professor of American Literature at West Virginia University, is the author of *Resistance and Reformation in Nineteenth-Century African-American Literature* (1995), *Liberation Historiography: African American Writers and the Challenge of History, 1794-1861* (2004), and *Chaotic Justice: Rethinking African American Literary History* (2009). His editions of texts by nineteenth-century African American writers include *Running a Thousand Miles for Freedom; Or, The Escape of William and Ellen Craft from Slavery* (2000), William Wells Brown's *The Escape; or, A Leap for Freedom* (2001), and *Narrative of the Life of Henry Box Brown* (2008).

Eric Gardner chairs the English Department at Saginaw Valley State University, where he is also a Professor and Braun Fellow. He is the author of *Unexpected Places: Relocating Nineteenth-Century African American Literature* and the editor of *Jennie Carter: A Black Journalist of the Early West* and *Major Voices: The Drama of Slavery.*